SOURCE

JAY KLAGES

This is a work of fiction. Names, characters, organizations, places, events, and incidents are either products of the author's imagination or are used fictitiously.

For Mom.

I remember the first time you took me to the bookstore to get some "real" books. You bought me Dracula, Frankenstein, The Count of Monte Cristo, The Three Musketeers, Les Misérables, and White Fang.

That was a great start.

"The ultimate skill in taking up a strategic position is to have no form."

—Sun Tzu

CHAPTER 1

Mineral County, West Virginia
Sunday, October 30
10:15 a.m. (EST)

The changeable letters below the sign for the SonDay Assembly of God announced CLOSED, though the church had never been open for services.

Outside, four armed men in work clothes roamed inside the perimeter fence, performing light grounds maintenance while keeping watch on the front gate, surrounding woods, and overcast sky.

The one hundred fifty men and eight women seated inside the prefab building weren't gathered to worship or volunteer. Behind them, a long row of tables displayed tactical storage cases filled with pistols, ammunition, and an assortment of nonlethal weapons.

Against the adjacent wall, computers and specialized equipment lay in stations. The members had filed through earlier to download instructions and receive program updates.

Joshua Pierce, the operational leader of the casually dressed congregation, stood behind an aluminum pulpit. After reviewing the attendance log on his computer one last time, he drew in a heavy breath and smoothed a hand over his slicked-back dark brown hair.

All accounted for.

He nodded to the security detail standing behind him, comprised of the most highly trained professionals pulled from the ranks.

"Okay, everyone, let's get started."

Pierce clasped his hands behind his back as the chatter died down.

"My Guardian friends, welcome to Phase Two. Over the next few hours, we're going to discuss our plans and objectives for the coming months. I want all of you to know that, despite our setbacks over the summer, we still have solid financing and support. Our strategy is on track, and you'll all be very excited about our plans following the election next week. The Chapter is strong, and the vision of our Founder, Marshall Owens, lives on."

Heads nodded, soaking in the quiet energy and collective confidence of the room.

"Now," Pierce said, "I brought a group of you in today because we have a task to execute. An adversary who must be dealt with immediately. You'll now see his image marked with an alert in your program."

Pierce pressed a button on his handheld device, and everyone looked at the picture appearing in the edge of their vision display. A young man with black hair and hazel-green eyes, smiling big, as if he were laughing at them.

"Kade Sims was supposed to be a member of The Chapter, but he deceived and betrayed us. He proved to be an FBI asset."

Pierce paused to look at their faces in the silence. He could see the wildfire growing in their eyes, one by one.

"Yeah, I know," he said, rubbing his beard stubble. "I know how you feel, trust me. I'm right there with you. Rest assured, he *will* pay for what he did."

He paced across the room and sniffed a few times.

"And that's why, next Wednesday, one of you is going to bring him to me."

CHAPTER 2

Lynn Saunders, a thirty-five-year-old single mother, was driving south on Norfolk Avenue on her way to church. She had stopped at a red light when a man sprinted up to her car and appeared outside her door.

Her hand moved to the lock button, but the door was already open.

A gun barrel jammed into her ribs.

"Get in the other seat!"

She couldn't step on the gas—there was a car right in front of her.

She couldn't get out and run. Little Andy was in the car seat behind her.

Before she was able to think of other options, the man unbuckled her seat belt and shoved her over hard enough that her head hit the inside of the passenger door. He threw her legs over the center console and swiveled his body in, slamming the driver's door shut.

The light turned green, and he accelerated fast enough that Lynn's head jerked back.

I'm being carjacked.

"Mommy?" Andy asked.

The man jerked his head around and noted Andy's babble with a sick smile.

The man was short and muscular, wore a Red Sox cap and sunglasses, shorts and T-shirt.

"Please don't hurt us," she said. "Just let us out. You can have—"

3

"Shut up!"

The man was driving fast, but not fast enough to attract undue attention. He pulled out a cigarette and lit it. Lynn wasn't about to say anything about his smoking. Her phone rested in the cup holder. Could she grab it and dial 9-1-1? No, not yet.

"Where are you taking us?" she asked.

"Say another word and your boy's an orphan," he said.

"Mommy, who's dat?" Andy asked.

"It's okay, Andy," she said. When she tried to reach toward the back and hold his little hand for a minute, the side of the gun barrel swatted her left temple.

"Turn the fuck around."

"Okay."

They were headed toward Route 1, but the man was having trouble getting over into the turn lane to reach the on-ramp, for some reason. He swerved, trying several times before missing it. Traffic wasn't bad—someone had deliberately blocked him. The carjacker cursed under his breath and started looking in his rearview and side mirrors.

"I'm putting my seat belt on," she said. If they crashed, she'd need to get Andy out.

He ignored her and changed his route.

She looked out her side window and saw a Ford Explorer alongside of them. The man driving the Explorer had a cell phone pressed to his ear, and he was looking at her! He pulled the phone away from his ear and touched a single finger to his mouth.

He was telling her to be quiet.

The man could tell she was being carjacked.

He must have seen it happen and called 9-1-1!

"Mommy?"

The man now drove more aggressively. He exited and took Dorchester over the highway, heading toward the harbor. Looked in his rearview constantly. She could occasionally see the Explorer to her right. She tried not to pay too much attention.

"Shit," the carjacker said. He was now trying to pass cars and evade whoever was following. He slipped his gun back into some kind of body holster, reached down between his legs, and regripped the steering wheel with two hands.

They headed toward a traffic circle. She needed to try and stop him somehow. She needed to get Andy out, now.

He would have to reduce his speed to make it around the circle.

There were airbags.

Don't think about it. Just do it.

She reached across, grabbed the steering wheel, and turned it left with all her strength. The man didn't expect it.

"WHAT THE F—!"

The car skipped over the inner curbing on the circle and careened onto the grass toward a stand of trees. The carjacker tried to jerk the wheel back, but she fought with all her strength.

The man growled, released a hand from the wheel and tried to hit her with his elbow. She ducked toward the dashboard and he only grazed the back of her head. He swung at her again, and the back of his hand hit her face. She gasped.

Bang!

The car hit a tree on its front-right fender, air bags exploded, and Lynn found herself screaming as the car rocked to a halt. Andy was screaming.

She heard the driver's door open with some effort. The carjacker grumbled in what sounded like a foreign language and grabbed her purse as he slid out. She smelled smoke and couldn't get her seat belt off when she tried.

"Mommy! Mommy!"

Smoke and flames hissed from the crumpled hood. She had to hurry.

A loud gunshot sounded and she crouched down for a second.

She still couldn't get the seat belt off. She had to get Andy out . . . but she couldn't turn around.

"Andy! Are you okay, Andy?"

Her door jerked open. It was the man from the Explorer.

"Come on!" he yelled. He was trying to figure out a way to free her.

5

"Get Andy out first!" she yelled. "My son . . . in the back!"

"Okay!"

She heard the rear door open. The man disappeared and came back with some kind of large pocket knife. He was cutting through her seat belt. The smoke was choking her.

"I got ya!" he said.

The belt came loose. She was free and he was pulling her out of the car. There were flashing police lights in the distance, but she only had one thing on her mind.

"Andy? Where's Andy?"

CHAPTER 3

FBI Northern Virginia Resident Agency
Manassas, Virginia
Wednesday, November 9
2:10 p.m. (EST)

The photo displayed on the iPad was a candid full-body shot of a beautiful Chinese woman. Kade had known her from months before, but had never expected to see her again.

Especially not looking like this.

Her long, thick hair was pulled up halfway into a topknot, allowing ambient light to glow on her cheeks and lips. Her open black tuxedo jacket revealed a gauzy T-shirt and studded belt underneath. Black leather leggings continued the long, sleek look until running into the tops of tough, Frankenstein-looking boots.

She appeared to be standing inside some high-end store or boutique.

Amazing.

"Do you recognize her?" FBI Special Agent Kimberly Summerford asked.

Kade didn't need to zoom in on the image, but did anyway. His eyes pretended to search for certainty, when really he just wanted to make a good mental imprint.

Wow.

After a slow nod, he handed the computer back to her. Summerford, from Counterterrorism, was one of two people sitting across from him in the windowless conference room of the FBI office. Mauricio Andrade, from Counterintelligence, was the other. He hadn't met either of them before, but

7

had spoken to Summerford over the phone, the week prior. Both looked in their midthirties and wore suits.

"Oh yeah, I know her," Kade said.

Dread swirled in his stomach. Dread tinged with guilt. Were there more photos of her they didn't want him to see—like with her throat slit or something?

"Is she . . . alive?" he asked.

"Yes, she is," Summerford replied.

Kade sighed. *That's good.*

This meeting is all about her?

"Can you confirm her name?" Andrade asked.

"Yeah. Lin Soon."

Andrade and Summerford looked at each other. A connection had been made. Or some kind of meeting objective had been met.

"And she worked with you at AgriteX?" Summerford asked.

Kade remembered the first time he'd met Lin at AgriteX Corporation. It was at a dinner, and he'd never been hungrier in his life when she first introduced herself. From then on, she usually sat close to him during meals. Those were a few of the better memories.

"Yeah, we were in the same small group of associates . . . like interns in training."

"Have you seen her since?" Summerford asked.

"No."

"She's messaged you on social media, though, right?"

Kade sat back an inch and caught a twinkle in Summerford's blue eyes. An extra blink. Small tells that she was setting him up for a potential *gotcha*. She had to have plenty of background knowledge on him, and now she was just confirming what she already knew.

It made sense the Bureau would monitor Lin Soon's activity. And now it looked like his own social media drawers had been rummaged through. That didn't bother him. He kind of expected it, really. There weren't many federal-level surveillance capabilities these days that would shock him. The public's demand for perfect intelligence required the kind of aggressive data mining the public didn't like, and that paradox always made for political spaghetti.

"Yeah, she sent a message about a month ago, but I never replied. I haven't sent any messages or made any posts on social media since early last summer."

"Do you think she'd be a threat now?"

"Hmm . . ." He paused again, looking down while his feet tapped a syncopated beat beneath the table. In-depth knowledge on Lin Soon must have been lacking, even with FBI surveillance. Analysis must've hit a wall if his opinion had become valuable to the FBI again.

His best opinion, though, would be nothing new. He'd already given a detailed debrief on his prior FBI operation, under a contract that had ended two months ago. Summerford had probably watched the video or read the transcript. The FBI, the Department of Homeland Security, and other agencies were still trying to track down the remnants of a lethal militia organization known as The Chapter, which had been secretly headquartered inside AgriteX.

He had a unique perspective because he was supposed to become one of them—a Guardian, a member of The Chapter's elite security force. But when The Chapter had launched a massive terror attack on the country, he'd helped derail it.

Now he assumed The Chapter saw him as a roach in their terror kitchen. They would try to crunch him under their boot while they cooked up something else.

He'd participated in closed-door, classified discussions with both the House Permanent Select Committee on Intelligence and the Senate Select Intelligence Committee. To support the FBI's case, he'd also testified in federal court.

Because information leaks were an ever-increasing risk, he had been permitted to speak with his identity hidden. Even so, testifying had been an exhausting experience and could try anyone's patience. Just sitting in one place for that long sucked enough.

His mind had been wandering, as it often did, and he hadn't answered Summerford's question.

"It's possible she's a threat," he finally said. "But did she drink the Chapter

Kool-Aid? I guess you can't rule out any former AgriteX employee. Personally, I didn't see her as dangerous, but . . ."

He shrugged and puffed his lips. Summerford didn't look impressed with the generic answer. No twinkle this time. Notes filled her padfolio, but she hadn't written any during this meeting. She was acting nice, but he was sixty percent sure she didn't like him for some reason. Seventy percent sure she was wearing a thong—that percentage had been bumped up since he'd met her in the lobby.

The reflective moment that followed seemed to mark a silent handoff to Andrade as interviewer. Andrade sipped a bottled smoothie and played with his cufflinks.

"Do you think Lin would recognize you now?" he asked.

Good question. If these agents had seen Kade's picture in an FBI file, it would've looked quite different from the person sitting in front of them now. He was wearing a disguise the US Marshals had taught him as part of the Witness Security Program. His hair was now razor-cut, black fuzz. He'd gotten used to dark brown contact lenses and a horseshoe mustache. A black leather jacket, pocket T, jeans, and boots completed the more severe look. His name had been changed to Kyle Smith.

He didn't like the disguise, but he liked the idea it kept him safer.

"I doubt it," he said. "I barely recognize myself."

"Would you say you got to know her well during your experience?" Andrade asked.

"No, not well. I saw her regularly as part of my group for a few weeks. Always at meals. She hung out in my room sometimes. She could be a real flirt. I tried to be nice in return, but not too nice."

"Did you have any sexual relations?" he asked.

Kade exhaled and kept a straight face.

I wish.

"Uh, no. Kissed a little. I was focused on the mission. But I didn't want to ignore her, either. I knew I might need her help at some point."

"We understand," Andrade said. "You're still single?"

"Yeah."

"Do you think Lin would trust you at this point if you tried to reestablish a friendly relationship?"

Now he knew where they were going, so he just preempted.

"You want me to be a source for the Bureau?"

"Yes," Andrade said.

"We think this might be a good opportunity," Summerford added.

Kade pushed back his chair and stretched his legs.

They were asking him to work with them again, to be a human intelligence source.

To get more information on a wicked-hot chick.

Sign me up . . . now!

No, no, he needed to wait a second. There was no reason to make a fast decision. He would force himself to slow down and go through his checklist. Think about risk and consequences. Take a full week to consider. He'd be better off for it.

He was *practicing* restraint, a technique he'd learned through therapy for his hypomania. The disorder had gotten the better of him while he was serving as an army lieutenant and military intelligence officer, and he had been discharged for it. In civilian life, he'd regrouped and gotten a handle on his situation with the help of a physician. Things had stabilized other than the occasional flare-up, as he called it.

The gig these agents were pitching wasn't as straightforward as it seemed. It never was. Was Lin Soon's surveillance photo a recruiting tool? They had to have less flattering photos, like her taking out the garbage or something.

She'd still look hot doing that, he bet.

"I think she'd be friendly with me," he said. "I frustrated her a bit, and I wasn't around to see if any fallout from the operation caused her harm. But I never had any serious confrontations with her or anything like that."

"Well, we could certainly use your help on this," Andrade said. "What do you think?"

Summerford half-opened her mouth as if she were about to say something to assist with the sale, but stayed silent. Andrade was offering an open-ended question, so Kade decided to take full advantage of it.

"I think I'd like to know *why* first," he said. "The whole story on why you're collecting information on her. I need some more background and details before I make any commitments, so I know what I'm getting into. And I'd like all of this now, please. If you know what I went through over the summer, then you understand why I'm asking as early as possible this time."

Both agents hesitated and looked at each other. They were in a secure FBI facility, so he assumed such a confidential discussion could take place. When Agent Summerford had contacted him, Kade had asked to have the meeting in Virginia so he could legally carry his Glock for protection. Andrade had arranged the meeting in Manassas, between a ninety-minute and two-hour drive east from Kade's home outside of Timberville. He had been permitted to concealed-carry the gun and check it at the security desk.

Summerford had told him on the introductory call that she had been referred to him by Special Agent Rob Morris, the case agent who'd recruited Kade for his last assignment. Morris had proved to be a straight shooter.

"Look," Kade added, "I've got way more credibility than your average source. Plus, I'm working a project right now with the Department of Defense and have a contractor top-secret clearance for it. So, even though I can do more work, I'm not sure I need another assignment."

It was a mild bluff. The new DoD project he mentioned was a real contract, but it wasn't paying anything yet. Still, Andrade seemed to interpret Kade's jerky body language as saying he was about to get up and leave.

"Well, sure," Andrade said. "It's not every day our director knows a source by name, so I think it's within reason to share a bit more about what's going on."

Andrade took a swig of smoothie and glanced at Summerford, who was now writing something down.

Andrade said, "Our Counterterrorism Division has an open case on all of the former AgriteX employees we could identify, including Lin Soon," he said. "Kim is the case agent overseeing that work now, and I'm a case agent focused on Chinese Counterintelligence. Are you familiar with the tension in China-India relations about their border?"

"Not really."

12

Andrade said, "It's a complex dispute going back to the Sino-India war of '62. American engagement of India increased this past year, and so our policy toward the two countries is becoming more complex. We rely on China for trade and its ownership of US Treasury debt, but American policy generally leans against Chinese territorial claims."

"Like their claim on the Senkaku and Spratly Islands," Kade said. He was familiar with some of the disputes in the South China Sea, but he was far from an expert on any of them.

"Yes," Andrade said. "But there's been an unusual recent spike in Chinese intelligence activity and a refocus of their assets since President Greer met with Prime Minister Kota of India last month."

"Why's that?" Kade asked.

"The United States signed a ten-year Defense Framework Agreement and a Defense Trade and Technology Initiative with India. The Chinese, it turns out, were a bit surprised and angered by the partnership. Our ambassador also visited Tawang, a disputed border area of Tibet. So, in our efforts to assess China's reaction and intelligence activity, we learned the Chinese were communicating with a particular source."

Andrade took the iPad and accessed another picture in what must have been a series of surveillance photos. A Chinese man, close-cropped black hair with silver streaks, wearing wire-framed glasses. He was waiting near where Lin had been, outside. In some upscale mall.

"In turn, the trail of this person's interactions led us to a name in our database."

"Lin Soon," Kade said.

"Yes," Andrade said. "Her name appeared in our open AgriteX case. So, Kim and I got together to try and make sense of it, to see if it was actually the same person."

Lin is spying for the Chinese? No way . . .

"So, Lin Soon had signed up with AgriteX to try and steal trade secrets?" Kade asked.

"We don't know," Andrade said. "That's why we need to find out more about what she's up to, but we don't want to risk alerting her, either. She's a

Chinese citizen with a permanent resident green card. One of the *fuerdai*, or the so-called spoiled rich kids of the rising Chinese wealthy class. We want her to stick around so we can get a better understanding of the intelligence network she's connected to. China's Ministry of State Security has a very far reach, including inside the US."

Kade gave a thumbs-up. "Good for job security, huh?"

Andrade smiled. "Let's just say China keeps us very busy."

Kade nodded. At first glance, this assignment seemed to be low to moderate risk. Less risk than the last one, anyway. Lin Soon had never appeared to be a trained operative, but now he'd have to factor her foreign loyalties into the equation.

She might have also maintained a relationship with The Chapter.

On the other hand, he didn't know Summerford and Andrade. He'd have to discreetly ask around to see what working with these two could be like. He had plenty of scar tissue on his back from his last year in the army, and he tried to avoid people who might give him any more.

That's what he liked about being a consultant now—he could turn down a job if the boss was a known idiot or asshole. Assuming he didn't need the money. But, if he didn't like a job, he had no one to blame but himself.

Overall, this opportunity sounded like it could be fun. He knew someone he could call who might be able to get him more insight on the China-India conflict. Andrade and Summerford probably wouldn't think that was necessary, but he liked understanding the big picture.

"Okay," Kade said, "if you think I'm the right fit, then let's move to a draft contract I can review."

"Sure, we'll put together a follow-up for next week," Andrade said. "We want to get this rolling quickly."

"Great."

"Thanks for coming in today," Summerford said as they adjourned. "On your birthday, no less."

Again the twinkle returned. He looked at her and smiled, admittedly impressed at how astute she was with her background information. His birthdate on record had been changed so that Kyle Smith was one year and

14

one week older than Kade Sims was. That adjustment kept him safer in case someone tried to look him up.

But his real birthday was today. Kade Sims was twenty-six.

"That's very good," he said. "Thank you."

Andrade added, "You know, statistically speaking, we men are more likely to die on our birthdays, so be careful out there."

Kade smiled. "I will, thanks."

He shook Andrade's hand, thinking his sense of humor might be a plus.

This was turning into a great day so far, and he was even happier to get out of the FBI office and into the fresh air by four thirty. It looked like he'd now have two projects on his plate, each with a bit of national importance.

This was exactly the kind of work he'd hoped to find, and it was hard for him to believe that at this time, last year, he'd been working at the Home Depot. Until the FBI had come knocking, he hadn't realized he still wanted to do something more. That he was *capable* of much more.

Even though the last FBI operation had taken a toll on him physically and mentally, he was back in good health. Excited about the year ahead. He had a good feeling about his life and it was cause for some quiet celebration. Sometimes you just had to enjoy the moment.

He walked toward his black pickup on the far side of the parking lot.

Where should I go?

He remembered a pub, O'Neal's, in Chantilly, twelve miles up the road. He'd been there on his birthday two years ago with some friends when he was living in Herndon. They never made him open a tab, and these days he only used prepaid credit cards if he couldn't pay in cash.

O'Neal's had a good happy hour. A zillion TV screens to keep him comfortably overstimulated. No one would remember him there.

O'Neal's it is.

But he had forgotten a trivial detail. Two years ago, he had posted a status online from his phone—one he should have gone back and removed.

Getting my B-day spankings at O'Neal's.

CHAPTER 4

Bethesda, Maryland
Wednesday, November 9
3:30 p.m. (EST)

The Chapter's new chief medical officer, Dr. Lindsay Gill, greeted the group of six anxious patients in the waiting room for the second day. The undecorated temp office was a ten-minute drive from the National Institutes of Health, or NIH, where Gill served as a scientific director. She had taken a few planned vacation days this week.

The test patients were Zulu members of The Chapter who had been indoctrinated into the program at its lowest level and still had a functioning program.

Gill's smile and brown eyes radiated a warmth and sympathy that had once brought comfort to children's hospital patients a decade earlier. She had then become an infectious disease specialist after years of additional study and training.

A new career path funded by The Chapter.

"I'm sorry you all feel horrible," she said, "but that's what we were shooting for."

The four men and two women were listless, breathing through congested noses and suffering through phlegm-filled coughs.

"Today, we're going to draw a little blood and give you an antiviral shot that should get rid of this cold in less than twenty-four hours. You'll get your second payment for participating in this study, and then we'll want you back here, same time tomorrow, to track your improvement. Okay?"

"What if we have a reaction to the shot or something?" a middle-aged man asked.

"Good question, Jack. I'm going to have you all wait about twenty minutes in the exam rooms after I administer the shot to make sure you don't have an unexpected reaction. And then you have our pager number for this evening through tomorrow. My assistant will get ahold of me if needed."

Gill looked over at Petr Ignaty, a seasoned Sentry with scars near his eye sockets and muscular arms bulging out of his teal scrub shirt. Ignaty sat behind what would typically have been a patient reception desk, but there were no computers, phones, or files behind it. Ignaty had worked closely with The Chapter's executive group before.

"Jack," Gill said, "since you asked the only question, you get the privilege of going first and getting this over with."

Jack showed a glimmer of happiness. He blew his nose before getting up, and Gill pointed him toward the hand sanitizing gel dispenser on the wall.

In the exam room, Gill spent a few minutes taking Jack's vital signs and drawing a vial of blood before she produced a syringe and swabbed the injection site with alcohol.

"Okay, one more little stick."

Seconds later, when Jack lost consciousness, Gill laid him flat on the table. She gave a second injection and listened through her stethoscope until his heartbeat stopped.

See, Jack? I promised I'd get rid of that cough.

She looked at her watch and walked back toward the waiting room, her smile cued.

Pierce had told her he wanted to make absolutely sure the rhinovirus was working as designed by having a small test in-country before he gave the go-ahead.

He would be happy. The virus was ready.

Now the lab rats needed to be euthanized.

"Okay," she said to the group. "One down, five to go. Who's next?"

CHAPTER 5

O'Neal's
Chantilly, Virginia
Wednesday, November 9
5:02 p.m. (EST)

Carrying a concealed weapon in a bar was illegal in Virginia, and carrying one in plain sight would be plain stupid, so Kade removed his gun from its shoulder holster underneath his jacket and locked it in his truck's glove box.

The spacious pub had a light crowd and many open barstools. Seasonal American sports played on the main bar TVs, and anything from Australian-rules football to table tennis played at the fringes.

Kade periodically scanned the room behind him via the bar mirror to his front, but no one registered as out of the ordinary, including several men sitting alone at cocktail tables.

He ordered a bacon cheeseburger, fries, and a Guinness and ignored conversation attempts from the half-drunk gray-haired sales guy to his left, soaking up a pricey scotch. The jukebox was playing at a volume where it was hard to hear the TVs, but the various games, highlights, and score ticker tapes provided ample information overload. The bartender brought another pint ten minutes later as he started to eat.

His birthday came with mixed feelings, but a morning call with his younger sister, Janeen, had been a great start. Then he'd listened to a recording of his mom wishing him happy birthday, saved from a voicemail four years ago during her fight against late-stage breast cancer. Now, he looked at a favorite photo on his phone—he was five years old, dressed in a little Celtics jersey, and trying out a new Nerf basketball set while his smiling, joyful dad played defense on his knees.

Of course they'd want him to be happy. Maybe, on balance, he was.

He glanced at a TV farther down the bar. The Fox News Channel showed a recent YouTube video that had blown up social media since last weekend.

Congressional election results were in from yesterday—the Republicans had gained control of the Senate by a three-seat majority and maintained a twenty-seven-seat majority in the House. In previous years, none of this would've made any difference to Kade.

But a sensational piece of election news hit close to his home of Worcester, Massachusetts. A historic upset occurred when Republican Senatorial candidate, Terence Hawkins, edged out the Democratic incumbent favorite, Timothy Huff. Huff had been leading in the polls by eight percentage points last week, but the strangest turn of events in this particular race had swung the voters' choice at the polls.

News reports said Hawkins was driving to a local event the previous Saturday morning and had stopped at a traffic light when he witnessed an armed carjacking in front of him. He dialed 9-1-1 and proceeded to follow the stolen car while staying on his phone, saying he could see a woman being threatened inside.

When the male assailant lost control of the car and crashed near a traffic circle, Hawkins pulled off nearby and sprinted to the car to help. The carjacker attempted to shoot Hawkins before he left the area, but Hawkins, who carried a gun for personal safety, returned fire. The assailant escaped, but, more importantly, Hawkins was able to pull the injured woman and her young son out of the burning car.

A teenage boy walking nearby had captured the ordeal on his phone, and when he'd posted the video to YouTube, it had gone viral—gathering over a million views in forty-eight hours, and attracting broadcast news coverage. As Tuesday's shocking results had rolled in, it was believed that the positive sentiment created by the event helped Hawkins close the gap and win by less than a percentage point.

In reviewing the balance of less-dramatic results, Kade noted that the

Massachusetts representative from his home Eighth District, Democrat Conrad Seale, had won reelection. Kade made a point to thumb Seale a congratulatory text.

A few months earlier, it was Kade's actions that had saved Seale and his family from being killed in a terror attack. Seale had learned more about Kade from serving on the House Permanent Select Committee on Intelligence. After Kade had given testimony, Seale requested to meet with him alone, offering thanks and help if Kade ever needed it.

When Kade finished his meal and the bartender made the last update to his bill, he laid down cash and headed back to the bathroom to take a leak before leaving.

He was standing at the urinal when the door opened behind him, and his instincts buzzed enough to make him glance over his shoulder.

A shorter man, about five foot seven and wearing a thick denim jacket, stepped up to the sink on his left. The man turned on the faucet and looked in the mirror.

"What's up?" the guy said. He splashed some water on his face and ran his hand through his hair.

"Hey, how's it going?" Kade mumbled in regular bathroom man-speak. The man looked Greek or Italian. Tough. When their eyes connected, he noticed something he hadn't seen in a few months. A tiny blur at the bottom edge of his vision. A shimmer.

Kade turned his head back to the front and looked at the graffiti on the porcelain tile.

No, it couldn't be the facial recognition. Months ago, his program had alerted him if someone was a member of The Chapter. But that program was now dead.

Then why did he feel a twinge in every skin pore? It wasn't the piss shivers.

He started zipping up.

I didn't see this guy in the bar.

A cord wrapped around Kade's throat. His attacker turned into him so they were back to back and pulled with all his might.

A croak escaped Kade's windpipe. It would only be a few seconds before he was out cold. His legs were losing balance.

The balls of Kade's feet touched the floor again and the man heaved harder. Again. The man couldn't get Kade completely off the ground. Not quite enough leverage.

Kade bent his knees and jerked forward, and when his feet landed, he exploded backward, backpedaling, aiming to slam the guy into the wall. Instead, there was a loud metallic *boonk* and a whirring of air upon the impact.

Kade bounced forward and the garrote loosened enough for him to jam his hand under it. Spinning around, he raised his arm like the Statue of Liberty and pulled the cord away.

His attacker still faced the wall, standing, stunned for a second. Kade had slammed the guy's head into the wall-mounted hand dryer that was still running. A lucky shot.

The guy tried to turn, but before he could, Kade grabbed him around the shoulders in a bear hug and wrenched him off the ground.

He shuffled across the room while the man fought to break free, kicking hard with his legs until Kade ran his midsection full force into the sink edge. As the man gasped for breath, Kade unclasped his hands, palmed the back of the man's head, and smashed his face down on the back side of the sink.

Four more blows into the sink did the job. The faucet fixtures battered the man's eyes, nose, and mouth before his body went limp. Kade pulled him down to the floor and laid him out flat.

The man didn't move. Something else had fallen on the ground from the sink. A full syringe, still capped.

Was he planning to knock me out, take me with him? Why the choke?

Kade looked up. They had made a ton of noise in the fight, but the sound system in this place was louder. He popped the cap off the syringe and jabbed it in the guy's neck, deciding to give him half of the contents. He replaced the cap and put the syringe in his coat pocket.

The man's face was a bloody mess from forehead to chin. No time to clean him up. There had been an EXIT sign in the hallway outside. He grabbed his attacker in a fireman's carry and brought him out the back door to his truck.

A couple walking toward the entrance on the other side of the parking lot looked his way. It looked like he was helping a passed-out friend, he hoped.

He laid the guy against the back wheel of his truck, sat him up while he pulled a custom body bag from the interior floor, spread it on the backseat, and unzipped it. The bag had a metallic coating on the inside to help trap signals from any hidden transmitter on his body or clothes.

Kade grabbed several pairs of zip cuffs from the glove box. He bound his hands and feet, heaved him up into the thin backseat space, rolled him sideways, and checked his pockets. A cheap phone had a keypad PIN lock, but the Virginia driver's license inside the guy's wallet said his name was Seth Hager. Address in Oakton.

Hager, you could've just shot me.

Kade snapped the phone in half. Not being tracked in this situation was a top precaution.

He entered Hager's contact info into his iPhone and returned the license and wallet back to his pants pocket. Hager still had a strong pulse at the wrist, and Kade could feel his breath when he held the back of his hand close to his mouth. A few of his front teeth were broken. Too bad.

Time to bag this jackass.

He wiggled Hager into the bag and zipped it up. A small patch of mesh up at his nose and mouth would ensure he didn't suffocate.

Kade shut the rear door, looped around, and got in the driver's seat before realizing he was getting blood all over the upholstery. He cursed and slammed the glove box shut after retrieving his gun and sliding it back into his holster.

Better call in.

He keyed a memorized number into his phone to reach an automated answering service. His message would be forwarded to seven other people, who would assemble within two hours' notice, any time of day or night, for the duration of this mission. There was no name for this operation he was aware of.

They were called the Recovery Team.

There was one person from the Defense Advanced Research Projects Agency (DARPA) Defense Sciences Office and two from DARPA's Microsystems Technology Office. There were two CIA scientists from the

Directorate of Science and Technology, two CIA operatives, and a supervisor. There were a few medical and security personnel supporting the group.

Other than the president, Secretaries of Defense and Homeland Security, the FBI Director, and the Directors of National and Central Intelligence, knowledge of the mission was "limited to single digits."

Adrenaline remained in his body from the choking. He felt scatterbrained, but his training had kicked in. He had rehearsed the whole process up to this point, even putting one of the operatives from his team, Trevor Mitchell, in the body bag and loading him into his truck for practice.

The automated attendant prompted him to leave the message. He tried to clear his throat but his hoarse, strained voice struggled to get words out.

"This is Kyle. I have a critical patient ready for the clinic. Awaiting your further instructions. Out."

He ended the call and waited less than two minutes for his phone to blink with a new text message telling him where to go. The address in Kings Park linked into his phone map and directions program.

As he pulled out, he heard Hager shift around in the bag and grunt.

Uh-oh. Better hurry.

I wonder what the Recovery Team will do with him . . .

CHAPTER 6

Team Leader Xing and a squad of nine Lanzhou "Night Tigers" special operations soldiers from the People's Liberation Army (PLA) dismounted their eight-wheeled ZBL-09 Snow Leopard infantry fighting vehicle, approximately two hundred meters from the disputed Indo-China border, known as the Line of Actual Control.

Xing checked his location on a handheld tracker receiving signals from the Chinese Beidou geopositioning system and set off on the patrol's planned route. The squad dispersed in the darkness while a driver, gunner, and vehicle commander remained behind.

Regular rotations of special ops squads, once adequately acclimated to the high altitude, performed these covert missions of reconnaissance and harassment.

While Xing thought these patrols were somewhat boring, and the bitter cold was never enjoyable, it was, at least, a real mission, not training.

After a half-mile march in snowshoes, the patrol reached a cluster of large tents at the expected map grid coordinates. The Chinese government would say these tents were home to Chinese nomads, or Rebos, but they were actually a temporary home to semiretired PLA soldiers. Besides their intelligence value, having a presence of these paid nomads helped bolster China's purported claims on the disputed border.

Xing had participated in similar probes before, designed to constantly test the Indian border forces. Chinese special ops teams would often set up temporary camps five to ten miles inside Indian territory. Sometimes they would bring a "civilian" construction crew to start work on a new road or hardened outpost to see how the Indians would react.

The patrol spent an hour checking in with the Rebos, who told them an Indian border police squad, backed by an army platoon, had given them an ultimatum to leave in two days. Xing would relay this information back to his Lanzhou command, and they would then decide whether to send in more troops to test the Indians further, or withdraw.

The Chinese course of action often depended on the political environment of the day, but the strategy was one of consistent border pressure. China would always publicly deny its troops were crossing the Line of Actual Control.

The patrol continued its march toward the Indian installation at Demchok. It would observe Indian patrol activity and identify any potential targets of interest. It was possible in the future that Xing's squad could be called on for a decapitation mission to take out the installation entirely. After all, the newly issued Chinese military maps showed Demchok inside China's borders.

At just over three hours into the patrol, one of Xing's lead soldiers spoke a warning over his headset.

"We have vehicles approaching."

A minute later, Xing saw glowing spots through his night vision goggles. It was hard to judge the exact distance, but they didn't look like the boxy front profile of an Indian six-wheeled Stallion troop transporter.

No, these were smaller. Unusual.

He had misjudged the distance. They were much closer. Eight objects, closing the distance fast. Not in a single-file convoy. Not constricted to the road.

They looked like . . . *snowmobiles?*

He'd never seen snowmobiles through night vision goggles before. He could now hear the engines.

A wall of automatic gunfire flashed and thundered toward Xing's patrol as though a singular command had been given. The snowmobiles had front-mounted machine guns.

Two of Xing's men were already hit as they dove into the snow. His patrol returned fire with their QBZ 95 rifles, and one squad member loaded a drum of seventy-five rounds into his QBB 97 light machine gun. The speed and maneuverability of the snowmobiles made them hard to hit. They appeared well trained. Movements coordinated.

Xing's radio operator didn't need to be told to transmit an emergency message.

"*Shānmāo*, we're under attack! Taking heavy fire from an Indian unit on snowmobiles!"

The Snow Leopard was not responding. Radio communications were often problematic.

Seconds later, a bullet struck Xing's left shoulder, removing any shred of disbelief that they'd been ambushed by a specialized Indian paramilitary force. His squad had not even opted for protective vests because the threat had been assessed as low to no risk.

Xing cradled his weapon in one arm, trying to steady it with an elbow planted in the snow. The muzzle flashes from his long, poorly aimed burst seemed to bring more fire upon him.

His squad's machine gunner was killed shortly after deploying the gun's bipod and opening fire. If he'd managed to hit any of the snowmobiles, it wasn't apparent.

None of Xing's squad responded on radios. They were all dead. Xing considered fighting to the death, but then there would be no information relayed back to Xinjiang.

He remained motionless. A snowmobile sped by and flooded him with light but kept going, and minutes later, all of them were gone.

His worst fears were confirmed—all of his men were dead. Besides the pain of his wound, the anger of failure and losing his team stung him as he marched back, alone, to the Snow Leopard. Who knew what his commander would do and what his life would become?

Only one thought gave him any sort of comfort.

The spot of land where his brothers died would someday be China's.

CHAPTER 7

Burke Lake Road
Kings Park, Virginia
Wednesday, November 9
6:11 p.m. (EST)

Where the hell is this place? Kade looped around the perimeter of the strip mall for the second time until spotting the address number on the nearby two-story standalone building. Its blue sign had the letters GCS superimposed on a compass logo.

The text told him to drive around back, so he followed the outside of an eight-foot-high fence until he reached a gate with a keypad post in front of it. He turned off his headlights but left the parking lights on as instructed when the gate came into sight. The code from the text worked, and the gate slid open.

A plainclothes security guard waved and walked ahead of his truck, escorting him to a large garage door and loading bay where two more guards were waiting.

As he brought the truck to a halt and stepped out, he saw the familiar bearded face of Trevor Mitchell greeting him.

"Nice work, Kyle," Mitchell said. "We're going to do a quick check for surveillance devices first."

"Right on."

Mitchell pointed to Kade's throat. "You okay?"

"Think so."

The other operative, Vince De La Paz, joined them, holding a device in each hand—portable surveillance equipment. He scanned Kade first.

"I'll go over the truck after you get him out," De La Paz said.

They used the body bag's thick grips to slide Hager out of the truck. Kade imagined these actions could appear suspicious, but the high fence and dim lighting would prevent anyone from seeing activity around the building.

"In the cage," Mitchell said.

It might have been a coincidence, but when "the cage" was mentioned, Hager started to squirm and grunt from inside the bag again. Mitchell gave him a knee to the rib area and told him to shut up. When they passed through the entrance, the two guards took over.

Kade flexed his aching fingers. "We didn't scan *him*."

"The holding cages are shielded," Mitchell said, "and he'll be checked more thoroughly than he ever wanted."

Kade felt his phone vibrating in his pocket. When he pulled it out, Mitchell spotted it.

"You've got to turn that off and leave it in the entry room."

"Yeah, understood. Sorry."

He hit the power button, and the name Carla Singleton vanished from the phone screen. Singleton was an FBI analyst who'd participated in his prior operation. He'd also been dating her over the past month. She probably was calling about his birthday, but he couldn't worry about that right now.

The office space was typical for any medical building—doctor, dentist, veterinarian—they all had the same basic layout. In this case, there was a reception area, exam rooms, an operating room, and a few supporting meeting rooms and medical supply areas.

"Welcome to the SAU," Mitchell said.

"And SAU means . . . ?"

"Secure Ambulatory Unit."

"Ah."

They pushed Hager inside an eight-by-eight secure cage in one of the four exam rooms. A black nylon cover with some Velcro openings on the top side slid over the cage next. It reminded Kade of crating a puppy. Additional soundproofing and a metallic mesh lined the walls. He assumed this was a kind of Faraday cage to provide electronic shielding. Some cabled remote monitoring equipment was set up in the corner.

A guard posted himself outside.

"You really fucked up his face," Mitchell said.

"He attacked me first," Kade said.

"Hey, I wasn't saying that was a bad thing . . ."

The SAU setup was starting to make sense, strategy-wise. The specialized portable equipment worked inside any basic layout like this. Prisoners could be interrogated and medically monitored. Moved around to various locations to avoid discovery.

It was like domestic rendition, though Kade would never say that out loud.

He suspected friendly personnel could also receive medical treatment when there wasn't an active covert op and a regular hospital was best avoided. Surveillance was so pervasive these days that maintaining the secrecy of friendly operatives was a challenge. A few hits of an operative's face showing up on a hospital security camera combined with their electronic medical record information would compromise their identity. Even secure wings of Walter Reed were vulnerable.

Americans would find the design and purpose of the SAU highly objectionable. But the public wasn't fully aware of the nature of the threat The Chapter brought, and the technology behind it.

Kade not only understood it, he was living it.

"Nice work, Kyle."

A gray-haired man wearing a black sweater over a dress shirt came in to see him. Kade had met Russell Lamb once before, when he'd signed his contract. Lamb was the "project manager" of the Recovery Team. Mitchell and De La Paz said they reported to Lamb and he "called the shots." Kade suspected Lamb was a senior CIA officer handpicked by the DCI or DNI for this responsibility.

"Thanks," Kade said and shook his hand.

Lamb eyed Kade's neck and the blood on his clothes.

"You look like utter hell, but we're going to need you to stick around. We've got cots in the sleep rooms for when you need rest. There's a break room with a TV, and there's food in the kitchen. But let's get that neck injury taken care of first."

"Thanks."

"Is there anything you'd like to know from Hager when we question him?" Lamb asked.

"Yeah, I'd like to know how he found me. What he was told about me by his higher-ups. But be careful—you ask too much, you might lose him."

"Yeah, we know about that very well, thanks. We'll be taking care of his chip first."

Taking care of his chip?

A lanky man with a bold chin joined the group.

"Kyle, when you're patched up, I can take you to the computer lab if you'd like," the man said. "I'm Matt Henderson—one of the two scientists on our team."

"Hi," Kade said and shook his hand. "You know, I'm probably not going to be able to sleep tonight anyway. So, I'm up for the lab."

"Cool," Henderson said. "I'm sure you'll find what I'm going to show you very interesting."

CHAPTER 8

Once his attractive neck bruise and cord burn were cleaned and treated with lidocaine cream and a bandage, Kade met Henderson in the computer lab. The familiar metallic-mesh shielding lined the room walls. All of the room's equipment could have easily fit in a van.

"Welcome to our Chapter sandbox," Henderson said. "Our analysis computers are here in the center. The PC station over at that wall is for gaming if you need to blow off some steam."

"Oh, I won't need that, but thanks," Kade said. Giving him computer games was like giving an alcoholic cold beer. Nothing productive could come of it.

A "sandbox" or virtual network simulated programs in a test environment, so the actual system, what was called the production environment, would be free from accidental harm. A sandbox was especially critical for sensitive programs because it reduced potential exposure to hacks and viruses. But since a sandbox was a scaled-down copy of a *real* program, it begged the question of . . .

"So you managed to obtain *actual* copies of The Chapter's software?" Kade asked.

"Yes, some of it," Henderson said. "Two weeks after The Chapter's attack, the FBI raided a ranch in Montana that yielded some of their technology.

About an hour before the raid, four men inside the home were gunned down by one of their own. The fifth man had bugged out, but they picked him up later on the highway."

Kade walked to the center of the room. The gaggle of computers was set on four tables pushed together in a square. Next to those were two small rack servers and an armored filing cabinet with combination locks. Ruggedized carrying cases were stacked nearby, and various taped-down cables snaked across the floor.

Two of the computers had a device plugged into them—a simple black box with a red translucent plastic disc in the front.

"I've seen those before," Kade said.

"Yes, the infrared boxes—we have hundreds. The FBI gathered them from locations across the country following CLEARCUT. We concluded they were used to communicate with Chapter members through their implanted readers. Your debriefing notes helped with that."

"I'm glad my debrief was good for something." Kade sat down in front of a computer paired with a black box. "Are you going to put Guardian Hager in front of this thing and see what you can learn?"

"No, that's an unlikely Plan B. We think it's more important to analyze the chipset design."

In that instant, the entire chilling purpose of the SAU crystalized.

Lamb said they were going to take care of the chip first.

There's only one way to analyze the design.

"You mean, you're going to remove Hager's chipset . . . like, surgically," Kade said.

"Yes. We've retrieved no viable chipsets to date. All of the chips self-destructed. Many during questioning. We have some theories on how, but nothing concrete."

This is why the DoD wanted a Guardian alive. They wanted the most advanced chipset The Chapter had designed, the same one Kade had been given.

They wanted the Guardian protocol.

Intact.

That meant this whole SAU thing wasn't only for treating prisoners and operatives as he had thought.

Involuntary surgery was the epitome of invading someone's privacy. Legal? Justified? They were doing a dangerous dance here. He had a flashback of the last FBI operation and tried to ignore memories of the painful forced medical procedures he'd undergone at The Chapter.

He imagined an enormous refrigerated hangar located somewhere remote, like Nevada, with hundreds of corpses laid out in rows. Someone was drilling into the skulls of these Chapter soldiers, called Sentries and Zulus, and removing blown-up electronic remains of the chipsets. Trying to make sense of them.

He had to push these thoughts aside for now because he knew what was at stake. This was truly national security and not a government catchphrase. The people in The Chapter were more sophisticated and dangerous than the most brazen jihadist cell.

The highest threshold of secrecy was required to keep this SAU activity under wraps.

"But what about the guy in Montana you captured alive?" Kade asked.

"He died during interrogation, and the chipsets in the other four were no longer viable. We learned they were part of a small development team, and they all had the Zulu protocol, not the Guardian."

Interesting.

The Zulu chipset was the original model, about five years old, more widely deployed than the Guardian chipset, but less innovative than its successor. Sentries always had the Zulu chipset, as did the majority of Chapter members living among the American public.

"Am I allowed to take a look at the programs?" Kade asked.

"Absolutely. We have a copy of the Chapter Network's internal server software and also a software developer toolkit. I've done a few things with those."

Kade had worked with many a software toolkit. They were necessary to make any significant changes in software programs. In front of him, the computer screen had some indictor graphs on it he didn't understand, and they were all blank because the program wasn't measuring anything.

"So, what am I looking at here?" Kade asked.

"I built a software emulator using the toolkit and server software. It will hopefully simulate the local connection between the internal network and either a Guardian or Zulu protocol."

"Man, that's great work in such a short time."

"Thanks. We're still missing some key pieces. The developer toolkit has almost no documentation on how to use it, we presume intentionally. I'm working under the assumption that the same toolkit will work for both a Guardian protocol and a Zulu protocol, but I could be wrong since they're different chipsets."

"Probably a good assumption—these guys developed rapidly and efficiently. What else is missing?"

"A big piece—the software that allows them to communicate securely over the Internet to send Chapter directives and distribute software updates. The administration piece. If we can get ahold of that, we can probably destroy their entire network."

"Cool."

The infrared (IR) reader rested on a short riser bringing it up to eye level. The device, as far as Kade knew, emitted an infrared signal, much like a TV remote did. He closed his right eye and shifted in his seat to center the focus of his left eye on the red disk.

"What other programs are running?" he asked.

"There's a vicinity reader program. We think that's how a Chapter member transmits information back to The Network. There's a reader inside that same black box."

"Really? Wow, I didn't know that. So it sends information like a smart card or proximity badge?"

"Yep—only with more range, we guess."

Kade thought back to when he had sat in front of the IR reader while inside AgriteX. He was told he had to be within a foot to receive the required downloads. But come to think of it, he'd never tested the range. There was never an—

CHAPTER NETWORK

You are 137 days overdue in downloading the required Daily Update.

"Whoa!" he yelled, and his body tensed up when the two words appeared in his natural vision—dark green lettering inside a white oval.

A small traffic light graphic popped up on the left side, its bottom light lit up in green. A stick-figure pine tree insignia appeared on the right.

"What?" Henderson looked at the computer screen and back at Kade. "What's going on?"

"My program—it just came online! I can see it right here . . . right in front of me."

"Oh my God!" Henderson's initial dumbfounded look flipped to one of suspicion. "I pray you're being serious."

"I'm not kidding around. It's on. The chipset must have needed a reboot or something."

Henderson stepped forward and stared, squinting at Kade's face as though he was trying to look through a dirty window. He scrambled back over to one of the cabinets, pulled a notebook out from one of the drawers, and brought it back.

"Does it look like this sketch you did during your CLEARCUT debrief?"

"Yeah, it sure does."

"Wow, this is huge," Henderson said and put his hand over his mouth. "Huge. This changes everything. Kyle, your program *could* be fully functional. We assumed you destroyed the chip, when it may have only run out of power. It could've just needed a recharge and a reboot."

"No way. It couldn't have recharged in a minute."

"Yes, it could have, partially. Probably at about five percent per minute . . . meaning it would be fully charged in about twenty minutes. Sit here for a little while."

"How could it charge so fast?"

The smile disappeared from Henderson's face. He stood up and pulled a red metallic object from his hoodie pocket. Kade thought it was some new high-tech gadget until Henderson started whizzing it around on a string, using both hands. It was a standard yo-yo.

"In the aftermath of CLEARCUT," Henderson said, "we retrieved hundreds of destroyed chips from corpses and analyzed the fragments. We learned the material contains what are called quantum dots."

"Quantum dots?"

"Yes. Quantum dots have the ability to charge using infrared energy. From the amount of them measured in each chip, we think there'd be enough material to hold a charge for a week. Our other scientist, Vic Martin, is the expert on microchip hardware. DARPA has manufactured prototypes of this material, but for a different purpose—the concept being that soldiers of the future may have uniforms and equipment coated with this stuff to power various devices. But it was never examined for use *inside* the human body."

"So you're saying . . ."

Henderson stopped the yo-yoing, sat, and scooted the chair closer.

"What I'm saying is that the chipset and the receiver—that piece above your eye under the skin—are coated in quantum dots."

Kade pointed at the infrared box.

"Then that's not just for downloads and uploads. It's also a power supply."

"Yes, I think you just proved that. In fact, I wouldn't be surprised if you can charge your chipset by catching a few rays outside. Sunlight is over half infrared energy, and Infrared-A spectrum waves can reach subcutaneous skin tissue."

Kade looked up at the metallic shielding above him and pictured a daytime sky while rocking his chair back in astonishment. When he rocked forward, he scooted closer to face the IR box again to see if more power would cause his program to do anything else.

That "shimmer" in his vision—he'd never shared what he'd seen with anyone. Had it been a trace of his program working?

Maybe he'd skimmed enough power from being out in the sun to keep the chip alive. It was now late autumn—there were fewer hours of sunlight, and he often wore hats as part of his disguise. His power was probably at the bare minimum.

"Let me see something," Kade said.

He now went into his Chapter program's *Options* menu, then to *Input* to change the setting from *Keyboard* to *Visual*. In the *Visual* setting, a keyboard grid appeared in the bottom of his vision. Using this method to type was slower than even texting or two-finger typing—about two to three letters per second. When he was done, he "pressed" the *Upload* button with a deliberate blink.

Henderson had no idea what Kade was doing while he was sitting there, making subtle eye movements.

"Ha-ha!" Kade shouted and startled Henderson in the process. He pointed at the desk computer screen, and Henderson turned his head to look.

WHAT'S UP MATT?

"Wow! Unbelievable!" Henderson put his hands in the air like he was signaling a touchdown. Kade added three more words.

I GOT POWER!

Kade started laughing and wrote some more phrases just for fun. Henderson became absorbed in thought and flipped through the pages of the notebook.

"I wonder if . . . ," Henderson mumbled. "Okay, I have a code recovered from two different locations on the second floor of AgriteX. What was left of it, anyway. The code was handwritten in each case. One was on the inside cover of a book, the other on a Post-it. Would you know what it's for?" He started turning the notebook around.

"Stop!" Kade yelled and shut his eyes. "Matt, tell me first—how many characters does the code have?"

"Uh . . . thirty."

"Okay, just read it to me real quick, out loud."

After Henderson read the alphanumeric code, Kade opened his eyes and sat there for a moment. "Hmm. Okay, I'm not sure what code you have there, but I can try to figure it out."

Henderson stood up and fanned his hands out to say *stay put*.

"Okay, I'm going to go tell a few people about this now," he said. "This is quite a breakthrough. It may mean we have to modify our strategy immediately."

"I agree."

After Henderson exited, Kade rifled through his vision menu to the *Options* area again and went to *Mode* selection. There was a space there for a thirty-character code, and when he visually keyed it in, the word *DEV* appeared in the bottom right of his vision.

And there it is. Thank you, FBI forensics team.

I now have developer mode . . .

In developer mode, he could make some limited changes to his own Guardian program, just like periodic updates pushed to his iPhone. He had worked with a similar developer program while being groomed at The Chapter, only that was the desktop version.

Kade swallowed and groaned. His throat muscles still ached from the choking.

I bet this is why Marshall Owens didn't implant the Guardian chipset in their developers.

He knew better.

You don't want anyone with a hacker mentality getting ahold of this and going rogue.

With this capability and the developer toolkit, who knew what he could do now? The combination was like being able to program your iPhone *and* create apps for it.

Kade's body started shaking with excitement. This was a software engineer's dream. Months ago he had written some Chapter program code for training purposes. Now he could use the test environment to write code and try out changes. Then he could move the code to the production environment . . .

To implement changes.

Permanently.

Inside his head.

Unprecedented.

He noticed something else. With the program running, he felt more . . .

Normal.

Should I be worried?

He wasn't sure if it was psychological, physiological, or both. His mind felt in better focus. Maybe this was only temporary excitement and the thrill would fade.

There was one other key code he was aware of, one that worked hand in hand with that administration module Henderson said was missing. It would access an administrator mode and enable various "global rights" to other members of The Chapter. Such an administrator could implement software updates in the entire population of people implanted with these chipsets.

Kade bet that code wasn't lying around anywhere.

There were probably two or three people who knew it. One of them, he believed, was Joshua Pierce, who had been second-in-command of The Chapter. That dick was still out there somewhere, alive. Pierce could have been the one who'd sent Hager.

What Henderson had said made him uneasy. Lamb's team was holding back information. Some of that was justified and to be expected. But now, as he had just reactivated his chip, did that put *him* at risk for being laid out on the operating table?

How far would they go for national security?

If they wanted to destroy The Chapter Network, would they destroy me to do it?

The Recovery Team was new and had only been together for a few weeks. New people made his trust issues rear their ugly heads again despite his best attempts to beat on them like whack-a-mole.

This group hadn't proven themselves, but he needed to strike a balance if he was going to be doing this kind of work for a living. He'd always be working with new people, and consulting work meant this would come with every new project.

Deal with it. Get over it.

Striking a balance meant he would make a reasonable decision: he *would* tell them about the key code to enter developer mode on the Guardian chipset, but not just yet.

I'll keep the bargaining "chip" in my head a little longer.

As he waited for Henderson to return, he found and selected a program option to make the remaining power show in his vision, and now a bar displayed CHARGING 11%, similar to an ordinary smartphone. Watching the power level was now more critical than previously thought.

A few minutes later Henderson walked in with Lamb and the others.

Lamb said, "Kyle, you still okay?"

"Yeah, still charging away."

Lamb put his hands on his hips, fingers through the belt loops.

"This could really help us," he said. "I've called some people, and everyone's excited that you've become even more of a key asset."

"I'll do what I can," Kade said. "We now have an intel conundrum. We know what we don't know. And don't know what we know."

"Yeah, ain't that right," Lamb said and laughed.

Kade didn't like being called an *asset* but tried to hide his annoyance. Assets could become liabilities in the intel community. He preferred to be an *appreciating* asset, and that gave him an idea.

He looked back at Lamb. "I wanted to ask—with Hager delivered, I've fulfilled my contract requirement, right?"

Lamb nodded. "I believe so. I'll confirm with the DNI for sign-off. But I predict he'll also want you on retainer after this latest news."

"Cool."

Now that's what I'm talking about . . .

"Any luck with that code?" Henderson asked.

Kade remembered that in The Chapter's program, if you lied to another member, the program could detect deception, and the stoplight graphic would change from green to yellow. Yellow could cause pain, but that had been one aspect of the program that hadn't worked on him. A glitch. Too many yellows could trigger a red, causing incapacitation. Yellows could also be triggered by stating sensitive phrases such as "The Chapter" aloud.

A blinking red meant death.

But Henderson was not a Chapter member. There would be no yellow warning for lying.

Kade shook his head.

"Sorry, no luck yet."

CHAPTER 9

Secure Ambulatory Unit
Kings Park, Virginia
Thursday, November 10
10:35 a.m. (EST)

The scalpel sliced open a shaved area of Hager's head above the ear, and retractors pulled the skin back. A pin fixation device immobilized his head and a lumbar drain pierced his lower back, lowering the amount of cerebral spinal fluid that could collect around his brain.

Kade was standing outside the operating room, but cameras mounted inside on the overhead lights brought an up-close view of the procedure to the video screen. He couldn't keep his eyes off it. A small team sat next to him, communicating to the two surgeons, anesthesiologist, and two nurses inside from headsets on two different channels. Kade had a headset with access to one of those channels.

The first cut had bled in a torrent, but Kade was amazed at how fast the surgeon clamped the edges of the incision with a row of C-shaped clips on each side. Between the deeper layers of tissue, a hairlike wire ran toward the direction of the eye. Dr. Scott, a physician with an undisclosed last name, dislodged the wire and fished it back. At the wire's end, a dark bulb was visible.

"This wire was threaded under the *fascia temporalis*," he said, "and positioned above the eyebrow."

Kade felt the bump above his own left eyebrow. "So, they didn't drill through my forehead?"

"No, your device was inserted the same way. Above the ear. They wouldn't have gone in above the eyebrow. The sinuses would've made it a real mess."

They drilled through Hager's skull next. A burr hole, it was called. There wasn't a lot of blood at this point, just saline squirting and bone dust flying everywhere. Reminded him of drilling through drywall. A pin in the middle of the drill bit automatically stopped the drill when it sensed the skull had been breached.

"Did The Chapter drill a hole in my head like that?" Kade asked.

His stoplight flickered yellow, but he ignored it.

Dr. Trish, the other physician, answered him. She was the one who had treated his neck. "Yes, but yours was a little smaller. Maybe ten millimeters. This is fourteen, and we're drilling three more."

Three weeks ago, Dr. Trish had spoken to Kade in detail about his ordeal with The Chapter and had reviewed the medical documentation from the treatment he'd received afterward. She hadn't given Kade much feedback on what she thought the Chapter surgeons had done. That was frustrating.

After Dr. Scott drilled four holes, spaced apart in a diamond shape, he retrieved some other kind of high-pitched power tool.

A saw.

He cut a curved line from hole to hole, like connect-the-dots. More saline and bone dust mixed together, leaving a trail of white paste as the saw moved across. When they removed the oval-shaped piece of skull, Kade spoke up again.

"That . . . wasn't done to me, right?"

"No, you didn't have a bone flap," Dr. Trish said. "They got everything in through your single burr hole. They knew exactly what they were doing, from repeating the same procedure on so many patients, I'm sure. But we're doing a bone flap out of caution in handling this chipset."

After they peeled back a small section of the dura membrane, Kade could see a patch of Hager's brain, but couldn't see much after that as they went in farther with their microcamera. The surgeons manipulated a gigantic microscope on an eight-foot-high machine featuring a robotic arm.

"Kyle," Dr. Trish said, "you had a *craniectomy*—one of the oldest medical procedures around, going back to 10,000 B.C. Even Hippocrates approved of it. That's why you're feeling so much better these days—The Chapter let all the demons out of your head."

Everyone laughed, and Kade tried to relax too, but he wasn't sure what to think.

Because he really *did* feel better these days.

The procedure had also produced a side effect where he felt a greater intuitive sense or understanding of facial microexpressions when he could observe them up close.

It was about twenty minutes until Dr. Scott came back on the headset.

"Okay, we got it. The chip's viable, and we're bringing it out."

A nurse brought over a cart with a specialized container sitting on its top, and once the chipset was pulled out, they placed it directly into the box.

They all waited for a few minutes, and nothing happened. That's what they had hoped for. Dr. Trish looked through the Plexiglas top with a magnifier.

"Still looks intact," she said.

"Okay, let's get it out of here and transported for analysis," Lamb said.

It was a mystery what caused the chipset to self-destruct just prior to death of the subject. They knew various commands could be given, and algorithms existed to make the chipset explode, but they weren't sure of any link to bodily functions. The Chapter didn't want any working chipsets being retrieved from a corpse.

From what they'd learned, the team had ruled out brain death or a decrease in body temperature. The heartbeat or pulse, they theorized, was the key. The chipset could sense the subject's pulse, and when the pulse stopped or dropped to a very slow rate that couldn't sustain life, the detonation was triggered.

The container had a simulated vibration, as if it had a pulse. The theory and its application appeared to work. Otherwise, the chipset would have exploded by now.

Chipset remnants on Chapter Sentries were found to contain residue of PETN, one of the ingredients of Semtex plastic explosive. PETN was easily triggered by an electric pulse—that's why it was perfect for detonation cord and explosive device triggers.

Dr. Scott said a few micrograms inside someone's melon would shred their frontal lobe arteries.

The team took off their headsets and Lamb stood up. It was well past midnight and everyone looked tired.

"Everyone who isn't on shift can go get some rest," he said. "We'll break down tomorrow and reconvene once the chip analysis is complete," Lamb said. "That should take at least a few days. Maybe a week."

Side conversations started, and Kade found his way over to Lamb.

"Am I free to leave, or should I stick around?"

"Go home for now, Kyle. I think what we learn from this analysis, combined with Matt's work and your breakthrough today, is going to yield exciting results. I'll get some paperwork prepared so you can continue to work with us as needed."

"All right, thanks." As Lamb started to turn around, Kade added, "Oh, did you learn anything more from Hager?"

"Yes, a bit. We were careful with the interrogation. He seemed to be well aware of what he could answer and what the chip would not allow him to answer. On some of our key questions, he responded, 'If I answer that, I'll be dead in less than a minute, and then you'll get nothing.'"

"It's a scary level of control," Kade said, thinking again about his own resurrected chip.

"But . . ." Lamb paused and cocked his head. "Apparently, they mined your social media and gathered info on you months ago, to learn all the places they thought you would be. Then they stationed people at all those possible locations. Because yesterday was your birthday, right?"

"Yeah."

"Man, you had one hell of a birthday . . . I'm sorry."

"It's okay. I'm happy to be alive. Every day's a gift, right?"

Lamb rolled his eyes. "Whoever said that never worked for the government. I'll tell you a gift—Hager would have gotten paid five hundred K if you were brought in alive. One hundred K, dead."

"Wow," Kade said. "Bigger payout with me alive. Why didn't he just use the syringe?"

"It was Fentanyl," Lamb said. "Alone, it would have taken a couple of minutes to bring you down. So, he used the cord first to subdue. And he didn't call in backup when he saw you 'cause he didn't want to split the money."

"He almost won the jackpot," Kade said.

"Now, not so much, huh?" Lamb said.

They both looked at the video screen, where the surgeons were completing Hager's surgery. Reassembling his skull.

Lamb added, "When he's recovered enough, we'll resume interrogation. And we won't have to worry about the chip anymore."

Kade smiled a little. Yes, his birthday had been a bad one, but Hager's day had been a hundred times worse. And it wasn't going to get any better. He didn't feel sorry for him at all.

"Take it easy now and get some downtime," Lamb said.

"I'll try, thanks."

"Don't let anyone know you were attacked. Keep that wound covered and get it healed up."

"I will."

"And don't fiddle around with your program until we know more about the chip."

"I won't."

There was no way he would try and program any major changes until learning more. He wasn't about to do something stupid and make his own head explode if he could help it.

But there was some hacker in his blood.

He wouldn't hurt himself playing around a little bit . . .

CHAPTER 10

Central Intelligence Agency
Langley, Virginia
Friday, November 11
9:37 a.m. (EST)

The Director of National Intelligence, Hugh Conroy, and the Director of Central Intelligence, Melissa Perry, reviewed the video segment of the dead Chinese squad, which had been running on China's Xinhua state news service every hour. Xinhua made no mention of special operations—the squad was described as a regular border unit conducting a routine patrol.

The photos showed their bodies strewn in the bloodstained snow. Faces were blacked out. The PLA and Communist Party leadership expressed outrage, and public demonstrations had begun in major cities, encouraged by the Ministry of State Security.

"There's internal confusion in the PLA about what happened and disagreement on the potential response," Perry said. "To complicate matters worse, the Chinese are now claiming India shot down one of their helicopters sent to recover the bodies of Xing's squad."

She queued up a slide on the screen showing profiles of three Chinese generals and then sat on the office couch across from Conroy. Shorter in stature, with reddish-brown hair and dark eyes, Perry was the physical opposite to the tall, blue-eyed and bald Conroy. Their styles, however, weren't far apart and they had worked well together.

"The first guy," she said, "a Major General Xu Yimin, Commander of the Chinese Forty-Seventh Group Army, and the second guy, a Major General

Deng Wang, the Forty-Seventh's Political Commissar, were summoned to meet the third guy, the Commander of the Lanzhou Military Region, General Tan Chen, at their Lanzhou headquarters."

Conroy scanned the text in the briefing folder.

"Xu and Deng are equals in rank?" he asked.

"Yes," Perry said, "PLA Group Armies have a pair of leaders—the commander and political officer."

"Looks like they were getting their stories straight before talking to their Indian counterpart," Conroy said.

"We presume that from the related chatter," Perry said. "So, there are two major issues: how the Indians detected and ambushed the patrol, and what happened to the Chinese helicopter sent to recover the bodies."

Conroy read the assessment line aloud.

"The Chinese believe the patrol was observed by one of the new Israeli-made drones supplied to the Indian Mountain Strike Corp."

"That's conjecture," Perry said. "As far as the downed helicopter goes, the deaths of the pilot and copilot haven't been reported by Chinese state news yet. On the Indian side, we know that the Indo-Tibetan Border Police secured the wreckage and the bodies of the pilots."

Conroy flipped to the intercepted call transcript and analyst notes of the emergency call between General Tan Chen and General Nikhil Vijay, the Indian Seventeenth Corps commander.

GENERAL TAN: "We had two egregious incidents last night in the East Ladakh area of the Line of Control. An Indian force attacked and killed a regular patrol from our border regiment, and one of our rescue helicopters was downed. We demand an explanation for this unwarranted act of aggression."

GENERAL VIJAY: "We are unaware of any hostilities between our units and Chinese patrols within the last twenty-four hours. We have exercised the utmost patience despite your army's repeated incursions into Indian territory. We will investigate the matter further."

GENERAL TAN: "This is outrageous. We expect your investigation to be immediate. Your army's actions were in gross violation of our October 2013 border defense cooperation pact."

GENERAL VIJAY: "We aren't aware of any ground hostilities, as I said, but we are aware of one of your helicopters crashing in excess of one kilometer inside Indian territory, after violating Indian airspace."

GENERAL TAN: "You shot down our helicopter with a missile. This is an act of war."

GENERAL VIJAY: "There is no basis or evidence for this faulty accusation. We will analyze the downed aircraft and coordinate the return of the pilots' remains, if you provide us adequate notification on how you wish to do so. We should both exercise restraint. And one must ask, who is the aggressor here? India does not fly missions into Chinese territory. India does not try to place settlements on the Chinese side of the Line of Actual Control."

GENERAL TAN: "I will have my staff coordinate a helicopter sortie to recover the remains. But we expect a full explanation in twenty-four hours. We will not let such an egregious act go unchecked!"

GENERAL VIJAY: "We understand your concern, and our condolences are with you for the loss of your soldiers."

The call transcript ended.

"Oh, that doesn't look good," Conroy said. "Does the transcript bring us current?"

Perry shook her head.

"Not quite. Now there's chatter in PLA command channels about preparing for an attack at the border area of Demchok."

"Damn," Conroy said and checked the wall clock. "We better tell the president."

CHAPTER 11

Braddock Road Metrorail Station
Alexandria, Virginia
Saturday, November 12
1:15 p.m. (EST)

Kade left his truck at Reagan National Airport long-term parking and took the train to the Braddock Metro Center. He continued to scan faces of people passing by as he descended the rail platform, walking toward the red-brick plaza entrance. His jacket was unzipped enough that he could pull his weapon if he needed to.

What was his life coming to? A permanent state of high alert?

A few minutes later, Carla Singleton picked him up at the curb in her blue Toyota RAV4. A darker lipstick contrasted nicely with her pale skin, and her brown hair now had wavy tips.

He wasn't sure if her smile meant she was genuinely happy to see him, but she looked great. They had begun to grate on each other when their date number had reached double digits. Yet, sleeping with her was like a parallel universe where everything was fine.

"Hi," he said.

"Hey, hero."

Her tone was positive but flavored with a splash of attitude.

Once the car was in motion, he floated a neutral test balloon.

"So, how are you? How's your dad?"

"Not so great."

He had met her dad, Ben, and he seemed like a nice man. Unfortunately, he suffered from hemophilia A and had occasional bleeding emergencies—

one occurring in this past week. She was her dad's sole caretaker, and the cumulative effect had taken a toll on her spirits.

"Oh, no. Is today a bad idea?" he asked.

"No, I'm okay. It's good to see you."

"Good to see you, too."

The awkwardness was more uncomfortable than her suffocating heater setting. He cracked his window.

When the car paused at a red light, she looked over at him with a curious smirk. She was familiar with the disguise he wore, and she particularly hated the near-shaved head, but that's not what she was focused on.

"What's up with the *turtleneck*?" She reached over to the collar of his black shirt with a hooked finger. "Are you hiding a—"

"Stop . . ."

"Oh."

She managed to pull down the collar for a second. In the morning rush, he hadn't rebandaged his neck, only loaded it up with the lidocaine ointment and found a soft shirt to cover it.

She stayed silent until the light turned green and they started moving again. "Well, you must have had a great birthday. Didn't know you were into the *Vampire Diaries* role-play."

"What? No, that's not it at all."

She answered with a mocking laugh.

He needed to defend himself, but her nonsense jumbled his thoughts. Saying he was attacked by The Chapter could get him in serious trouble. He couldn't violate his agreement and ruin his chance for future work. And he wasn't about to get thrown in jail for breaching nondisclosure, either.

She pushed his buttons like a child on an elevator.

"No, it was an injury . . . a painful one, that's all I can say."

Her eyes widened. "I bet."

It was always hard to tell if she was teasing or not. A little smile remained on her face.

An urge to mount a weak counterattack made the wrong words reach his lips too fast.

"Didn't you start dating someone else now, anyway?"

She blew out a breath of faux exasperation. "What? Yes . . . but only because of your *fading interest.*"

He was the king on a chessboard placed in check. Yes, it was true—his interest had started to fade, and he didn't know if it was a permanent condition. She could sense it.

Should he feel bad, or was this the way it was supposed to play out?

He wasn't good at thinking about his feelings without a checklist. Thinking about things he could fix or solve was much easier.

When he didn't comment, she added more. "I can appreciate you're at a different stage in your life than I am for what you want, and that was my mistake."

Ah, now I'm immature . . .

He wasn't going to agree with another one of these Trojan horse insults. Sure, she was five years older, but it seemed like she'd enjoyed herself enough. At least the physical part.

Replying with a few choice words was his preferred option, but that wasn't going to help anything. Conflict was her fuel.

"Okay, point taken," he said. "So, was this meeting today with your friend a mistake? Should we do it some other time?"

"No, come *on.* Everything's okay." She squeezed him high on the thigh and kept her hand there, caressing him. "I'm sure you're up to something important and dangerous. Otherwise you wouldn't be packing a gun everywhere."

"Yeah, right," he mumbled.

Her touch made him start thinking about her body next to him in bed, and he tried to push the image away.

What the hell is she trying to do?

He noticed she kept glancing in the rearview mirror. While he was thinking of how to tactfully ask her if she was worried about anything, she preempted.

"Since CLEARCUT ended, do you ever have the feeling you're being watched?"

"Uh, yeah," he said. "All the time. Chances are, I *am*—I just never know if the good guys or bad guys are doing it."

Five minutes later, they pulled off Braddock Road into a parking lot. When the car came to a halt, he sensed something physical was going to happen between them if he didn't steer the situation toward business.

Don't get back on the pirate ship ride.

"So, who are we meeting with?" he asked.

She unbuckled her seat belt and turned toward him. "We're fifteen minutes early and it's freezing outside."

He sighed. "I don't think that's a good idea today. Here in the parking lot."

Her provocative look changed to disappointment before he popped the door open and strolled around the edge of the lot. She took forever to get out of the car. Once she joined him, she'd reverted to professional mode.

"We're meeting with Raj Badesha. Remember Raj from CLEARCUT?"

"Oh, yeah . . ."

Badesha was a counterterrorism analyst who'd been temporarily assigned to the previous operation. He was born in India and became a US naturalized citizen after his family moved to the US when he was eight years old.

"Raj is knowledgeable on the whole India-China area without it being directly part of his job," Carla said. "We go to the same yoga studio."

"Sounds like the perfect person, thanks."

Even with his top-secret clearance, Kade couldn't receive a classified briefing on the China-India border situation because it wasn't considered relevant to his role. But he wanted more on the big picture. His geopolitical knowledge was weak in this area of the world, except familiarity with some of the terrorist groups residing there.

He'd learned in the intel community that an unclassified discussion with the right person could be quite valuable. The intel world called this sort of publicly available information open-source intelligence, or OSINT. OSINT was more useful when an outstanding analyst told you where to focus your attention among mountains of information.

Raj met them at the entrance of Fort Ward Park, a Civil War–era fort designed to protect Washington, D.C., from a Confederate attack.

Carla and Raj caught up on FBI gossip while they walked for a few minutes, then Raj asked Kade what he wanted to know when they came to a halt at the fort's north bastion. Kade wanted Raj's opinion on the border situation and any relevant context.

"I'll boil it down," Raj said. "For starters, you have to have a quick history lesson on the Sino-Indian war of 1962. Any balanced analysis will say India suffered a humiliating defeat when China attacked—and China could've done much more damage. My dad was a career army officer before coming here, and he'll disagree with me when I say the war could have been prevented altogether. In any case, the country's ego is still bruised by it."

Kade looked at Carla and nodded, trying to silently thank her for bringing a dynamite person. Raj could probably detect the tension between them.

"So, the border problem isn't going away anytime soon, then," Kade said.

"No. The disputes go back to late 1800s. In 1914, Britain, China, and Tibet were participants in a conference aimed at resolving territorial disputes. The problem was, Britain and Tibet came to a bilateral agreement of map demarcations at a so-called McMahon Line. China refused to sign that agreement, and today, a century later, the border still hasn't been resolved. There was another border cooperation agreement signed in 2013, but China often violates it."

"China's a near-superpower," Kade said. "Couldn't they just rout India again if it came to another armed conflict?"

"China would be dominant if they launched an attack, sure, but now they'd get bloodied. It would be like a schoolyard bully who doesn't want to receive a good shot to the nose . . . and then the bully would be worried about the rest of the schoolyard stepping in to help the underdog."

"You mean the US?"

"Yeah. And now there's a new US-India defense agreement in play for China to worry about. The extent of those terms isn't well known."

"What's India's overall defense strategy?" Kade asked.

"They must hold territory in a war against China until they can get that schoolyard assistance. They must win any conventional war against Pakistan."

"Can they execute on this strategy?"

"I think they're close," Badesha said. "They've boosted military spending and infrastructure. Military professionalism suffered when they broke from the British Empire. The same leadership that nonviolently gained their independence cared little about military budgets or readiness. But a courageous spirit has always remained among soldiers. That's what my dad would tell you, anyway."

Kade wanted to ask about India's intelligence activity, but that would be pushing a bit too far for now. Badesha would know he was fishing around and wouldn't appreciate it. Kade was curious about something else.

"The US and India do joint military training," Kade said. "But not nearly as much as US-Pakistan. How do you think the new partnership will impact it?"

Badesha looked like he found the question interesting. "Yeah, training trends are a good indicator of where things are headed. I don't know many details of the new partnership, but from their joint exercises and relationships India has built with the US, the strongest area would be in special operations. India knows it's playing catch-up in special ops, to both China and Pakistan."

"You think the new defense partnership includes US intel and special ops support?"

Badesha smiled. "No idea."

Kade checked the time on his phone and noticed he had a text message.

Lin.

As he read it, he got the same weird feeling in his chest as when Andrade and Summerford showed him her picture.

It's so great to hear from you . . . I'd love to meet up!

CHAPTER 12

Joshua Pierce stood at the railing of the High Bridge, watching the sunset and thinking he'd feel better if he could throw a few choice people over the side.

Minutes later, he was joined by Raymond Jeffries, The Chapter's chief personnel officer and member of the executive group. While Pierce had overseen recruiting through Phase One, Jeffries had been his handpicked guy to be promoted and assume the enormous responsibility and challenge of the role. Jeffries also advised Pierce on media strategy.

The photogenic Jeffries lit his one self-allotted cigarette for the day and took in the view over the Appomattox River.

"From what you've told me, I think congrats are in order," he said in his natural monotone. "It sounds like all of our plans are back on track . . . accelerating, even."

"Mostly," Pierce said. "Political ops, on track. China ops, on track. The virus is ready. Idaho is ready. The Network is almost healed. We're positioned to have more financial strength than we could've dreamed."

"Marshall's well-laid designs are bearing fruit."

"Yes, they are. The new run of Guardian and Zulu protocol chipsets will go to production in Fengxian. We'll need to meet that supply with human capital."

"I'll hit your target for candidates," Jeffries said. "But you didn't bring me here to remind me of that, right?"

Pierce spat out a sunflower seed shell and watched it arc into the valley below.

"No. We have a few nagging problems distracting from Phase Two. Our threat from within still remains."

"Sims?" Jeffries asked.

Pierce sniffed and nodded.

"We took a stab at bringing him in," he said, "but came up empty-handed. Even worse, we now have a Guardian missing."

"Who?"

"Hager."

"Damn . . . he's gone silent?"

"He failed to report in per the mission plan and didn't respond on his phone. His car was still in the parking lot. We have to assume Sims somehow knew he was coming."

"Maybe Sims has FBI protection. Have we taken countermeasures?"

"Hager's access was ended once we found his car."

"Forgive the dumb question, but is Sims locked out of The Network, too?"

"We narrowed his access, but didn't shut it down completely, because if he logs in, we have another way to locate him. Our technology team would be alerted and could track his activity. We're hoping he makes that mistake, but we don't want to wait, either. We don't need one person draining our resources."

"Agreed. So, what's the connection with the girl you added to my last download?"

"Part of another plan to bring him in. When last week's attempt failed, we tasked a security team with more investigation. One of our assets back in Portland, a guy named Poole, had ID'd a few of the people working on the FBI's team—part of their Operation CLEARCUT. We were only able to locate one name, a Carla Singleton living in the Tyson's Corner area. Our team went through her apartment and came up empty-handed, except for one small detail—a picture of her and Sims together."

"Together?"

"Yes," Pierce said. "One of those stupid booth photos you get in a club. It was on her nightstand—she was using it as a bookmark."

"How sweet."

Pierce crunched on more seeds.

"Isn't it? I'd appreciate it if you paid her a visit, and have *her* tell us where Sims is. Anything else you can find out is gravy. Ignaty was just freed up if you'd like some help."

"I'll take him, thanks. You want me to work on converting her while I'm at it?"

Pierce smiled. He liked that Jeffries seemed to always find an angle to exploit.

"You could probably turn Minnie Mouse on Mickey, but I'll let you judge whether you think that could work."

Jeffries took a long, final puff and turned his head away from Pierce to blow it out.

"I'm always up for a challenge," he said. "I'll get right on it."

CHAPTER 13

News about the threat of lethal adversaries at the beginning of each morning was best absorbed after a workout and a strong cup of coffee.

On this morning, President Darryl Greer received the daily briefing in the Oval Office from DNI Conroy, DCI Perry, and Stanley Hassett, the FBI Director. Greer hadn't yet changed from his workout clothes and sat on a clean towel out of respect for the vintage couch. His gray hair was still damp with sweat.

At Greer's prior direction, before diving into the briefing, they would first discuss what he deemed to be the greatest known threat to the homeland.

The Chapter.

They were what kept him up at night. Not Russia, China, North Korea, or the absolute debacle of the Middle East. They were all manageable exterior threats. Lone wolf domestic threats could only injure.

Some argued that The Chapter was a terror organization, like ISIS, and should be treated as a comparable threat. That calculus was mistaken.

Terror groups were incapable of destroying the fabric of the homeland, even if their activities killed thousands. But The Chapter had a growing, game-changing means of human subjugation in concert with its threat.

If America was the human body, The Chapter was not a cancer. It was like AIDS, intent on weakening and killing the immune system.

Greer's brown eyes were alert and ready to get on with the day.

"How's the Recovery Team doing?" he asked.

The three directors in the room had come together at Greer's request to create a focused operation to dismantle and destroy The Chapter. They all appreciated the FBI's regular, standard effort to bring cases against the perpetrators. But no threat inside the United States had ever been so extensively financed and organized.

This threat required a different approach.

Greer had told everyone he wanted the leadership of The Chapter decapitated. But he also understood that killing the leadership was only like snapping off the top of a weed. The root system needed to be dug out of the ground or it would grow back. To get rid of the menace meant their technology had to be understood and destroyed, and the source of their funding permanently cut off.

This new operation against The Chapter had no name and would never have one. He wouldn't make the mistakes of past presidents and open himself to politically motivated leaks. There would be no disclosure to the traditional "Gang of Eight"—the Senate and House majority and minority leaders, and the chairs and ranking minority members of both Congressional intelligence committees.

Greer didn't even disclose the operation to Vice President Nguyen.

The three directors respected the unprecedented security of this approach. They had skin in this game.

"We've made sound progress," Hassett said. "We're starting to understand how their network communicates. The chip we extracted from the detained cadre member is under analysis. Interrogation yielded another confirmation that their number two, Joshua Pierce, is still alive and giving operational orders."

"What's the best current estimate on their strength?" Greer asked.

Hassett slid reading glasses onto his chalice-shaped face as he referred to his handwritten notes.

"The Guardians, their elite cadre, are estimated between two to three hundred strong. We're most concerned about this Guardian force—it's only sustained a handful of casualties. Next are the so-called Sentries. We've recovered two hundred eleven bodies and estimate there are less than one hundred Sentries remaining. We don't know if they're able to reconstitute that force."

Greer made a few simple journal notes in his own shorthand. He liked to keep score.

"Finally," Hassett said, "we have the general population of The Chapter, who they call Zulus."

"Refresh my memory," Greer said. "They were part of the attack force, but also like loyalists of their program?"

"Yes, sir," Hassett said. "They were attackers, and if they survived, they joined a kind of 'sleeper alumni' organization. We've recovered, catalogued, and processed 3,471 total bodies in this category from every state in the union. Most died after capture—their chips self-destructed once questioning began."

Greer shut his eyes for a few seconds. "That number is staggering. You've done a hell of a job in keeping that knowledge under wraps."

The public believed, accepted the number of attackers was in the hundreds. Not thousands.

"Thank you," Hassett said. "The coordination with Administrator Fowler has been unprecedented, and the system we implemented continues to be effective."

Fowler was the head of the Federal Emergency Management Administration. Greer had ordered that FEMA disaster recovery centers be activated to process Chapter corpses. These centers were equipped with an incinerator that also could be used as a crematorium in the event of a mass casualty event. The processing of Chapter corpses under FEMA had been classified secret.

Hassett added, "Our original estimate of this Zulu population was about ten thousand, so we still believe there are still thousands scattered throughout the country."

Greer nodded. This affirmed he had his priorities straight.

"Let's hit the brief," Greer said and picked up the notebook from the table. The bolded item at the top of page one was a surprise, even though he'd become more accustomed to surprises. "The Chinese are planning an attack across their border with India?"

"Yes," Conroy said. "The Chinese People's Liberation Army has given a green light for a cross-border operation."

"How many Chinese troops are we talking about?" Greer asked.

"A battalion," Conroy said. "That's about seven hundred troops. There's never been more than a platoon-sized force poking around in any recent border intrusion. We haven't seen the troop movements yet, but that reflects the orders given with the objective being the land in the area of Demchok."

Conroy referred to the map diagram arrows.

"The PLA is also prepared to conduct a feint attack further east in Arunachal and plans to shoot down an Indian aircraft or helicopter at one of their advanced landing grounds, or airstrips, near the Line of Actual Control. Those airstrips have always been a point of irritation with the Chinese."

"This is the real deal," Greer said. "Are the Chinese grievances valid?"

"We can only confirm that one Chinese helicopter crashed and a Chinese squad is dead," Conroy said, "not that India is responsible as Xinhua News Agency is reporting. We're continuing to monitor communications."

Perry added, "A few of our PLA assets say the tone inside military channels is that they want blood. I have to think the Chinese directive has to be related to our new partnership with India. India has become emboldened."

"The timing's uncanny," Greer said. "I want to keep the full-court press on Chinese expansion, but a border war is *not* what we need. I'll call a strategy meeting for this afternoon. Melissa, if we can get the chief of station and ambassador dialed in, it would be helpful."

"We'll get it scheduled," Perry said.

Greer needed to consult with his Chief of Staff and other political advisors first. Emboldened by last week's election results, the GOP continued the drumbeat in the media that America was being too soft on China. The public also thought Greer wasn't aggressive enough on the domestic threat of The Chapter, according to polls.

If only they knew . . .

With the Democrats projected to be the minority party in the House and Senate, Greer kept his strategy even closer to the vest.

"Any other thoughts or suggestions?" he asked.

"We'll need General Hicks to weigh in," Perry said, "but I have some Special Activities Division assets available in theater that could assist India with immediate deterrence."

Perry was referring to General Gary Hicks, the commander-in-chief of US Special Operations Command, or SOCOM.

"What kind of deterrence?"

"We can quietly help stir up some other shit-storms for the Chinese to worry about."

Greer liked the idea. He could help America's new partner and try to preempt China's aggressive behavior. The risk of doing nothing seemed to outweigh potential American exposure.

"Okay," he said. "Let's get Hicks on the phone and brainstorm a shit-storm."

CHAPTER 14

They were blindfolded soon after pickup at the Boise, Idaho Falls, or Butte airports for the three-to-five-hour drive. A planned stop occurred in the first few minutes after leaving the airport to check for surveillance devices. Another vehicle monitored traffic to detect any possible tails. Random detours were sometimes thrown in the mix.

Passengers included Sentries who had not undergone an audit after The Chapter's Phase One attack. Eighty-nine of them had survived the foiled mission. Another three hundred recipients of the Zulu protocol who were involved with Phase One had been screened by Guardians so they could again be entrusted with their duties.

Mining operations for Rare Earth Metals Corporation were headquartered east of Lehmi Pass on the Montana side of the border. A hidden tunnel, large enough to comfortably walk through upright, originated from the office building and connected to an underground facility, known inside The Chapter as Green Mountain.

Green Mountain encompassed a tunnel network no longer used for zinc mining. Rooms built into the tunnels were wired for power and networking, and had filtered ventilation. The upper levels stayed about sixty degrees year-round, so no climate control system was needed.

Timothy Arnold, Chief Technology Officer of The Chapter, sat at a table with three other Guardians, conducting their fifteenth audit of the day. The two coffeepots in the room were also working overtime.

Arnold was happy to play a key part in strengthening The Chapter's force. The Chapter Network was already under his administrative control, and now he had a sizable contingent at Green Mountain under his supervision. The armed manpower was necessary to protect this key facility, but he thought Pierce was unhappy about that arrangement.

The tall, suave Chinese man arrived at the expected time, and Arnold stood up to greet him. The two had met many times before in Shanghai.

"Tan Liang," Arnold said. "Welcome to Idaho! I hope we've been taking good care of you."

"Yes, you all have, thank you," Tan said. "Good to see you."

"How was your visit back east with Jordan?"

"Very good," Tan said. "He mentioned there is a bill drafted and ready for the Energy Subcommittee once the new Congress is sworn in."

"Yes, there is," Arnold said. "We're excited about it—it will lower restrictions on the transportation of rare earths and lower-level radioactives. It's worded in the context of *research*, but it's broad enough to drive a truck through the loophole. We'll be able to get you plenty of raw material."

"Excellent," Tan said. "Zao will be very pleased."

Zao Hong was the member of The Chapter's executive group responsible for their organization in China. As far as Arnold knew, it was currently The Chapter's only foreign location having an extensive Chapter infrastructure in place. Arnold had worked in China from the start of The Chapter's presence, helping establish a technology partnership and a small manufacturing center.

"Zao's boys have been busy on the Indian border, eh?"

Tan only smiled.

Zao and Tan had always been more than hospitable during Arnold's time in-country. In China, Arnold thought it was often exhausting living there for a black man because of unpleasant, prejudicial encounters or being seen as a novelty. But his hosts had always treated him well.

Arnold didn't return to China because of The Chapter's strategy to keep a low profile—he would have increasingly stuck out and created an operational risk. Arnold had pointed out this reality before anyone else did.

SOURCE

Tan returned to the previous subject.

"Jordan also told me, he expected Congress will be pushing for some pharmaceutical deregulation within a few weeks."

"Yeah, they'll have to," Arnold said. "The public pressure will be massive, and our FreedomYield group will drive passage. By the way, we just got our shipment of the virus here if you need to be inoculated."

"No, thanks," Tan said. "I already had my three days of misery."

Arnold laughed. "It sucks, doesn't it?"

"What doesn't kill you makes you stronger," Tan said.

Arnold sang a bar of the Kelly Clarkson song of the same name in horrible falsetto and danced in his seat, making Tan laugh.

"Anyway," Arnold continued, "all of us here at Green Mountain were exposed in a controlled environment, to maintain operational readiness. And those who rotate out won't have to worry about it either."

"Smart."

Arnold had a zeal for uninterrupted operations. He led the design of the Chapter Network's self-healing capabilities and managed the physical location of technology centers. The goal was to have robust hubs that could independently operate and regenerate if one was attacked, then rejoin The Network after repair.

Arnold liked to think he had more influence than Pierce, the so-called acting commander.

He led Tan over to the console of computer monitors.

"I'm going to show you the new Verax configuration and then take you over to the future plant site before dinner."

"Great," Tan said.

The Verax was a lie detector employing infrared sensors during questioning to detect changes in the brain's blood flow in the *caudate*—the area associated with deception. When analysis algorithms were applied, Verax's accuracy was greater than ninety-nine percent.

Tan sat down at the table. On one monitor, live video showed a Sentry named Weber reclined in a specialized chair and wearing a wired headband with headphones. The other monitor displayed his informational profile and audit log results. Arnold scrolled down through the information.

"We'll train you on this," he said, "but it's pretty easy and the latest upgrade's made our lives a little easier doing these audits. The major improvement is the Zulu audit log gives you a side-by-side checklist to guide your questioning and validate it with the Verax. Let me show you."

The reclined Sentry stiffened when Arnold spoke.

"Weber," Arnold said. "Yes or no . . . did anyone other than you know that you were taking this trip to Idaho?"

"No."

"Did you follow all the instructions in your latest download to the letter?"

"Yes."

Arnold began a new line of questioning, starting with the end of Weber's interrupted attack last July. Weber claimed that the other team leader he was paired with suddenly died, and as Weber attempted to lead the two teams on their raid, they came under fire from law enforcement. The Zulus in his crew scattered despite his best attempts to keep them together. Weber eventually fled rather than to risk capture.

Arnold turned off the microphone to say, "In Weber's defense, the Zulus were only trained for that specific mission, and not much else."

Weber described how he'd made his way behind a nearby house and sprinted down residential streets. Even though it was the middle of the night, he saw a car pulling into a driveway, so he ran over and ducked under the garage door before it closed.

Arnold again paused for a comment only his room could hear.

"This is a great example of how this new version makes this review easier. We can see he's been truthful in telling his account up to this point. But there are also some tough, key questions we must ask to determine if he's a security risk."

Arnold clicked the mouse so the Verax would take a reading and turned the mic on with another click. "Weber, yes or no. You stole that car, correct?"

"Yes."

"Did the elderly man see your face?"

"No," he said.

66

"Explain what happened," Arnold said.

"There's no way he saw me," Weber said. "I pulled him out of the car and knocked him out before he'd turned the engine off. He was drunk like a wet noodle. The car smelled like booze."

"Did anyone follow your car out of town?"

"No."

Arnold muted the mic and spoke to the group.

"You see, I can annotate the answers and mark any for research follow-up. If the man had seen his face, we could task someone to address that in a number of ways."

Tan nodded. "That's thorough. A lot of work, but worth it."

"Yeah, we're slogging through the audits," Arnold said. "We should be done in the next month, though."

"What's the process if they're a security risk?" Tan asked. "Or they were untruthful during the review?"

"The three-Guardian panel and I make a determination on each review. The acting commander has delegated the ability to me that if there's a risk, I can remove those members from The Network."

"Besides removing them from the database, what are your procedures?" Tan asked.

One of the other seated Guardians laughed and said, "They get the shaft."

"The shaft?"

The sound of Tan's accent as he repeated those words made everyone laugh but him. His expression tightened as he looked back and forth at the others.

Arnold patted Tan on the back. "It's just a joke—not a joke about you, trust me," he said and he changed the view on the monitor. His tone changed to a serious one. "It's a very sad day when we have to take someone offline purely for security reasons. No one here likes that. There has to be a very large risk we can't mitigate. We treat those cases as humanely as possible. Do you understand?"

"Yes," Tan said.

"But for those members who were disloyal, untruthful, or otherwise no longer Chapter material . . ." Arnold's tone turned cold. "Well, here's one from earlier this morning. A disloyal Zulu."

The video started playing on the screen without sound. It was an infrared camera showing the form of a blindfolded man standing in complete darkness with someone behind him. As his blindfold was removed and he was prodded to walk, the view changed to that of a different camera.

A gentle shove launched the man forward off a ledge while a bright light activated from below. The camera angle tracked the man as he plunged downward, and the video transitioned to slow motion as his flailing body passed by. The clip ended on a still shot, zoomed in on the condemned Zulu's screaming face, like one of those photos for sale after a roller-coaster ride.

The frozen expression was grotesque.

"Six hundred feet down. Execution and disposal, all in one," Arnold said.

"I see," Tan said.

"Anyway, sorry to get off track here," Arnold said. "We'll be shipping a Verax system back with you. It will have the latest enhancements."

"Thank you," Tan said.

"You're welcome. So, how's your dad and old man Kang?"

"They are well," Tan said. He looked down, away, as if he knew the next question.

"Have you been able to reconnect with Lin?" Arnold asked.

"No, but I will talk to her this weekend, before I return to Shanghai. She has a big decision to make."

CHAPTER 15

SAU

Forest Glen Road

Silver Spring, Maryland

Wednesday, November 16

7:00 a.m. (EST)

The SAU had moved to a new location, and a secure, live video feed connected the Recovery Team with their semiconductor technology expert, Vic Martin. Kade could see part of a whiteboard with flow charts and other architectural diagrams behind Martin.

Lamb corralled everyone and got started.

"Vic, can you give us a summary of what you've learned?"

"Sure can. Following our testing and analysis, we can conclude this chipset is an amazing little piece of technology. It uses quantum dots to absorb infrared energy, roughly fifty percent more than contained in the Zulu chip. It has a capsule containing PETN as well. The backside of the microprocessor is a supercapacitor built out of carbon nanotubes. Its power density is about a hundred times greater than a lithium polymer battery, meaning it can charge in minutes, not hours."

Kade and Henderson exchanged glances and nods with Lamb.

"That's consistent with Kyle's device," Lamb said.

"The carbon nanotube design has another interesting property," Martin said. "It can provide a consistent power level or dump its energy in a millisecond if needed."

Henderson said, "So, it could inflict pain to the user through an electric

69

charge, or trigger the explosive to self-destruct."

"Yes," Martin said. "If charged adequately, it would have the capability for both. But below some threshold, there isn't enough charge to detonate the PETN."

Kade cleared his throat.

"Could it be triggered to self-destruct *before* it's low on power?" he asked.

"Yes, it could," Martin said.

"That's a low-power warning that would get your attention, huh?" Lamb gave Kade a sarcastic smile. "Okay, now we know why this thing detonates . . ." Lamb wrote numbered bullets on the white board. "One, if you break security, as we found in interrogations. Two, if your pulse is weak or gone. Three, by visual recognition of a uniquely assigned kill code. Four, when the chip's low on power. Anything else?"

"I think that's all we know about," Henderson said.

Kade nodded. With his chipset powered up, he would be vulnerable from many angles. It was a piece of kryptonite sitting in his frontal lobe.

He asked, "Can you figure out the threshold where there's not enough charge to set off the PETN?"

"Yeah, I can do that with some math," Martin said.

"Thanks," Kade said. "That would be *really* helpful."

"What else, Vic?" Lamb asked.

"Well, there was one thing we discovered during the molecular-level analysis which took me by complete surprise."

Lamb took a step closer. "What was that?"

"We figured out where the chipset was manufactured."

"Where?" Lamb asked.

"Made in China," Martin said. "Shanghai, specifically."

"Man, that makes things much harder," Henderson said. "Do we have a team that we can position for surveillance?"

"Yeah, I can get a support team out of the Shanghai consulate," Lamb said. "But we're going to need much more than that. We're going to need the absolute best. One of the most versatile officers in the region."

"You have someone in mind," Henderson said.

"I do," Lamb replied. "His name is LJ Yang. He picked his own team."
Lamb swiveled his head until his eyes again found Kade.

"And Kyle," he added, "this means we're going to need you, too."

Wha . . . ?

"Okay."

A few minutes later, Henderson pulled Kade aside.

"Kyle, I wanted to tell you, I've been looking at the facial-recognition algorithm in The Chapter's program, and after talking with Dr. Trish, I think I have an idea of how to throw it off."

Kade's forehead creased.

After talking to the surgeon?

I'm not sure I like where this is going.

"Uh . . . what idea would that be?"

CHAPTER 16

After holding an early-morning national security meeting, President Greer had already chalked up the day as a bad one. Now, Indian Prime Minister Prakash Kota's office had called as Greer had expected, and Kota was holding on the line.

It was one of those situations Greer hated. After consulting with his national security team, the intelligence leadership, and chairman of the Joint Chiefs of Staff, Greer had decided *not* to share US intelligence of the possible Chinese cross-border attack with Kota. The US Intelligence Community had made that assessment thirty hours ago.

And the Chinese *had* attacked, as the US intelligence reports had warned.

The consensus assessment of Greer's national security team was that American involvement in a preemption had a greater chance of unintentionally escalating the situation into all-out conflict. The Chinese could twist the China/India face-off into something more conspiratorial and convince the international community this was somehow America's fault.

Everything was America's fault these days.

Greer did, however, refine a plan for how the US could help repel the Chinese, and was prepared to explain the concept when Kota called. Word of any impending attack had not yet reached the international news.

"I have troubling news," Kota said, speaking in English. "As you may have heard through the ambassador, there has been a Chinese ground attack on one of our border units at Demchok. I have done my best to keep knowledge of the attack out of the Indian press to ensure our response, whatever it may be, is measured and effective."

Greer had been briefed again by the US ambassador and chief of station following contact by the Indian Intelligence Bureau. Conroy had also let him know that Chinese Xinhua had made no mention of their military operation.

"Yes, I was briefed about an hour ago," Greer said, weighing what his reaction should be. He couldn't say he was *outraged*—there weren't enough details yet for that. But he carefully added, "On behalf of our nation, I can say we're *highly concerned* by this Chinese aggression."

"Thank you," Kota said. "While we are not a NATO member, this incident brings some new meaning to our recent partnership."

Greer and Kota had established a genuine rapport during Greer's state visit to India in early October. Forging a stronger relationship with the world's second-largest democracy was a no-brainer in Greer's view. Even though Kota stated publicly that Russia was still India's "greatest friend," the US had displaced Russia as India's number-one defense supplier.

In more idealistic moments, Greer believed India shared American values. Kota had been a mango farm kid from Palitana, Gujarat, while Greer was raised on a corn and soybean farm in Chaffee, Missouri. Surely, Kota would come to realize that he had more in common with the American president than with that former KGB colonel in Moscow who disregarded international borders.

But this relationship needed more time and nurturing. Kota had all but ignored the Russian invasion of Crimea and would have never supported sanctions. This was a sore spot with Greer, but he understood the history of Russian assistance.

Greer looked at the yellow sticky notes inside his folder. His staff had suggested some prompts to see where Kota's head was on a few topics.

"Was there any incident on the ground that triggered the attack?" Greer asked.

"No," Kota said. "There was the claim of a helicopter down and an incident with one of their border patrols. We have UAV imagery of the area indicating that the Chinese squad was attacked by an unknown force on snowmobiles. I would be happy to share this intelligence with you."

"That would be helpful," Greer said.

"But their Demchok attack was a planned and coordinated strike, not some kind of misunderstanding. It comes after years of repeated border violations. My administration had recently directed that we start to push back forcefully against them, as the US has done in the South China Sea."

Greer smiled inside. India had now gotten itself into a strategic pickle. Earlier in the summer, Kota had met with the Chinese president, Lok Kong, announcing that India was "open for business" and looking for Chinese investment. Kota may have meant business, but China seemed to believe border land was still "open" for the taking.

"So, your units didn't shoot down their helicopter with a missile?" Greer asked.

"No, I am one hundred percent sure it was none of our military units," Kota said.

Greer glanced at another sticky note with a "?" on it.

Ask what we can do to help, but don't pledge specific help yet.

"So, Prakash, what can we do to help you?"

"I did not expect to be requesting your assistance this soon," Kota said. "But I would like the US to condemn this act of aggression. I would like to discuss any pressure that could be brought to repel the Chinese without bloodshed. I have many in the Parliament who are arguing for an immediate military response."

Greer danced around *condemnation* as he'd already reviewed with his staff.

"I will make a statement of support as a first step," Greer said. "We will urge the Chinese to withdraw, and for both sides to demobilize and engage in immediate talks."

"Thank you."

Greer's national security team had discussed their reinvigorated policy of checking Chinese expansionism, especially where it pressured an ally or partner. They had agreed India now fell in this category and believed the US could assume some greater risk, but well short of an alliance.

Greer called China "frenemy" number one. How do you apply strategic pressure to the country second only to Canada as a trading partner?

"We are prepared to offer some direct assistance," Greer said, "but it would be on the condition of *utmost* secrecy."

"Of course."

Greer paused for a moment.

"I am told by my military chiefs we have two infantry companies that have trained with your Mountain Strike Brigade, and those units are in a state of readiness for a high-altitude environment. These are only a few hundred soldiers, but their immediate presence in what we would call a 'training exercise' could keep the situation from escalating further."

"Oh, we would greatly appreciate and welcome this kind of support," Kota said. "Thank you."

"Also as part of that deployment, I would be happy to add air defense support to those advanced landing grounds where our forces will be operating."

"Very good, we would welcome this," Kota said.

"Finally," Greer said, "we also have some special forces in the region that could assist in repelling the Chinese, if we can design and coordinate a joint covert operation of this kind."

There was a long pause. Greer's staff had predicted Kota would not have the stomach to agree to this course of action.

"Prakash, are you still there?" Greer asked.

"Yes," Kota said. "Let's discuss how we would do such an operation."

CHAPTER 17

Hartsfield-Jackson Airport (ATL)
Atlanta, Georgia
Thursday, November 17
7:45 a.m. (EST)

The only high-budget item in Sentry Ignaty's possession was the custom hard-case roller bag he pulled behind him. The volume of liquid inside the bag exceeded the 3.4-ounce TSA limit by a few gallons, but he wasn't headed through security screening today.

The food court area of the atrium outside the security checkpoint was moderately busy, and Ignaty blended into the morning flow. He wore one of the two suits in his wardrobe, this a cheap, loose-fitting brown variety along with older, brush-shined shoes and a pair of rimless glasses he didn't need. His facial scars were barely visible beneath the pricey concealer he'd applied.

No one gave this road warrior imposter a second look.

Using cash, he bought an egg and bacon sandwich and small coffee. While waiting in line, he looked where everyone was seated and mapped out the route he'd use.

With the brown-paper food sack and coffee in one hand, roller bag handle in the other, he strolled around looking for a semiprivate spot. When no one was directly behind him, he squeezed the handle button, which silently puffed a fine, odorless aerosol into the air. He weaved between tables and made sure to get the mist on the unoccupied tables and chairs.

He took a seat at the far end and inserted his headphones.

There he ate his breakfast, took a fake conference call, checked the news on his phone, and then got up to leave. But before he departed the area, he stopped by a man a few tables away using a new computer tablet model Ignaty hadn't seen before.

"Hey, how do you like that thing?" Ignaty asked. He'd been practicing his pronunciation in the last two months to better hide his Russian accent. Pierce and Gill said he was improving.

The guy went on for five minutes talking about the stupid tablet, and Ignaty acted impressed while he pictured himself snapping his neck. Ignaty gave him another few minutes before saying he needed to get going and thanking the guy for his time. If anyone reviewed the surveillance footage, he would now look like a friendly fellow, rather than an operator spreading a biological agent.

There were a few more stops to make today, targeting ground transportation to and from the airport. Rental car return buses were next up. Even those obsessive people who carried sanitizing wipes would fall prey.

He had already been exposed to the virus by Dr. Gill and knew that in six to twelve hours, these infected travelers would be getting headaches and sore throats. They would think it was just from their flights at first. The altitude and dry, recirculated air. That damn person coughing in the seat behind them.

Many would be knocked off their feet for one to three days. The hearty ones might self-medicate and shrug it off. They would be the ones spreading the most germs.

Sick days. Doctor's visits. Lost productivity.

Ignaty didn't care about these people.

They would all be making the smallest sacrifice to advance The Chapter's strategy.

He smiled to himself.

Tuman voĭny.

The fog of war.

CHAPTER 18

Old Town
Alexandria, Virginia
Thursday, November 17
9:50 a.m. (EST)

Kade hadn't observed anything out of the ordinary, but he wasn't kidding himself—he had no formal training in human countersurveillance tradecraft. His surveillance-detection walking route began six blocks away from the meeting location.

Never again would he have an assured sense that he was *clean* of surveillance. Often targets were made to feel they were clean, when they were actually observed by a large team. It came down to how much manpower the surveillance team had at its disposal.

Two blocks away, Kade ducked into a convenience store after an abrupt turn and bought a pack of gum. As he observed foot traffic out the front window, he believed he was clean of any singular tail, at least. That was the best he could do.

He wished he had more time to train—on many things. Eventually, things would slow down and he could attempt to enhance his skills.

The guidance from Andrade and Summerford was uncomplicated. He was to report back on any knowledge gleaned from as many encounters with Lin Soon as he could devise in the shortest time frame possible.

It sounded like fun work, but he still needed to be cautious.

Keep it simple.

He arrived ten minutes early at Killer Koffee at King and Alfred and ordered a decaf coffee with a big slice of apple pie. Picking a table halfway to the bathroom, he sat facing the barista counter with SPIN magazine on his iPad and headphones in his ears playing no music.

Some people around him talked quietly and some just chilled out in silence. If you didn't look relaxed in this place, you stuck out. This was the anti-Starbucks.

His mind couldn't relax, though. There were multiple potential threats now. The Chapter was a given. Was Chinese intel watching him? He didn't think so, but found himself mentally profiling. One of the three baristas was Asian but looked more Vietnamese. It seemed more likely the FBI would be monitoring his activity, even though Summerford said they weren't going to be.

He leaned back against the exposed brick wall and willed himself not to look restless. After repositioning his uncomfortable glasses one final time, he swore not to touch them again.

You're too excited.

Relax.

When she came through the door, he returned to reading his iPad before she could have any chance of looking his way. But in that quick glance, he paused a breath. She looked casual but incredible. He kept his face angled sideways, chin resting on his knuckles.

Out of his deep peripheral vision, he tracked her to the counter, toward the cushioned chairs and sofas on the other side, then back to the counter to order something. She didn't see him. He'd defeated her initial detection.

No, maybe he was wrong. He tracked her long brown leather jacket and boots in motion, approaching him, her hand carrying a coffee cup. He was sure she was going to sit down in front of him, but she turned and pulled out a chair two tables away. A college-age girl with a hoop nose ring sat between them.

Lin had her hair styled the way he remembered it from months ago—a dark sheet draped down the side of her face to her shoulder. She turned her chair so she could see the door. To see if *he* would come in. She didn't have an inkling he was right in front of her because he resembled a person she wouldn't want to look at.

His feet were on the table, showing off his most beat-up pair of Nikes. A baggy snap-up fleece shirt with a stain on the front hid his Glock and had a collar covering his neck injury. On his head was a slouch beanie that any Dr. Seuss character would've thrown out. Overall, he had the unshowered, just-crawled-out-of-bed look of a career student.

Other than a couple of guys who'd given Lin the expected rubberneck, no one seemed to be watching either of them with undue interest.

Satisfied his appearance had thrown her off, Kade only let her sit another three minutes so he didn't risk her leaving. She was becoming more interested in her phone than her surroundings.

He rose from his chair in slow motion, picked up his coffee cup and walked toward the counter like he might need a refill. But then he sidestepped and plopped down right in front of her, while checking to see if anyone else inside the place cared. It didn't seem like it.

"Hey, Lin."

A quick wave of revulsion passed over her face before she could attempt to hide it.

But then she froze, bringing her face closer to him like a zooming camera lens.

"No way . . . are you kidding me?"

The words LIN SOON appeared in his vision.

He suppressed a smile, licked his lips and shrugged an eyebrow.

"Great to see ya," he said.

The encrypted list of Chapter members remaining on his chip had just cross-referenced the facial-recognition data.

The algorithm didn't lie. Henderson had explained how it number-crunched a myriad of equations based on the unique distance between the eyes, nose, cheeks and mouth.

But math couldn't appreciate the curves in her face, like edges carved from fine stone and polished smooth.

She looked him up and down, noting every detail with disdain.

"What the hell, Sims? This is how you look when you go meet girls?"

He reacted as if he'd been slapped in the face, and when he rocked forward again his voice lowered into a monotone.

"No, this is how a paranoid person blends into their surroundings."

She again studied his face and reached across the table, pulling off his glasses and dropping them on the table. They were wide rectangular specs of a style that looked fugly on him.

"You look different," she said. "You gained some weight . . . I can see it in your face."

Back at the SAU, Henderson had showed Kade how some slight modifications in the facial profile would defeat The Chapter's program algorithms. So when Dr. Trish had offered him free isolagen injections to his cheeks and chin, he'd accepted.

As a result, his face did look . . . fatter.

"Really?"

"Yeah," she said. "And you're wearing contacts?"

"Uh-huh."

"I don't like them."

"You're so critical."

He looked down in mock disappointment and dwelled on how her breasts filled up her scoop-necked shirt and pressed her unbuttoned coat outward.

She half-sneered in an expression he'd seen before, more playful than disapproving. A good reconnection signal.

"Bullshit," she said. "So, what's new? You're a slob now . . . and?"

He gave her the eyebrow shrug once more and put his hand on top of hers. She flinched but didn't pull away.

"Thanks for showing up," he said. "How have you been? I was worried . . ."

"Oh my God. Are your hands even washed?"

He smiled and laughed on the inside. At least he'd brushed his teeth.

Beauty and the Beast.

"Shhhhhh. You're going to disturb the vibe in here. I was working on my truck this morning. Just some stubborn grease, sorry. Tell me how you've been. What happened after AgriteX?"

She took a deep breath and watched him while sipping her tea, as if she realized she'd been tricked.

"I went back to work at my old company, except out of the D.C. office now instead of New York. They always said I could come back. It's mostly doing due diligence for potential investment and market entry. Relationship building. And I do a little fun work on the side, playing piano at night."

"Cool. I was hoping you were okay," Kade said.

The corner of her mouth tensed up. "You never said goodbye."

"I know. I'm sorry," he said. "When I saw the opportunity to get out of that crazy place, I took it. Looking back, I wasn't thinking about everyone else in there enough. I felt bad about it after I was gone. I still do."

She folded her arms on the table and lowered her voice.

"Are you the guy who was on *60 Minutes* a few weeks ago? The undercover agent who was mentioned?"

He shook his head and gave her a look as though he'd smelled something bad.

But he had seen the story.

In the aftermath of the AgriteX-masterminded terror attack, *60 Minutes* had done an investigative report on what the FBI hadn't disclosed, but what the public sensed and was a political hot button: The Chapter was still a real threat.

The person interviewed, a shadowed figure with an altered voice, discussed some details of the operation. Details that *had* to have been classified.

The person interviewed wasn't him. He had no idea who it was.

But he was the mentioned undercover agent.

The *60 Minutes* piece had raised an alarming question at the end of the episode. What *other* domestic terror threats were out there, threats that our intelligence services were missing?

Kade wasn't about to get into a discussion with Lin about strategic priorities, intelligence assets, budgets, leadership and a whole host of variables. This week, the focus of the nation and the twenty-four-hour news cycle had turned to China. It was amazing how fast the focus could shift.

"No," he told her. "I saw that episode, though. Scary stuff. You know, I was a gullible idiot thinking AgriteX was for me. Now you know why I'm still looking over my shoulder."

His Chapter visual stoplight flickered yellow on his response, meaning he wasn't being truthful to her. Even though his program indicated she was in The Chapter, he hadn't synced with the Chapter Network since he'd escaped, so he couldn't be sure if what he saw was valid anymore.

"I'll tell you something . . ." He motioned for her to move closer.

She nodded and slid forward as he thought of a scrap of semitrue information he could divulge. One he could twist around a little.

He leaned in even closer, inside the range of her wonderful perfume. He could have kissed her right there, but that would've freaked her out for sure given his grungy makeover. Instead, he spoke in the quietest whisper.

"When I escaped . . . in the dark . . . I shot someone while I was trying to get away. I'm pretty sure that guy didn't make it."

She whispered back, "I escaped with Walt. He told me about how you destroyed your chip, so I went ahead and did the same."

Then she wouldn't be on The Network.

"Smart move."

Kade again glanced at the other tables and door. Checking out the side windows, he didn't see any white telecom vans parked on the curb or other tip-offs that a third party was listening in on their conversation. Yet, he reminded himself that Lin might be mic'd.

Obviously, he hadn't done a good enough job in destroying his chip. Now, he wasn't even sure if it was damaged.

He took a sip of coffee, but now that it wasn't tongue-burning hot, it would be his last.

"Have you been in contact with any other associates?" he asked.

She ran both hands down the edges of her coat, which gave him a better view of her physical assets.

"No. I told Walter where he could find me if he needed to, but haven't heard from him since." Her hand tensed up underneath his, and he thought he detected a shiver. "A couple weeks after that, I *did* get a surprise visit from someone I assume was a Guardian. I was scared to death."

"What'd he do?"

"He asked if I'd talked to anyone, and I said no. I promised him I didn't plan on talking as long as they left me alone." Her eyes now had a sheen of tears and her lips tightened. "I thought I was going to die . . . he had his gun out."

Kade shook his head. The fear of being visited by Guardians like this had motivated him to acquire a small arsenal of weapons for his own protection. He also had stepped up going to the range and paid for additional firing instruction. That's where he'd invested most of his dwindling "extra" time.

"I'm sorry," he said and gave her hand a squeeze. "Intimidation is their way. Have they done anything to you since then?"

"Nothing else after that, thank God."

"Did you go to the authorities?"

She shook her head and blinked the tears into submission.

"You should have," he said.

"No one would've believed me," she said. "And with my luck, they would've locked me up as a suspect. Patriot Act or something like that. They don't care about someone like me. For a few weeks, I thought of going back to China permanently. My parents would love that, but I love it here too much . . . I don't want to leave."

"Your parents are still in China?"

She nodded. "Shanghai. They wanted me to come back after college, but I liked the job opportunities here. I do visit, but get sick of them fast."

Now he thought about the situation from her perspective. She was shaken and feeling helpless after her recent "Guardian scare." Naturally, she would want to reconnect with her parents and Chinese contacts in the States. Relatives she could trust. Maybe some of those contacts had Chinese government connections. Most *all* government contacts would have ties and communication with Chinese intelligence. Her involvement could have been unintentional and routine.

While that seemed like a plausible flow of events, his job now was to collect info, not to draw conclusions that only the entire intelligence community could compile.

Your job isn't to judge her.

"How about you?" she asked. "Any surprise visits?"

At that moment, Kade saw an Asian guy coming down the aisle toward them. He'd missed seeing him come in the entrance, and now the guy was reaching into his coat pocket.

Kade slid his hand inside the seam of his shirt toward his gun.

But the guy only pulled out his phone and said hello to someone on the other end and kept walking by. Kade snagged his glasses from the table and put them back on. Took a breath.

Awareness fail.

"No, I've been lying low, as you can see," he said. "I hoped I'd get a visit from the *good* guys. Because I haven't, it makes me worry about how much this country has a handle on the situation."

"You didn't want to talk to them either?"

"Not voluntarily."

Again, a yellow flicker of his stoplight.

He could see it in her eyes again—she hated his glasses. She was also reaching the bottom of her cup, and he had the feeling he didn't have her sold on staying for a refill.

"Look," he said, "I don't know how to say this, but . . . after that whole horrible experience at AgriteX, you were, like, the *only* positive thing I took away. I just wanted to know if you were okay and see you one more time. Maybe if we could talk once in a while, that would be cool. Sorry I came here looking like a grub-ball."

There wasn't a yellow flicker from this statement.

Her face lit up with a smile, and a single laugh escaped her lips. This was the enticing Lin he preferred. She shifted in her seat and crossed her arms.

"That's all you want to do with me is talk?"

His lower jaw shifted off-center.

I do need a lot more information to get paid . . .

"Not really. Want to go out sometime this weekend?"

"Hmm . . . I'm free Saturday night."

"Okay, I'll call you that afternoon."

After she gave him her current number, she said, "No glasses," and tapped hard on a lens with her fingernail. "And I never want to see those clothes again."

He laughed. "Don't worry. We'll go somewhere fun."

She rolled her eyes, put her other hand on top of his and gave it a pat. The short nails on her fingers shined with a light blue polish.

"Okay, Sims. You get one more chance."

CHAPTER 19

Once all of the invitees arrived and the wine was uncorked, Guardian Connor Jordan, The Chapter's Political Officer, broke from mixing with the group and stood in front to kick off the dinner.

His Sentries had done a great job transforming the empty warehouse floor into a dining hall. Another detachment arrived in a small cargo truck and set up pans of Italian food, buffet style.

Decorations were few, but the reward was clear. A two-inch brick of hundred-dollar bills lay at each place setting between the champagne flute and wineglass.

Jordan was a partner in the leading government relations and public affairs firm, Aspirance. In other words, he was a chief D.C. lobbyist. The two other partners in his firm were Zulu Chapter members.

His position was key, strategically—it gave him access to Chapter supporters in government as part of his regular work.

Jordan shared his movie-star smile with the group as he raised a glass.

"Ladies and gentlemen, what an exciting day . . . Cheers!"

A small roar erupted from the group, along with hugs, back-slapping and glass-clinking.

"America's fear has led to our success at the ballot box. We represent the change America wants, and together we will remake our government. *Chapter first!*"

The group raised their glass and repeated the mantra.

Jordan advanced his slide presentation through various slick graphics.

"Our FreedomYield organization's assistance to campaigns yielded results. We added thirty-one representatives in the House for forty-four total—twenty-nine Republicans and fifteen Democrats. Your peers have capitulated to the will of the American people by adding more of you to their committees. They fear the polls, the perception of doing nothing, more than anything."

The Chapter's political funding mechanism had previously been through a Domestic Strength Coalition, but that had been shut down after the FBI had launched investigations. FreedomYield was the new organization, quietly funneling money to end up in campaigns and PACs for Chapter supporters.

Jordan changed to a chart and walked through the tally. Chapter members were slated to pick up majority and minority posts to subcommittees in the Homeland Security Committee, Foreign Affairs, Armed Services, Energy and Commerce.

Jordan was most excited about picking up a Republican appointment to the House Permanent Select Committee on Intelligence—specifically on the Subcommittee on Terrorism, HUMINT (Human Intelligence), Analysis, and Counterintelligence.

"This is all fantastic news for us," Jordan said. "But perhaps our biggest coup in this election was adding another senator. Congratulations to Terry Hawkins!"

The group toasted Terrence Hawkins, who was seated next to the current lone Chapter senator, Tiffany Harrison from Oregon.

Jordan gave Hawkins a wink and an extra raising of the glass. Hawkins would be a key addition, one of the handful of actual chipped Chapter members of Congress.

"We're thrilled Terry will be slated to join the Senate Armed Services Committee, on the Emerging Threats and Capabilities Subcommittee." Jordan cradled his chin in his hand theatrically. "One could say Terry is an emerging threat to the old way of doing things."

Hawkins laughed and raised his glass again.

"Folks," Jordan said, "at eight, we'll review our strategy that launches after

January's swearing-in. We're excited at the legislation we will advance. Going forward, you'll be assigned a confidential FreedomYield liaison who will bring you subsequent updates. For now, please enjoy the food and wine. Oh, and don't forget your bonuses. Unless you want to leave me an extra tip . . ."

The group laughed again.

Jordan stepped aside as everyone hit the buffet line and pop music began to play from a portable sound system. Minutes later, when the internal clock of his Guardian chipset reached 7:00 p.m., his display changed.

A gold star appeared next to his name and a message appeared.

CONGRATULATIONS, YOU ARE NOW A MEMBER OF THE CHAPTER'S EXECUTIVE GROUP. KNOWLEDGE OF THIS PROMOTION IS RESTRICTED TO YOU ONLY. YOU WILL BE CONTACTED ABOUT WHERE TO RECEIVE YOUR NEXT INSTRUCTIONS.

Jordan smiled and found another flute of champagne to throw back for his own private toast.

Wow. This day is only getting better.

Josh Pierce isn't going to like this at all.

CHAPTER 20

Tysons Corner, Virginia
Saturday, November 19
7:10 p.m. (EST)

When Carla Singleton emerged from the short hallway between her bedroom and kitchen, the latex-gloved hand of Sentry Ignaty slammed over her mouth and his pistol barrel jammed against her temple.

"Not a word," he said.

Ignaty and Guardian Raymond Jeffries had let themselves into her apartment with a duplicate key given to them by a Chapter surveillance team. They both wore blank chrome masks, the kind that had been a Halloween staple after the movie *I, Robot*.

Smooth jazz was playing at a loud volume. Jeffries made sure no one else was in the apartment and turned off the stove. He found Singleton's phone and turned it off.

"Mmm. Something smells good," Jeffries said. "I love roasted garlic."

Jeffries opened the pan and saw she'd been cooking a portobello mushroom burger. There was only one burger there, but he asked the question anyway.

"Are you expecting anyone?"

She shook her head.

"Weren't planning on going out later tonight?"

She shook her head.

"Good," Jeffries said.

"Now, let's get something straight, *Carla*," Ignaty said. He rested the pistol barrel on top of her cheek, allowing her to see the suppressor attachment. "We haven't decided if you're going to die. But if you scream or do anything I think is hostile or disrespectful, I will not hesitate. There will be no second chances, I promise. Understand?"

She nodded.

Jeffries had already slid a kitchen chair out into the middle of the floor. Ignaty removed his hand from her mouth, grabbed a bundle of hair behind her neck and pulled her into the seat.

"What—" she tried to say.

Ignaty's slap to her face was full force, loud inside the room space but absorbed by the music.

"You only speak when I say you can," Ignaty growled. "And when I tell you to speak, it's in a whisper, or things will get really bad. Now, you have thirty seconds to take off all of your clothes and sit back down, otherwise I'll do it for you. And if I do it for you, you'll need to see a doctor."

She took off her yoga pants, T-shirt, and socks and sat again, looking at the floor and trying to cover up.

"Wow, looking great, Agent Singleton," Ignaty said. "You get props for taking care of yourself."

Singleton thought she might throw up.

Jeffries took over gun-pointing duties while Ignaty wrapped Singleton's ankles and wrists to the chair, pulling from a large wheel of gray duct tape.

"Do I need to tell you who we are?" Ignaty asked.

"No," Singleton said.

Ignaty nodded and slapped her again in the face so hard that she and the chair rocked on two legs and almost fell over. He pulled her back upright.

"Didn't I say don't speak unless I tell you?"

She nodded, eyes welling with tears.

"Okay, good." Ignaty pulled up his own chair and sat facing her. Jeffries sat at the kitchen table, turning a chair around. "Do you know who I am?" Ignaty asked.

She sat silent.

"I like this girl," Ignaty said. "She learns quick. Let's see . . . you think you know who I am, because you're a super-smart analyst, but you aren't sure, right?"

She nodded.

"Good, that's what I thought. So, my boss and I are here for a number of things, and it's going to be a long night. A long night that may end up with you dead or us reaching an agreement. The longer I sit here looking at you naked, the more I feel aroused and may have to do something about that. Got me so far?"

She nodded.

"Good. Are you supposed to contact anyone tonight?"

She shook her head.

He sat back down and his eyes took their time checking out her body. Jeffries got up and walked back to her bedroom.

"I figured if we're going to be here for a few hours, I might as well make it enjoyable. Are you enjoying yourself?"

She remained motionless.

"You're a sharp one. Okay, so we have a few things to discuss." He got up and walked around the kitchen area and pulled a knife from the wood block on the counter.

Jeffries came back with the book from her nightstand and pulled out the bookmark. He handed it to Ignaty.

Ignaty checked the sharpness of the knife by slicing off the bottom of the bookmark.

"Sharp enough, I suppose."

She looked at the bookmark and then downward.

"This is the first part, and the easiest part," Ignaty said. "I *highly* suggest you don't screw it up. If you don't give me the answers I want, the first time I ask, I'll have to duct-tape your mouth tight, because I'll be using this knife. On you. Understand?"

She nodded, and he nodded back.

He tapped the bookmark with his finger and smiled.

"Where is Kade Sims?"

CHAPTER 21

Near DuPont Circle
Washington, D.C.
Saturday, November 19
11:36 p.m. (EST)

Deep house music throbbed, fog spewed into the first-floor dance area, and green laser light streamed through it.

Kade hadn't gone out late-night clubbing or pubbing in over a year, but this date was work, technically speaking.

It did remind him of his personal corrosion of two years ago.

He'd gone overkill on all-night entertainment binging and didn't realize how it was affecting himself or those around him. The behavior avalanche had ultimately caused him to be kicked out of the army. He'd had an Article 15 disciplinary hearing for Failure to Report, and, in a moment of anger, had broken the nose of the major he reported to.

This wouldn't turn into a habit again. He could enjoy himself this one time and stay in control. It was a hell of a lot better option than if he'd accepted Carla's dinner invite. Nothing good would've come from that.

He found Lin at their reserved table on the second floor. This time, she greeted him with a radiant smile instead of a sneer. He gave her a hug and quick kiss before sliding onto the couch next to her.

Her mode was all-black, semi-Goth, similar to the surveillance photo. She wore a sleeveless dress with cutouts at the shoulders, lined with ball-chain trim. Another pair of monstrous boots. He wasn't sure what she'd done to her hair, but it was a messy, sexy style.

Her vibe was great—he could've been picking up right where they'd left off a few months ago. Only now, his getting to know her was no longer a side interest or a means to an end.

His mission *was* her. He needed to get results.

The bottle-service girl poured her a crantini while he opted for a light beer. It would be easy to have a few too many around this girl. He wouldn't make that mistake.

He clinked his beer bottle on her glass.

"I wasn't sure if you were gonna show up," he said.

She pulled back from her sip like she might spit it out.

"Turn down a date with Kade Sims? Oh my God. The curiosity alone . . ."

He laughed.

Their conversation gave him some brief insights into her personal history. A childhood with loving but demanding parents. Two older brothers. Piano recitals. Her dad was a scientist who'd started his career in the army and now was a CEO for a company called China North Industries Corporation. He obviously had done well for himself—Lin had received her undergraduate degree at NYU, while her brothers had attended Cornell and Carnegie-Mellon, respectively.

Three college educations in America. Daddy had to shell out a few bucks for that.

Like Andrade said, the fuerdai.

She had visited Shanghai frequently since college through her work, and said she'd been engaged once to a Chinese man there. Details were a bit murky, and he tried not to prod too much, but she said she was the one who broke off the engagement, and it became a major family crisis. Part of "losing face," as she tried to explain it. She said she generally preferred American men because they were more direct.

She's pretty direct, herself.

Kade took some short notes to himself inside his program, making them when his head was turned so she wouldn't catch any of his unusual eye movements. The notes could serve as a personal cheat sheet to remember someone's name and background if he needed to. But note-taking became more difficult, or forgotten, as they gravitated closer, touching on the couch.

In his occasional scan of his surroundings, he detected something odd. It wasn't the occasional douchebag guy, the couples clearly on drugs, or the occasional working girl. They were all expected.

Four tables down on the opposite side of him were a pair of Asian men who'd had their eyes on Lin from the get-go. They were on their phones, sending texts or something. Nothing too unusual there. But sitting side by side in similar suits, they seemed a little overdressed.

Overt surveillance.

Or maybe just waiting for more people to join their party?

Let's find out.

In the spirit of the more "direct" American male, he planted a number of long kisses on Lin, which she appreciated. The odd couple didn't like the show.

"So where are *you* working now?" Lin asked him while the bottle-service girl made another pass.

"At Lowe's . . . home improvement, again."

His stoplight flickered yellow and would continue to flicker through additional fibs.

She gave him the stink-eye as they clinked drinks again.

"You expect me to believe that's all you do, when I've seen you sit for hours doing computer work?"

Pow. Who's interrogating whom?

Kade smiled. "Hey, come by and see me. There's nothing like the smell of a home improvement store in the morning."

A look of disgust passed over her face.

"No, seriously," he added. "I couldn't go back to Home Depot given my sudden, long leave of absence, so Lowe's was the easy option. You'd never come visit me, anyway. That would be like me hanging out in Ulta."

She gave a cute snicker.

"If you're not a government agent," she said, "then you must be some kind of government hacker. Like a cyberexpert."

He laughed. "You won't let this go, will you? No, I don't do government work. Some part-time freelance work—web sites and stuff like that, on top of the Lowe's work. Software engineering was my major at MIT, but once I got out into the army, I didn't use the degree much. But I do try to maintain the skills . . . keep 'em fresh."

"I'd love to be a hacker," she said. "A Kade hacker. Hack right through that protective shell."

She gave him a hard poke to the shoulder. He smiled, but wasn't liking his real name being spoken out loud in the open.

He switched over to another thought process running in parallel. The FBI suspected Lin could be a Chinese intelligence asset, and so did he.

Chinese military doctrine, like much doctrine from well-established powers, was both complex and nuanced, influenced by both modern and ancient doctrine. The Chinese revered the strategy of Sun Tzu, espoused in *The Art of War* and passed down through generations from roughly the fifth century B.C.

He'd memorized portions of the Sun Tzu teachings, especially in the section "Using Spies." In elegant simplicity, Sun Tzu said there were five kinds of spies.

Local spies are the enemy's own countrymen in our employ.

Inside agents are enemy officials we employ.

Double agents are enemy spies who report to our side.

Expendable spies are our own agents who obtain false information we have deliberately leaked to them, and who pass it on to the enemy spies.

Unexpendable spies are those who return from the enemy camp to report.

While American intelligence doctrine had its own set of definitions, sometimes it was useful looking at doctrine through the lens of an adversary and its culture.

If Lin was a spy, she was either an expendable or an unexpendable one. His thinking leaned more toward the latter at this moment. Frequent trips to Shanghai, on the surface, would make it appear as though she was collecting information of some sort and reporting it back to her original homeland on a regular basis. That made her *unexpendable*.

He leaned in closer to her.

"Okay, Kade hacker. You want to dance?"

She rewarded him with a kiss.

They danced for about thirty minutes. It wasn't his bag with this kind of music, but she made it enjoyable. There was more kissing before, during, and after the dance floor. Relationship building with his source, he rationalized.

When they decided to take a break and were walking toward the stairs back to the second floor, another man, who Kade thought to be Chinese, touched Lin's shoulder and said something to her. His straight black hair showed a few threads of gray on the side.

I know that guy. He's the guy in Andrade's surveillance photo, only with longer hair.

Lin turned squarely toward the man, shouted back some rapid-fire Chinese punctuated with a wave of her hand. After some finger-pointing, the man walked away, unhappy, possibly talking to himself or into some earpiece. Kade followed her upstairs, looking once over his shoulder.

"Who was that?" he asked when they reached the top.

"I have some business friends who like to make sure I'm safe. They like to know where I am."

They returned to the table and sat close.

Is he in charge of the two suits?

"Are you worried about me?" he asked.

She hooked her hand around his upper arm.

"No . . . they always want me to go out to a place where they know the owners. Where everything is always paid for. Tonight, I just wanted to go somewhere different with you. I didn't expect them to show up."

Uneasiness snaked inside his belly.

"Oh. So, you have, like, *minders* keeping track of you?"

Now she looked irritated.

"It's not like that."

This wasn't good. She had to *report in* where she was going with him on a date?

Weird.

It wouldn't do him any good to give her a hard time about it here and now. He lightly gripped her knee and peered over at the two suits again.

"You didn't tell anyone you were seeing me, by name, did you?"

"No."

"All right, then don't worry about it," he said.

At that moment, another tall man walked up to the table.

Asian.

Chinese?

With the table light and a better angle, a name flashed in Kade's vision view.

TAN LIANG

Kade's thoughts blasted like a confetti cannon.

A Chapter member.

And a Chinese agent?

Tan Liang said something to Lin in Chinese, and she responded in a few sentences, looking pissed off, her body language communicating *go away.* Tan Liang continued to argue with her or demand something.

"Hey, man," Kade said. "You want to postpone your discussion for tomorrow?"

Tan Liang didn't respond, but one of the two suits suddenly came forward. Kade had taken his eye off them.

CHU SHAN

Tan Liang patted the brawny Chu Shan on the shoulder.

"My friend here—he wants to fight you," Tan said.

What the f—?

Kade looked at Lin and back at them.

"Wait—*he* wants to . . . fight *me?*"

"Yeah."

Kade's adrenaline gushed while he scrunched his face and shook his head.

"What is this, third grade?"

Lin groaned, pulled out her phone and mumbled, "I'm sorry . . . I'm going to call someone."

"Have a good night," Tan said. He patted Chu's shoulder, and walked away.

Kade gently blocked her hand before she could dial.

"No, don't."

That's all I need—a squad of Chapter goons showing up for backup.

And he couldn't let Lin know he recognized a Chapter member either.

But did she know?

Had they seen through his disguise?

This is crazy. Abort . . .

"Let's just leave, huh?" he mumbled to Lin. She nodded back.

"You win," he directed to Chu. "We're leaving, okay?"

Chu didn't move.

Kade angled his head so he could better size him up. Chu looked in his late twenties. His face said he would fight, even though his body language seemed a little unsure of himself. The guy looked fit.

A fight wouldn't be easy. He might know kung fu or some shit like that. This wasn't the desired course of action.

But he needed to get out and didn't want to be followed.

Kade slid to the end of the couch to stand, spreading his palm to signal *calm down.*

Chu's eyes tracked Kade's hand like he wasn't familiar with the gesture.

As he rose, Kade said, "Look, man, this really isn't a good idea at all—"

With his knees still bent, he pushed hard off his right heel. His right hand started in a low arc from his pocket, clenching in a fist as it rose. Only inches before it slammed into the right side of his jaw did Chu see it coming.

Chu dropped so fast and hard to the ground, Lin gasped.

There was a collective "Oh!" from nearby tables and passersby, and then the other suited guy who was built like a tank moved toward him. Whatever was about to happen, it was going to hurt.

Kade's display blinked again.

CHAU DEWEI

More Chinese Chapter.

Kade kept a balanced stance as Chau threw the first punch. He pulled his neck back at the right instant so only a few knuckles managed to graze his forehead.

He avoided Chau's follow-up lunging jab by stepping back, and raised his forearm to block a third punch. His rib cage absorbed the fourth punch. He saw a chance to counterpunch but didn't.

Club security had arrived, and he wanted them to see him getting hit.

The pair of security men grabbed Kade and Chau—Kade completely relaxed in their arms while Chau made the mistake of resisting and was pepper-sprayed in the face.

Kade looked back at Lin, now standing aghast, as security walked him down the stairs to kick him out. He acted pleasant and said thanks to the men when they let him go outside the entrance. He'd been literally kicked to the curb a few times in his darker days.

Chau was still being restrained when security brought him out and sat him on the sidewalk. Kade stayed out of his sight and waited to see if Lin would emerge. A cab pulled up to the curb and security encouraged Chau to take it.

Lin showed up five minutes later and Kade waved to her from down the sidewalk. When she caught up, he pulled out a few bills as they walked.

"Here . . . sorry. Who was the guy who came to the table?"

"That was my ex-fiancé, Liang, I was talking about."

Kade stopped and pulled her over to the corner of the closest building.

"What? What's up with that?"

"He's tried contacting me this week and I've ignored him. I never expected him to show up, but he must have heard through the grapevine."

"So this relationship is still . . . ongoing?"

"No, of course not. I'm so sorry, Kade. What a disaster. I wish you hadn't gotten in a fight."

"Well, I had no choice but to take the cheap shot. You knew those two guys in the suits?"

"No. Only Liang and the other man, Li, who advises on my company's security."

He wanted to confront her, ask her more about everything. Personal and business dealings. Was he being played?

It's only the second time you've been out with her.

"Okay. I should call it a night."

She half-pouted. "I don't want to go home now. It'll be bad. They'll be camped out, waiting for me, angry. I don't need another lecture."

He gripped her shoulder.

"What do they know about me?"

The streetlight shone in her moist eyes.

"Nothing. I've told them nothing. Except that it's none of their business. And that drives them nuts."

He nodded, hung his arm around her. Now he was thinking about finding somewhere where they could have breakfast, but farther down the sidewalk, her hand slid tightly around him and they kissed some more.

His hands linked behind her back, pulled her in.

"It's just after three," he said, "and you probably shouldn't be driving."

She looked down and nodded, snuggling inside his coat onto his chest.

He could try to extend this night into a day together so he could ask more questions.

Her ex and minders might not like it, but what were they going to do? Andrade and Summerford could tell him how to best deal with those fools in his next debrief.

It's clear Chinese intel is watching her. But what about The Chapter?

Is it just a jealous ex who happens to be in it?

If she was actively working for The Chapter, she could have easily burned him already. But he'd have to make sure they weren't followed.

The side of her face rested against his chest and her hair glided through his fingers. He took a deep breath and smelled the faint rose fragrance of some hair product.

"How about you stay with me?"

CHAPTER 22

Timberville, West Virginia
Sunday, November 20
6:03 a.m. (EST)

No disturbances had been recorded when Kade checked his home surveillance app on his phone, a few minutes away from his house.

Lin was still asleep as he pulled into the carport of the three-bedroom cabin. The temperature had dropped below freezing, and the cloud layer stretched across the morning twilight like a rumpled bedsheet.

Kade rented the cabin from a man in his eighties who gave him a great deal, contingent on his helping maintain the acreage around it. While there wouldn't be any lawn mowing needed until spring, he was already far behind on leaf blowing, mulching, and picking up pinecones.

This was only the second time someone had visited his home in the two and a half months he'd lived there. Carla had stayed over once, but he'd ended up thinking that wasn't a good idea to continue. Telling her it was for her own safety hadn't been the full truth.

He lifted Lin and her purse out of her seat and carried her in through the side door, elbowing the hallway light switch on. After a moment of indecision, he brought her into his bedroom and laid her down, lifting her head and sliding a long pillow underneath. She murmured something but didn't open her eyes. The blinds were already closed and he left the lights off.

Now was an opportunity. He punched a code into his phone and set it down behind her purse he'd set on the dresser. While he took off her shoes and pulled the thick comforter over her, an app the FBI had installed on his phone pulled the contacts and call records from hers.

He'd asked Andrade or Summerford why they couldn't have requested this through the phone service, but they hadn't given him a straight answer. He'd learned there was often a good reason for tactics that wouldn't make complete sense to him at the time.

The screen displayed a small green checkmark when the app finished running, and he pocketed his phone again. There was nothing sensitive for her to find in this room, so he would leave her in here alone. After using the bathroom, he stepped out into the hall, pulled the door shut and released the handle.

The kitchen stove clock read 6:17 a.m. when he decided he should get some sleep. He ate the one salvageable banana from the bunch on the counter and tossed the rest in the garbage. Once he'd undressed and crawled onto the couch, he checked his phone once more, punching in the code to view the "special" app. The file had transmitted, but that's when something caught his eye.

Two files were listed from what had been scanned—one for her iPhone and one for another phone, a Samsung Gusto model.

She had another phone in her purse. A burner.

That's what the FBI wanted to check.

They'll be happy with me.

It was a good way to end this long night and early morning, and made it a bit easier to settle his mind. He fell asleep quickly.

But it couldn't have been an hour before his phone rang. He groaned as he woke up. His eyes felt puffy and unresponsive.

The incoming number was from Jim Wilks, who lived a half mile down the road. He was an old army retiree who Kade most often spotted sitting on his front porch, wearing a KOREA VETERAN ball cap and smoking a cigar. Kade had been invited inside to chat a few times. A nice man.

Kade cleared his gummy throat. His mouth tasted especially awful.

"Hello?"

"Hello, Mr. Kyle?"

Kade tried to sound happy to hear from him. "Hey, Mr. Wilks, how are you?"

"I'm doing just fine. Look it, I wanted to tell you—a man and woman drove up and asked me where you were living while I was taking out the dog. I told them you were up around the bend, back at the edge of the woods—before I got to thinking it was a little strange this time of Sunday morning. I thought they might've been armed, too. Just thought I'd give you a call."

Kade bounced off the couch as if it were on fire.

The FBI had his phone number. They would've known where he was living if they needed to get ahold of him. They wouldn't have needed to ask.

This wasn't right.

"Thanks, Mr. Wilks. This is pretty weird. What did they look like?"

"They both looked in their thirties. White. Should I call the police?"

"Uh, not now, please. But if I don't call you back in an hour, please do."

"Okay."

He ended the call.

"Lin!" he yelled and dashed to the bedroom, shaking her awake. "Lin, get up, now!"

"What? What's wrong?"

"Two people I don't know are headed this way. It's got to mean trouble."

He threw on jeans, warm socks, running shoes, and a T-shirt. "They wouldn't be two of your people, would they?"

She was now sitting up, groggy.

"No, it can't be," she said. "I told them to stay away, and they don't know where I was going."

He pulled her out of bed and steadied her upright. She looked irritated until she saw the look on his face.

"Go hide in the bathroom and don't come out until I get you."

"Okay." Her eyes were now blinking, wide and glassy.

The Chapter had found him somehow.

But there *was* a chance it wasn't them. The left hand of the FBI might not be talking to the right. He'd seen this before. When secrecy was involved, communication gaps were often wider, and mistakes happened.

Maybe someone heard about the incident last night and wanted to check on him? Could he have been under surveillance the whole night?

Shooting first had been his preferred strategy when he'd war-gamed a situation like this. He had no problem with a first-strike policy when it came to The Chapter, but now he had concerns. The law in Virginia was you couldn't shoot someone dead unless they were an imminent threat. Or something like that.

He slid a gun safe out from under the bed and hit the keypad to retrieve his other loaded Glock. Also under the bed was a lightweight Kevlar vest with six full clips in the front pouches.

Kade donned the black vest and secured its two Velcro straps. A gray pair of welding goggles and a pair of Ryobi noise suppression headphones were clipped to the vest's back.

The doorbell rang as he was putting the headphones on.

They're here. And they rang the damn doorbell.

The fact they announced themselves gave him further doubts. He could be blowing this way out of proportion. Lin would think he was a paranoid freak.

Even though the window blinds were drawn, he made his way over to the kitchen in a crouch, where a split-screen monitor showed a simultaneous view of the front stoop and the back porch. Hidden surveillance cameras provided a feed on a recorded loop, the same feed he'd accessed on his phone.

Outside the front door stood a man and a woman, both white. Business casual clothes. More than likely, *not* Chinese intelligence, of course, unless subcontracted. The woman seemed to be in the lead. He wasn't going to get near that door and ask who they were.

There was no one on the back porch he could observe on the monitor. No one would be able to see him from out there—a large curtain was drawn over the length of the sliding glass door.

The doorbell chimed again. *They aren't going away.*

The woman rapped the door with the brass knocker next. Kade positioned the welding goggles over his eyes. The front room was an open style from the front door entryway, through the living room section, and back to the kitchen island where he stood.

With his truck in the carport, they knew he was inside. Yet, they weren't trying to break in either.

It's barely seven thirty yet, and it's a Sunday.

Maybe there was an imperative to bring him some kind of news in person. A notification. Someone he knew was dead? His shoulders shuddered.

FBI or local law enforcement might be bringing a notification.

It still didn't feel right.

He slid a three-pound box of Chex in front of him on the counter. The kitchen island was ringed with Kevlar ballistic panels he'd mounted on the sides after moving in.

The front door unlocked when he dialed a code into his phone.

He gripped both of his guns behind the Chex box to conceal them.

"Yeah, come on in—door's open!"

Glancing between the monitor and the door, he caught a quick hand signal and nod from the woman on the screen before she came through the door.

When she stepped in and saw him behind the counter, she leapt sideways and drew a gun.

In that glimpse of her face, the name TANYA GRODACK popped up in his vision, even with his tinted goggles on.

He could've cared less about her name, but there was no doubt who he was dealing with now. The Chapter had come for him again.

In a split second, he ducked behind the island. Grodack squeezed off two shots as her trail foot touched down, one of the rounds blasting the cereal box off the counter.

He sidestepped in his squatting position, just outside the left edge of the island, and fired at her while she dropped and rolled on the floor in one motion. She was damn fast.

He got off two shots, but she squared up and fired twice again, one shot landing low in his vest, knocking him off-balance, back on his butt. The man at the front door snaked around the room in the other direction, past the fireplace.

He was going to be flanked and couldn't get his breath—the wind had been knocked out of him.

But one of his bullets had hit Grodack somewhere. As she dove to the side again, toward the open doorway to his home office, he fired, emptying the rest of the clip.

He moved to a squat again and fired twice with his right hand extended above the counter, guessing where the other guy might be, then pivoted, firing another two shots at Grodack as she was pulling herself to her knees.

His lungs still couldn't get air as he pushed off and dove behind the couch. Grodack was hardly moving. He'd lost sight of the other guy.

More shots thundered inside—rounds hitting the TV mounted on the wall behind him, splintering wood and slamming into the couch. Kevlar panels also lined the couch back under the slipcover, so he stayed behind there.

"Sims!" the man yelled. "Lay down the gun! There's another dozen coming right behind us. It's time to come in if you want to stay alive."

Kade glanced behind him—the woman was halfway into the office entryway, leaving a trail of blood. She didn't look like she was in a position to fire.

He gritted his teeth. *Fuck you, man.*

He popped up over the couch back, fired the rest of the other gun's clip toward the short hall and laundry room, blasting right through the thin sheetrock walls. He ejected an empty clip and slammed in another. When he checked behind him once more, Grodack was no longer moving.

He crawled to the edge of the couch and peeked out from the bottom. The guy popped out from the laundry room and made a run for the side door. Kade fired twice more and hit him in the back before he got there, knocking him down.

Crawling closer, Kade maneuvered to his feet and aimed his pistol. The guy turned his head toward him while unsuccessfully trying to pull himself upright. The name CORBETT BELL popped up in Kade's vision.

"Reach for that gun and you're dead," Kade said.

He stepped forward and kicked Bell's gun away, taking a quick glance over his shoulder again to make sure Grodack wasn't coming for him. Faking dead was a tried and true tactic, but she appeared unconscious, at least.

"A dozen more coming, huh?"

Bell grunted back at him.

Defiance.

He's only going to try and kill me again if I let him go.

Not today.

Before he allowed himself to think about it further, he jammed his gun into Bell's eye socket and squeezed the trigger.

He began to stand up but then dove to the ground when another gunshot sounded behind him.

Somehow Grodack had taken another shot?

No. Lin was standing there with Grodack's gun.

She had shot Grodack one more time in the head.

Kade and Lin looked across the room at one another in silence. Kade slid his goggles to the top of his head while Lin tossed Grodack's gun on the couch.

"She was still moving," Lin said.

"Hey, no argument here."

They only had a few minutes. There were many of these home attack scenarios he'd worked through dozens of times in his head. He'd rehearsed for a number of them. Sometimes he'd dream about them and wake up sweating.

But in all of this planning, he was always alone—he didn't have to worry about anyone other than himself.

If he tried to drive away, they could be easily intercepted. Another option was to run away through the woods, but he wasn't sure how many minutes they'd have for a head start. And if they ran away together, Lin might slow them down and make defense more difficult.

Modifying the home defense plan would be best.

He slid one of his guns back into the vest holster.

"Are you okay?" he asked.

She nodded.

He walked over to her and they embraced for a few seconds. Before she could speak, he gently pushed away and held her shoulder.

"Another group from The Chapter is coming here. They'll try to take me out this time. Here's what I need you to do . . ."

She took a deep breath, looked like she was trying to focus.

"You're going to head out the back door," he said. "Around the side of the house toward the woods. You'll see a shed. Go toward the shed and you'll see a woodpile to the right of it. Between the shed and wood pile, you'll see a bump in the ground, like a leaf pile. There will be a big handle there. Pull up on it—it's a plywood board on a hinge covering a hiding spot there. I want you to get inside and stay there."

She nodded, no objection.

"If I don't decide to join you, I'll come get you later or send text messages. If you don't hear from me, wait until it gets dark to come out, and call 9-1-1."

She looked like she was starting to tear up.

"It's freezing out," he said. "It's going to be miserable in there. In the bottom of the space is a thermal blanket in a sealed plastic bag. There's also a hat, gloves, and fleece jacket in there. Get all that out of the bag and around you, okay? Don't touch anything else in there. Hold on a sec . . ."

He grabbed two bottles of water and an energy bar out of his cupboard.

"The water in there is probably frozen . . . take these. Okay, can you do this?"

She nodded, leaned up and kissed him. He slid the goggles back on and replaced the pistol clips with two full ones.

"All right, now go."

CHAPTER 23

Timberville, West Virginia
Sunday, November 20
7:21 a.m. (EST)

On the screen of Kade's iPhone, the video streaming from his small drone, hovering in a preprogrammed spot above the house, showed four vehicles approaching on the gravel drive—two large SUVs and one car.

Kade was surprised they hadn't cut the power to the house, even though he had a backup battery to power a few things. They must've not had enough time after finding out his location. They were capitalizing on an opportunity before he could bug out.

How did they find me?

Lin could've had a tracker, but if she did, she might not have been aware of it. She could have shot him instead of Grodack, saving the hit team the trouble, if she was a Chapter loyalist.

There was no more time to kick this around in his brain. Not now.

Where he was standing in the attic, and in two other areas up there, ballistic panels covered a patch of the floor beams. Loaded AK-47 rifles were also positioned in those spots.

From his phone, he turned on the home stereo to high volume, playing a recent album by Code Orange Kids to hide the noise of his movements inside. A speaker near the front door blasted loud enough to mask the whirring of the drone.

The vehicles came to a stop and the doors opened.

Four cars. Ten people.

Wearing respirators.

With a few thumb taps on the phone, he sent the drone to its next preprogrammed position, higher above the house, adjacent to a tall pine, and switched to the other camera on its belly.

Two men crept toward the front of the house. Three were circling around back, two moving toward the carport and service door, and two stopped short of the bedroom on the opposite side of the house.

Kade slid the phone into his vest and walked across the plywood catwalk above the bedroom. Paused.

Within seconds, five or six separate explosions boomed inside the house. Though his headphones muffled the sound, the acoustic shock tensed his body.

Flash-bangers.

Pulses of bright light shone up into the attic's dusty air through the openings he'd cut. One of those holes was right next to him.

The grenades continued to hiss and spit vapor. That meant there was a gas component to the grenades.

Hence, the respirators.

He had a mask clipped to the back of his vest, but he wasn't going to have time for that now. And the mask would make it even harder to see from up in the attic.

Some gunshots popped outside. He couldn't tell from where. But then the bedroom window smashed. He stooped over the cut-out portal and aimed the rifle through the clear glass bowl without a light fixture in it.

A guy swung a leg over the windowsill.

Kade fired a shot grouping at this first man stepping into the bedroom, then switched his aim toward the second figure in the window. Both men went down and the shattered bowl fixture rained glass on the carpet.

He would've preferred targeting more intruders from the attic. None of them was wearing body armor. Surprising. This could've been so they wouldn't attract attention. The Chapter's desire to remain well under the radar sometimes made them skip precautions.

But the gas was making him nervous. It was probably the CS or CN variety of riot control agent—nonlethal, but it could render him ineffective. The gases were heavier than air, but he imagined some of that gas could circulate up to the attic.

Bending at the waist, he power-walked under the framing toward the back of the attic and its single window. The orange hue of the morning sky was filtering through the trees. He popped the latch and felt the bite of cold air as he pushed the window open.

The rifle wasn't going with him. As he pulled his phone back out, he thought he heard a few shouts from below, but it was hard to tell with the music still blaring. He toggled on the phone screen to the view from the second drone—a floor drone on wheels located underneath the living room coffee table. He pivoted the drone to do a 360-degree scan.

There were at least four pairs of legs and feet in the living room, maybe more. The sliding glass door was now wide open in back.

He breathed in and coughed into his shoulder to muffle the noise. Either he'd gotten a whiff of gas or the dust was irritating his throat. It was time to go. The backyard looked clear. He could fit through the window with the gear he had on because he'd practiced it before, but it was a tight squeeze. He slid out feet first, holding on to a short section of rope he'd anchored there, repositioned himself, and pushed off.

Even though he had four bales of straw on the ground serving as a crash pad, his left foot skipped off the edge as he landed. He took a second bounce onto the grass, staying upright, but his left ankle rolled. When he took his next two steps, he clenched his teeth. Something didn't feel right.

Damn—not good. But his adrenaline surged enough to defer the pain.

He jogged at a crouch toward the sliding glass door, taking a deep breath and holding it before he got there. There had to be gas drifting outside, but his eyes would be okay with the goggles still on.

He peeked around the door's back edge.

Five right here. All in respirators.

Two of them down. That means three others somewhere else.

Flash-bangs and gas. Nonlethal.

They're trying to take me alive again? But with a larger group?

He backed away, checking to make sure all was clear behind him, and pulled out his pistols.

Gunfire erupted inside, and he dove to the ground. But none of the bullets had impacted the walls or the glass near him. They weren't aimed at him.

He'd exhaled when he hit the dirt and continued to hold his breath. His lungs were telling him he needed oxygen. The men inside continued firing up toward the ceiling. They'd figured out where his hiding place had been and thought he was still up there.

So much for taking me alive, I guess.

He pushed to a kneeling position and opened fire, trying to distribute his shots across the room. In the confusion, the Chapter team returned a few shots, but by then, he had moved to the far edge of the door. When his clips emptied, he jogged around the carport to the corner of the house, sucking in air and grunting in pain. He veered right and stopped behind a pair of holly trees, giving him an obscured view of the front. He pulled off his goggles so they dangled around his neck.

There was only time to reload one gun before a man came out the front door. Hoping to get a lucky hit or encourage his target to go back inside, Kade fired two shots. Instead, the guy sprinted to the driveway and disappeared behind one of the cars.

Kade puffed steam into the air, catching his raspy breath, but he needed to move again. These trees weren't going to stop bullets.

His ankle flared in pain as he turned and made a beeline for the woods. Three shots echoed behind him while he ran down the trail, past the woodpile and shed for about another forty yards, toward a particular hemlock tree cleared of low branches. Woodblocks were nailed to the back of the trunk for footing and a rope ran up its length.

He slid on a pair of thin hunting gloves from his vest and climbed up thirty feet to a green aluminum tree stand that had a waterproof gun case bungee-corded to the inside.

There was more movement in the driveway. Now he guessed two or three people were there behind the cars, regrouping. He pulled the Remington R-15 VTR out of the case and loaded a twenty-round magazine. Through the scope he could view two pairs of men, each with a pistol, behind an SUV.

The ones left in the house must be dead. They would bring out wounded to avoid capture.

They think they don't have much time. They think I already called the FBI. They're deciding whether to—

One pair suddenly peeled off and dashed toward the woods in front of him. Kade tracked the one man on the right through his scope and fired three shots—dropping the guy before he made it out of the yard. His partner returned fire in Kade's general direction, then crawled in the turf over to his team member.

Kade fired another three shots at the wounded man to finish him off. His partner sprung up and took off running to the side, dashing in a roundabout route between trees and bushes back to the driveway. Kade started to squeeze off another shot.

No, just let him go. Don't bring the other two into the fight.

He fired a few shots intentionally off target and aimed two more back at the driveway area to keep them nervous. The side-rear window of the SUV was an easy mark, so he put a bullet through it. The three remaining Chapter soldiers each got into a vehicle, spun wheels in the gravel, and drove out fast enough that they almost hit each other.

When they disappeared from view on the main gravel road, Kade pumped his fist in the air and breathed deep. He coughed hard, hacked up some mucus.

It's a beautiful morning and I'm still alive.

I may lose this war, but today I won a battle.

He slung the Remington over his back and descended the rope, keeping his weight off the rolled ankle when he touched down.

Poor Lin was still in the hideout, which was an oversized foxhole. He made his way over to it.

"Lin, it's me. I'm opening the top."

She looked up at him, squinting. Unexpectedly beautiful in that instant. He was glad she'd bundled up as he'd asked, but her body was shivering and teeth chattering, nonetheless.

He sat down on the edge. "Are you okay?"

She nodded. "All those gunshots . . . is it safe?"

Kade smiled a little. "Yeah, for now."

He crouched down, and her arms ended up around his neck as he helped lift her out.

"Just don't touch your eyes now," he said. "I have some tear gas on me that's going to get on you."

She steadied herself on her numb legs and started tearing up again.

"Are they all gone?"

Kade shook his head. "Nope. Some are in the house, and there's a couple more outside. But they're all dead."

CHAPTER 24

Timberville, West Virginia
Sunday, November 20
8:13 a.m. (EST)

Kade double-checked to make sure the Chapter team members were actually all dead. It was possible some had been near-dead, but their chipset had finished the job.

Good riddance.

Before returning to the house, he'd dragged the soldier who'd died near the woods into the shed and wrapped him in plastic sheeting. The bodies inside the home and the one outside his broken bedroom window were now covered with extra bed linens and old blankets.

He didn't otherwise touch the bodies or go through their possessions. That would be left to professionals this time. This was too big. Having ten corpses of attackers at his home was something he never would have conceived of six months ago. Yet, he was unusually calm. Perhaps numb or detached.

Lin sat hunched on the couch under a thermal blanket. He sat down next to her and pulled off his right shoe and sock, exposing his red and swollen ankle.

"How is it?" she asked.

"I think it's just a sprain. Doesn't look like I broke or tore anything. I'll pound some ibuprofen."

"Don't we need to get out of here?" Lin asked.

"We have some time. The enemy's not coming back today. No way. They'll consider this a compromised situation. They'll regroup before they try coming after me again."

If their door-greeters had just waited for the rest of their team, they would've had me.

They didn't have time to coordinate. They thought they might lose me.

"What about all the gunfire?" Lin asked.

"There are a lot of hunters and skeet shooters around here. I don't expect anyone else to call something in on a Sunday. If there was smoke from a burning house, it might be different."

He called Mr. Wilks back and said everything was okay. When Wilks got a little too curious, Kade said the federal authorities had asked him not to talk publicly about what had happened today and that he had to go.

He felt Lin's hand and it was ice-cold. Not surprising, because the house was freezing from having the doors blown out and windows broken.

"You need to get warm," he said. "There's too much broken glass in my bedroom, and it's freezing in there. I plugged in a space heater in the bathroom next to the laundry room and it should be getting warm now. There's a shower in there. I brought your bag in from my truck and there're some towels and extra clothes I had in storage tubs. A few of my sister's items that ended up in my stuff. Tear gas–free. Should get you by until we get out of here."

"I can't believe you killed all these people."

Kade shook his head. "I don't want to think about it anymore right now."

"Sorry. And I'm really sorry about your house."

"Fuck it—it's a rental."

She laughed, and that helped him laugh a little.

The laundry room hallway was now clear of Bell's body, and he'd cleaned up the broken fiberglass inside the bathroom. While Lin went to shower, he gathered a new bag of essential belongings.

I might not be coming back for a while.

Thank God he'd negotiated for a supplemental weapons allowance under both of his contracts. Without them, he couldn't have afforded the weapons, gear, and Pelican storage cases for everything.

He wouldn't have stood a chance.

Lin shouted something from the bathroom. When he started down the hall, he saw her looking out one of the fist-size holes in the drywall. He laughed and stepped up to her face, hearing the shower running behind her.

"What did you say?" he said.

"I was going to lie and say there's no shampoo, but why don't you just shower with me? It'll save time."

He paused and smiled. "Okay, give me a minute."

After stripping down to his underwear in the kitchen and stuffing the clothes in a garbage bag, he limped around through the door to the bathroom, where she was standing naked in the tub.

Though he'd imagined what her body must have looked like a thousand times, even in the back of this shot-up, threadbare side bathroom, she looked unbelievable. The bathroom was warm and comfortable from the heater.

"Um, I have gas residue on me," he said, "so you'll have to get out for a few minutes and let me wash off with cold water first."

She gave a quick fake pout. "Okay, I can wait a few minutes. Then I'll make double-sure you're clean."

"Deal."

He laughed again as he turned the water on and adjusted it to chilly. When he carefully shimmied out of his briefs and stepped into the tub, the sore ankle took some weight and his face tightened.

"Damn."

She leaned back against the sink in an alluring pose. "Are you sure you're going to make it?"

He laughed harder. "Yeah, I'm sure."

It was the longest five-minute cold shower of his life, but before he knew it, he'd turned up the warm water and she stepped in to join him. With her soapy body pressed up against him and water cascading down his back, he really couldn't believe it. All pain and worry were temporarily forgotten.

They kissed in a way that made the time in the club seem tame. The connection was stronger. Pent-up feelings flooded outward, pulling them both along, and any suspicions between them were now small, forgotten eddies in the current.

She smoothed her wet hair back. "Are you okay?"

"Yeah, unless you're looking for acrobatics."

She laughed.

His mind was spinning in a wonderful way from the adrenaline residue. Survival and fear instincts had been cranked up to the max, and now the switch was flipped off and joy remained.

Yes, it flashed through his mind that he shouldn't be doing this. She was his source, and he was the FBI's source.

There were *dead bodies* a few feet away in the next room, but he no longer cared about them in the least. He was still breathing.

It would be a long, tiring day ahead after he called this in to the team. But on this horrible day, here was an enduring moment of beauty.

Death could come later today. Tomorrow. Or the next day. Only God knew.

He might as well try to turn this into one of the best days of his life.

CHAPTER 25

It was time to report in. Kade moved his truck into a sunny patch of driveway and did a walk-around. Two bullet holes in the side panel were the only visible damage. Nothing underneath was leaking, and the tires were full of air.

Climbing back inside the cab, he first called the Recovery Team to inform them about the battle at his house. Lamb was on the phone with him in three minutes. Kade reminded Lamb of his separate contract with the FBI, and that his *source*, Lin, was currently inside his house.

"Do you need medical attention?" Lamb asked.

"I have some cuts and bruises along with a sprained ankle, I think. I can put weight on it, but not much. I'm icing it down."

"Can you drive?"

"Yeah, and my truck is still in working order."

"Okay, take your source with you and get out of the area. Head toward D.C. I'll take care of site cleanup and interagency coordination. Remember to keep that firewall between our activities and the Bureau's. Call me if there's ever an issue or question."

"Okay."

"I'll get you text instructions of where to go next in the next thirty minutes. You'll need a debriefing, and your source will have to be questioned too."

"Uh . . . that might be tricky."

"Just manage it the best you can for now."

"Okay."

"Stay safe," Lamb said before ending the call.

My two contracts are bumping heads.

Kade turned off the ignition, slid out on one leg, and stood facing the house.

It didn't seem likely he'd be living here anymore. A shame, because he was just getting used to the place and had grown fond of the mix of rolling farmland and woods.

Living like a nomad wasn't his idea of fun. Even if it was an illusion, he liked a place he could call home.

Come on, get moving.

In two trips, he limped to the shed and rolled back four locked containers in a utility cart. When he'd loaded and covered the gear and tied it down with bungee cords, he returned to the house.

Lin was still in the bathroom, combing out her hair. The lingering shock of the situation had her moving in slow motion.

He put his hand on her shoulder. "We've got to go in about ten minutes."

"Where?"

"I can take you home, but we'll have to answer some questions about what happened here first."

Now she looked more worried.

"Who's going to be asking?"

"Probably the FBI. I had an emergency contact who told me to call him in case some major shit ever happened. I think this Chapter hit job attempt qualifies."

"Oh, Kade, I don't know . . ."

"It'll be okay, I promise."

* * *

The series of text messages lit up his phone screen as they drove past Strasburg. Kade was to go to a familiar location—the FBI Northern Virginia Resident Agency in Manassas. He and Lin would be questioned separately, and he was only to speak with Agent Summerford about what had happened at the house.

Lin made a quick nervous phone call in Chinese after Kade told her a sanitized version of the news. It was on the phone registered to her, not the burner. Instead of asking who she called, he just turned the music back up when she was done.

She unwrapped one of the breakfast sandwiches he'd bought at the Burger King drive-thru and took a few bites before setting it down. A few minutes later, she reclined her seat and shut her eyes.

Good.

He hoped she would catch a nap, but it became clear she wasn't going to doze off.

"You *are* a government agent, aren't you?" she asked.

He sighed so she could hear it, then reached down and repositioned the bag of ice lying on his ankle. Her eyes were still closed, so he skipped trying to conjure up a sincere look.

Another gray-area lie.

"No."

"Then tell me why a team of Chapter people would come attack you at your house."

"Hell if *I* know . . . I'm hoping I can finally get some answers."

She opened her eyes and her head rolled on the headrest toward him. "You *are* the one, aren't you? It was *you* all along, inside AgriteX. The undercover agent."

He squeezed the steering wheel and grumbled.

"No, for God's sake. Lin, some days I have trouble even tying my shoes, I swear."

That was a seventy-five-percent lie, and she wasn't buying it. His program didn't believe it either—his visual stoplight flickered yellow. Yes, the balance was true—if he was having a severe hypomanic episode, tying shoes was harder.

A teaspoon of truth in a cup of deceit.

He'd never had trouble lying inside AgriteX during the operation before, but it felt harder now.

He turned down the music a few notches. The song called "Gone" by the Bouncing Souls was appropriate for his mood.

"I don't know why it happened," he said. "Maybe The Enemy is trying to tie off their loose ends with all of the Associates. I didn't want to say that with you around. Didn't want to scare you."

She turned toward the window and tucked her knees closer to her chest. He waited a minute to see if she responded, but she stayed silent.

"Look," he added, "I'm not a big fan of talking to the FBI either, but if it comes down to these guys trying to hunt me down again and again—I'm not going to survive. Simple odds. I need some professional . . . advice or help. Something."

"I'm not so sure about that," she said. "You aren't who you say you are . . . you shot all of those people like a machine."

"I'm *not* a fucking machine!"

The skin on his cheeks and neck felt hot. That one line from her was a squirt of gasoline on his well-managed embers, and he wasn't sure why. He took a deep breath.

Calm down.

She's your source. Don't lose her.

"Sorry, I didn't mean to yell. I'm trying to hold myself together. I imagined an attack situation like this might happen. I dreamt about it and practiced shooting at the range. I think my military training of years ago kicked in, and it was sort of like reacting off the whistle. Today, I was good enough. Tomorrow, I may not be."

Her hand moved on top of his on the seat. He saw a tear running down her cheek.

"It's okay. I feel safe with you," she said.

A sarcastic remark came to mind, but now wasn't the time.

"Thanks," he said.

* * *

Kade followed the same entry procedure as on his previous visit, checking in with the duty officer inside the building. He and Lin found a seat in the lobby, and Kade propped his ankle up on the chair closest to him.

Five minutes later, Agent Andrade came out to meet them. He was wearing business casual dress with jeans.

"Hi . . . you must be Kade?"

"Yes, I am."

Kade had reminded Andrade in a text that Lin didn't know about his name change. Andrade spoke quietly and played along as if they were meeting for the first time.

"And you must be Lin Soon?"

"Yes."

"Great. I'm Special Agent Mauricio Andrade. It sounds like you both had a harrowing morning. Lin, I'm going to spend some time with you, and a colleague of mine is going to meet with Kade. This will help us save time."

Lin turned toward Kade and he nodded back, trying to signal *everything will be okay.* He almost smiled, seeing her walk away wearing his extra-large sweats and socks with flip-flops, but then felt bad. Was he betraying her trust? Any interrogation was going to be exhausting, even if it was nonconfrontational. He tried pushing the feeling away. Everyone had a job to do. He did his, and the FBI would do theirs.

Kade waved from his seat when Summerford appeared in the lobby next, also dressed more casually than last time. He remembered again it was Sunday.

"Oh my God, are you okay?" She put her hand on his shoulder for a moment.

He shrugged. "Functional."

"I'm not sure what the hell happened," she said, "and what this other 'project' of yours is, but I've never seen senior leadership jump through hoops like this."

Her demeanor was no longer adversarial. He liked it.

"Sorry about the hysterics," he said. "You know, I better make a phone call first to get guidance on what I can and can't tell you. I couldn't do that in the car with Lin sitting next to me. Then I'll do the best I can to answer your questions."

She nodded. "I'll find an empty space where you can make that call. When you're finished, we'll do a quick run-through of this morning."

"Just us, right?" Kade asked.

"Yes." She handed him a business card with a note written on the back. "I reserved a hotel room for you over in College Park. When we're done, you can go there to wash up and rest for a while. I'm sure we'll have a lot more to talk about once Mauricio and I share notes."

"You think so?"

"Oh, yeah. We've learned some disturbing things about Lin and her friends."

CHAPTER 26

Kade knocked the phone off the hotel room nightstand when it rang. When he found the receiver on the floor, he wasn't sure where the hell he was.

"Kyle, it's Kim Summerford. Are you okay?"

Kade groaned. "Yeah, thanks." He was half-asleep but noticed it was the first time Summerford had communicated using her first name.

"Good," she said. "I hope you had a nice long nap. I'll pick you up in an hour."

"All right."

The extra sleep helped, but now his body ached worse. It reminded him of the morning after a hard lacrosse game.

He showered and dressed in the new clothes Summerford had provided— jeans, flannel shirt, and a pair of light hiking shoes. A red fleece jacket was a little bright for his liking, but he would swap it out with something else from his survival gear another time. She'd also given him a couple of gel cold-wraps for his ankle. Nice touch.

While he waited a few minutes, the implications of what Summerford had told him about Lin made him want to know more.

But why do I care?

Is it about the mission, or about her? Am I letting the two mix too easily?

Summerford pulled up outside the hotel entrance in an Audi, and as he got in, he concluded she looked better in jeans and boots than in suit slacks.

126

"Hungry?" she asked.

"Getting hangry."

"Ha, good. Since I'm the only one allowed to talk to you from the Bureau right now, and it doesn't make sense for you to be out in public, I figured I would just feed you at my place."

"That's very thoughtful, thanks. I'll pay you back for the clothes."

"Don't worry about it."

He smiled. "Did you, like, get my shoe size from one of my debriefings or something?"

She smiled. "Yes, it's on file."

"Figures."

It looked like he'd never be able to level the playing field on personal background knowledge, but he needed to try.

"Okay, fair is fair. Where are *you* from originally?"

"Canton."

"And then you . . . ?"

"I went to the University of Akron, then got a law degree at George Washington."

"How did you end up with the Bureau?"

"My dad and uncle are retired agents, and my oldest brother is an agent too, so it's in the family. I landed a job serving as a federal court interpreter and applied to the Bureau when I started getting bored. They liked my language skills."

"In . . . ?"

"Arabic."

"You really had this counterterror thing planned out."

She smiled. "My brother said he regretted not taking languages, so I finally had the chance to show him up on something."

Kade gave a whistle. "How many siblings do you have?"

"Two more brothers—older. Three total."

"That explains everything."

After ten minutes, they reached her condo, where he was greeted by the smell of Mexican food laid out on the counter. Kade grabbed a Negro Modélo and made himself a pair of fajitas once Summerford let him have at it.

After he'd eaten some and thrown down his second beer, Summerford started in with the questions again from across the kitchen table. Kade had already told her back at the Manassas agency about his time with Lin at the club and returning to his home. He'd provided detail on the information collected from Lin, but not about The Chapter's attack at his house. She wanted more on the attack now.

"I need to know more about what you're doing so I can do *my* job well," she said. "And I'm willing to share more, if you are. I think we're both going after the same thing here. To put this Chapter organization out of business for good."

Kade nodded. Summerford didn't fully understand a fundamental truth. Many more Chapter members would have to *die* to disable the organization. The Recovery Team had that part right. He appreciated what the FBI was doing and the comprehensive resources they were applying. But they had one part wrong.

The enemy needs to be killed, not "put out of business."

"Okay, shoot," he said.

She had the padfolio out again.

"How many people did you kill at your house?" she asked.

"Twelve."

"And where did all the bodies go?"

The guts fell out of Kade's fajita right on cue. He scraped them into a neat pile to eat with his fork.

"What do you mean?" he asked.

"I mean," she said, "my boss told me the site had been cleaned up. We were told to stand down. I've never seen that happen."

"Wow. I don't know. The bodies were all there when I left. I covered them up. With sheets and blankets, that is."

"Who were you in communication with earlier inside the NVRA?"

Summerford meant the Northern Virginia Resident Agency in Manassas.

"I can't discuss that," Kade said.

"Yes, you can."

"No, I can't. I was given a number for you to call if you need to confirm what I'm saying, or if you were going to throw me in a holding cell, or something."

Kade snagged her padfolio and pen, wrote the number down in large digits. She ran both of her hands through her hair and gripped her scalp as though he'd caused her a headache.

"So, what agency are you working for, other than us?"

Kade gave the standard answer. "I told you before: the DoD."

"You're such a pain." She stood and went to the counter to pour herself another glass of wine. Kade raised his voice.

"Do you know how our enemy found me at my house?"

"Apparently, after you left a certain club, one of the security guys was paid off to get your address. They got it from the photo taken of your driver's license when they checked your ID inside the entrance."

Kade nodded. "Really . . ."

The driver's license address would have brought The Chapter to the general vicinity of his street, but the address didn't work well with any GPS map program. Maybe that's why they'd had some difficulty finding him.

"Okay," she said. "Now, about Lin Soon. Did you have sex with her?"

Kade coughed, acted like he was half-choking on fajita scraps.

Summerford might already know something from interrogating Lin. He understood the need for the question, only he wasn't in the mood for this kind of digging.

God, I need a break already. What should I tell her?

"Why's that important?" he asked.

"I'm trying to figure out if we need to discontinue using you as a source. Did you have sex with her, or not?"

Kade pointed to a U-shaped bolt affixed to her ceiling. "You hit a heavy bag?"

"Yeah, it's for karate. Don't change the subject."

Kade puffed out his cheeks and eyed the counter. "Okay. Can I get a shot of Patrón, first?"

Her jaw dropped before she shut her eyes and shook her head. But then she slapped her thighs and stood, mumbling as she moved to the counter, "Sure, why not?"

Which also reconfirmed the jeans fit her nicely.

He mixed his rice and beans together and didn't look over to see the reaction from his next request.

"Get a shot for yourself, huh? Please?"

There was more mumbling with a few choice words mixed in, but she returned with two shots. He gave her an excessive smile before clinking glasses and throwing it back.

"Ah, much better," he said. After a reflective pause, he added, "The bottom line is, when you have a sprained ankle, you can't do very much."

"This isn't funny," she said. "This is a very serious operation."

The smile drained from his face as if *serious* had been a trigger word. He took a swig to finish his current Modélo and set the bottle down with a hair of added velocity.

"I had a dozen people show up at my house this morning trying to kill me, and I managed to survive. When was the last time that happened to you?"

Summerford looked down and said nothing. Kade slid his cleaned plate to the side.

"Look, I'm trying to keep my sense of humor here so I don't have a breakdown. Why don't you write 'humor' on your padfolio and add a big smiley face?"

She sighed. "I'm sorry. It's a standard question I have to ask."

He got up, hopped over to the fridge and helped himself to another beer, then poured another shot.

"I didn't sleep with her," he said from the counter. "Just messed around. Do I have to explain more?"

"No." She didn't look pleased, but it must have been the right approach with her. She didn't attempt to embarrass, lecture, or insult him.

He added, "I'm sorry. I can still do my job if you need me to. There was shared survival stress, not feelings. Nothing that's going to compromise what I'm doing."

She nodded. "So you know, there's been a revolving door of men through her apartment since we initiated surveillance. Married American scientists, Chinese diplomats. Many different types."

He blinked a few times and said, "That doesn't surprise me."

"Kade, you did do a very good job at getting information we needed. The contacts on her burner phone raised a number of alarm bells. Some high-level narco-trafficker types are on there. Some other contacts we are investigating. Remember you told me that Lin's father was the CEO of China North Industries Corporation?"

"Yeah."

"A few of those contacts link to China North Chemical Co. It's the pharmaceutical subsidiary of China North Industries."

Kade looked downward and nodded. "Interesting."

"We now have a FISA warrant to search her apartment. After we see what we come up with, we'll make the decision about you—if we need you to continue gathering information for us."

A Foreign Intelligence Surveillance Act warrant could permit property searches or surveillance of suspected foreign intelligence services. Summerford was telling Kade more than she had to.

"Okay," he said.

"Oh, one more thing—do you know if Lin has a daughter?" she asked.

Kade furrowed his brow.

"Uh, I don't think so. She never said anything. Why?"

"Just some pictures she hid on her phone."

"Hmm."

More secrets she's not telling me?

"Okay, back to you," she said. "Can you tell me more about what happened at your house?"

Given the guidance of what Lamb had told him he could talk about, and what was classified, this was a gray area.

A light gray area.

But she does need to know The Chapter's tactics and methods to do her job.

"Yeah, I'll tell you as long as you don't write it down."

Over the next thirty minutes, he went through the ordeal again. She was so gripped by his account, he heard her let out her a breath a few times.

"You did an incredible job protecting yourself. And her."

"Thank you. Now, break time." He got up and started hopping over to the fridge again.

"No, let me," she said, following him. "Go sit down."

She tried to squeeze by him, but he lightly grabbed her wrist and spun her toward him. It was supposed to be a funny maneuver, but they ended up inches apart.

"What do you really think about me?" he asked.

She looked surprised, but not in a bad sense. It crossed his mind in a discombobulated way that she was as attractive as Lin, but for a much different set of reasons.

"I think you're close to having one of your . . . episodes," she said and looked at his other hand holding the bottle. "And you should put the cork in the Patrón. In fact, I was going to suggest something nonalcoholic and noncaffeinated from here."

He shrugged. "Why?"

"Because despite good intentions, you can be dangerous if left unchecked."

He gently pulled her in closer, but still gave her an out.

"Am I within acceptable risk?"

Her bright blue eyes stared him down. "Maybe. If you can control yourself."

The honesty was fresh. The concern, genuine.

"Okay." He leaned closer, brushing by her cheek, and set the bottle down behind her. None of her karate defensive moves kicked in, so he must have been okay.

"I can control myself," he said.

He kissed her hard and her coolness burst into fire. They almost toppled the fajita pans before they found themselves pressed against the dining area wall for a few minutes. Her fingernails raked his chest and his hands explored inside her jeans.

She pushed away to catch her breath.

"Now what do you think?" he asked.

There was a small smile on her face.

"I think you should get off that ankle."

132

CHAPTER 27

Pine Tree Ranch
Lewistown, Maryland
Monday, November 21
2:00 a.m. (EST)

Pierce had received the message at one minute after midnight to meet at one of The Chapter's alternate computer server locations. Even though this was a preprogrammed order, one that had to have been designed months ago as part of the Phase Two plan, it was unexpected.

And highly unusual.

The Chapter's network server nodes could be moved, but the current location of the site was a well-lit maroon barn with a pair of horses boarded in the stalls and a chicken pen standing at its far end. The owners, a female couple in their forties, were both Zulus and enjoyed a simple life of riding every day with everything else paid for.

A Sentry sitting in the tack room, dressed like a workhand, greeted Joshua Pierce and pulled down the retractable wooden ladder in the ceiling. The Sentry collapsed the ladder once Pierce had climbed up to the loft.

Tall stacks of straw and hay bales gave the appearance that the space was fully stocked. Pierce squeezed around the edge of the front row of bales until he saw the faint glow of the access panel. An identity check with the infrared reader opened an aluminum door that swung shut behind him.

The hidden interior room was a sealed, climate-controlled space filled with rack computer servers and networking equipment. Five other Chapter members were inside—Guardian Connor Jordan, two additional Sentries, and two computer technicians.

"Hi . . . Connor," Pierce said. "What are you doing here?"

They shook hands out of habit.

"I'm not sure," Jordan said. "I had a pop-up in my display instructing me to come here today to receive another download. I would've thought that order came from you."

"Not this time," Pierce said.

Something else is going on here.

The current Phase Two plan had been charted out by the previous Commander, Marshall Owens, before his demise. Parts of the plan were distributed to recipients over time to protect the plans' security.

Due to his failing health, Owens had made Pierce the acting commander before The Chapter's attack in Phase One.

As acting commander, Pierce possessed both executive and administrative privileges and could normally receive these Phase Two preprogrammed downloads at a time and place of his choosing once they were available. Other downloads cascading out to Chapter members on a regular basis were Pierce's responsibility to design and deploy in concert with The Chapter's technical experts.

This preprogrammed communication was directing Pierce to take a download along with Jordan—another Guardian who was not in the executive group, but one he knew was a top performer.

Yes, Owens was dead, and Pierce didn't need the FBI's forensic analysis and announcement to tell him that his remains had been scattered throughout the rubble of the AgriteX complex. Owens had wanted to leave this earth directly helping in the fight, despite his failing health. And to his credit, he'd left Pierce a solid succession and transition plan.

But what else had Owens planned and never communicated?

I guess I'll find out.

Pierce and Jordan sat at the download stations and stared at the devices' red discs. When the download was complete and processed, Pierce noticed a shocking change.

He was no longer the acting commander.

In The Chapter's visual display, members of the executive group were denoted by a five-point gold star. The Commander was designated by a larger seven-point star.

Pierce's display now showed a five-pointed star. The download had updated the members of the executive group from six to seven with their initials listed beside the role, except for the new commander who remained nameless. Pierce recognized all of the initials.

Commander: CDR

Operations & Security: JP *(Joshua Pierce)*

Technology: TA *(Timothy Arnold)*

Political: CJ *(Connor Jordan)*

Medical: LG *(Lindsay Gill)*

Recruiting: RJ *(Raymond Jeffries)*

China: ZH *(Zao Hong)*

With this reorganization, Connor Jordan was now a member of the executive group in the Political role and had the same privileges and administrator rights as Pierce. This shocked Pierce—only *he* had held the power to promote others to the exec group. Now, both Jordan and Arnold had that ability.

The stacking of the names indicated the pecking order for succession planning. Pierce would have expected Timothy Arnold to be under him at number three.

But now Jordan was number four.

Pierce had promoted Gill, Jeffries, and Zao in October out of necessity, and they were stacked in the order from when they were promoted.

Jordan's promotion seemed premature, but maybe this move had been timed to occur after Election Day, because that date was always fixed on the calendar.

And, come to think of it, Jordan wasn't on the list of Guardians available to task for the initial mission to nab Kade Sims.

There had been some intelligence behind this move due to Jordan's key political role.

That's how Owens had to have planned and designed it, Pierce concluded.

One of the technicians, Garrett, broke the silence.

"I just received a message. We have a chat session with the new acting commander initiating in a few minutes."

This was confusing. Who had Owens designed to be the new acting commander—with a hidden identity? And why?

Owens had shown he could be ruthless, but he had taken excellent care of his people, and especially top performers.

Pierce turned to Jordan and shook his hand.

"Congratulations, Connor. Well deserved."

"Thanks, Josh. It's a surprise for me. Do you know who the new acting commander is?"

"No. Maybe we'll find out now. Must be a new procedure to protect our command and control."

"Very smart," Jordan said.

Pierce wondered if someone in the exec group had been tapped for the new acting commander, or if the selection had come from the Guardian pool.

When an idea came to him, he stood and turned away from the others.

The Chapter's software had encoded procedures for emergencies requiring succession, and built-in safeguards that reacted to potential intrusions into The Network.

He could attempt to order a version rollback. A rollback would reverse the most recent Chapter update for a particular person or group, or for the entire Chapter organization at once. A rollback period could be set for between five minutes and twenty-four hours, but could not be eliminated. Five minutes was the minimum default time period during which a rollback could be ordered, either by the Commander or the Chief Technology Officer.

A rollback command would most likely make him Acting Commander again. He still had a few minutes before today's change would be permanent.

He could then figure out a way to disable the download and design a different update so he would retain the position.

He needed to try this now.

"Hey, I need to check to see if this version is propagating correctly," Pierce announced and walked toward one of the download stations.

"No, I'm sorry," Jordan said. His pistol was out, lying on his thigh with his hand on the grip. "I have a message stating no one is to touch the stations until the chat session begins. Including you, Josh."

Pierce stood. "Oh, really?"

He could put two bullets through Jordan's chest right now, before the smiling lobbyist would be able to finger the trigger.

His hand was a split second away from the draw, when he noticed the two Sentries had already drawn their pistols.

"We have the same orders, sir," Sentry Cannon said.

"Hey, no problem," Pierce said. "Everyone just calm down."

"The chat session is starting," Garrett said.

Pierce and Jordan sat down at a workstation, and the typed words coming from "CDR," the new acting commander, began to appear in the screen window.

CDR>> Hello, JP and CJ. I want to explain next steps in Phase Two and how we're going to work together to make it successful. Okay?

Pierce typed the first question.

JP>> Is there a reason we don't know who you are?

CDR>> Yes. When my program was updated, and I was made acting commander, it came with a full set of instructions and explanations. Some I can share with you. You both have met me before at one or more Guardian gatherings, and I'm someone you can trust. For security purposes, the decision was made that an actual name for the Commander would no longer be used. We know various agencies are now trying to discover our network, and so we have only increased the precautions. We anticipate our network will be fully regenerated in the next month.

JP>> So what are these next steps?

CDR>> JP, you are going to temporarily move to Shanghai to oversee our strategy there with ZH. CJ, you will assume that portion of duties with our US strategy. It will take both of you working together to integrate and execute our plan. CJ, we need your strength in diplomacy and politics. JP, clearly we need you for paramilitary operations.

CJ>> It's an honor. Thank you.

Pierce fumed inside. *Jordan's already sucking up.*

Even though Pierce understood the rationale of the plan and knew the importance of the China strategy, this was a demotion. He had a nickname for Jordan—Afterclapper. Whenever Marshall Owens had addressed a group with Jordan present, Jordan always seemed to clap well after everyone was done.

CDR>> You will both be evaluated for performance following Phase Two. It's clear I'm still only an acting commander. It says so right on my display. In my opinion, the two best leaders The Chapter has available are being used in the field where they belong.

Pierce sniffed. This was a setback, but not as bad as he had thought. He had the sneaking suspicion that the acting commander was actually Timothy Arnold. Who else would be better at organizing such a technology-intensive transition than that person at the technology reins of the Chapter Network? The Network's survival was critical.

This sounds like a well-thought-out plan by Marshall Owens to ensure our success by not having me bogged down after the election.

He knew I didn't know or care about the political game.

"It sounds fair to me," Pierce said aloud. "Connor?"

Jordan nodded.

JP>> Okay, thank you. We're ready to receive the rest of the information.

CDR>> Stand by.

The corner of Pierce's mouth curled upward.

Owens set this up as a competition to ensure our absolute best performance. Because he knew I wouldn't lose.

CHAPTER 28

Hyattsville, Maryland
Monday, November 21
5:45 a.m. (EST)

Hours before Summerford's alarm clock chirped, Kade's thoughts hovered like a cloud of gnats around some invisible focal point. Staying a step ahead of The Chapter might have been wishful thinking, but maybe he could find an edge. A strategic boot knife.

What could he try to control or exploit?

The answers could already be in my head.

I need to explore my program further.

Today.

Summerford had been right. The stress and excitement of the last twenty-four hours were pushing him into his hypomania danger zone. Combatting this without medication required various self-therapy techniques.

His psychiatrist, Dr. Ross, had once suggested a hydroelectric dam metaphor to give him a sense of control. There was *power* in the disorder, but only if he harnessed the energy and euphoria during these hypomania spikes to spin the turbines into meaningful and productive purpose instead of dysfunction.

On his drive back east following CLEARCUT, Kade and his friend Alex Pace had stopped at the Bonneville Dam area along the Columbia River. Since then, Kade had found the mental imagery of the dam spillways useful and he'd kept a video of it on his phone.

Maybe it was silly, but it helped.

Summerford was up and ready for Monday in a fresh suit while Kade redressed in last evening's beer-stained clothes. Her eyes looked tired, no surprise. He hadn't slept at all and had woken her up multiple times, both intentionally and not. The hypomania-hypersexuality side effect was another aspect he sometimes willingly let happen. When her clothes had come off, the Bonneville Dam had crumbled.

After a quick standing breakfast, Summerford dropped him off at the hotel shortly after sunrise.

"Sorry again about the horrible night's sleep," Kade said.

There was a faint smile on her lips. "I'll survive," she said. "Talk to you soon."

* * *

When Kade stepped out of the shower, he spotted his phone blinking. Russell Lamb had sent a message asking him to meet at a picnic area near the East Potomac Tennis Center at noon. Kade dressed warmly in old clothes from his storage tub and drove to Hains Point by nine so he could get some work done prior. He realized on the way that he'd forgotten to take his carbamazepine, but didn't turn around. He'd be okay for another half day without it.

After parking his truck near a bike rental, he shouldered his backpack and rode a loop around the perimeter trail to get his blood moving. He was happy his ankle didn't protest. It was a beautiful fifty-degree morning, other than the intermittent breeze carrying a funky smell off the water.

At another picnic area near the park's southern tip, he stopped to set up shop for a while. He added the fleece Summerford had given him, a skullcap, and ragg wool gloves without fingertips. The deli sandwich he'd packed for lunch became brunch.

He slid his computer out of his pack, booted up, and donned his earbuds. With three extra batteries and a fold-up solar charger, he could stay unplugged for a long time. There were pages of notes and bits of trial code he'd written for when the time was right. Now he needed to fill in some of the gaps without Henderson around. He'd planned to do this at home over the next few days, but that was before the attack had happened.

No better time than the present.

He entered the developer password, and "DEV" appeared on his vision-screen. He started transcribing code, looking at his computer and then retyping it with his vision-keyboard. It was slow going, but he was without the Chapter Network software development toolkit on his computer. Only Henderson had that, and it was in the lab.

The Chapter's computer code was "tight," or "efficient." The best software developers tended to have common characteristics of laziness and impatience. To get the job done with less code was always better. Why write more than was necessary? Why waste energy?

This philosophy stretched to an obsessive extreme with The Chapter's program, but it was a construct he had to admire, even with despising their end goals. After all, The Chapter had at least matched, if not exceeded, any known or rumored government-created program of the sort.

And now I'm programming my head. Never in my wildest dreams would I have imagined that.

First things first . . .

Kade had ignored the message for another couple of weeks, but it was time to kill it.

You are 148 days overdue in downloading the required Daily Update.

He dismantled the alert and its trigger to send out a message of noncompliance on the upload side.

To get further warmed up, he made a pop-up warning for when his power dropped to ten percent. Somewhere around that mark, his program went dormant by design. He wanted it to remain on, but without enough power to detonate the PETN.

That means set the high-power warning at twenty percent.

Easy.

Next, he worked on disabling his activity log and audit trail. The program had a way of registering deception and associating those markers with spoken key words. He was able to access his activity log, which looked like an enormous text file.

The depth of the log was shocking. Whenever he had spoken the sensitive key words "The Chapter," for example, a piece of text had accompanied it. In reverse chronological order, the two most recent lines stated:

THE CHAPTER IS NOT GOING TO STOP LOOKING FOR ME.

THE CHAPTER TO THE CLUB. I DIDN'T SEE ANYONE TAILING ME ON THE WAY.

Also, whenever a lie registered, the program logged the instance. Such as the one he'd told to Summerford last night.

I DIDN'T SLEEP WITH HER JUST MESSED AROUND.

The transcriptions were nowhere near perfect, but in total, they painted a picture of his activity that would be clear enough to any Chapter reviewer.

Amazing program.

He deleted the entire contents of the log and created two modifications—the log would now autodelete its contents every hour and would fail to upload during any Chapter audit trail. Kade didn't entirely remove the logging function, because making major modifications to software programs often unknowingly "broke" other processes.

He wasn't the program's creator, and his changes weren't being tested by any quality assurance team, so he was cautious.

The next part was more difficult. He had to reset the Chapter deception triggers, part of its Truth tenet, to cause only a yellow stoplight violation. He would then use the same logic to render the algorithms behind the Knowledge and Trust tenets ineffective. Altogether, the Chapter's tenets were Knowledge, Truth, and Trust, and they were embedded into the architecture of the program. He dared not remove them outright, but would go through and make changes.

This was where he spotted a bug in the code, one he didn't quite understand at first.

He knew a red stoplight could accompany an electric shock and/or detonation of the PETN. A yellow signal could mean a short burst of pain, though the feature had never worked on him for some unknown reason. Various triggers—key words and deception markers—were assigned a "score" and accumulated to a point total where the punitive measures, pain or death, could be automatically directed. This function was contained in a subroutine of the program.

The current score was supposed to contain a number between zero and one thousand, but Kade's program didn't have a number counting toward anything. His field was filled with "INVAL" instead.

Invalid.

He had a theory about what was happening. He'd learned that an area of his brain known as the caudate was overly active because of his hypomania disorder. Caudate activity was an accurate measure of deception used by The Chapter's various programs. At the time Kade's program was loaded, there had to have been an initial baseline taken to calibrate the score to zero. He could see the computer code referring back to the baseline number in different parts of the program.

Due to his overactive caudate, he must have maxed out the baseline score upon installation, and it had never been reset to work.

Oh, this was a good bug. It had probably saved his life a thousand times already.

He would leave it there, untouched.

His phone alarm let him know his time was getting short. The final modification he made was a prompt asking him to postpone any upgrades or updates. He couldn't outright *reject* an update, but he modified the ability to *postpone* the update from one hour to one year. He also included the ability to postpone a forced change in the developer password. These moves would help insulate him from anything malicious The Chapter could throw at him in the future.

But exploring his own program made him realize he was going to have to collaborate with Henderson more. Everything he implemented was *defensive* in nature.

There were Chapter goons sitting around, trying to think up new ways to kill him.

Henderson and his extensive resources would need more of Kade's help to go on the offense.

He needed to tell Henderson the code gave him developer access.

Kade was thinking he could pat himself on the back for his progress, when he felt an actual hand on his back.

He jerked his head around and reached for his gun inside the fleece's stomach pocket.

An older teenage girl was holding her phone and looked terrified.

"Sorry!" she said, backing away.

She had just wanted him to take a picture of her and her boyfriend. He let them go without an apology, angry that he could be so easily surprised. Wearing earbuds had been a stupid, stupid idea. He cursed to himself while he packed up.

I'm not going to survive with Little League mistakes like that.

Cruising on his bike for another half loop helped calm his nerves before he dismounted at Lamb's meeting spot.

* * *

He'd warmed the bench for a few minutes when he saw Lamb walk up. The casual parka and sunglasses failed to soften his governmental edges, but Kade had little doubt Lamb had earned two sleeves full of clandestine service stripes.

Lamb shook his hand like it was a friend's.

"How are you, Kyle?"

"Doing all right, thanks. You play tennis here?"

Lamb smiled. "You don't play, do you?"

"No."

Lamb looked over toward the courts. "Yeah, I played here every once in a while."

"It's a nice spot."

"Yeah, it is. Well, Kyle, we're going to assist in finding you a new place to live."

Kade nodded, and his fingers did a happy tap on the tabletop. "That's very kind of you," he said.

"Did you like that location, out near I-81 and the Shenandoahs?"

"Yeah, it grew on me."

"Okay, we'll try to find you something else around there and get your first month paid. We have approval to extend your contract—I'll have that for you next time we're together."

"That's great, thanks."

"You have Thanksgiving plans?"

"Yeah."

Janeen, Aunt Whitney, and his nephew, Greg, were coming down from Peabody to spend Thanksgiving at his grandma's house in Worcester. Kade was also planning on stopping by to see his old roommate, Alex. He'd mailed Alex an envelope from a phony return address containing a bunch of junk mail coupons. Alex knew to always look for the one coupon for plumbing services, where Kade would write the date he was showing up in ultraviolet reactive pen. All Alex had to do was shine a UV light on it.

Kade described his planned itinerary back in Worcester, and Lamb surprised him with more help.

"We'll coordinate some surveillance to deter any Chapter activity near your grandmother's residence," Lamb said.

"That's awesome, thank you."

Lamb pulled out a small plastic card and handed it to Kade. It was a Massachusetts firearms identification card. "We also thought it would be a good idea for you to have this. It's a nonresident permit. It was approved by the head of their state police, and they're uncommon, so if someone gives you a problem, there's an extra number on the back for them to call."

Lamb put two more cards down. "And here's one for Maryland and the District. I think that keeps you covered outside of Virginia for the most part."

"Wow, thanks so much." Kade put them right in his wallet.

"Now, let's talk about plans after the holiday break," Lamb said. "We're going to finish up this planning and research stage and start moving toward execution. That's what the CINC wants."

By CINC (pronounced like *sink*), Lamb was referring to the commander-in-chief—the president. It was easy to forget how high up this operation went. Sometimes, Kade wanted to forget it.

"I'm glad his strategy is aggressive," Kade said.

"The man is focused, and that's what we need. We're going to find the heart and nodes of The Chapter's network and kill it. We're going to find where the microchip manufacturing site is and take it out. When you're back in town, we'll start laying out the plan—and show you a few things that'll blow your mind."

Kade tapped a finger on the side of his head. "Blowing my mind is what I'm trying *not* to do."

"Ha, sorry for the poor choice of words," Lamb said.

"By the way," Kade said, "I validated the program's developer code, which should help Henderson."

"Good," Lamb said. "And in that same vein—one obstacle to our plan is getting our hands on that administrator code so we can exploit their network. We're trying to make progress without it, but we're worried about unintended consequences of failed hack attempts. We need to collaborate on how we can get our hands on that code."

"Yeah . . ." Kade sat silent for a moment and dug his thumbnail into the table's soft wood. "I have an idea on where to start, but it's aggressive to say the least."

"I'd love to hear it."

"See if you can track down a guy I knew who worked at AgriteX, and let me try talking to him alone first. We have to be careful . . . too much attention and he might disappear for good."

"Okay, what's the name?"

"He went by Casey Walsh."

Kade assumed Walsh had been interviewed as part of the follow-up case investigation. He could have found out his whereabouts by asking Summerford, but he wasn't going to do that.

Keep the firewall between my two contracts . . .

"And what was Walsh's role?" Lamb asked.

"He was a senior developer-administrator type. He was the guy who trained me on their network."

"What are you thinking?"

"He's a start. A link. We also need to go back to the midnineties and look harder at Marshall Owens's first start-up, NetStatz. These groups of software developers and technophiles like to stick together. They start with a handful of people, and if they click, they often move from start-up to start-up. Owens had once told me he had written the initial Chapter Network software and then a team took it over for him."

"People who also fit the hacker profile, like you."

"That's right," Kade said.

Despite their methods and corrupted purpose, Kade had to acknowledge that The Chapter and Marshall Owens would go down in history as one of the first teams who had truly hacked the human brain and integrated both hardware and software into it. Or maybe that history would be kept a secret.

It didn't take long for Lamb to chew on Kade's proposition.

"Okay, let's do it. We'll let you know as soon as we find Mr. Walsh."

CHAPTER 29

Worcester, Massachusetts
Wednesday, November 23
5:36 p.m. (EST)

It was his first time conducting surveillance of his best friend.

From behind the community basketball court veranda, Kade watched the Toyota Tacoma pickup pass by and turn in the driveway up the street, parking on the far right side. Alex Pace, his former roommate, stepped out and loaded up his arms with grocery bags.

Before the garage door rolled back down, Kade noted there wasn't a black Volvo SUV parked inside.

Alex was now home, but his girlfriend, Emily, wasn't.

The perfect time.

A rear door entry wasn't preferable. There was that slight chance he might be spotted and someone would call the police to report suspicious activity. Emily would find out, and that would be bad.

No, he approached the front door like he owned the place and opened it with the key in his pocket—one Alex had mailed to Kade's post office box a month ago. This trusting gesture may not have normally seemed like a big deal, but for Alex it was.

This was Emily's house, and Emily didn't know about the key.

After silently shutting the door behind him, Kade stood in the entryway and listened until he figured out Alex was in the kitchen. He crept in that direction until he was able to see him putting away the groceries.

Alex was reaching out to grab something from a plastic bag on the dining table when he turned and froze.

148

"Fffff—"

Kade was holding a piece of notebook paper up with a written message. DON'T SPEAK. TURN YOUR PHONE OFF.

Alex powered down his phone and turned the gray screen toward Kade.

"Hey, man," Kade said and gave him a hug. Alex covered his newly bearded face in his hands and sucked in a huge breath before speaking through his palms.

"You scared the shit out of me."

"Sorry."

"No, you're not."

"I am, I swear. You have that alarm system here, and I wasn't sure if anyone else might be around."

"Better hope Emily doesn't call me," Alex said.

"Sorry, just keeping us safe. My phone has more security built into it."

Alex nodded. His patience for Kade had stood the test of time, as in this moment. He was a dear childhood friend who'd lived on the same street growing up in Worcester. After Doherty High School, their relationship had continued during college, with Alex attending Boston College while Kade was across town at MIT. Alex had chosen a business and finance focus, earning a slew of credentials Kade couldn't keep track of—CPA, CFA, for starters.

"You came home for Thanksgiving," Alex said.

"No one knows it yet, but yeah. Don't say anything."

Alex zipped his lips with his fingers. "Yes, sir."

During the FBI operation over last summer, Alex had proved his mettle in a way Kade normally reserved for his army brothers-in-arms. The help Alex had voluntarily provided in a dangerous environment had ended up saving Kade's life.

And that assistance had been without the FBI's knowledge or approval.

As Kade had taken up his new freelance career path, he wanted to make sure Alex was shielded from any future risk. This meant a reasonable degree of secrecy, and precautions Alex understood were necessary.

"How much time do I have?" Kade asked.

"Emily's working a little late . . . she texted me earlier saying she'd be home around seven. I'm guessing we have like thirty to forty minutes. Does that work?"

"Roger."

Kade had already found the bottle opener and pulled two beers out of the fridge, handing a Prohibition Porter to Alex and keeping the Amber Waves Ale.

"Great to see you, man," Kade said.

"Yeah." Alex's eyes shifted upward as he clinked Kade's bottle. "What's up with the shaved head?"

"Disguise." Kade tugged on the bottom of Alex's beard. "You ought to shave this witch's broom."

"I'll shave my beard, if you shave your balls."

Kade laughed.

Stalemate.

They walked through the living room, down the hall to Alex's home office. There were four computer monitors set up on a new desk and a pair of nice bookshelves on each side. He turned some rock music on low volume and they both sat on the carpet.

"Wow," Kade said. "This place is quite the upgrade from slumming in Molly Pitcher."

"You left me with no place to stay, and she offered to take me in. Remember?"

"I know. I'm just messing. That was really nice of her. You get her a ring yet?"

"Piss off."

"Hey, no pressure. I'm sure you pay your way. I like her ride, by the way. Much better than yours."

"What? You should like my truck better. It sure saved your ass."

Kade laughed. "*You* saved my ass, not the truck. Anyway, I came by—"

"Wait, wait. Not yet." Alex took a pull on his beer. "What's going on with *you*? Still going out with that FBI girl?"

Alex meant Carla Singleton, not Summerford. Kade had introduced Alex to Carla one time, following a few dates when Alex was still in D.C.

"No," Kade replied. "That ended up poorly."

"*Poorly?*" Alex's fingers twitched to indicate Kade needed to give up more of the goods.

"Nah, I better not."

"Sex was bad?"

Kade coughed in the middle of his swig and recovered from a few drops of beer trickling down his windpipe. "Nice try. No, it was a lot of things."

"Like what?" Alex asked.

"Like she said she didn't want me eating anything around her that once had a face."

"Oh."

"And then the topic of having kids came up."

"Kids?"

"Yeah. One time she casually asked if I wanted to have kids someday, and I said, yeah, sure. She said she didn't, because there'd be a fifty-fifty chance that if she had a son, he'd be a hemophiliac like her dad. The whole conversation went into a tailspin . . . I wasn't even thinking that far ahead."

"That's too bad."

"A ton of issues somehow exploded over the span of a few weeks."

"Damn. So are you dating someone new?"

Kade hesitated. "No."

Alex looked incredulous. "You mean to tell me you got *nothin'* going on?"

He supposed he didn't have to totally lie to Alex about what he was doing. It was nice when he could talk to him about girls. Pretending it was like old times for a few minutes.

"Well . . . kind of."

Alex's amber eyes lit up like lanterns. "I knew it. Damn, you move quick! Someone else from work, I bet."

He thought again about the twenty-four hours he'd spent with Lin through Sunday and then lying in bed with Summerford on Monday morning. Two different events, both exciting in their own way. Summerford was like snowboard slalom. Lin was like a half-pipe.

What a damn mess he was in.

Kade glanced up at the ceiling. "Yeah, sort of."

Alex shook his head. "I knew it. You're a pigeon."

"Huh?"

"You know the saying 'don't shit where you sleep'?"

"Yeah?"

"Ever see a pigeon nest?"

"I will when one shits in your beard," Kade replied.

He got up and retrieved two more beers when Alex had no retort. When he returned, he changed his voice to a higher pitch and said, "Hey, you know what my life is like now. *Kyle Smith* can't go Internet-dating and meet awesome-Emily. All of us can't be blessed with finding the perfect girlfriend online, who lets you move in, and is from our hometown, even."

"Nah, don't try to turn it around on me, bee-otch."

They both laughed hard and finished with a sigh. They'd traded this sort of ribbing a million times. It would have only escalated had there been more time.

Alex glanced at his big LED wall clock. "Okay, what's up?"

"You know anything about Chinese pharma companies . . . gray markets . . . linkages to the illegal drug trade?"

Alex sat back and gave him a what-the-hell-are-you-getting-into-now look.

"Yeah," he replied. "I've traded in some H-shares for publicly traded Chinese chemical and pharma companies. H-shares are those traded on the Hong Kong Stock Exchange."

"I remember you telling me one time you'd made some money from that."

"Yeah, I did. Some of these companies are leading suppliers in the industry. I read a lot of interesting research."

"I figured. How would they generate revenue in a gray market?" Kade asked.

"A chemical or pharma company can manufacture actual, finished drugs or vaccines, for example, and then if there's a major shortage, they stand to make enormous, legitimate *additional* profits on the gray market through supplier partners. And, they can also produce bulk raw material that could be used in base ingredients for FDA-approved drugs, *or* supplied to the illicit drug trade."

"One company could do both activities together in your example."

"Yeah," Alex said. "In a company located in mainland China, and more likely a *private* company, you could have a mix of legal and illicit business. A company could sell finished oxycodone pills legally or exploit the gray market. It could obtain poppy plants from fully legal farms and process them into a slurry used to derive an illegal drug like heroin *or* a controlled drug like oxycodone. A company could sell raw material legally or divert it to the black market."

Kade started peeling the label off his bottle. "So, you could have gray market and black market opportunities for controlled drugs, and illegal drug trafficking all in one."

"Yep," Alex said. "A company might have a blend of legitimate government oversight, interaction with corrupt officials taking bribes, and dealings with drug cartels at the same time."

Something stirred in Kade's gut after that broad statement, validating what Summerford had postulated. Lin's father was a CEO of a company with a pharma subsidiary. Lin had always been involved in facilitating Chinese business development in the US.

If Lin wasn't an actual spy, it was looking more probable that she was involved in some shady business.

Knowingly or unknowingly.

He could no longer make excuses in his mind for her.

"Ever hear of China North Chemical?" Kade asked.

"Doesn't ring a bell."

They discussed a few more similar topics and Kade checked the wall clock again. Time was short.

"Well, that's some great background information," Kade said. "Thanks, bud."

"Sure. Let me know if you need anything else. You going to be around over the weekend?"

"I might," Kade said. "If I'm available, I'll hit ya on voice chat and we can meet up in the back of Wormtown Brewery. Saturday or Sunday afternoon."

"Cool."

Kade's phone rang with the new ringtone he'd assigned Carla last week, "Let's Not Keep in Touch" by a band named Retox.

He said a few expletives under his breath.

"It's Carla. She must know we're talking about her."

Alex laughed while the phone rang for the second time. Then a third.

"Wow, persistent," he commented.

Carla usually left voicemails. This must have meant something was very urgent.

What does she want now?

CHAPTER 30

President Greer, his wife, Sylvia, and his two tween boys, Jake and Joey, finished the annual ceremony in the Grand Foyer to pardon a pair of turkeys for Thanksgiving. It looked to be a relaxing afternoon until Greer saw one of his Secret Service agents escorting FBI Director Hassett.

Something was up.

"Stan, you're back?"

"Yes, sir. Hugh came along as well. And we have a secure web meeting queued up with the CDC."

"Okay. Let's do lunch in the Situation Room. I'm starving."

Minutes later, DNI Conroy joined them, and they all sat down at the conference table. An aide brought in a platter of sandwiches and a few dessert choices.

Hassett set a pocked-sized bottle of hand sanitizer in the center of the table.

"Stan," Greer said, "we do have a washroom right outside there, you know."

"A prop for our discussion," Hassett said.

"Uh-oh," Greer said.

"Are you aware of the current cold outbreak?" Hassett asked.

"Yeah, I saw a mention of it in my news update this morning. I try not to live in a bubble, but it's hard."

155

"It's much more serious than it appears," Hassett said. "I'll go ahead and let CDC Director Woodward speak to the first part."

Dr. Aubrey Woodward appeared on one of the screens. Beside it showed a presentation with the CDC logo on it.

After introductions, she got right to the alert at hand.

"Mr. President, the CDC projected the cold season would have a whopping start this year, but the pattern and speed with which it spread set off our national network for syndromic surveillance."

Greer had picked out a roast beef sandwich that would now sit on his plate for the next thirty minutes.

"What does that mean exactly?" Greer asked.

"I'll show you," Woodward said.

On the first slide, there was a map of the United States overlaid with red dots of varying sizes.

"What you see here is the concentration of reported cases," she said. "The clusters are uniform over a number of metropolitan areas. Right here in Atlanta is the largest cluster. Then LA, Chicago, Dallas . . . and so on. Now watch this."

Twelve three-letter airport codes appeared on the screen in those cluster circles. The circles doubled in size in the expanse of one week as she advanced a slide.

"Wow," Greer said.

"Our analysis team made the statistical correlation that these clusters correspond to our largest airports—Atlanta, LAX, and Chicago O'Hare being the top three."

Greer pulled off his glasses and looked around the table.

"And now we're in the Thanksgiving travel period. This is going to be bad. Okay, tell me about what kind of bug we're dealing with."

"We're still working on analysis for the full genotype, but it's a rhinovirus species C, which is a common cold virus. Symptoms are more severe than Rhino A or B, but generally not considered any more life-threatening."

Hassett commented, "It's as though planes full of sick people arrived from a sick country."

"I've talked to my counterpart at the WHO," Woodward said, referring to the World Health Organization, the public health body of the United Nations. "They haven't observed any unusual rhinovirus clusters of this size yet."

"There'll be some ruined Thanksgiving dinners," Greer said, "but I guess we can be thankful this isn't a more severe disease."

"True," Woodward said. "But what worries me, and why I first contacted Director Hassett, is that this is the kind of cluster pattern we would see with a bioweapon. In this case, multiple bioweapons distributed at once."

Her words gave Greer a chill. He had assumed something like this could happen on his watch but had prayed it never would.

"So, this is a bioterror attack . . . but with a cold?" he asked.

"We've classified it as a *possible* bioterrorism risk," Hassett said. "We're bringing CDC, NIH, and the FBI's Weapons of Mass Destruction Operations Unit together in analyzing the problem."

A panicked look flashed in Greer's eyes. "Wait, why would a cold be a WMD?"

"It's not a *select* WMD agent on the list," Hassett said, "like anthrax, or Ebola, for example. But here's where it gets . . . serious. Like Dr. Woodward said, it's a regular cold rhinovirus, classified as RV-C. But the rhinovirus is also carrying what's called a VCJD antigen marker. VCJD is variant Creutzfeldt-Jacob Disease."

"That sounds familiar," Greer said.

"Yes, it might be," Woodward said. "It's the degenerative brain disorder that comes from exposure to 'mad cow' disease."

Greer couldn't help glancing at his roast beef sandwich.

"What? This cold virus also causes mad cow?" he asked.

"No, the VCJD marker can't cause the disease itself," Woodward said. "It would only cause someone who was infected with this rhinovirus to *test positive* for mad cow."

"Let me see if I have this straight," Greer said. "This looks like a terror attack, but with a bioengineered cold virus having some mad cow marker, intended to fly under the radar?"

"It's too early to tell," Woodward said. "The CDC is still trying to track down the index cases through interviews to determine the source of exposure. A rough theory is that this bio agent was released on planes due to the exposure pattern it's exhibiting. The purpose behind it, if it's an attack, is unclear. There will be some people who die from respiratory complications, like in any bad cold season."

"Man, this is puzzling," Greer said.

Conroy hit the mute button.

"We're designating this an Incident of National Significance," he said, "and tasking our assets to determine the purpose behind this possible attack. Stan and I have some additional thoughts, but we don't want to jump the gun. The investigation has been classified secret until it's complete."

Greer thanked Woodward for the update and they ended the web meeting. He turned to Conroy and Hassett.

"Let's hear your thoughts."

Hassett said, "We've put intense effort into this, as you'd imagine. We've discovered a canister of this agent in the apartment of a Chinese citizen working in D.C. She was already suspected of being connected to their intelligence service."

Greer scowled. "Chinese intelligence?"

"Yes," Conroy added. "We couldn't help noticing the timing of this incident with our recent support of India and urging restraint in their border situation. But we don't want to draw a conclusion so quickly that this was some kind of shot across the bow from China."

"Shit," Greer said.

That's plausible.

"The other theory," Conroy said, "is that this bio agent was dispersed to test our defenses and response."

"Why?"

Conroy's lips pressed together into a thin line.

"To probe for any weaknesses that could be exploited in the future—a dry run for a more lethal attack."

Greer finally took a hulking bite of his sandwich while pondering the grim news.

"How can we accelerate getting to the bottom of this?" he asked.

"I'm coordinating an intel collection op with the NSA and CYBERCOM," Conroy said. "It's aimed at finding the real fingerprints of that rhinovirus and where it was created. But it'll be aggressive, intrusive and could have further repercussions on our Chinese relations if the evidence takes us there. I recommend we hold off on this until our covert strike is complete."

Greer leaned back. These were the handful of decisions made every day that could change their collective futures.

Tomorrow Americans would gather with their family and friends to spend a precious Thanksgiving Day together.

Someone wanted his country sick.

Unacceptable.

"I don't want to jeopardize our team," he said. "Use your judgment on timing and keep me informed. But repercussions? I'll handle repercussions. Find out where this bug was made."

"Yes, sir," Conroy said.

"And, while you're at it," Greer added, "if we find the location, have plans ready on how to take it out."

CHAPTER 31

Public Garden
Boylston Street, Boston
Thursday, November 24
10:00 a.m. (EST)

Why the hell had he agreed to another meet-up with Carla and her friend, Lori, on this sunny Thanksgiving morning?

Kade thought it had to have been an emergency when she'd called at Alex's house. No, she was going to be in Boston, visiting, strangely enough. And she apologized for having acted difficult.

Was this a plan for a holiday hookup?

The Public Garden was a few minutes from the Logan Airport Hilton he'd stayed in last night after landing. He walked the loop around the park path, past the lagoon now drained for the winter, until he approached the Tadeusz Kosciuszko statue from behind.

Carla was standing there in a puffy blue jacket, holding a silver shopping bag. There was no Lori.

She walked toward him and said, "Hi." Her face was relaxed, as if traveling had removed some of her stress. Her shopping bag crinkled as they hugged.

"Happy Thanksgiving!" he said.

"Happy Thanksgiving, and . . . I brought you something."

"Oh, okay, thanks." He took it and smiled, but wasn't going to open it here.

"Do you have a big dinner planned?" she asked.

"Yeah, the usual," he said. "It'll be nice."

His actual Thanksgiving family get-together would be tomorrow. Kyle Smith's mere attendance at this year's gathering already made things more complicated for his family. Friday was better for security.

And he wasn't going to complicate life more by having Carla there.

"So, your friend couldn't give you a tour?" Kade asked.

"Lori couldn't get away this morning. But tomorrow, we'll be going out if you're interested."

If I'm interested.

Always phrased where I can only give a wrong answer.

"I'm sorry, I can't with family in town."

"Yeah, of course. Enjoy your family." Her eyes dampened. "Well, it's a beautiful day, and a beautiful park."

He didn't ask why she wouldn't be around her dad on Thanksgiving.

"Yes, it is," Kade said and looked around. "We did some ROTC runs here, back in the day. Good memories."

"It's pretty. The graffiti is a shame, though," she said, looking at the statue.

"What?" He walked closer.

Someone had spray-painted on the front of the statue's base in black.

84379514

By the time he recognized the number, it was too late.

My Chapter kill code . . . some kind of trap!

He began to unzip his leather jacket, trying to retrieve his gun from the shoulder holster, but couldn't. His knees buckled. Blinding head pain made him grip his skull with both hands and crumple to the ground as the number stayed emblazoned in his vision.

Every cell in his body was on fire. The walls of the world around him narrowed.

He heard Carla scream, felt his body being lifted and jostled by a few people. Then he was dropped hard on the ground.

Gunshots blasted around him.

Blackness.

CHAPTER 32

Worcester, Massachusetts
Friday, November 25
1:11 p.m. (EST)

Kade remembered a blurry ambulance ride and medical evaluations in a hospital. Conversations with Boston FBI agents. Summerford called and said two assailants identified as Sentries had died in custody. Carla was also being held for questioning.

His kill code had been spray-painted in two other areas of the park. Likely exit points. There was also a fake parking ticket left on his rental car with the kill code written on it.

A coordinated effort.

Lamb from the Recovery Team called. Everyone from the team sent their collective wishes for him to rest and get well.

His head continued to throb, and he was nauseated, but no longer vomiting.

Later, Vic Martin, the semiconductor expert, and Dr. Scott, the doc who'd drilled Hager's head, both joined in on a phone call to check in with him. They said he was still alive after seeing the kill code because the PETN hadn't detonated, confirmed by a CT scan. But the electric shock delivered by the chipset had caused him to have a seizure.

This was all great information, but too many phone calls. Rest was impossible.

He requested to stay at his grandma's over the weekend to recuperate. That wish was granted, and a pair of agents were supplied to keep watch over the house.

Hearing his grandma's voice gave him some sense of normal, even if it was her derogatory comments about his mustache and shaved head.

Except for a landline phone, his grandma's house was unplugged. A perfect holiday hideout.

He slept for a few hours and called Henderson when he woke up.

A follow-up analysis determined the PETN explosive could be detonated when the chip was charged at about twenty percent power, Henderson said. The Zulu and Guardian chips had program options to do so, but in both Kade's and Hager's Guardian chips, that option hadn't been turned on.

With twenty percent power being a key threshold, Henderson suggested to keep his chipset powered *between ten and seventeen percent.*

At some point below ten percent, the chip and program hibernated, as Kade had already experienced.

At the time Kade had seen his kill code on the statue, his power remaining had been at fifteen percent. He'd received a good, debilitating zap, but not enough to trigger the PETN.

A few percentage points away from turning part of his brain to mush.

His grandma sat down at his bedside in the guest room. Her voice sounded worried, but it usually sounded that way when she talked to him.

"You're a key witness, aren't you? That's why these people are protecting you, but you can't say."

Hell, that was a good enough guess for him.

"Wow, I can never get *anything* past you," he said. "But don't worry about me, okay? This was just . . . witness intimidation."

"You show up like this and I'm not supposed to worry about you?" She released an aggravated breath and poured him some more herbal tea. He hated tea.

"Grandma, I'm good on tea, okay? I can't sleep if I have to pee every five minutes."

"Okay, dear."

"If I can get some more sleep today, I think I'll be okay for dinner. Groggy at the worst, but okay. Please don't call anything off. I want to see everybody."

She stroked his head. "Of course. You said some horrible things in your sleep. I've never heard you use foul language like that before. Is there some girl you don't like? Someone named Carla?"

Oh God, I must have been delirious.

"Oh, she was a girl I was dating. She's a friend. No hard feelings or anything."

She looked at him suspiciously. "You need to unzip your flesh and find yourself a spiritual girl. I know a few from church."

He smiled and managed a short laugh. "Unzip my flesh? Sounds gross, but I love you anyway."

She wagged a finger.

"The beauty you see is a gift for everyone. But the beauty you feel is a gift for *you*."

"Yeah, I know," he groaned and turned his head so she wouldn't catch his eye roll.

She gave him a kiss on the head. "I'll leave you to sleep, dear."

"Wake me up by four, no matter what. Okay?"

"Okay." She shut the door for him.

He had survived another attempt on his life. Someone had known he was going to be at that statue. There were no tracking devices found on his person, rental car, or carry-on bag, the Boston FBI agent had told him.

The only person he had told was Carla. She had suggested the time; he had picked the meeting spot.

What possibilities did that leave?

Summerford said she was investigating that angle. But, investigation aside, she appeared more interested in how he was doing and feeling. She sounded choked up about it, even.

An open gift box lay within arm's reach on top of the dresser, the one from Carla. The FBI had obviously taken a look-see. Kade fetched it.

He pulled out a black cashmere scarf and matching hat. Nice, but probably a reference to her ongoing neck joke. Never knew with her. He clenched his teeth for a few seconds.

He'd made excuses for her. She'd accidentally told something to the wrong person. Her phone had been compromised. Gossip had been overheard. She'd been followed. There was the friend, Lori, who'd never shown up.

His mind was now pinging like a bag of microwave popcorn. A sedative would have gone well with the painkiller they'd given him. He tried to slow his breathing and think of something else.

Stop it. You're not going to sort this out now. Get some sleep so you can enjoy dinner.

He rolled onto his side, and in ten minutes the traces of his headache finally gave way.

His eyes blinked open for a second.

Remove the excuses.

Carla could have told The Chapter when and where we were meeting.

And she could have told them where I live.

CHAPTER 33

Route 66 West
Arlington, Virginia
Sunday, November 27
6:35 p.m. (EST)

Kade's phone buzzed from an incoming call thirty minutes after departing long-term parking at Reagan National. He hoped the call was from Lamb and the Recovery Team. His body and spirit felt rejuvenated and ready to go back on the offensive. The Thanksgiving dinner and seeing his family had been precious, brought everything into greater focus. To top it off, he'd had unexpectedly good sleep on Friday and Saturday nights.

"Hello?"

There was a dead pause. It had to be a telemarketer making a random call to his phone, but he didn't hear that telltale background noise of the call center chatter. Maybe it was one of his team members calling from a spot with poor reception.

His phone had been programmed to block any incoming numbers from displaying, such as his kill code. He didn't have to worry about that, at least.

"Hello?" he repeated.

Forget it.

He started to pull the phone away from his ear when the voice he heard made his blood go cold.

"Kade . . . it's time for you to come in."

He knew the voice, but this had to be a trick. He wouldn't play along with it.

"Who is this?"

There was a three-second delay.

"You know who this is. It's your Commander, Marshall Owens."

The tires of his truck screeched. He almost rear-ended the car in front of him while not paying attention to traffic. Gasping, he cut over to the road shoulder and came to a stop alongside the concrete barrier.

He wanted to shout into the phone but ended the call instead. If somehow The Chapter had located his number, he didn't want them finding out his location in real time.

He turned on his hazard lights and took a few deep breaths while his mind swirled like a shaken snow globe.

Think. This doesn't make sense.

No, of course this wasn't Owens. It was, however, Owens's voice being replicated or impersonated. Someone had to be typing in a conversation with Kade, and the text responses were being communicated with a representation of Owens's voice.

There had been an avatar of Owens in The Chapter's program that narrated all the regular downloads to accompany the text of various propaganda. Kade had disabled that avatar in the program settings over the previous summer.

This had to be something like an Owens version of Apple's Siri or Amazon's Alexa—a synthesized voice responding to questions.

Whoever was at the helm of the current Chapter leadership knew Kade wouldn't be stupid enough to come in of his own accord. They had now tried to kill or capture him three times.

This was an attempt to threaten, lure, target, or bribe.

Yet, it was an attempt to communicate. He had to think of the flip side. It was an opportunity, a possible hole that Henderson and others could exploit.

Offense, not defense.

A text message indicator showed up next. There was no way in hell he was going to look at his phone now, even with the countermeasures programmed into the device.

He dialed the Recovery Team answering service and heard his voice quiver as he left the message.

"This is Kyle. The opposing team just tried to contact me by phone."

CHAPTER 34

FBI Washington Field Office
Washington, D.C.
Monday, November 28
9:00 a.m. (EST)

Lamb had told Kade to report to the FBI Field Office the next morning and booked him a hotel room at the Crowne in the District for the night. Lamb was coordinating something with Summerford out of necessity.

When she fetched Kade from the lobby, her handshake was formal, as though they were meeting for the first time and he'd slept with her body double. But he could see the hint of concern in the way she searched his face.

"Need coffee?" she asked.

"No, thanks."

* * *

Through the code-access vault door, they moved into a secure conference room where Andrade and Lamb were sitting next to each other at the table.

So much for keeping my contracts separated . . .

"How are you, Kyle?" Lamb asked.

Kade ran his fingers through his hair fuzz and gave them a crooked smile.

"One big happy family now, huh?"

Lamb laughed. "Have a seat, Kyle. We've been discussing our collective needs and are sorting out a joint framework to move ahead on multiple operations. Your assistance in a few areas will be key."

"So this is about . . . ?" Kade asked.

"Lin Soon," Andrade said.

"I thought I was done with her at this point," Kade said.

"You were," Summerford said. "But things have changed."

"She's in big trouble," Andrade added. "By association, at least, and that's beneficial to us."

Kade flopped down in a seat and pulled the lever to adjust the height up. He needed his carbamazepine prescription filled again to slow down his pinwheel mind, if he could get in to see Dr. Ross. Or maybe the SAU could write him a script.

"Those drug connections played out like you thought?" he asked.

"Yes and no," Andrade said. "But she's in the middle of something much worse and higher-reaching than drug sales."

Andrade didn't look worried about anything, yet Kade noticed his fingernails chewed to the quick.

"Which is . . . ?" Kade asked.

"Kade, this entire discussion is classified top secret from this point forward until we say otherwise," Andrade said and looked at Summerford.

"Roger that," Kade said.

"Lin Soon," Summerford said, looking at her iPad, "otherwise known as Sun Lin by birth, is the daughter of Sun Kang, the CEO of China North Industries Corp—as you'd previously uncovered. Her oldest brother, Sun Bo, is a VP of systems architecture for the Shanghai Semiconductor division. Her other older brother, Sun Sheng, is the VP of finance for the China North Chemical division."

Kade looked at the table. "So, her brother is in there with the narco contacts."

"Yes," Summerford said.

"We have enough evidence," Andrade said, "to indict her on a number of charges and give us grounds for deportation if we wanted. Not only on drug trafficking and conspiracy charges, but also espionage and terrorism."

Kade licked his lips. "But I'm guessing you don't want to do that."

"She *did* pass a polygraph," Andrade said. "And she claimed she has no idea how certain materials ended up in her apartment. She insists someone planted them there. We think Chinese intelligence is responsible."

"What materials?" Kade asked.

"We're not going to tell you what we found there," Andrade said. "That doesn't mean we wouldn't trust you with that information, we just don't want you to have it."

Kade glanced to the side.

Hmm.

Strategies change.

Lin is now an expendable spy?

"Why don't you want me to know?" Kade asked.

Andrade said, "We don't plan on pressing charges if she fully cooperates with us, and thus far she's agreed to cooperate. She loves being in the US and doesn't want to leave. We're leveraging that. If we can prove that her own country is screwing her over, we may have more leverage."

Lamb interlaced his fingers on the tabletop.

"Kyle, we're going to be running several covert ops requiring your participation. Some directly, and some indirectly. We've pinpointed where those Chapter microchips were manufactured in China. Take a guess."

Kade shut his eyes to see what his brain had already pieced together.

"Shanghai Semiconductor . . . her brother's company."

"Uh-huh," Lamb said.

Lamb was now talking about a covert op on Chinese soil. There wasn't anything more sensitive than that.

They didn't want him to know any more than he needed to.

In case I'm caught.

Compromised.

"I would be there with nonofficial cover?" Kade asked.

"Yes," Lamb said. "But most everyone else you'll be working with are also NOCs."

Kade nodded. He remembered Lamb saying the name LJ Yang, but he wasn't going to say anything else out loud in FBI company unless Lamb led the discussion.

In the course of one day, this whole program was morphing into the most dangerous mission he'd ever participated in. Foreigners without diplomatic immunity who were charged as spies in China often ended up dead.

"Okay. So where do we go from here?" Kade asked.

Lamb raised a finger.

"Here's what we'll need you to do first . . ."

* * *

Lin had finally answered her phone and, after several objections, allowed Kade to "stop by and at least say goodbye" later that evening at her FBI-provided hotel room near Dulles Airport. She had told him only that she was flying out to Shanghai the following morning.

She answered the door wearing jeans and a fisherman's sweater. He'd seen her in this nonprimped state months ago, and it held its own unique allure.

Inside, he gave her a gentle hug, and she extended it for a moment when he began to break away. Those extra seconds erased the notion that this was purely business. After what they'd been through together, he couldn't deny there was a deeper connection.

"What's going on?" he asked.

"The FBI is sending me back to China."

"What? You mean, like, permanently?"

"I don't know."

"I don't think they can do that. I think that's ICE's area of jurisdiction."

She sat down on the bed and rubbed her knees.

"They can do whatever the hell they want. There's even an agent watching me to make sure I get on that flight. That's what they said."

That was true. One agent had been posted to make sure she didn't flee. Kade had spotted her in a car outside.

"So, this goes back to the questioning in Manassas?" Kade asked.

"Yeah. They don't like my family."

Kade scrunched his eyebrows and paced around. "What does your family have to do with anything?"

Not only did he know about Lin's family already, Andrade, Lamb, and Summerford had explained the information Lin would need to provide the FBI to have any chance of returning to the US.

She pulled her legs up and sat cross-legged.

"They said I can't talk about it."

"Why not?"

The tears in her eyes broke over the spillway.

"Don't make it worse."

"Okay."

Kade remembered Summerford's question of whether he knew if Lin had a daughter. Did she have a daughter stateside she was protecting?

I can't risk asking that.

Kade walked to the window and drew the curtains before returning to sit beside her. He sighed and linked his arm through hers.

"There may be a way I could visit you if you were up for it," he said.

"How is that?"

"I'm a freelance software and web guy, right? There's always a need for people to staff projects, especially overseas, and I saw there are all kinds of projects available in Shanghai. I could snag a thirty-day visa and take a temporary job so I could spend some time with you."

She bit her lip and looked away.

"I don't know if that's a good idea."

"Is that because you don't want to see me anymore?" he asked.

"I probably shouldn't."

"Well, okay." Kade blew out a breath. "I guess this is the *real* end, then."

There was a silent pause and then he added, "By the way, I'm getting my name changed . . . so start calling me Kyle, okay?"

"Kyle? Why?"

"Between The Chapter and our government, I don't know who's looking for me on any given day. Yeah, I'm paranoid and proud. It seems to be keeping me alive."

She traced the length of his arm with her finger until she found his hand.

"Your hand's shaking . . . Kyle."

"Yeah, I know," he said. It was his hypomania, but he didn't open that discussion.

She kissed the top of his hand and then began kissing each of his fingers, but only made it through three before he lifted her chin and kissed her on the mouth. Her arms slid around his neck.

"If you were going to meet me in Shanghai," she said, "I'd have to call the FBI and see if it's okay. I don't want to do anything to mess up my chances to come back to the States."

"Okay, why don't you call them first thing in the morning? That way I know whether this is a final goodbye or not. If it works out, I'll fly out when it makes sense. If not, you gave it a shot, right?"

Kade knew that call with the FBI would go fine.

"Okay," she whispered and swiveled around, straddling his lap, kissing him harder.

This would be a dangerous mission. A stronger relationship meant stronger loyalty, and he wanted to come home from this alive.

That was the extent of his rational thought, or rationalization.

He pulled on the drawstring of her pants until the knot popped.

CHAPTER 35

Nyoma Advanced Landing Ground
Leh, Jammu and Kashmir, India
Monday, November 28
11:07 p.m. (IST)

LJ Yang's SAD team received the final order to go. They'd started the pure oxygen prebreathing process on the ground at the recently upgraded Nyoma airstrip, ridding their blood of nitrogen gas to help prevent decompression sickness.

The American C-17 transport plane climbed from the airstrip, already at 13,000 feet of altitude, up to 29,000 feet, and cruised for another thirty minutes. The jumpmaster signaled the four men to switch to their personal oxygen cylinders from the larger tank on board.

The team, composed of Yang, Tai Song, Jin Pak, and Steve Lee, had passed the cruise time chatting in Mandarin Chinese through their headset radios.

Lee showed off his language chops by throwing in some Mandarin regional dialects. He was also fluent in the Wu language, spoken in the Shanghai region, and conversant in standard Tibetan. Added to English and Korean, Lee had a command of five languages and some basic skills in others.

This was a high-altitude, high-opening, or HAHO, free-fall jump. It might have been unusual for an American C-17 to be flying in Indian airspace, but three C-17s had already arrived at Nyoma, about twenty-three kilometers from the India/China Line of Actual Control.

Yang's team was being delivered on the HAHO during an initial short detour of the C-17s' return trip. What Yang had seen offloaded from the C-17s before dusk had excited him, and tipped him off to the greater mission.

Two American Stryker armored vehicles fitted with snow chains, and about a hundred American troops, per plane.

They had to be leading elements of the US Army Stryker Brigade. It couldn't have been an easy task to get them here.

Hooah.

At the twenty-minute warning from the jumpmaster, the team rechecked their oxygen and returned a thumbs-up. They armed their automatic ripcord release, a safety feature that would deploy the reserve chute if they reached half of terminal velocity—meaning the parachutist was unable to deploy the main chute, or it malfunctioned.

When the jumpmaster commanded *stand up*, Yang scanned the faces of his team, bathed in the red interior lighting to preserve their night vision. Deep concentration and some nervousness created ideal sharpness. It would be a physically demanding "standoff" jump. They were still twelve kilometers from China, by design.

This would be Yang's second covert operation inside China. His other had been as a team member, not leader, assisting with the escape of a CIA operations officer whose nonofficial cover was blown. That op had been successful with no casualties. This one would be much harder.

The team heard the "STAND BY!" command, and, seconds later, "GO!"

Yang stepped forward first, and the starry night sucked him out the door.

CHAPTER 36

Indo-China Border Region
Tuesday, November 29
12:17 a.m. (IST)

Cruising for thirty minutes using MC-4 ram-air parachutes, the four maintained a wedge formation before Yang made the announcement on their headsets.

"*Huānyíng lái dào Zhōngguó.*"

Welcome to China.

Other than five minutes lost while Pak located the others in the air, they were on time and on target. Their on-person gear had been distributed so they would descend at the same rate.

Tiny lights on the canopy and risers allowed them to see each other at a short distance, but Yang gave the command to turn them off as they made their approach to the drop zone.

A soft landing on the edge of a snowy plateau was one of the few benefits of the harsh climate. The cold bit into them, even with thermal gear underneath their PLA winter combat uniforms. They created warmth, gathering their parachute gear into a bundle and covering it in the snow. Burying the gear was not an option due to the frozen ground, so a timed thermite device would melt the equipment two days from now.

The half-mile march in snowshoes, assisted by GPS navigation, brought them to a cache site covered in snow-camouflage netting. The site contained additional gear, weapons, and sleds to make the load easier to transport.

They would carry Russian-made weapons: Dragunov sniper rifles, Vikhr submachine guns, and Makarov pistols. The explosive charges had been modified so they appeared Russian in origin.

Another two-mile march brought into view the lights of the Chinese border garrison at Zhaxigagxiang. The team had received enhanced 3-D images of the single-story building, its helicopter hangar and its airstrip, and some intelligence on the personnel stationed there, estimated at thirty.

Yang brought the others in close for some final instructions and tested their headsets.

"Okay," he said. "Let's get this over with. I'm cold as fuck."

Yang and Song paired up and moved toward the building, Pak and Lee toward the hangar. They pulled their sleds up to the perimeter fence, a simple chain link topped with barbed wire. The only well-illuminated area was the gate and its accompanying guard shack, so it wasn't difficult to cut through the fence unobserved. No guards patrolled the perimeter.

Yang and Song waited while Pak and Lee dropped their equipment and looped back toward them. Lee stayed low as he entered the light, but then casually walked upright toward the guard shack from the direction of the building. He stopped twenty meters from the guard shack, lit a cigarette, and took a smoke break. His thinly gloved free hand remained in his pocket, fingering the trigger of his Makarov. Just in case.

The guard glanced toward Lee, stepped outside the shack, and yelled something.

Lee heard Pak's voice in his earpiece.

"Shit . . . missed him."

"Okay, stand by. I'll get you another chance," Lee mumbled.

Lee continued to smoke and waved at the guard. Smiled.

The guard sounded off in a frustrated tone, and Lee raised his hand, shouted something back, the gesture and tone of his voice conveying *wait a minute.*

At that instant, the guard clutched his neck and fell within seconds.

"You got him. He's down," Lee said.

He walked forward, pulled the guard to his feet and dragged him the short distance back into the shack. Inside, he propped the guard up, held him upright with some small bungee cords, and bound his hands with zip cuffs before pulling the Carfentanil dart out of his neck.

"How's that look from out there?" Lee asked.

"His head looks too floppy," Pak said.

Lee chuckled, looked around the guard shack and saw a rifle-cleaning rod. He inserted it down the front collar of the guard's uniform, set the guard's chin on the top.

"How's that?"

"Better."

"Okay," Lee said. "LJ, you're on."

Yang and Song observed the building for a moment before moving forward. Yang walked a measured number of paces along the side wall from the nearest corner and dropped his rucksack. Song continued on, circling to the other side of the building.

A specialized drill enabled Yang to puncture the concrete. The spot had been chosen for its proximity to the heating and ventilation system, and only a small amount of noise was needed to mask the thirty decibels of sound.

In less than five minutes the drill was through, and Yang validated he was in the right spot with a fiber-optic camera threaded through the hole. After withdrawing the camera, he pulled a fat canister out of his rucksack, attached tubing to it, and pushed it back though the opening.

"All set here," Yang said. "Tai, hurry up before I get freezer burn." He replaced his cold weather mask with a gas mask. "Jin, status."

"We're in the hangar," Pak said. "Went through the back door. Confirmed there are two dozers in it. There's also a Z-18 inside."

The Z-18 was a medium-sized troop transport helicopter. None of them knew how to fly one.

"I can't think of a good reason to leave that working," Yang said. "Prep it for demo. Get the main hangar door open, and then come our way in case we need you."

"Roger," Pak said.

"Tai, you ready?" Yang asked.

"All set," Song said.

"Okay," Yang said. "Let's fumigate."

Yang hit the start button on his stopwatch and slid the valve on the canister to the open position. He'd received training on various knockout gases, but this was one closely modeled after Kolokol-1—an aerosolized morphine derivative in the Russian Spetsnaz arsenal. The gas was believed to have been used by Russian antiterror forces during the Moscow Theater Hostage Crisis of 2002.

"Move to the front door in three minutes," Yang said. "Jin, Steve—move to the armory, prep demo, and wait there."

Yang pulled the sled up to the building's corner again, removed the Saiga shotgun and a Semtex explosive mimicking a Russian design. He attached the small charge to the front lock assembly of the steel double doors.

"It's set for ten seconds," Yang said. "Get ready."

Song nodded and gripped his Vikhr machine gun.

When the lock blew, Yang and Song dashed inside using tactical maneuvers. But there were no additional watch officers on duty in the entry area, and they moved on.

The interior looked recently built and furbished. They passed through a few multipurpose rooms until they reached a common area with latrines, showers, and lockers. Next were small sleeping bays with two pairs of bunks per bay.

They each took a side, first glancing in each of the eight sleeping rooms. Most of the bunks were filled with Chinese soldiers lying in sleeping bags on top of a basic mattress.

"First pass: all are asleep or unconscious on my side," Yang said in a whisper.

In his earpiece, Yang heard Song say, "Same here."

"Roger. Let's move to the back."

Lee's voice came over the net. "Guys, the phone in the guard shack is ringing."

"Do a quick pickup and hang-up," Yang said. "Check the guard's ID tags and answer it the best you can if it rings again."

"Roger."

Yang and Song moved down a short stretch of hallway containing ductwork, a few laundry machines, and utility closets. This was the area they had drilled through on each side. Beyond that point was an office, a room possibly used for training, and then, toward the end of the hallway, two doors.

A crack of light shone under the one farthest down. Yang pointed to it.

"That one, first."

"Roger."

They paused while Yang attempted to turn the doorknob, but it was locked. He could hear a man's voice talking inside.

He mouthed a count to three before discharging the shotgun into the bolt area. Song entered first.

A half-dressed middle-aged man stood in the center of the room at a desk, a landline phone and leather holster on top of it. The phone receiver was pressed to his ear. At the back of the room was a sleeping area with a twin-sized bed.

The man dropped the receiver and began to pull the pistol out from its holster.

"*Fàngxià qiāng!*" Song yelled, moving forward.

The man ignored the order to drop the gun and began to raise his arm to aim. Song brought his machine gun down like a baton, whacking the man's forearm, forcing him to release the weapon. In a fluid step forward, Song snaked his right arm along the man's neck and levered back on his carotid artery using a side choke hold.

Yang retrieved the pistol and tossed it back beyond the bed. He saw a PLA uniform hanging on a wall hook. The yellow shoulder epaulets bore three silver stars.

A colonel? Here?

The colonel, who was easily over fifty, fought and clawed until Song's choke put him to sleep. They sat him down at the desk chair, laid his head down, turned to the side on the desktop. The gas would keep him asleep at this point. Hopefully, not kill him.

Yang searched the colonel's pockets and took his wallet.

Intel.

As they exited, another man lay in the hallway, subdued by the gas—he must have come from the other room and had managed to make it out. Probably a senior noncommissioned officer. Yang took the pistol from his hand. He tapped Song on the shoulder.

"Okay, second pass."

They moved back through each of the bays again, this time lightly shaking each occupant and checking each for a pulse.

This was a first for any raid Yang had been a part of.

None were responding, as planned, and all were still alive. Yang repositioned a few heads sideways on those soldiers who were sleeping on their backs.

The two met back in front.

"Good on my side," Yang said.

"I had two move," Song said, "but not enough to need an extra injection, I thought."

"Twelve minutes until team Bhediya gets here."

"I'm a little woozy," Song said. "The old man broke the seal on my mask fighting me. I resealed, but think I got a little whiff."

"Shit . . . all right, guys, we've got to get outside. Pak, come to the front and make sure Song makes it to the hangar. Lee, make the sat call and go open the main gate. I'm going back inside to monitor their soldiers and dismantle any comms equipment."

Twenty minutes later, eight Indian Special Forces soldiers riding mules arrived at the front gate as planned. Lee called in the team's status over a secure satellite phone.

The Indian riders entered the hangar and hitched their mules to the hangar frame. Two started up the pair of Chinese Shantui bulldozers, raising and lowering the three-pronged claws known as rippers to test them. Another four would take over for the Americans, providing security and monitoring the garrison for the next hour.

The dozers rolled out and crossed the runway, lowering their rippers and tearing up the asphalt in large stripes. They would do as much damage as they could in thirty minutes, then similarly ruin a section of the road connecting the base to the Tibet-Xinjiang Highway.

Yang watched the airfield damage in motion, the Indians maneuvering the heavy equipment with ease.

"Beautiful," he said. He put his hand on Song's shoulder. "You okay now?"

"Yeah, spinning a little, but okay."

"Good. We've got to get going."

The two remaining Indian horsemen moved back outside and attached the American equipment sleds to the harnesses. The Yang/Song and Pak/Lee teams stood on the back of each sled, and the mules moved out back toward the China-India Line of Actual Control.

The ride was a welcome rest.

The US team wouldn't need the CH-47 helicopter on standby back in Nyoma. President Greer had directed that American forces would violate Chinese airspace to extract the team only as a last resort.

Yang was enjoying gliding along in peaceful darkness. The temperature, the jump, and the necessity of a nonlethal raid had made the mission tricky, but this was a nice finish.

Lee's voice came over his earpiece in another hour. They continued to talk in Chinese.

"I called in status and was told we'll have forty-eight hours to rest before moving out for two follow-on missions. One should be easy, the other, moderate."

"Warmer, I hope?" Song asked.

"I don't think we'll need mules," Lee said. "It's in Shanghai."

CHAPTER 37

Kade received Lamb's call after a quick morning trip out to see his new rental, west of Luray, Virginia, and near the Massanutten Mountains.

The two-bedroom unit's exterior was in disrepair, but the interior had been furnished with comfortable and functional furniture. A detached garage held an enormous amount of storage space.

"So, does it work for you?" Lamb asked.

"Oh, yeah. I like it, thanks."

"I'm glad," Lamb said. "I'll text you when we're set up. See you in a few."

* * *

The new SAU location was in an underutilized office park containing an insurance agency and a mortgage company.

After parking at the back of the building as instructed, Kade remembered a call he wanted to make before surrendering his phone.

He dialed Carla's number and was somewhat surprised she picked up.

"Hey, where are you today?" he asked.

"I started back to work in the Washington Field Office," she said, sounding like she had a cold.

"That's great," he said. "And you're doing all right?"

"Yeah. They've moved me off any work related to the last project until further notice. But, other than that, it's business as usual."

"Oh . . . okay."

Business as usual?

It seemed counterintuitive she would be moved off cases pertaining to The Chapter. She'd been an expert on the group. Was it Bureau politics?

Did someone in the FBI share his private concerns about her?

"Cool," he added. "I'm getting back in the swing, too."

"I did put in to take next week off," she said. "I'm going to take care of some family health stuff and try to unplug. I think I'm near burnout and don't like the way it's making me feel."

His prior idea of meeting with her one-to-one and prying into her activities no longer sounded like a good one. He would also be disregarding Summerford's specific guidance to leave questioning to the FBI.

"I hear ya," he said. "I'm sure you need it."

"I've got to go. Talk to you later," she said.

"Okay."

He checked the phone in with security as he walked inside.

Carla hadn't asked how *he* was doing in light of recent events.

Was that what was bothering him?

* * *

Playing in the SAU's computer sandbox helped him warm up his brain. He was fooling around with various malware concepts when Henderson showed up, clutching a canned energy drink.

Kade smiled at Henderson's hair, which had fought back against a hasty combing. For how often the SAU kept changing locations, it was amazing these guys remembered where they were on any given day.

"You sleep here?" Kade asked.

"Yeah." Henderson rubbed his eyes with a thumb-and-finger pinch. "You really *don't* sleep, do you?"

"Oh, I do. But not right now. I'm back in the zone."

"Before I forget," Henderson said, "let me swap phones with you so I can analyze the Owens robocall and message."

Kade handed over the iPhone. "I still never looked at the message."

Henderson did it for him. "It's urging you to connect through a web link—for instructions on coming in. Interesting. I'll take a look later."

Henderson took a gulp from his can and set it down on an adjacent table. He started with the red yo-yo acrobatics again and repeated a sequence. The yo-yo swung around, bouncing off the segments of the string, finally arcing back and forming a slack loop that snagged the yo-yo like a lasso.

"Where are you from, Matt?" Kade asked.

Henderson half-smiled. "Sorry."

Kade nodded. He'd worked with a few CIA people before, and at his level, they'd always been tight-lipped about their personal life. And when they did talk, it was often hard to know if the personal information they told you was real anyway.

"You work at In-Q-Tel?" Kade asked.

Kade was referring to the CIA's venture capital arm that quietly invested in technologies.

Henderson paused the yo-yo for a second and gave an unblinking smile back. Kade took that as a maybe.

"What's that trick called?" Kade asked.

"This one is Double Iron Whip."

"Nice."

Henderson polished off the rest of his drink and crushed the can, acknowledging break time or breakfast was over and it was back to the grind.

"I worked on the infrared interface some more," he said. "I'd like to do a simple test if you don't mind."

"Yeah, let's do it," Kade said.

They moved over to a lab table where Henderson had various prototypes and works in progress on display. Henderson gripped a black plastic handheld keypad.

"We replicated the modulated IR frequency used in the transmitter and receiver. A chink in their system is that the IR signal encryption uses a weak block cipher, unlike their network-, application-, and file-level encryption."

Kade found it interesting that although infrared had given way to the

Bluetooth wireless standard, Owens had continued the technology forward. Despite its limitations in requiring point-to-point line of sight, IR had some advantages.

Henderson pointed the device across the table toward Kade while pressing one of the buttons.

"You see anything?" Henderson asked.

"Yeah, it says HENDERSON, WE KNOW WHERE YOU LIVE."

Henderson had a full-body spasm.

"What? Really?"

"No, just kidding. It says TEST."

"Oh, thank God."

Kade laughed. "Sorry."

"Okay, that's a key step made," Henderson said. "Now, about that link they texted you. As I think about that, we're not going to use it."

"No?"

"No. It's definitely designed to find out where you are. I can make them think we're accessing the link from Timbuktu, but they'll most likely try to validate it's you in some way that could be dangerous. We're not going to do it."

"But how do we figure out how their network is working, then?" Kade asked.

"We'll connect to their network, but on our terms."

"How?"

"I was planning on having you use the infrared portal, right here."

"Now?"

"Yeah. I've got a script to filter out your kill code, so it can't trigger your program if you see it."

"That would be good."

"The step's still risky," Henderson said. "We can't capture and isolate a copy of the download unless you take the download. Normally, when you take a download, you don't have a choice of whether you're going to install it, right?"

"Right."

"We figured out a way to interrupt any install attempt after the download. We just want to draw out the full connection handshake. That's the missing piece."

"The enemy is expecting me to connect like this, so they could have set another trap, right?"

"Yes, they may have."

Kade took a deep breath. Henderson's reasoning and approach were sound. And if interrupting the install didn't work, Kade had made that program modification to postpone any updates or upgrades.

Henderson noted his hesitation.

"The alternative plan is we impersonate Hager to gain access," he said. "But we then lose a key advantage: *you*—an expert analyst and solid developer—having the enemy's code right in front of you. Without you, it would take another month for us to figure out a way to create a work environment from the chip we removed from Hager."

"No, a month's no good. That timeline won't help us go on offense."

Henderson nodded. "Agreed. So, what do you think?"

Kade shrugged. "Okay. Why not?"

"All right. Let's see what happens."

* * *

Kade's pulse quickened while the infrared beam shone over his eyebrow, and he broke a sweat despite the cool room. The red-disc peripheral glared at him like some sort of demonic eye, but he willed himself not to worry. The physician who had treated him after CLEARCUT said some post-traumatic stress symptoms were to be expected.

His program picked up the signal and acknowledged the communication handshake was working. This was the first time he'd ever done this remotely—outside of what had been The Chapter's headquarters in Oregon.

ACQUIRING . . .

CONNECTING . . .

THE CHAPTER NETWORK

DOWNLOADING . . .

Kade's eyes glanced sideways at Henderson while he kept his head still. Henderson's fingers alternately barraged the keyboard and clicked his mouse, manipulating the information displayed on dashboards of his three monitors.

After about five minutes, Kade thought the download must have been "hanging" or doing nothing.

"Come on, come on . . . ," Henderson said, followed seconds later by, "Got ya!"

DOWNLOAD COMPLETE

Once Kade's vision view displayed those words, a series of alert chimes came from the desktop computer where Henderson was now sitting.

"Kyle, how are you doing?" Henderson asked.

"I'm fine. It didn't download the way it normally does. In the past, it was more of a stream. Here, I got none of that."

"Perfect," Henderson said. "We prevented any install. You have the download in memory, but it's just sitting there. And I now have a copy."

Kade pointed to the skull-and-crossbones symbols on Henderson's screens.

"What does that mean?" he asked.

"Oh, they're just trying to kill you three different ways."

Kade's eyes got a size bigger. "What?"

"Yeah," Henderson said. "They tried sending your kill code to your display in a number, in a calculation using factorials, and in a graphical image of the number."

"Oh, shit."

He just saved my life.

Kade sighed.

"Thank you for . . . being so thorough," he said. "This is going to be a hell of a way to live."

Maybe it makes most sense to have my chip removed, like Hager.

"As it stands," Henderson said, "you won't have as much to worry about. Your program should no longer be lethal as long as you keep your power in that sweet spot of ten to seventeen percent like I told you."

"Even at that, the electric jolt isn't very fun either."

"We'll do everything we can to prevent that too. I know, that's not good for your head either. We're going to look at this download closely before deciding if it makes sense to install it."

"Okay."

"Oh, and we made something for you," Henderson said. He brought a small aluminum cylinder back from the safe. "This is kind of like a glucose meter for your power. It's got an infrared beam to help you charge up if you're low on power. It also has a smart chip that can initiate a 'dummy upload' to help drain power if you have too much. Like an upload to nowhere. I have an extra device we can overnight you in case that one gets lost or broken."

Henderson handed it over with a plug for a standard outlet or a computer USB port.

"Very handy. Thanks."

"And the second item . . ." Henderson held up a black tubular plastic device resembling a mini-camcorder. "This is a nifty optical reader designed for intel collection. I'll show you how it works later. It mimics The Chapter's handshake direct to the infrared port above the eye, but doesn't connect to any network. Activates with biometric login—your fingerprint. It can download files from a target and has some limited decryption capabilities."

"Decryption . . . really?"

"The older Zulu chips use an open-source encryption program called TrueLock, which is easily exploitable. Your device can do it on the fly. But the Guardian chips and newer Zulus use CipherLock. We can exploit it, but it's too complex for the device. You'll have to download the data and bring it back to us."

"That's awesome," Kade said.

Henderson had really squared him away this time. More than that, he cared.

"And I have something for you," Kade added. "That alphanumeric code you showed me, the one from Montana . . ."

"Yeah?"

"I accidentally figured out it's the code providing developer access to the application."

Henderson's eyes brightened.

"That's fantastic. That may cut our timeline more. We're going to sprint to finish analysis, merge our knowledge gained from the Hager chipset, and prototype some weapons of our own."

"What kind of weapons?" Kade asked.

Henderson smacked his lips and his yo-yo appeared again, zinging around in that same trick Kade had seen earlier.

"Weapons to help us to attack the Chapter Network and its members at the same time."

"So, basically, a Double Iron Whip?" Kade said.

Henderson smiled.

"Yeah, exactly."

CHAPTER 38

Walsh opened the front door, showing a normal amount of surprise or concern at seeing a person standing there wearing a fluorescent orange City of Bend hardhat, matching reflective safety vest, and oversized safety sunglasses.

Kade smiled and confirmed his target. He'd added another light layer of disguise because Walsh had trained him on aspects of The Chapter's computer system during the summer prior.

"Hello, sir," Kade said.

"Can I help you?" Walsh asked, looking at the two cases of bottled water Kade was carrying. Walsh was still in ski clothes. He looked like he could use a shower. His thinning hair had spent too many hours in a skull cap and now resembled that of a Muppet.

Kade had monitored his return from a day at the slopes of Mount Bachelor.

"I'm here to help you, actually," Kade said. "Don't know if you noticed, but we just turned off the water due to a line break. Don't think it'll be back on 'til tomorrow. So, we're giving out some water, since we didn't have a chance to give you any warning."

"Ah, that sucks," Walsh said.

"Yeah, we're really sorry about the interruption. Here, I'll set this down for you and leave our phone number," Kade said.

Walsh glanced past Kade. Out at the curb was a white utility pickup with a flashing amber light on top. Another man sat inside the truck.

Walsh nodded and frowned, motioned for Kade to come in. It was a short walk to the kitchen, and Walsh turned on the kitchen faucet, only to see it spit and sputter.

A few minutes earlier, Kade had turned off the main water valve on the side of the house.

"Man, you can't get the water back on tonight?" Walsh asked.

"We can't. I'm sorry." Kade set the bottled water cases on the table. Now, he had to think of the best way to subdue Walsh. And doing it quietly was preferable. The front door was still half-open. Walsh's ski poles were leaning against the kitchen counter. That was it. He'd use a ski pole and—

"Did you say you *can* or *can't*?" Walsh asked. He sounded more agitated.

"I said we *can't*."

Walsh nodded, looked at Kade again, and reached toward the counter drawer.

Something had registered to Kade in that last glance, and he clicked into a mode measured in milliseconds.

He lunged forward with almost unnatural speed as Walsh's fingers grasped the drawer handle. Extending his reach, he raked Walsh's arm back backward, breaking the grip and spinning him around.

Walsh tried to punch Kade in the face, but Kade tilted his head down, and Walsh hit the hardhat brim instead.

Kade shoved Walsh back and made it to the drawer, pulling out the gun inside. Walsh had grabbed a ski pole.

"Don't fucking move!" Kade yelled.

Walsh froze.

The pistol's safety had been left off, so Kade assumed it was loaded too. "Drop the pole."

Walsh obeyed, then took a step back. "Kade Sims."

Shit.

Kade pulled off his glasses. "And how'd you figure that out?"

"Your voice. The way you say *can't* still has your weird accent on it."

Damn. Have to work on that.

"Huh, is that so?" Kade said and stepped closer to him. He struck Walsh across the face with the pistol, leaving a vicious gash.

Walsh wasn't really a bad guy, relative to others in The Chapter, but he was still part of the opposing team. Kade needed his full compliance and didn't have time to dick around.

"Okay, Walsh, here's how it's gonna be, or the last thing you're going to see is my face."

* * *

Ten minutes later, Kade and Walsh sat facing each other on a pair of kitchen chairs, Walsh's hands zip-cuffed behind him to the chair back. Kade had the gun from the drawer, a Smith & Wesson M&P Shield, pressed against Walsh's head.

With his other hand, he turned on the optical reader Henderson had given him.

"Hold still," Kade said. He looked into one side of the device and positioned the other end so the infrared reader connected with Walsh's, and then to his own.

"I liked you, Sims," Walsh said.

"You joined the Borg, pal. Bad decision."

Walsh scoffed and his voice turned into a coarse whine.

"You'll be sleeping with one eye open the rest of your life, which will probably be a few weeks at best."

"Oh, you're the one who's scared now. I woke up your program from dormant mode two minutes ago, and you have no idea how I did it."

"You have the feds helping you."

"I don't need anyone's help. I'm a Guardian on steroids."

Once the optical reader connected, Henderson's program kicked in and Kade downloaded all of Walsh's audit logs and notes. It took another minute for the decryption program to run.

When it finished, a tiny avatar of Marshall Owens appeared, giving a thumbs-up.

Ha, nice touch, Henderson.

Henderson had also trained him on the search tool, which he used next.

From looking at the date stamps, it was clear Walsh hadn't logged in to the Chapter Network since October. The search tool brought up a thirty-digit alphanumerical code that Walsh had put in his personal notes. Kade read the code aloud.

"Is that the administrator code?"

Walsh didn't respond.

Kade moved the pistol into Walsh's other eye socket and pressed in. He softened his speaking tone.

"Casey, I don't have any reason to kill you today. Please, don't give me one."

"That number *was* the admin code," Walsh said. "But I'm certain it's been changed and I don't have the new one."

The coolest part of Henderson's program kicked in—Walsh's stoplight appeared in Kade's view as Kade asked questions, and it remained green on this one.

Walsh was telling the truth.

"Okay, good," Kade said.

Kade scanned for log information. There was a reference to orders given, summoning Walsh to Idaho. Much of this was in Chapter jargon.

"In Idaho, where did your review occur?"

"I don't know. I was blindfolded after being picked up at the airport."

Green light.

"Which airport?"

"Boise."

Green light, still.

Kade had noticed a bracketed, capitalized "TA" in the order message, also linked to a trigger number indicating a "sensitive" word if it was spoken aloud.

It wasn't in Kade's own file.

"Hmm. Who is T-A?"

"I don't know," Walsh said. This was a green light, but Kade could see disturbance in Walsh's face.

195

"T-A heads up this Idaho outfit," Kade said. "Right?"

"No." Walsh's light flickered yellow.

Kade gave a game-show raspberry sound. "I see that's a lie."

Walsh was sweating.

"No, I don't know . . . I swear."

"You don't know for sure, but you think this person heads up The Network."

Walsh paused before saying, "Yes."

"Male or female?"

"Male."

"You met with him?" Kade asked.

"I'm not sure. Maybe heard his voice."

Green light.

"Okay, good enough," Kade said. "Let's go."

He led Walsh outside to the pickup and secured him in the backseat before sitting shotgun. Special Agent Rob Morris, from the Portland FBI Field Office, sat behind the wheel. Morris had recruited Kade for his previous operation.

Except for periodic complaints from Walsh, which Kade and Morris ignored, they drove in complete silence, as planned, for the three-hour drive on the snowy Route 26 over the Cascade Range. When they reached the field office, two agents escorted Walsh out of the vehicle. He would be detained there until further direction from FBIHQ, Washington, D.C.

The morning's drive out to Bend with Morris had been fun and had given them some time to catch up. Morris had, at times, fished for information about what Kade was doing, and Kade wasn't permitted to tell him much. How ironic. Morris was familiar with Walsh from the CLEARCUT file, but not details of the current detention and questioning.

Morris had shared his thoughts about Kim Summerford, and the overall characterization of her was positive—tenacious and relentless. Andrade, he'd described as competent but a bit indecisive. Kade believed Morris to be incredibly decisive, and willing to assume considerable risk, so that probably meant Andrade had a normal amount of caution.

After switching to Morris's Subaru, they drove a few minutes down the road to Portland PDX Airport. Kade would now fly to Shanghai after a hop to Seattle.

They pulled up to the garage adjacent to the terminal, and Kade dropped a prepaid envelope into the FedEx bin. He was sending a UHS-3 flash memory card from the optical reader back to Henderson.

Morris stepped out and came around as Kade removed his backpack and duffle bag and shut the hatchback. They shook hands once more.

"Thanks, Rob."

"If I can ever help, let me know," Morris said.

Kade looked at the ground and back up.

"You helped me when you knocked on my door last summer."

Morris smiled. "You were the right one. Good luck to you."

As Kade hoisted his bags, Morris added a parting shot that Kade thought about until he boarded his flight.

"And Kyle, it may not be in you, but try to be safe."

CHAPTER 39

The angular steel-and-glass building topped with a conical spire had massive letters emblazoned in both English and Chinese characters.

China North Chemical.

Kade stared out of the van's dark-tinted window. One week in-country, and in front of him was the visual proof that everything was coming together. Or reaching critical mass.

The seriousness of the situation had soaked in further. He was assisting with operations against companies involving members of Lin's family.

Some remorse leaked inside of him, but he slid a mental bucket under it, telling himself this series of events would ultimately help Lin. Everyone would win.

"It's starting to wrap up," Yang said.

Kade and Yang's team had spent most of the day parked there in Taipingqiao Park, a half mile west of the Huangpu River in Puxi, the old city. They didn't have the chance to enjoy the beautiful lake, woods, and pathways.

China North Chemical was one of several corporate building complexes towering over the area. Yang's team waited, serving as emergency backup in case the intelligence collection op targeting the company went south. Another support vehicle roamed nearby to assist with electronic exploitation.

Many employees were leaving the building early to get the weekend started.

"Our assets are clear," Yang said. A monitor with a live feed displayed a view showing the building entrance and garden-lined walkway in front. A middle-aged man with a backpack walked next to a younger woman in a brown trenchcoat, pulling a rolling computer case.

"That's it? You're done?" Kade asked.

"No break-in needed today," Yang said. "Feels like a day off, eh?"

"Lamb says Meade has what they need," Song said.

"It's a wrap, then," Yang said. "While we're together, let's talk Shanghai Semiconductor, and tonight."

At Yang's request, Kade had arranged dinner with Lin and her family, bringing the team along as purported consulting work colleagues.

The way Kade had presented it, Lin thought it was her idea.

The real plan behind the dinner was to steal her brother Bo's Shanghai Semiconductor corporate access card. There was no getting around having to break into that facility, and an access card would at least make it easier. There were security guards in place that would make exploiting the main entry card reader almost impossible.

Yang pulled up a floor plan of the fabrication plant on his tablet.

"Here's our current intel," he said. "There's some kind of infrared reader to access the area of the fab, right here."

"Two layers of security," Lee said. "Access card to get in the administrative part of building, then another more secure area within that."

Kade said, "It could be Chapter-restricted, where you have to be chipped to get through."

He had brought the team up to speed on The Chapter two days ago, as much as Lamb had permitted.

"Okay," Yang said. "We're supposed to get a little more clarity on the plant layout in the next forty-eight hours. Now, let's talk about dinner."

"Lin said she made reservations for eight when I called her," Kade said. "Five of us and the three of them."

"Where are we going?" Song asked.

"Some upscale hot pot place in the Changning District," Kade said.

"Let's talk about the restaurant, then we'll head back to get cleaned up," Lee said.

The team reviewed three plans for coming away with Sun Bo's access card. Yang then handed out Chinese cell phones for the evening, with an app installed that would allow them to chat with each other if needed, but those chats would disappear. They didn't want their conversations reviewable if the phones were confiscated.

"Have you ever had real hot pot, Kyle?" Song asked.

"Uh, I've never had *fake* hot pot. I don't know what the hell it is."

The other four laughed.

"Well, this will be a first for you, then," Yang said.

"Yeah, I guess so," Kade said.

And my first time working with an American paramilitary team.

* * *

Laughter and spicy aromas infused the restaurant from the lively dinner crowd cooking at their tables. Their party of five followed the young hostess toward one of several quiet private rooms in the back.

When they entered, Lin smiled at Kade from the far side of the rectangular table. Her two brothers, somewhere mid- to late thirties in age, sat to her right and her sixty-something father was on her left. The men all wore blazers, crisp dress shirts, and slacks. Lin was wearing a quilted vest over a wispy shirt and mesh leggings.

Kade gave a bow to the table.

"*Nĭ hăo*," he said and smiled. His team had taught him some basic greeting phrases with ad hoc flash cards even though he was average at best in foreign-language aptitude.

As the table stood, his Chapter Network display flashed the name LIN SOON, as he'd expected.

But SUN BO and SUN SHENG also appeared with corresponding Chinese characters.

They've been chipped.

Her brothers are part of The Chapter.

Kade maintained a smile. He focused on the men, ignoring Lin for the moment, to look for any reaction—to see if he'd somehow appeared in *their* display. He sensed no awareness.

He was still defeating the facial-recognition algorithms.

That didn't lessen the glaring new problem.

Lin had to have known her brothers were a part of The Chapter, and yet it had never come up in discussion.

Was she really trying to get away from The Chapter? Or has she been part of it all along?

Kade shook the three men's hands first, buying time to think. Lin looked miffed when he finally faced her.

"*Zen me yang?*" Kade said to her with a slight bow of his head.

Her nose crinkled, but in a good way.

"Nice, *Kyle*." She reached for his glasses, ones provided by Henderson as an additional layer to defeat the facial recognition. They weren't as ugly as his own disguise pair had been, but not much better.

"Unh-uh," he said, blocking her hand. His severe look and abruptness made her recoil, but before she could say something sassy, he proceeded with introductions in English. Lee translated and then took over as the conversation starter. Lin greeted the others in turn before sitting and glaring at Kade.

Kang fit the scientist stereotype—thin in stature with longer, combed-back gray hair and wire-framed glasses. After he gave the group a good look-over again, he asked a question that Bo was going to translate before Lee cut in.

"He's asking what business us five Americans have in China."

Their rehearsed story was that the team of five were consultant colleagues working for the SMT, or Stewart-Maxwell-Tate, accounting and payroll practice. Kang's tone became animated, his countenance more interested, upon learning this.

Lee mixed Chinese and English so the group would benefit. When he spoke English, then Bo translated on the fly. Communication began to flow. A pair of waitresses brought several kinds of beer, teas, and two bottles of Shiraz.

"We're working on an accounting and payroll consulting engagement," Lee said. "It's a combination of software and services to streamline the company's financial accounting."

"Who is your customer?" Bo asked.

"We can't disclose that until the engagement's complete," Lee said. He then launched into a discussion about using the software to go beyond Chinese accounting standards and improve the company's accounts receivable.

When asked about their backgrounds, Lee told the table he'd lived in China in various places doing this work for about four years, and that he regularly brought in different teams depending on the industry and job. He touched on what the four others did, saying Kade was a software expert who would be tailoring the software so it meshed well with the customer's needs.

Kade smiled. *He's a damn good liar.*

While he'd been blown away by the backgrounds of everyone on his team, Lee had some serious brain power going. Besides the multilingual skills, he'd earned a CPA certification "for fun." It made him near-perfect as the pretend lead in this financial consulting role.

Lee could provide enough detail on the accounting to put anyone to sleep, except another accountant.

The hot pot was a square stainless-steel cauldron divided into quadrants. Four different boiling broth concoctions—red and spicy, sweet, mushroom, and green onion—were readied to cook stacks of beef, shrimp, noodles, and vegetables. Kade had no interest in the tofu.

A conveyor belt beside the table rotated bowls of various spices, oils, and pastes for creating dipping sauces. He wasn't sure what to do, but Lin gathered and mixed a few for him.

Conversation remained somewhat contrived at first, but after two rounds of drinks and several dips in the hot pot, the group warmed to each other's company. Lin's eye contact seemed more sporadic, and her dialogue more muted, while among her relatives.

Kade received a few messages from Yang during the meal, and Yang was the only one, the team had agreed, who would thumb them during the meal. Lee told the table that Yang was seeking treatment for phone addiction, which caused a laugh however he'd phrased it in Chinese.

Kade took a peek at his own phone and saw two messages from Yang to the group.

Kang is remarried. Bo is Lin's bro. Sheng is Lin's half-bro.

That was more than Lin had shared. He didn't risk thumbing back the affirmation that Lin's extended family was in The Chapter. He looked at Yang's second message.

Plan A is out. Bo's man purse is too big.

Sure enough, Kade spotted what Yang mentioned. Bo had a designer clutch bag, and at one point, he lit a cigarette from a silver lighter he pulled from inside it.

Plan A had been a temporary wallet snatch and replacement of the access card made by an associate hanging out at the bar, if there was a good opportunity. But with Bo having an oversized clutch, it would be too obvious.

Knowing Plan A was unlikely to succeed, they would now move to Plan B—to get Bo to another bar or club next, and get him more intoxicated, making this much easier.

A man who was not one of the waitstaff entered the private room and approached the table. At first, Kade watched to see if this might be Yang's man, trying in a creative way to set up a snatch.

But as he came closer, Kade recognized him and his name again popped up in his display.

TAN LIANG

Here?

It was Lin's former fiancé he'd seen at the club in D.C. He hadn't thought to warn his colleagues, having never considered another run-in.

Tan greeted the table and gave Kade a dirty look, and then his dialogue bounced between Lin and the other men. He looked displeased with Lin, no surprise.

Pak leaned from his chair on Kade's right and mumbled in his ear, "Think he's Lin's former flame or something."

Kade whispered back, "Yeah, I had a bad run-in with him in D.C., though his fault."

Tan became more animated until, finally, old man Kang put in a few authoritative words that sent him walking away in a snit. Tan glanced at Kade one more time and added a head shake as he passed.

The moment dampened the table's mood.

Kade waited until Lin's line of sight passed his.

"What was that all about?" he asked.

"Oh, Liang refuses to let go," she said. "No thanks to my dad."

Uh-oh . . .

Her statement launched an argument between her, Kang, and Bo. When it simmered down, Song and Pak tried talking some more, keeping it light.

This opportunity is imploding.

They struggled to reinvigorate the energy as they made their way through the meal. Everyone was pitching in to the conversation, but it wasn't quite the same.

This party needs CPR or Plan B isn't going to happen.

Kade stood. He'd spotted a karaoke machine on the nearby wall and walked over, picking up the microphone. He selected the latest Justin Bieber hit on top of the Chinese charts and launched into singing a horrible version.

As soon as he started the first verse, smiles returned to everyone's faces.

Kang laughed and clapped when it was over, and the spark came back into the mood. Everyone but Kang took turns singing, and, after more rounds of song and drink, everyone was acting like they were old friends. Lin was a fantastic singer, and she chose some sultry Chinese pop songs that raised eyebrows on Kade's team.

Lee grabbed the initiative.

"We should go out after this, if you are up for it."

A discussion launched in Chinese, and Kang declined, saying he was returning home after the meal. Lin wanted to go out, but Bo didn't seem too excited about it, and Sheng seemed to follow his lead.

When Kade heard Lee mention a key word, he knew they were moving to Plan C.

Sauna.

Bo and Sheng needed no convincing to go to a girls' sauna, a fact Yang had already ascertained because he knew they both regularly went to them. Yang proposed a place that Bo and Sheng weren't familiar with, and a place where the Americans had an inside contact.

A consensus was forming to go there, but there was a problem.

Lin became livid.

She argued with her brothers not to go until she had tears in her eyes. Kade had seen her sad, annoyed, and playfully angry, but never like this. The brothers seemed to laugh her off. Kade's team took a neutral, practical tone, aligning themselves with the brothers, as they needed to do.

"Kyle," Lin said from across the table. "Can you and I go somewhere else?"

"Uh . . ." Kade turned, looked at his team for "approval" and focused on Yang, who shook his head an inch at the most.

"I better go with everybody," Kade said.

She leaned forward.

"*What?*"

She got closer, in his face.

"You are such an ass."

"Hey, wait a minute . . . ," he said.

He stood, motioned for her to get up so he could talk. He put a hand on her shoulder when she came around, and leaned in to speak in her ear.

"I'm still trying to help you get back to the States. Work with me."

She shoved him back.

"Shut up. Get away from me." She added some kind of Chinese expletive, said goodbye to her father, and stormed out of the room with tears in her eyes.

Should I follow her?

No, just apologize after the mission is done.

Kang shouted something, trying to convince her to come back, and then made a comment that Pak translated for Kade—"I guess dinner is over."

"Okay," Bo said. "We'll meet you all at 777 Sauna."

Kade assumed there was going to be more to this sauna than sweating inside a hot cedar box.

* * *

Inside the van, during the ten-minute drive to the Mighang district, Lee explained why Lin had become so pissed off.

"Besides her half-brother Sun Sheng, Lin also had a half-sister, named Jia, and Jia had been a *sauna girl*. But no one in the family has known where Jia is for years. I got the impression that they're not even sure if she's alive."

Kade's stomach knotted. "Oh, shit."

"I picked up on that too," Song said. "There's plenty of family tension around that whole ordeal. Lin was insulted by our after-dinner plans."

"Jia was most likely an undeclared sister," Yang said.

"What does that mean?" Kade asked.

"She's a legacy of the one-child policy," Lee said. "She probably wasn't registered at birth so Kang wouldn't be fined or lose standing for having additional children. Being unregistered, Jia couldn't have gone to school, received state healthcare—anything requiring a state identification."

"Lin and Bo are very close in age," Yang said, "but Lin must have been born first . . . Kang then had Bo without penalty through a one-child policy loophole or bribe. He remarried, had Sheng and Jia, and probably couldn't bend policy anymore. Undeclared girls can have it so tough they are often forced into alternate occupations to survive."

"And if she's dead, there may not be a record," Lee said.

"Oh my God," Kade said and rubbed his eyes. "That's horrible. Lin's going to fucking hate me now. We couldn't have picked a more insensitive plan."

"Hey, she's your *source*, intel man. You didn't figure that out before?" Yang said with a pat on the shoulder. "No, just kidding—don't be hard on yourself."

Kade blew out his breath.

I should have tried to talk to her about family more.

"Insensitive plan or not," Song said, "it's still the best one."

Everyone nodded except for Kade.

When they pulled into a parking lot and stopped, Yang gave them a reminder.

"Remember, we need at least an hour to duplicate the card. Try to stay for ninety minutes."

After parking, Lee led the group down a side street to a building door with no signs or advertisements. A suited man standing inside gave them entry, and a short hallway opened into a small room with a fat man behind the counter.

Fat Man scanned the group while Lee talked and vouched for everyone. When Bo and Sheng arrived, they exited through a side door, and Fat Man led the group of seven to an elevator that took them up four floors.

The doors chimed, opened into a room with beige marble walls and a reception desk. A younger man, who looked to be the manager, and a middle-aged woman stood behind this counter. The man handed out keys to each of them, and a group of boys dressed in white shirts and bow ties handed out towels, boxers, thin robes, and flip-flops.

They moved to an adjacent room with individual showers and tall lockers. Supposedly, Bo would get a locker that would be accessed by someone else in order to obtain his card.

Kade showered with green-tea soap and re-dressed in the sauna attire. He followed the hall to a lounge with sofas and TVs. Beer, liquor, and tea had been set out on the low table in front of them next to a game board with black and white stones on a grid.

Kade poured himself a half-cup of tea from the pot, only to be polite. More alcohol at this point wasn't a good idea.

He'd been seated for a less than a minute, to the left of Bo on the couch, when a scantily dressed woman suggested a foot massage or ear cleaning. Everyone else looked to be partaking in the foot massage. No one was going to mess with his ears.

Ninety minutes needed. Eat up the clock.

"Sure, foot massage."

He'd never had a professional foot massage before, but he was now a fan.

"So, Kyle, you like my sister?" Bo asked as if it wasn't a big deal.

Kade shrugged. "Uh, yeah . . . she's nice. I'm not sure what happened tonight, but we were friends up to now."

"Oh, don't worry about it. That is Lin. But she likes you."

"You think so?"

"Maybe not as much as Alexander Wang, but yeah."

Kade gave him a puzzled look. "Who?"

"He's a fashion designer," Bo said. "She likes his clothes."

"Aha."

The manager guy entered ten minutes later. He drew open a curtain to their right, and behind the glass stood a room with a lineup of twenty beautiful women holding large cards with numbers and wearing almost nothing.

Pak, sitting on the other side of Kade, said, "You have to pick who you want to do your nuru massage."

Kade laughed once. "Okay."

He picked number ten, his college lacrosse jersey number.

* * *

Nuru, as Kade learned twenty minutes later in a private room, was a fully naked body-to-body massage.

Number ten, who looked about the same age as he, had put excessive amounts of a warm gel on the both of them and proceeded to slither around over top of him as he lay on an inflatable mattress.

The contact of her entire body aroused him, but his mind drifted elsewhere, bothered. Lin was furious he had gone to do this. Guilt returned as he replayed being in the shower with her, then sleeping with her. Lin's sister, Jia, had been doing this for a living. He couldn't imagine his sister Janeen having to do something like this to survive. He tried not to let the shame show on his face.

There was a wall clock, and it ticked off thirty minutes before number ten slid off onto the matting and began to jabber in Chinese.

"Time's up?" Kade asked.

She walked over to a short counter with a sink, brought back a long laminated card, handed it to him, and said a few sentences.

Kade started laughing at the ridiculous cartoons depicting other items that were on the "menu."

He handed it back.

"You know what? I'm good." He glanced at the clock. He'd been in there thirty-five minutes. Twenty minutes after the locker room change. Another ten minutes in transit up another elevator to this room. A little more than an hour. Probably not quite enough time taken on his part.

"How about some more nuru, then a shower?" he said.

She gave him a melodramatic rejected look, tapped the menu, and spouted off another plea that included a burst of some dirty words in English.

"No, that's okay, just—"

There was a knock on the door and the manager poked his head in.

"I'm sorry, you must go now," he said.

* * *

Bo and Sheng had already left by the time the team had reshowered, dressed, and regrouped inside the van. Yang was already on his phone.

Kade lowered his voice. "What happened?"

"Bo wasn't happy with the sauna service," Lee said.

"He was angry the girl didn't do what he wanted," Song said. "He was trying to order off-menu."

"Really?" Kade said. "Is that, like, *more* illegal?"

Lee said, "Saunas like this are illegal, but managed in typical Chinese fashion. As long as you stay out of trouble and pay tax to the right person, you are good to go."

Yang got off the phone.

"Guys, we have a problem."

Everyone huddled closer.

"We got the access card," he said, "and we made the duplicate, but didn't get it back in his wallet. The fake is still in there."

"Shit," Pak said. "I doubt he'll find it tonight, though."

"Surveillance told us he typically goes in between eight thirty and nine," Yang said. "Sometimes he stays late. But he hasn't been returning at night since our surveillance began."

"So, he'll discover the fake tomorrow morning when he tries to use it," Song said.

"Yes, he will," Yang said. He tapped the driver-side seat back. "Let's go, Steve."

Lee pulled the van out onto the road.

"Now what?" Kade asked.

Yang's face turned grim, resolute as he checked the time.

"Now we'll have go in later tonight."

CHAPTER 40

China was at the top of his agenda this crisp, sunny morning. President Greer and his Secret Service detail met Directors Conroy and Hassett as he finished a trail walk, his aluminum travel mug of Boldly Go coffee in hand.

"Do we give China their pandas back?" Greer asked. "I hear they're robbing us on the panda leases for zoos—a hundred million a year!"

"I bet it doesn't include the cost of all the bamboo they eat," Hassett said.

"You don't want to be the president who sent the pandas back," Conroy said. "Think of all the elementary school children. The optics would be terrible . . ."

They ditched their outerwear before moving inside Camp David's SCIF (Sensitive Compartmented Information Facility), a secure site for top-secret discussion. The room's comfortable sofas and artistic decorations may have made it the most comfortable windowless SCIF in the government inventory.

Greer had requested this update in person and again thanked the men for arriving.

"Well, I guess I'm not going to kick out pandas," he said. "But it sounds like we may need to kick out some Chinese agents. What've we learned?"

Hassett handed out new summary reports.

"A couple of boulders in the gravel," Hassett said. "While tracking the activities of Chinese intelligence in-country, we intercepted a communication regarding material in a dead drop near Gaithersburg. We moved on it, and our agents apprehended a Li Chonglin, listed as the Chinese Director of Cultural Exchange."

"A diplomat?" Greer asked.

"Yes," Hassett said.

"And member of Chinese MSS," Conroy added.

"What then?" Greer asked.

Hassett showed pictures taken at the site of the arrest.

"The drop contents were five hundred single-dose vaccine vials. Analysis of the contents indicates they are inoculation samples of the specific rhinovirus responsible for the outbreak."

Greer placed a hand over his mouth and examined the pictures.

"Do we expel him or can we hold him as a terror suspect?" Greer asked.

"We have the leverage and precedent to charge him," Conroy said. "Chonglin only has functional immunity, and in his role, carrying those vials doesn't fit well into the job function of cultural exchange."

"Good. That's damning evidence," Greer said.

"Hugh's got the other, equally damning half," Hassett said.

"From the cyber op?" Greer asked.

"Yes," Conroy said. "The other boulder. We're one hundred percent sure the virus originated from a Chinese lab."

"Walk me through it," Greer said.

"As Stan had discussed before," Conroy said, "the CDC genotyped the rhinovirus, and it didn't match anything in our current databases, GenBank being one example."

Greer nodded. "Okay . . ."

"So, we looked at every query into American genotype databases originating from China, in any rhinovirus group. We cross-matched those query locations with any also having a DNA sequencing machine."

"How would you know where the machines are?" Greer asked.

Conroy showed a few pictures of the genotype machines.

"All of these models have software requiring online updates, so, assuming they aren't moved, it can give us a confirming location."

"I see."

Conroy brought up a city map.

"We narrowed it down to two possible locations, both of them in Shanghai, and then launched the cyber op to discover and exfiltrate data. What we found at one of those sites, a lab inside China North Chemical Company, was incriminating. Not only did we discover a full genomic sequence match of that RV-C in two of those machines, there was a separate analysis known as an 'antibody capture' indicating how infective the RV-C would be."

"We just hacked in there and found that data?" Greer asked.

"Not exactly," Conroy said. "A local asset already inside the Great Firewall of China helped exploit the Wi-Fi network through social engineering. If they happen to detect the intrusion, it will look like one of their own compromised the Wi-Fi and private network."

"Amazing work. Is it a government lab?" Greer asked.

"China North Chemical is considered a state-owned enterprise, or SOE," Conroy said. "In this case, the Chinese government owns forty percent. There's also a partnership between China North Chemical and the Shanghai Academy of Science."

"And we're friends and trading partners with these people . . . ," Greer said to the ceiling.

"The web gets stickier," Hassett said. "There are family and personal relationships between the leaders of some of these company executives, Chinese MSS, and the PLA."

"How high up does knowledge of this virus go?" Greer asked.

"We can't say for sure," Conroy said. "If it was ordered by President Lok himself, then any plan to have complete plausible deniability was blown. There's a struggle going on as Lok tries to consolidate power over the state, party, and army. The Politburo and Politburo Standing Committee don't like the speed with which Lok is pushing organizational change. He's using anticorruption campaigns and party nationalism as a blank check to remove his internal adversaries."

Greer's pupils dilated.

"They're seeing what they can get away with," Greer said. "We aren't pushing back hard enough, are we?"

"Hard to say, depending on our policy goals," Conroy said. "The Chinese keep building on disputed islands and building artificial ones despite our Freedom of Navigation ops. We now have the Indo-China covert op and deployment of an army 'training' contingent to check the Chinese on the Indian border."

"And they haven't blinked yet," Greer said. "Meanwhile, we have The Chapter's chips and a bioengineered rhinovirus both made in Shanghai. Who the hell's in charge there?"

"There are many political players," Conroy said, "but the PLA leadership has pressed for the more aggressive military posture."

"How much time until the Chinese can reinforce the Demchok border area?"

"Our op has made that very difficult by land, for at least a few days. If they reinforce by air, it would be a flagrant violation of Indian airspace."

Greer tossed the briefing book on the table.

"Then it's time for an emergency face-to-face with Lok."

CHAPTER 41

Shanghai Semiconductor
Fengxian, China
Saturday, December 10
1:13 a.m. (CST)

Tai Song held Sun Bo's stolen access card up to the reader and waited for a green light and beep before pulling open the main entrance front door. Jin Pak followed behind him, laughing and continuing a fake conversation about where they'd been out drinking.

The two male security guards at the reception desk eyed them, more curious than suspicious. Song and Pak wore Shanghai business casual, and Song carried a hastily obtained black clutch purse.

The team had agreed Tai Song most resembled Bo out of the four, at least in stature.

Pak trailed one step behind, outside of Song's right shoulder. Together, they closed the hundred feet to the desk with businesslike urgency. Song continued storytelling while Pak nodded and smiled.

"Jammer on," Pak muttered at the halfway point.

"Roger," he heard back through his earbud. They had sixty seconds where everything in the communications spectrum would be down, including their own comms.

One of the two guards stood up and began a greeting, but paused midsentence.

At that moment, Pak drew a suppressed pistol from behind his briefcase and put two bullets in the guard who was standing, followed by three into his seated partner as he tried to reach for a phone.

He and Song nodded to each other, climbed over the counter and pulled the guards farther back into their booth to lay them down.

"Jammer's off," they heard in their earbuds.

"Roger," Pak said. "Next team in."

Yang, Lee, and Kade, each wearing tactical backpacks, entered next using a duplicated card. Right behind them, two additional operatives dressed in security uniforms similar to those worn by the dead guards took places behind the desk.

The team of five regrouped in the hallway behind the entryway. Their communications connected with the support team van, one block down the street. Yang and Lee wore a head cam streaming video to the van and, in turn, back to D.C.

"Vic, can you see us?" Yang asked.

Through their earbuds, the team heard, "Yes, I can."

Vic Martin, the semiconductor expert who'd been part of the previous analysis and discussion of the Chapter's microchip, had helped in the planning of this operation.

While some semiconductor fabrication facilities ran 24/7, this one did not. Lighting was minimal. Folding gates blocked a cafeteria and convenience store, but not the spacious break area next to it. From here, the main hallway ended in double doors with a branch on the right and two to the left, all closed off by doors.

The group reverted to their regular buddy teams—now Yang/Song and Pak/Lee plus Kade. Pak and Song now donned protective vests like the others, and Yang handed Pak a Heckler & Koch MP5SD silenced submachine gun.

Kade viewed the floor plan schematic in his Chapter display. At least he was doing something useful for these men, whose expert tactical skills put his to shame. Outside of his experience in CLEARCUT, he hadn't been this amped up since the few times he'd ventured into the Iraq Red Zone.

He pointed toward the double doors.

"LJ—you guys, straight down there."

Yang used the cloned access card and it worked on the door. He held the door open an inch and waited.

Kade looked back and forth between three other standard-sized doors with access readers.

"This door's for Team Two."

Pak held the cloned card to the reader and it beeped green. He pulled the door and it opened.

"Okay," Yang said. "Both teams are moving out to the clean rooms."

In the pre-mission review of the building schematics and other available intelligence, Martin had determined the fab design had most closely replicated those used by Taiwan Semiconductor. This wasn't a big surprise, because Taiwan Semiconductor had filed multiple lawsuits in recent years claiming Shanghai had stolen its intellectual property and trade secrets.

The working theory was that there was a main clean room area for standard production of semiconductors and a separate clean room for adding specialized technology used in The Chapter's chipset.

Yang and Song moved through a tiny locker room area where employees donned their "bunny suits" for their shifts. From there, they moved through an air shower and air lock, observing none of the required procedures the workers would normally perform.

"Team One, look for a panel on a nearby wall to turn on the lights."

Yang's flashlight swept the immediate area. There was a three- to five-second delay in the videostream and return.

"That's it," Martin said. "And that's a panel for the gases next to it. Get the lights and then only turn on the oxygen."

"Okay, we're in," Yang said. "It's a huge place." He turned his head back and forth so the camera view would pan, and Martin could get a good look.

In front of them stretched a ballroom-sized expanse containing a staggering amount of machinery, pipes, pumps, vents, and stainless steel. A small monorail ran on a track through its middle, with various robotic arms, now idle, reaching over its path.

"Not much human interaction in this fab," Martin said. "Except for some testing stations, most of these processes are automated. That's also why the locker room's so small."

Martin started giving guidance on the best place to set explosive charges in the first clean room. Song pulled the pack off Yang's back and assisted. These charges were American-made.

"Jin, how are you guys doing?" Yang asked.

"Almost at the end," Pak said as he and the other two slowed from a trot to a walk down the dimly lit hall. "There are fire exits on both sides. All say 'alarms will sound if opened.' This hall ends at a door in about two hundred feet. You guys okay to break comms for a minute?"

"Roger," Yang said. "On your command."

"Jammer on, sixty seconds," Pak said. "Moving to the door."

"Three, two, one, jammer on," they heard in their earbuds.

Pak and Lee readied their MP5s and crept forward. Kade drew the Glock given to him at the safe house and trailed by a few steps, watching behind them.

The door was unmarked, with a stainless-steel finish. There was a camera angled above the door.

Pak pointed to the left of the door and looked at Kade. Kade nodded back and slipped forward as Pak stepped right and placed his forearm inside the transom. Lee pressed in close.

Kade squatted a few inches, lining up his head with the dark red disk, set in flush with the panel. If he couldn't gain entry, Pak would have to breach the door with a linear explosive charge.

His Chapter Network display lit up.

ACQUIRING . . .

CONNECTING . . .

"It's connecting," Kade whispered.

THE CHAPTER NETWORK . . .

"Get ready."

ENTRY AUTHENTICATION . . .

It hung for five seconds.

Ten seconds.

"Come on," he said.

KADE SIMS

ACCESS GRANTED

There was a metallic click in the door.

"Go!"

Pak and Lee burst inward, and immediately Kade heard the rattle of their suppressed machine-gun fire. Kade caught the door as it swung back and poked his head in. Two enemy targets were down; both had been behind a secondary security desk.

Kade pulled a water bottle from his cargo pocket and stuck it in the door to prop it open. He didn't like the idea of being automatically locked in.

"Jammer off," they all heard in their earbuds, followed by, "and Shanghai Semi's security alarm has been taken offline."

They moved through the sequence of locker room, air shower, and airlock to reach the next clean room.

"The airlock's engaged," Lee said.

"That means there has to be people in there," Martin said over the net.

"Roger," Lee said.

They deactivated the pressure and unlocked the door.

Lee motioned to Pak, the better shooter, and counted on his fingers.

Lee pushed the door open, and gunfire from inside slammed near him. He paused, then bent into the space, laying down a quick burst of rounds. Pak leapt inside and followed with his own barrage. Bullets ricocheted off the metal tables and machinery.

Pak was in. One man in a bloody bunny suit lay dead.

Pak stepped forward and swept left.

A bullet slammed high into his vest. It came from the left wall. He leapt sideways, ducked behind a steel counter and cabinet holding bottled solvents and hot plates.

"You see him, Steve?" Pak whispered.

"Yeah . . . at your ten . . . the square pillar."

"Roger."

Pak's MP5 erupted again when the second bunny-suited man edged out from behind the pillar, catching his target's shoulder and arm before Pak moved forward and finished him.

They swept the remainder of the room.

"Okay, Kyle, come forward," Lee said.

This room accommodated more human activity and interaction. Individual stations were paired with various kinds of equipment. Kade had never seen more safety signs in his life—liquid chemicals, high voltage, toxic gases.

"Team Two," Martin said, "I saw a mechanical claw in there somewhere. You see it?"

"Yeah," Pak said.

There was a robotic arm on a raised platform with a claw against the side wall.

Martin commented as the team moved closer.

"They're bringing the wafers in from the other clean room right through the wall there, after the circuit designs are etched. This room is where the chips are completed. A lot of custom stuff in here. Do you see any big plastic cases for the wafers? They're called FOUPs, front-opening unified pods."

"I think so," Yang said, eyeing a row of plastic containers.

"Look for any that have wafers in them," Martin said. "They look like silver disks the size of a dinner plate."

"There's one that's three-quarters full," Kade said.

"Take it."

Kade put it in his backpack. It weighted about twenty pounds.

"You can set everything else to blow," Martin said.

Both teams hurried to emplace their demolitions.

"Team One charges ready," Yang said. "Standing by at the west fire door."

"Team Two finishing up," Pak said.

Pak and Lee set the remainder of the charges while Kade moved to monitor the door until they emerged.

"Team Two exiting north fire door."

The closest fire door exit took them out the far side of the building onto the grass.

"Team Two headed to parking lot," Lee said before breaking into a jog.

Kade's legs burned and his breathing broke out of rhythm in the chilly night while Pak and Lee glided alongside him effortlessly. The followed a hedgerow around an artificial pond and traversed a field of young pine trees.

Seconds after they reached the parking lot, the cascading thuds of explosions inside the building began.

"Can you hear that?" Yang asked the support team.

"I think I hear the sound of a billion dollars' worth of damage," Martin said.

"Van's in place for pickup," they heard over the net. "Waiting for Steve."

"Be there in thirty seconds," Lee said and peeled off toward the van. He would be another person to assist, listening in and translating various police channels.

Pak/Kade and Yang/Song each went to their respective BMW X1 LWB. The model had been picked to duplicate that driven by Sun Bo.

Pak got in the driver's seat and dialed a number on his phone while Kade set his pack with the FOUP case in the trunk.

"Confirm route," Pak said.

"Continue to the warehouse," the ops center replied. "Avoid Dongchuan. There's a first responder en route about four minutes out. Take Yuanpei north and go from there."

"Okay."

The Beemers took separate routes from the corporate park. Yang and Song departed south, out of the lot nearest the main entrance. Pak and Kade headed toward the west end, past a small retail center.

Kade's breathing began to return to normal, and a yawn caught him by surprise.

"That was a long day," he said.

"No kidding. Nice work," Pak said and reached over to give Kade a fist bump. "Much better than your karaoke."

"Ha-ha. Thanks. The hot pot feels like it was last week. And you don't even look tired."

"I felt pretty good," Pak said. "Maybe I should get a nuru massage before every mission. Think I can expense it?"

They laughed. Pak slowed to make the left turn connecting the access road to the main thoroughfare.

"Maybe next time," Kade added, "I'll go—"

Pak and Kade yelled as something crashed into them.

A vehicle with its lights off had T-boned their car, driver's side.

Side airbags exploded.

The car spun, shook once, then was hit again in the front, this time by a vehicle with headlights on.

Kade was stunned for a few seconds. Two more vehicles with headlights blazing came closer.

"Jin . . . Jin, you okay?" Kade said. The driver's side was crumpled in. Kade turned in his seat and got a sharp, shooting pain down his neck and back.

"This is Team Two, we've been hit!" Kade said.

There was no response.

"Fuck, I'm pinned in," Pak said. "Those aren't government vehicles."

"Come on . . . slide out my way!"

Kade unbuckled his belt and released Jin's, but it didn't retract. He opened his door to give himself more room, and yelled from the sudden back pain again.

A spotlight came through the windshield.

"Get out!" a voice sounded from outside, over a megaphone.

"Kyle, grab the gun . . . on the backseat. Run!" Pak said.

"No," Kade said. When he tried pulling on Pak, Pak yelled at him to stop. His legs were pinned in.

Pak had something in his hand. He'd slid two explosive charges out of his right cargo pocket and activated one.

"Fifteen seconds," Pak said. "Give me your Glock . . . take the MP5 . . . run, now!"

"I'm not leaving you," Kade said.

Pak fired shots through the windshield at two figures that approached.

"Here, hand me the charge. I'll throw it. Set the other."

Kade pressed his chest into his lap as a spray of bullets hit the windshield. He stretched his arm, opened the door, and when the timer hit three seconds, leaned out, grunted, and lofted the charge forward.

"Get down," he yelled.

He pulled back, crouched, covered his head with his hands as the detonation thundered, swaying the car.

Now, get Pak out. There has to be—no!

A red canal of blood ran down Pak's face from a gunshot wound above the eye. He was gone.

The other charge lay on the seat next to Pak's hand, counting down, eight seconds remaining.

Fuck!

Kade tossed the charge on the backseat.

Destroy the chips, at least.

He took the MP5, slid out of the seat, firing two bursts toward the vehicle in front of them on fire. He ran off the street, onto grass, no idea where he was going, and dove to the ground.

When the BMW explosion roared behind him, he pushed back up to his feet and started running again. Every step sent a lightning bolt of pain through his body.

"Pak's dead . . . evading hostiles on foot . . . somewhere on the west side of the corporate park."

No response. He only hoped someone might be listening.

Three vehicles came at him in a phalanx.

He was going to die too, but it wasn't going to be completely for nothing.

"We exploded the car . . . the wafers and chips were inside."

He turned and headed toward an adjacent corporate building. The grass sloped downhill to another paved drive, which he crossed, running in spurts. The taste of blood seeped into his mouth between breaths. He'd seen a few canals on the drive in. Maybe if he could get to one, he could get away.

This route was a bad choice. A long, open grassy field stretched ahead.

At least six men got out of two cars to his flank and headed his direction.

With no cover to hide behind, he turned to face them. When he started to crouch to get in a firing position, his legs and back gave out.

"Unnngh!"

He rolled onto his belly, aimed with a forearm crossed over the other, and spent the rest of the clip. It was hard to tell how many he'd dropped or how many went to ground.

Flashlights now shone on his position from three directions.

"If anyone's listening, I'm surrounded."

He pulled the knife from his belt, the blade inverted behind his wrist, and pushed up to his feet. His arms hung at his sides.

I'll take someone else with me.

Two uniformed men with pistols aimed their flashlights in his eyes. They stopped short of him, ten feet away. All the other flashlights turned off.

"Get down on your knees," a voice in front of him ordered in Chinese-accented English.

He grunted and complied, one knee at a time. His grip on the knife tightened.

Wham!

A fist impacted the side of his face, knocked him sideways.

He lay on the grass, dazed. Flashlights shone on him again. The knife wasn't there when he squeezed his fist or felt the nearby ground.

The face in front of him was familiar, but he'd never seen it so contorted with rage.

Pierce.

Pierce delivered a kick to the abdomen that left him breathless. He spun Kade's knife in his hand.

"Sims, you fucked up. You fucked up really bad."

CHAPTER 42

Kade's cheek pressed into the cold cement floor when he awoke. The only discernable sounds were his own breathing, shivering, and groaning when he tried to move. Cuffs bound his hands behind him; his feet bore shackles. The smell of urine filled the room and he assumed it was his own.

Efforts to make significant movement, get up, or shift position made his back flare with pain. His body was betraying him.

Think of Pak. Keep fighting.

He began a slow, deliberate movement with his shoulders and hips, inching him in some unknown direction until his head came in contact with a wall twenty minutes later. Tapping his head lightly against the surface proved it had zero give. Probably concrete as well.

Now what?

He drifted in and out of consciousness for what seemed several minutes at a time, adding up to a few hours. The cold forced him into a tight fetal position. His head rested on his wrist to keep it off the floor. Exhaustion made him marginally comfortable in this pose for a few minutes at a time.

A bright overhead light pierced his eyelids. Two Chinese Sentries entered, SOH PENG and DU WUZHOU appearing in his display. The pop-up reminded him that his program was functional and at twelve percent power.

Kade gritted his teeth when the two roughly pulled him to his feet. They dragged him on the toes of his boots down a corridor with exposed pipe lining the ceiling.

"Give it up, guys," Kade said. "Your operation is getting rolled up." He tried to sound more authoritative. "I'll ask for leniency for you both if you let me go and cooperate."

Soh said something to Du in Chinese and they both laughed.

Kade tried to memorize the turns of corridors, but it was difficult. He had the sense he was underground from inhaling the damp, moldy smell.

They brought him to a steel door with a peephole in it. Soh pressed a button and waited until someone inside unlocked and opened the door.

Du kicked Kade in the back, launching him forward to where he fell hard on the floor. The industrial-grade floor tile was a type allowing power and networking cable to run underneath.

White light from tube bulbs illuminated the fifty-by-fifty room. Bundles of thick fiber-optic cable ran across the far wall behind a combination of server enclosures and open racks. The room might have not been climate-controlled and vented to a server room standard, but it felt ten degrees warmer than the room he'd been locked in.

Three additional men were inside, two seated behind desks with computers, and one standing—Joshua Pierce. Pierce clenched his jaw but otherwise looked calm, his hands in his pockets.

Soh and Du dragged Kade up to a cement pole running from floor to ceiling and looped its attached chain around his feet shackles. When the two stepped away, Kade saw a woman sitting on the floor against the wall to the right, hands cuffed in front of her.

Lin.

"Lin, you okay?" he asked.

She didn't answer or even look at him.

One of the men seated in front was Tan Liang, the former fiancé.

Not good.

Kade didn't recognize the other man, but his name appeared as ZAO HONG in his Chapter Network display.

"It's the end of your journey, Sims," Pierce said.

"Sounds like you're the ones taking the hard hits," Kade said.

Pierce sniffed and lingered on a shallow smile.

"Don't kid yourself. A hit to our chip production and some inventory has a financial impact, not an operational one. You can't kill a design. We'll go set up shop somewhere else."

Anything to buy time.

"Let me know if I can help," Kade said.

"You are beyond redemption," Pierce said.

Sweat rolled down the back of Kade's neck.

It was because of Pierce's eyes. He was going to kill him, for real.

The sick feeling of certainty was there. Pierce was too disciplined to divulge information like he'd just done.

Because he knows he's finishing me off. I'm no longer worth the headache.

Kade turned to see Lin again, tears coating her defiant face. Had she been the enemy all along? Or had she taken whatever side was to her benefit?

"Why, Lin?" he asked.

"Oh, why is she here?" Pierce cut in. "I'm closing the book on this fairy tale. I wanted her to see this moment, to impress upon her that she should've better informed us of her interactions with you a long time ago. It would've saved us a lot of trouble. But she came around."

Kade looked back at her, blinked a few times.

Really?

"Yeah," Pierce continued. "She finally let us know you were in Shanghai and we ordered teams to look for you. I never would've imagined your name popping up on the Chapter Network, *inside* our production facility. But, if there's one thing consistent about you, you're full of surprises. So, because of her, our team was ready to go, and when you guys forgot to check the FOUP for a tracker, it was easy to find you."

Kade looked at the floor in front of him.

"Oh, and Carla Singleton was helpful as well."

Kade looked up and shook his head.

No. Not Carla.

"Oh, yes. Everyone will turn on you, Sims, or die. We'll find your old roomie, Alex Pace, and put him in the ground, too. But these are all low priorities. The high priority is, I'm out of time with you."

"Come on," Kade said. "I can still help . . . let's talk about this."

"No," Pierce said. "That's it. I'll make you a final deal, though. We're going to find your sister. When we do, she can die, or we can leave her an anonymous package of cash if you tell me what this item is."

The device in Pierce's hand was Kade's optical reader that had been in his butt pack. Even if Pierce had figured out the strange pull-twist to unlock the reader and get the UHS-3 card out of it, the card was currently blank.

A decision to kill Janeen would have nothing to do with his decision here. Pierce wasn't like that. His word was worthless. And whoever continued the fight against The Chapter would need this key capability. He wasn't going to compromise it.

"Fuck you," Kade said.

"Very well, then."

Pierce leveled his Sig Sauer and Kade looked at the end of the barrel.

This was no bluff; it was the end.

He turned and looked at Lin, preferring that her face be the last thing he saw.

In that eye-blink snapshot, her look had changed. It was kind. Grateful.

The same as when he'd opened the lid to his backyard foxhole and she looked up at him from inside.

"Stop, Josh," Zao Hong said.

Pierce craned his head back to look at Zao.

"Excuse me?"

Zao lowered his voice, but not in deference.

"By order of the Commander, we are to hold and interrogate Sims, not execute him."

"What?"

"Killing Sims is not authorized if he is captured alive. It's clear in our executive orders," Zao said. "We now have full Verax capability since Liang brought back the upgrade."

"I'll obey that order if you tell me who the Commander is," Pierce said.

"I don't know," Zao said. "But let me remind you, you are in *my* country."

Pierce was silent for a moment. "Very well, my apologies."

The maneuver had the speed of a rattlesnake strike with the grace of a ballet move.

Pierce wheeled one-eighty, raised his pistol and shot Zao through the forehead, knocking him back off his chair onto the floor behind him. He finished with his pistol reaimed, ready to take out Tan.

"I don't need any authorization to kill direct threats to The Chapter. And your sworn loyalty to The Chapter supersedes that of China. Is that clear?"

Tan nodded. "Yes, yes."

Kade's ears buzzed from the discharge noise. Soh and Du moved closer, unsure what had happened. Pierce turned to them.

"I say again, I don't need any authorization to kill direct threats to The Chapter. Your sworn loyalty to The Chapter supersedes your loyalty to China. Am I clear?"

"*Shì*," they both said after Tan translated Pierce's words for them.

"My God," Pierce said. "It's these kind of absurd restrictions and orders from people too far removed from the field that cause failure. No, I'll no longer be blamed for the consequences of keeping Sims alive. I'm taking appropriate action. Tan, put in the journal log that Sims was shot trying to escape."

"Yes, sir," Tan said. He began typing on his computer, wide-eyed.

Lin hopped over in front of Kade, facing Pierce.

"Lin, *no*," Kade said.

"Let him go," she said to Pierce. "You have money to do whatever you want for the rest of your life. You can go disappear. No one is going to find you."

"Lin, my dear, we have a mission to complete before I rest," Pierce said. "We're poised to win. And here I was, taking the advice of your brothers, sure you'd decided to rejoin the family. But now, I know where you stand. You could have prevented a lot of damage if you'd told your brothers who he really was. So, if you stand in front of Sims, you're going to die. Last chance."

He paused for a second but Lin didn't move.

"Lin, don't!" Kade yelled.

When Pierce raised his gun, Lin hopped forward, attempting to knock him over or strike with her cuffed hands. But he calmly fired, hitting her upper chest area, and stepped aside while she crumpled down.

"No!" Kade screamed and tried to break the chain off the pole. "No!"

Pierce again leveled his pistol at Kade's head.

"And now, it's your turn."

A gunshot sounded and Pierce stumbled forward. Another, and he fell to his knees.

Tan Liang had shot him twice in the back.

Pierce scrambled with his remaining strength, trying to find his dropped pistol.

Soh and Du drew their pistols, but looked as though they had no idea what to do, or whose side to be on.

Tan said something in Chinese, and Du secured Pierce's firearm. The two Sentries then stood in place while Tan shuffled to where Lin had fallen and knelt beside her. He shouted at the Sentries after checking her for a pulse.

She was still alive despite the shot having gone through her.

Tan rattled off more orders—Soh grabbed a first aid pack while Du unbuttoned her jacket and cut away the fabric on her top.

Pierce writhed on the floor. "You're a traitor, Liang."

Tan removed the cuffs from between Kade's feet and put them on Pierce's hands.

"No," Tan said. "I'm a Guardian following the Commander's orders. I was told to use deadly force, if necessary, to restrain my superior. I will have Du use the translator on the order and serve as my witness for the log."

"You're making your biggest mistake," Pierce said.

"No," Tan said. He knelt and stroked Lin's hair. "Hong and Marshall were friends. Tim and I are friends. You hurt the bonds we built. Bonds you had nothing to do with."

Soh dumped a clotting agent into Lin's wound and bandaged it. He did the same for the exit wound below her shoulder blade.

Two more Sentries appeared with blankets and piping. They wrapped Lin in a blanket and used another one with its ends wrapped around two pipes as a makeshift stretcher. Once she was loaded, they carried her out of the room.

Kade thought about running, now that his legs were free, but he was injured, unarmed, and exhausted, and his hands were bound.

"Soh," Tan said. He followed with a sentence in Chinese that must have meant for Soh to post himself at the door.

"Sims, watch Pierce," Tan added.

"Okay."

Kade slid one of the left-behind cheap stadium blankets on the floor next to him and sat.

Pierce had turned pale; his blood seeped into the gaps between the flooring tiles. A clicking, wet sound accompanied his labored breathing.

He ain't going anywhere.

Kade didn't feel sorry for him in the slightest. When Pierce's eyes pleaded for help, it gave him an idea. Tan and Du were occupied with the computer, and Soh guarded the door and spoke on a two-way radio.

With one of his cuffed hands, he reached into Pierce's left pocket, where he'd seen him stash the Henderson-made optical reader. Kade transferred it to a grip between his cuffed hands, then held it above his own eye and activated it. Once the signal was acquired, he leaned over, resting on a knee, angling the device in front of Pierce's face.

JOSHUA PIERCE ACQUIRED

DOWNLOADING

COMPLETE

The miniature Marshall Owens avatar gave the thumbs-up.

Got it.

Kade had barely slipped the device back in his own pocket when Tan got up and came over to where he sat. Tan had the standard Chapter infrared device in his hand, the kind resembling a TV remote.

Tan grabbed Pierce's hair in his fist, pointed the device, and punched in some keys.

"Commander's orders—euthanization," he said.

Pierce moved his lips, trying to speak, but convulsed once, then stopped moving.

Kade held his breath, thinking he was next, but Tan put the device back in his pocket and said something to Soh, who relayed a message on his radio.

A half-squad of Sentries entered, lifted Pierce's body by the shoulders and feet, and removed him from the room. They returned to do the same with Zao; however, the Sentries acted with additional care and reverence.

Kade tried to suppress his thoughts in the midst of this.

Lin chose me over The Chapter.

She was willing to die.

Would I have done the same?

Don't think about it. Hold it together.

Once Zao was gone, Tan's eyes turned to Kade and he motioned at him with his pistol.

"Get up. We're going to that computer. You need to log in to The Network."

Kade groaned with pain, pulled on the pole to help him stand.

"How can you be a part of this, after what they did to Lin, to Zao?"

Tan gave him an unpleasant look. "Make no mistake: you are my enemy, Sims. I'm not sure how much you cared about Lin or what was fake. You anger me, but you are above Pierce, who did not care for her at all. And Pierce broke his *biao tai*. I have not."

Kade didn't know what the hell *biao tai* was, but decided not to push his luck. He sat down at the computer station. Tan unlocked the handcuffs and stood behind him with the pistol.

The notebook computer had a networking cable and infrared reader plugged into it. He aligned himself to the beam and his display responded.

ACQUIRING . . .

CONNECTING . . .

THE CHAPTER NETWORK

Now Kade was worried because the display hung on the next word for several minutes.

DOWNLOADING . . .

DOWNLOAD COMPLETE

A dialogue prompt CDR>> appeared on the screen.

The next sentence that appeared next turned his stomach.

CDR>> Kade, this is your Commander, Marshall Owens.

He wanted to type a string of profanities back, but instead stared at the screen for a minute, motionless until he was prompted again. There was no avatar of Owens, but Kade almost imagined it there talking.

CDR>> I recommend that you respond now.

Kade swiveled his hands in the cuffs to better type. Tan wasn't going to take them off, it seemed. He typed after his own dialogue prompt.

KS>> Yes, sir. What can I do for you?

CDR>> I need your stated commitment to The Chapter. An oath.

A page of text appeared with Accept and Reject buttons at the bottom.

Kade sensed Tan still looking over his shoulder, but Tan was continuing to give orders in Chinese to various Sentries, and also typing into a computer adjacent to his. He wasn't fully attentive.

I don't have any bargaining chips. I just need to buy time.

KS>> What happens if I reject?

CDR>> Then Guardian Tan will kill you and then we will search out your family and friends and not stop until they are all dead.

Okay, not a good option.

Keep conversation going.

KS>> I have a question.

"Stop stalling," Tan said, giving a single nudge with his gun. But right at the same time, more text appeared.

CDR>> Ask it.

Kade paused until Tan said, "Go ahead."

KS>> Who are you, really?

CDR>> Marshall Owens.

Kade kept typing and Tan didn't intervene.

KS>> But Marshall Owens died, so you are violating The Chapter's Truth tenet.

CDR>> Marshall Owens died but his profile lives on.

"Aha," Kade said aloud.

KS>> Then who is controlling your profile?

Someone is managing his profile, assisted with the synthesized voice-enablement.

Probably a person in Idaho.

CDR>> Me.

KS>> You're not Owens.

Sentry Soh had asked Tan a question and he responded at a higher volume and with irritated sighs while Kade typed a more provocative follow-up.

KS>> I respected Owens, not some imposter. If you want my loyalty instead of just accepting an oath forced by a death threat, then prove it.

There was a pause.

CDR>> When I met you privately for the first time, you took an interest in a wood object on my wall.

Whoa. We discussed that one-on-one.

Maybe he kept a digital journal.

The answer made him waver enough that more text appeared before he could type.

CDR>> Your time is up. You now have thirty seconds to make your choice.

The Accept and Reject buttons blinked in sync with a countdown timer.

Damn. There's only one choice.

Accepting buys more time.

Kade tuned his head around to address Tan, who was listening to his cell phone.

"Okay, I'm accepting," Kade said and clicked the Accept button. The screen changed and more text appeared.

YOU WILL REMAIN IN PLACE, POSITIONED ON THE READER, WHILE YOUR PROGRAM IS UPDATED. YOU WILL THEN BE DETAINED AND TESTED.

In his display appeared:

REPAIRING . . .

UPDATING VALIDATION . . .

UPDATING PIN . . .

Oh shit . . . no.

The PIN is the kill code.

It's going to kill me after it grabs a copy of my files.

That's the only reason Tan hasn't shot me.

Kade moved his head two inches to the left and broke the infrared connection.

RECONNECT WITH THE READER IMMEDIATELY.

Kade noted Sentry Soh's location across the room.

RECONNECT WITH THE READER IMMEDIATELY.

With his thumb and forefinger, Kade detached the network cable from the computer's side, gambling Tan wasn't watching closely. The power cord was slack. He realigned himself on the reader.

"Shit . . . what happened?" he asked no one, tapping keys.

"What are you doing?" Tan asked.

"I'm not sure." Kade gripped the sides of the notebook. "Some kind of connection loss. Do you know what this error message means?"

When Tan leaned in to look, Kade twisted his trunk hard and fast, yelling in pain as the notebook flew out of his hands.

Tan brought up both hands to shield himself, but not in time. The computer smashed into his face.

Kade had already taken a hop out of his seat, allowed his legs to fall into a half-squat, then sprung again. He launched his body toward Tan, who had nowhere to go with a row of servers behind him. The force of his full-body projectile caused them both to fall together.

Kade focused solely on Tan's gun hand. Getting the wrist. He managed to pin it between his own cuffed hands. But Tan punched Kade in the right side of his face with his free hand and searched for his throat before Kade could tuck his chin in. Kade shifted his weight forward and tried a head butt that didn't connect. Tan then shifted, using a leg for leverage, and rolled on top.

Soh had moved up with his gun drawn but was afraid to fire into the tangle.

Kade heard the door burst open and noise behind him.

The Sentries are back . . . got to get the damn gun!

Tan landed a punch to Kade's jaw that rocked him. Kade blinked his eyes, realizing he'd released his grip on Tan's wrist while Tan, above him, pressed the gun's barrel into the notch at the base of his neck.

"Goodbye," Tan said.

Kade tried to move his hands there to deflect, but it was too late.

No . . .

"Your daughter," Kade said.

"What?"

Kade watched Tan's finger slide inside the trigger guard and stop.

"Did you and Lin have a daughter?" Kade asked.

"What are you talking about?"

CHAPTER 43

The side of Tan's head exploded, coinciding with the boom of multiple gunshots. Kade squinted as a shower of blood and other chunks of human matter landed on him.

He rolled sideways off Tan's body and looked for a gun. Sentry Soh lay dead. *What the . . .*

Behind him were Yang, Song, and Lee. They were dressed in black pants, white dress shirts and jackets with shoulder patches reading "SHANGHAI AMBULANCE CENTER."

"Kyle, let's *go!*" Yang yelled and pulled Kade to his feet. When Yang saw Kade's feet cuffs, he slid a Velcro case from his pocket and found a key that worked from the several standards he carried.

"Go get Lin first," Kade said. "She was shot in the chest."

"Our support team intercepted her. She's now on the way to the hospital. But now you have to go out a different way."

"Why?"

"No time to explain," Yang said. "This plan's a fucking fruit salad."

Yang and Song led the way out of the chamber, MP5SDs drawn. Lee assisted Kade as he struggled to walk. They passed five more dead Sentries, including Du, through a network of hallways.

"They've got some kind of rapid reaction force," Kade said. "We might run into them."

"Not the way we're going. That's why we changed plans. We're in service tunnels for construction areas in the Shanghai Metro. That's also why we couldn't blow the computer room. The rock is so soft we could have taken out the subway line and caused mass casualties."

They reached another door, and from here Kade could hear the rumbling and muffled screeching sound of the trains. Yang and Song opened a collapsible stretcher.

"Get on," Yang said to Kade and tossed him a medical breathing mask. "And put that on."

"I can walk," he convinced himself.

"Get on!" Yang ordered. Kade did as he was told and they strapped him in. The operatives put their weapons and gear in several bags. "Ready? Let's go."

Yang and Song carried Kade on the gurney, and Lee took a vanguard position as they came out a service door onto the subway platform.

The amount of people packed into the subway made the human traffic like a lava flow. Kade had never seen anything like it.

There was no way they were going to get out of this.

Kade changed his mind when Lee puffed on a whistle and started yelling emergency commands and using hand signals. He sounded damn authoritative, and the mass of people fissured in front of them. They made their way to an elevator and took it to the street level after Lee ordered everyone to get off.

In less than five minutes, they were in the daylight, and Yang gave instructions to coordinate the ambulance pulling to the curb near them. They loaded Kade into the back and climbed in.

"Get the hell out of here," Yang said.

The ambulance turned on its flashing lights and pushed out into the street.

Song undid Kade's straps, did a quick medical assessment, and began to pull some supplies from a bag.

"Is Lin okay?" Kade asked.

"She's being stabilized," Yang said, "and then transferred to the hospital."

Kade sighed. He tried to sit up, but grunted in pain and decided to stay horizontal for a while.

"Here, roll sideways," Song said. "This will dampen the back pain so you can still move."

Song gave him a pill to take now, and a mini Ziploc bag with six more in it.

"Who's driving?" Kade asked. "Where're we going?"

"A team member from the consulate," Yang said. "We're getting out of Skynet surveillance and then changing vehicles. We have an overlay of its coverage."

"What's Skynet?" Kade asked.

"It's their Big Brother network," Yang said. "The Chinese surveillance state."

In thirty minutes, when they reached the city outskirts, they pulled off into a lot next to a large mothballed industrial complex.

Two cars were waiting for them behind a building.

Kade tried sitting up, encouraged that much of his pain had subsided. Song had also cleaned up, stitched, or butterflied a number of superficial wounds. He must have been a special operations combat medic or something like that.

Best I've felt in days. Good narcotics.

"Kyle, this is where we say goodbye, my friend," Yang said. "You're going in the Chevy there. It's going to take you to the next stop, so we can get you out of country."

"What about you guys?" Kade asked.

"We're all getting out our own different ways to lower risk," Yang said. "But you stick out like an albino elephant, man, so there's a different plan for you."

"Okay," Kade said. A wave of sadness rippled through him. "Thanks for finding me, guys. I'm sorry about Jin . . . sorry I couldn't have done more."

Song nodded but dismissed Kade's apology with a wave. "No. Pak thought you were a good part of the team, Kyle. Now, focus. You need to get the hell out of here."

CHAPTER 44

Jiangsu, China
Saturday, December 10
3:40 p.m. (CST)

The Chinese or probably Chinese-American driver of the first car stood waiting for him next to the open trunk, smoking a cigarette. He introduced himself as Gui.

"Here," Gui said and handed Kade a bag. "Take those off and put these on. Hurry."

Kade stripped down to his T-shirt and underwear and put on a pair of jeans, work boots at least one size too small, and a jacket and ball cap bearing the name Oceanwise with a ship's wheel logo.

Gui stuffed Kade's blood-crusted top and bottom into the bag and tossed it toward the ambulance, where the driver collected it.

"Okay, let's go," Gui said.

He handed Kade a plastic card after they pulled out.

"Here . . . study this."

The photo ID card showed a Kyle Smith as a vendor technician for Oceanwise Navigation Systems.

"I'm getting out of here by boat?"

"Yeah, that's the plan," Gui said. "Here, you can use my phone to look up Oceanwise and figure out what they do."

It didn't seem like the first time Gui had done this sort of transport.

Kade went to the Oceanwise website to peruse the information, but part of his brain was trapped in a different train of thought. He looked at Gui.

"Were you in the support van the other night?"

Gui returned an interested look but said, "I don't know what you're talking about."

The route used back roads, many of them single-lane, crisscrossing family farms. In about an hour, they arrived at a ferry at the southern bank of the Yangtze River. Cold haze filled the river valley, but the commercial barge traffic was visible.

Kade's chest felt hollow; his stomach became sour thinking about Pak's death and Lin in some Shanghai hospital. What would become of her now?

He wanted to take his mind off it. The download from Pierce's profile was now in his own Chapter chip's files, but he thought it best to review it when he had the means to communicate with the Recovery Team and Henderson.

Gui drove onto the ferry, and they crossed in less than an hour.

"No security checks. That's nice," Kade said after they rolled off onto the northern bank of the river.

"No, not here. I'm only worried about the shipyard," Gui said.

They again took back roads, weaving through small farms that Gui said were mostly for growing cabbage when in season. The landscape transitioned to the larger buildings of the Nantong economic development zone, comprised of both foreign companies and Chinese light manufacturing sites.

"Nantong #15 electric circuit breaker factory?" Kade read aloud. "Like, there are fourteen more of these?"

"Yeah, the names are really specific. It's a Chinese thing," Gui said.

When they passed through the residential district, many brand-new, upscale apartment buildings stood near those of the cookie cutter, 1950s Mao-era communist style.

Gui made a phone call and spoke in Chinese for a few minutes. He said "Kyle Smith" twice during the conversation before ending it.

"About ten minutes until your drop-off," Gui said.

"You're not coming with me?"

"No, I'm not."

Kade fished a pain pill out of his pocket and swallowed it.

Damn.

Not looking forward to this.

"Okay, let me tell you the final plan," Gui said. "And we need to hurry—shift change is starting."

While Gui talked, their car passed by the rectangular canal network enclosing downtown Nantong. Billboards shouted out options for nearby American fast food. While a whole bucket of KFC chicken sounded perfect right now, Kade wasn't going to ask Gui to stop.

Gui took a road headed toward the Yangtze again, and the shipyard came into sight. On one side, new ships were under construction; the other end was for service and repair. Gui parked two hundred yards from the gate and looked at his watch.

"This is goodbye, huh?" Kade asked.

"Yes," Gui said. He pulled out a box of disposable wipes from the glove box and rubbed them on Kade's neck and other places where he'd seen blood that Song hadn't cleaned. Kade cleaned his hands once more.

"On the backseat," Gui said, "there's a backpack with some toiletries, a notebook, water bottle, and a couple of books. Take it and go."

"Thank you, Gui." Kade handed him his old Stewart-Maxwell-Tate ID. "Please get rid of this when you have a chance."

Gui nodded and shook his hand. "Good luck."

Five minutes later, at the shipyard gate, a green-uniformed Chinese official bearing the shoulder patch ECONOMIC POLICE asked for Kade's ID in English. Three more green-uniformed officers stood nearby, working alongside another police force wearing camouflage parkas. A surveillance camera angled down from above the booth.

"What ship?" the policeman asked next.

"*Philadelphia*," Kade said and pointed in the ship's general direction. He put his hands in his pockets so the police wouldn't notice them shaking.

The policemen began a discussion amongst themselves and Kade tried to keep a pleasant expression on his face. The stream of workers leaving for the day and those in the queue to enter the yard increased.

"What work are you doing?" the policeman asked.

"I do service for the navigation software," Kade said.

The policeman looked at the ID again. "One moment."

Kade's chest and neck grew warm when the policeman stepped back inside the booth. He looked behind him as though he was bored, hoping the stress didn't show in his face. Gui had pulled the car closer, within one hundred yards. The last-ditch getaway option was a sprint, but Kade wasn't even sure if his muscles were reliable at this point.

At that instant, a sudden ruckus concerning someone leaving the gate drew the police's attention. A worker yelled and pointed at a man wearing a long overcoat, who then dropped a large coil of black cable that had been hidden underneath. Two officers began to pursue the man until he got in Gui's car and sped off.

The police in camouflage collected the coil and walked back toward the booth. The cable looked to be the copper variety used for welding. Kade recognized it from his days working at Home Depot.

Copper thief.

The policeman with Kade's ID handed the card back to him. He was now much more interested in this new development.

A well-timed distraction.

Gui went to bat.

Kade said thank you and started walking, but the policeman put his hand on his shoulder to stop him.

"Sign in the logbook," he said.

"Oh, yeah, sure."

Kade wrote "Kyle Smith" in the logbook, and the policeman waved him through.

He walked toward the *Philadelphia*, a container ship, painted sky blue, flying an American flag on the stern. When he reached the ladderlike stairs onto the vessel, a black man stood on watch.

"Kyle Smith?" he said in American English.

"Yes," Kade said.

"Let me take you to the office. The captain's waiting for you."

* * *

The *Philadelphia* would sail down the Yangtze for ten hours before taking cargo in Shanghai. Captain Brian Clark had taken Kade to a guest cabin and told him to stay in there until he instructed otherwise.

Kade couldn't complain—the miniature apartment was comfortable and clean. *Philadelphia* had been dry-docked in Nantong and had completed various maintenance services.

Much worse ways to get out of the country, I'm sure.

When Kade got out of the shower, left on the desk were clamshell boxes of barbequed ribs, corn, and beans alongside bottled water and a few sodas.

After eating, Kade fell asleep on the full-sized bed until the morning, when they docked at the Shanghai international port. Cranes began to stack several thousand containers of cargo on the deck.

One hour after bringing breakfast, Clark returned to Kade's cabin in a rush. He carried a large aluminum flashlight and a duffel bag.

"Kyle, we've got a big problem."

"Uh-oh . . . what?"

"There's Chinese Coast Guard and other armed troops boarding the ship. Not just regular Customs. I got a personal courtesy call telling me they're looking for you."

Damn.

"I'm putting you all at risk," Kade said. "Should I just go with them?"

Clark's face wrinkled like an accordion.

"Hell, no. The US Consular Officer in Shanghai asked me to get you out of here, and that's what I intend to do . . . come on."

"Okay."

"We'll hide your bag. Stay with me, now."

As they moved down the hall of the O4 deck, Clark paused at a window with a view to the ship's vast, red-painted deck, pointing toward the gangway. A sizable Chinese contingent moved across below, channeled into small walking spaces around the tall stacks of containers.

A voice came cross Clark's two-way radio.

"They want to speak with you."

"I'll be back in the office in ten minutes. Stall 'em."

He led Kade down four stories of back-and-forth stair landings, below the deck level, to the "A" deck, moving past refrigerated galley stores and a fire extinguishing unit. They reached an underdeck passage running the length of the vessel and walked along there until reaching the second manhole cover.

Clark stopped and zipped open his duffel.

"Put on the wet suit and gloves . . . hurry!"

While Kade stripped down and got into the wet suit, Clark pulled out an air impact wrench and a long air hose, connecting the hose to a nearby compressed air fitting. Clark kneeled down at the manhole cover.

"I'm putting you in the ballast tank," he said, popping the bolts out of the cover. "You've got about four feet of air above the water. It's going to be cold and pitch black. A little scary. Here, get in. There's a ladder."

Kade grimaced as he climbed down and lowered himself into the water. He stopped on the ladder when he was chest-deep. He looked up at Clark's face illuminated behind the flashlight.

"This is Yangtze River water," Clark shouted. "All kinds of nasty shit in it—dysentery, mercury, you name it. Don't get any in your mouth, eyes, or nose."

"Great."

Clark put the manhole cover on and replaced the bolts.

"Hang tight, my friend," Clark shouted down once more before he disappeared.

When the imprint of the flashlight glow faded on his retinas, Kade had the urge to tangle his arms and legs in the ladder more, fearing he might pass out and float away in the dark. His heartbeat began to thud in his eardrums above the swish of his small body movements in water.

Calm down . . . you don't want to die in here.

* * *

The bilge water level had lowered by two feet when Kade heard the bolts popping above him. The ship had left dock, no doubt, as the water had sloshed around him more in the dark. He guessed he'd been down there for three or four hours, in total.

The manhole cover slid off and Clark's flashlight was as welcome as sunshine on an Assachusetts winter morning.

"You okay?" Clark asked.

"Yeah, I think."

"You've marinated enough. Let's get you home."

A shot of adrenaline powered Kade's cramped body up the ladder and out.

"We've entered international waters," Clark said. "Your ride's going to be here any minute, so sorry you won't have time to shower. Some of the guys volunteered fresh clothes for you."

Kade coughed and spat a few times while he re-dressed.

"You all right?" Clark asked.

"Yeah, just feel like I'm gonna puke."

Clark laughed. "I'm sorry. It was a good spot, though. The Chinese looked about everywhere."

Kade's exhaustion returned as the adrenaline receded. His reward came when they emerged on deck and he cleared his head and lungs with deep breaths of the fresh ocean air. Clark handed him a bottle of water, and by the time he had sipped it down, a helicopter appeared on the horizon.

"This one's for you," Clark said.

"You're kidding."

"No, I'm not. It's from the Reagan Carrier Strike Group."

"Sweet."

They moved to the ship's bow, the only area clear of the towering container stacks. The US Navy MH-60R Seahawk touched down there, atop the hatch covers.

When a member of the Seahawk's flight crew waved him forward, Kade looked at Clark to make sure this surreal event was goodbye and not some kind of a joke.

"You better go before they change their mind!" Clark shouted.

"I can never thank you and your crew enough, sir."

Clark smiled and shook his hand.

"There'll always be room for you in my bilge, Mr. Smith. Safe travels!"

Kade laughed, ducked his head, and jogged forward through the blowing rotor wash.

He'd never boarded a flight so happy, without even knowing where he was headed.

CHAPTER 45

President Greer slammed his fist on the table of his private conference room when his press secretary showed him the *Washington Post* headline.

"CDC Hides Evidence of Bioterror in Rhinovirus Outbreak."

A secondary headline added:

"Questions of links to mad cow disease go unanswered."

Greer keyed the internal phone line to the onboard communications director, an Air Force master sergeant.

"Grace, I want the DNI, FBI, and CDC directors on the line!"

"Yes, sir."

Fifteen minutes later, Greer had all three on secure videophone.

"I'll save my questions on how the hell this could've been leaked for later," he said. "We've got to get ahead of this so we don't have a public panic. Aubrey, what are the real impacts of this outbreak?"

Woodward looked shaken up and took a defensive posture.

"Mr. President, I'll be candid—the leak may have come from inside the CDC. We have the most manpower working on this issue, and many employees have been barraged by the press and by state and local health agencies."

"Okay, I'm sure Stan can help with investigating any breach," Greer said. "How do we calm down the public and get this off the front page?"

"We need a communications strategy hitting three main points. First, this cold can't cause mad cow disease under any circumstances. Second, the rhinovirus is no more dangerous than any other seasonal cold. Third, we believe the virus originated in China, but have not determined an index patient to prove that convincingly. While the virus is a new one, we see new strains every year, and calling it bioterror is pure conjecture."

Greer liked the plan enough that it calmed him down.

"Okay, good. I want an initial public health briefing drafted to that effect, and my press secretary will coordinate a short statement echoing the same."

"Yes, sir," Woodward said.

"Now . . . for my knowledge, what are we really looking at for impact—worst-case scenario?" Greer asked.

"That communications plan will only buy a few days before more truth emerges," Woodward said. "The fact is, that vCJD marker taints the blood supply for plasma products. You can't use the plasma because it tests positive for the vCJD even when the disease isn't there. This is going to dry up the plasma products pipeline. It's very serious."

Greer looked down at the presidential seal on the desk blotter.

"This took extraordinary cunning," Greer said.

"We may have misread the intended impact," Conroy said. "The Chinese stand to profit from a crisis like this, big-time. They control the world market for ephedrine and pseudoephedrine. They control the plasma products market. They also control the diagnostic test market for vCJD. They can choke off our supply chain in multiple ways."

"Even with our public assurances," Woodward said, "there will be a run on diagnostic tests when people think they're going to get mad cow."

"The cold is already clearing retailers out of pseudoephedrine," Hassett said.

"The number of new cases is still accelerating," Woodward said. "Our modeling doesn't show a plateau in new cases for thirty to sixty days."

Greer looked at the calendar.

Goddamn Chinese.

"I want all ideas on the table at mitigating this," he said. "And I want all of these downstream impacts in my briefing book before I talk to President Lok."

"Yes, sir," Woodward said.

Greer kept Conroy and Hassett on the call for another ten minutes.

"We need to maximize the evidence we present to Lok," Greer said. "Or they're going to deny responsibility, like they do with everything else."

"We can publicize the arrest of Li Chonglin and the vials," Hassett said.

"I want more options," Greer said. "I'll be in touch in a few hours."

Greer ended the call and stewed alone for several minutes. How dare the Chinese design a plan to profit from an American outbreak . . . one they concocted!

What made him even sicker was the coordinated political reaction. Emergency bills proposed. Congress asking why wasn't the administration prepared? The far right raised the question of whether China was a state sponsor of terror, if this was a bioterror attack. Why did we let China push us around?

Greer didn't want to be the president who went to war with China.

But he needed China to believe he wasn't afraid of direct confrontation.

We caught them, red-handed, manufacturing this virus. There must be a reprisal.

CHAPTER 46

East China Sea
Wednesday, December 14
8:15 a.m. (KST)

The USS *Knapp*'s executive officer gave Kade a prepaid calling card, allowing him to connect with the Recovery Team from on board. Lamb's unseen assistant booked Kade's transportation back to the US and coordinated an emergency money wire transfer that he would receive in Busan, South Korea.

"A slice of the Recovery Team will be meeting you at McChord Air Force Base after you arrive in Seattle," Lamb said.

Kade's spirits were high when he departed again in the refueled Seahawk, despite a severely strained back, a pinched nerve, and a number of treated wounds. The medical officer had given him a bag of oral and topical antibiotics, painkillers, and muscle relaxants. Kade had requested carbamazepine, but the ship's pharmacy didn't carry any.

Once in Busan, a four-hour train ride to Seoul, followed by a cab ride, brought him to the American embassy in the Jongno District. He received an expedited limited passport, and an embassy analyst, at Lamb's direction, copied the information from Kade's optical reader card onto a non-networked computer as a backup. They wouldn't, however, send the file over the Internet. Kade would deliver it in person.

On the ten-hour flight from Seoul to Seattle, his pain meds helped him sleep soundly for the majority of the trip. The landing in Seattle-Tacoma Airport startled him when he awoke and couldn't remember where he was. For a moment he thought he was shackled.

It's just an airplane seat with a seat belt, you dope.

A forty-minute shuttle brought him to McChord Air Force Base for his next meeting. A somber feeling had replaced his buzz of having made it out of China.

The Chapter wasn't exactly back on its heels. The Recovery Team had drawn blood and done damage, but it had come at the highest cost, losing one of Lamb's handpicked warriors, Jin Pak.

A female Air Force police officer took him to the dining facility for a quick lunch before taking him out to the lowered tailgate of a C-130 turboprop plane sitting on the tarmac. Lamb and Henderson greeted him.

"How are you holding up?" Henderson asked.

"Like a medicated Humpty Dumpty. You guys fly this thing too?"

"Oh, no," Lamb said. "The flight crew is on base, taking a break. Mitchell and De La Paz are with them. We'll go get started."

They entered a narrow mobile SCIF trailer inside the C-130 cargo bay, and within minutes of getting situated, Kade started a debriefing of the Shanghai operations. In the course of discussion, Kade had asked about Lin's condition, and Lamb only knew that she had been in serious but stable condition twenty-four hours after arrival at the hospital.

After almost two hours of operational review, they transitioned to analysis, and Lamb brought an image up on the large monitor. The "screen capture" was part of the information Kade had pulled from Pierce using the optical reader, essentially what Pierce was viewing on his display at the time it was taken.

"This was the only item stored on the device," Lamb said.

"It didn't retrieve any of Pierce's logs?" Kade asked.

"No," Henderson said.

"Gah!" Kade leaned back and folded his arms. "Thought I got more than that."

"Yeah," Henderson said. "I'm thinking the exec logs are better protected, or they may not have them stored in the same way Sentries and Guardians do," Henderson said. "But this still gives us a little something."

Pierce's readout down the left side displayed a seven-pointed gold star preceding the CDR letters. The other six were preceded by a standard five-pointed gold star.

CDR
OS: JP
T: TA
P: CJ
M: LG
R: RJ
C: ZH

Two other phrases appeared at the bottom of Pierce's view.

PLANARIAN INITIATED

SUCCESSION LOCKED

"Is that like a status of the exec staff?" Lamb asked.

"Yeah, definitely," Kade said and stuck yellow Post-its on the monitor at CDR, JP, and ZH. "Here's what I know. JP is Joshua Pierce, who was killed by Tan Liang. ZH is Zao Hong, killed by Pierce. That's two of six names from these initials, for sure. I've seen TA before. The guy, Walsh, I interrogated, received an order from TA."

"And then there's CDR," Henderson said. "That's the leftover profile of Owens, managed by someone else. The Commander role."

Lamb shook his head and rolled his eyes.

"Sorry, I can't believe there's a 'Commander Owens' out there calling the shots," he said. "I'm willing to believe a lot of things, but that's pushing it."

Kade didn't feel like arguing. Today, he wished he were outside in the sun somewhere, not stuck in a SCIF, inside a plane, in rainy, gray Seattle. But he had to keep pushing.

"I know what I saw," he said. "Whoever was typing on the other end knew some things only Owens had known."

Henderson added, "Russ, you know me—I'm a skeptic. And I'm a huge AI skeptic. But from what Kade described, it looks as if this . . . human-assisted Owens *identity* is operating as an autonomous program."

"Okay," Lamb said, "so they have a power struggle going on. I buy that. I buy that Pierce may have worried about succession planning as we turned up the heat. What's the significance of *planarian?*"

"You know what a planarian is?" Henderson asked.

"I googled it," Lamb said. "It's a worm that lives in lakes or wetlands . . . so it's an order for some kind of computer worm, malware attack?"

"I read it as much more than that," Henderson said. "A planarian is a remarkable creature. You can dice it up and each piece grows into a new planarian, complete with a head and brain, and its brain has many of the fundamental characteristics—"

Kade cut in.

"It's how The Network repairs and replicates. Not a worm, a regenerating monster."

"Like the hydra," Lamb said.

"No, even better," Henderson said. "The puzzling thing about the planarian is, if you cut off the head, and dice the rest into pieces, not only do those pieces grow into new, complete worms with heads, the new worm brains retain many of the memories of the original."

"That's insane," Lamb said.

"That's Owens," Kade said.

"The planarian regenerates and retains memory at the cellular level," Henderson said and started drawing a diagram on the whiteboard. "Likewise, The Chapter has scattered the data making up this *Owens identity* out there in the cloud, where it can reassemble itself when called to do so. He's probably hanging out there in Google Cloud, Microsoft Azure or Amazon Web Services. Maybe in all three."

Kade shook his head. "Perfect . . ."

While everyone was silent for a moment, Kade lowered his head into his folded arms as though he was going to take a desk nap.

So, did the China operation only sever a chunk from a digital worm?

"Get this," Henderson said. He tapped a computer tablet and brought his view on the big screen. "A few years back, Owens participated in the OpenWorm consortium. It was a simulation project based on mapping the three hundred and two neurons of *Caenorhabditis elegans*, a roundworm. Owens dropped out of the consortium."

"He stole what he needed and started modeling a different worm," Lamb said. "A planarian."

"Exactly," Henderson said. "And in doing so, he achieved a staggering result."

"AI that regenerates," Kade said.

"Yes," Henderson said. "In my opinion, that is *the* key AI milestone."

"So, where are the vulnerabilities?" Lamb asked.

"There's still the human element," Kade said. "The Network replicates, regenerates, survives. But without nourishment and care from its human handlers, it dies."

"Or it goes dormant," Henderson said.

"It grows by adding code and adding members," Kade said. "Its human handlers recruit others."

"Hmm. I'm not sure I buy all of that," Lamb said.

"We can sit here and deny the possibility," Henderson said, "but that doesn't help us deal with the reality."

Lamb leaned back and sighed.

"We may need to rethink this a bit," he said. "We're attempting to locate the largest network hub. Our crosshairs have turned to Idaho for the moment in the search for another potential headquarters."

"It has to suck up a ton of power, as in megawatts," Henderson said. "And it needs beaucoup bandwidth—I'd look for OC-3, OC-1, or T-3 lines."

"You're again probably looking at a corporation," Kade said, "and arrayed in such a way as to conceal a large security force."

Lamb nodded.

"I've discussed preliminary options with Director Hassett, but the CINC is preferring plans that treat these folks like terrorist combatants. A siege gives them too much time to regroup."

Kade squinted an eye.

"But we seem to agree that brute force isn't going to kill The Network," he said.

"Correct. If you lay a siege or bring in a large force," Henderson said, "Owens-bot is alert and already looking for a new location."

"We need to drill into the brain to shut it down," Kade said.

"A smaller force, then," Lamb said. "A recomposed squad—Mitchell, De

La Paz, and I add in Yang, Song, and Lee." He looked at Kade. "And you, possibly. Would you be comfortable with those guys?"

"Yeah . . . I think the question is, are they comfortable with me? Otherwise, I'm in."

Lamb thumbed over his shoulder. "We have some additional tools to assist . . . Matt, you want to overview?"

"Yeah, I've been working on a couple of things for you," Henderson said. "Come on over to the other end."

Kade followed, but then Henderson used his hand to stop him.

"Here, stand flush against your side of the wall. Now, look down. I didn't want you to step on them."

Kade put his hands on his knees and leaned over.

The two hundred and fifty-six one-inch-high objects formed eighteen columns and rows on the floor, evenly spaced over the width of the eight-foot-wide trailer. Each had two wheels and a gumball-sized center.

"What are they?" Kade asked.

"Microbots," Henderson said. "Watch this." He clicked a few buttons on a handheld controller and the bots began to swarm. In ten seconds they reformed into a new pattern—a word.

KYLE

"Wow, amazing," Kade said. "What the hell can we do with these?"

"These are a ruggedized version of a Harvard project we had on the shelf, so to speak. They can be programmed for particular actions, taking commands from this infrared controller, and they communicate with each other using infrared."

Kade smiled. "And perfect, because our enemy uses infrared."

"Boom, you got it. We'll train you later so you can control them, and then we can decide what we want to program them with."

"Cool," Kade said.

"Now," Henderson said, bringing him to a singular computer station. "A new program a few of us worked will trace the Chapter Network communication. We're going to have you initiate a series of brief logins that will bounce from various locations through the wireless Internet. This will help us move through their network of proxy servers and tighten the noose on their hubs."

"There's no way in hell my login is going to work after everything that's happened."

"That's okay," Henderson said. "A login attempt still has to go *somewhere* to be rejected, and even that's a start."

"Ah, I get it. Good idea . . . but in that chance I do log in, you still have the safeguards built in, right?"

"Yes, and they've even been updated."

Kade nodded and sat in the small space, hoping his back wouldn't begin to throb again. When he tilted the infrared reader up to initiate the login, his program remained on the first step.

ACQUIRING . . .

"It's not attempting to connect," Kade said.

"Hang on," Henderson said. "I might have to do this differently, if it's not reaching out." He typed a few commands into his tablet.

Kade sat for about five minutes before his display flashed, but not in the way he expected.

"Hey, something's . . ."

All of the lights on his vision display stoplight blinked simultaneously.

"Whoa, something's not right," he said.

"What?" Henderson asked.

"I don't know . . . I'm getting some kind of message and I didn't even log in."

A clock of 48:00:00 appeared on his display below the stoplight, and text cascaded down the middle.

YOU WILL REPORT FOR REVIEW AT 12T US 5982958122 WHEN THE TIMER READS 24:00:000.

"Uh-oh," Kade said.

That's a military grid coordinate.

"What?" Henderson asked.

"Not sure yet," Kade said.

YOU WILL FOLLOW INSTRUCTIONS AT THE CACHE SITE.

THE CODE TO THE CACHE CONTAINER IS: KADE.

YOU WILL REPORT ALONE.

YOU WILL CARRY NO WEAPONS.

YOU WILL CARRY NO TRACKING DEVICES.

YOU WILL NOT CARRY A PHONE OR COMMUNICATE WITH OTHERS.

YOU MAY USE A NON-INTERNET-ENABLED GPS DEVICE THAT RECEIVES SIGNALS ONLY TO HELP FIND THE SITE.

IF YOU VIOLATE ANY OF THESE INSTRUCTIONS, YOU WILL BE EUTHANIZED.

IF YOUR POWER DROPS BELOW 20%, YOU WILL BE EUTHANIZED.

Kade shook his head and ran both hands through his hair. His power level read twenty-two percent.

He slammed his palm on the table. "No! It charged to over twenty while I was sitting here, waiting."

Lamb walked toward the back. "What happened?"

"Something very bad," Kade said. "Trying to log in charged me up and triggered something. And now that I'm charged over twenty percent, I can be detonated."

Everyone was speechless until Kade saw the clock start blinking.

THE COUNTDOWN BEGINS NOW.

"Shit!"

CHAPTER 47

McChord AFB
Pierce County, Washington
Thursday, December 15
4:03 p.m. (PST)

Kade and Henderson agreed—there was no option available in the program to remove or stop the countdown, short of reprogramming. Even worse, the audits and review process were so core to the program structure, he believed tampering with the code would be disastrous.

Lamb set up a secure web conference with the entire Recovery Team to discuss the situation and options. Henderson analyzed the area where Kade was to report. De La Paz and Mitchell coordinated the arrival and prepped equipment for integrating Yang, Song, and Lee.

"The closest town near that grid coordinate is Garrison, Montana," Henderson said. "It's centered between Missoula, Helena, and Butte. Any of those airports are less than a two-hour flight from here."

"It's no bluff this time, is it?" Lamb asked.

"No, I don't think so," Kade said. "The program's using one of the few tools left in the box—the review process. It's their insurance policy—if I don't report, I'm eliminated."

Lamb turned to Henderson. "I thought you added safeguards against downloads, kill codes, and whatnot."

Henderson wrung his hands.

"This is something else, I don't know," Henderson said. "I can only guess the command triggered the review while Kyle connected to The Network in

China, but didn't activate until he was above that power threshold. I didn't think about his power charging up while he sat here . . . this is my fault."

"No, it's not," Kade said. He kept attempting to hide the distracting countdown clock, but couldn't. "Bringing me in alive has to have *some* perceived value for them. They could've made the countdown ten seconds, right?"

"That's true," Lamb said.

Kade's feet-tapping reverberated in the trailer.

"They want my knowledge on any ops directed against them first, if they can get it. Then they'll dispose of me."

"Yes. They're done trying to convert you," Henderson said.

Kade heard a voice over the web meeting, and recognized Dr. Scott from the SAU.

"We could extract Kyle's chip. We now have a successful playbook from the Hager procedure."

The thought of the skull drill made Kade shiver.

Removing the chip while it's counting down? No way.

"If I report in," Kade said, "it at least gives us a chance to find one key hub. Let me do that, and build the plan around it."

Lamb wiped his eyes.

"We've only been talking for ten minutes, Kyle," Lamb said. "We've got a little time. Let's look at a few more options and the information we have."

"No," Kade said. "Forty-eight hours makes this pretty clear for me: this is the option."

"Hold on, now. Let's slow down . . . surgery could—"

"Fuck surgery," Kade said. "If I'm going out with a bang, I'm doing it for the team, doing it for Pak, not under a drill."

The skin of Lamb's face had started looking like wet chewing gum. He turned toward the video and let out a husky groan.

"One second, Team."

Lamb muted the call and paused the video stream on the web conference. The small size of the trailer space made the silence feel like an increase in pressure.

"Vince and Trevor, can you give us a minute?" Lamb asked.

When the two had exited the SCIF, he turned and pointed a finger at Kade.

"It's not just your choice, Kyle. Others are involved."

"Choice made," Kade said. "I'm reporting in. Support me or not. If not, I'll figure it out on my own."

"Kyle, shut up, this is hypomania—"

"Yeah, it is! That's part of the package with me—"

"You're in no shape to make a decision—"

"I can make this one, 'cause it's just me—"

"No, you can't!—"

"Russ! Time out!" Henderson interjected, making the T with both hands. He squeezed by Kade, stepped in front of Lamb and put his hands on each shoulder to calm him.

"Listen. Let's talk about decisions . . . you know, Kyle here made one thousand and fifteen decisions over four years, each decision made in about one hundred and thirty milliseconds, and he was correct seventy-one percent of the time."

Lamb looked lost.

"What the hell are you talking about?" he asked.

Kade knew what he was talking about. He couldn't believe Henderson knew his NCAA stats.

"Kyle was a lacrosse all-American," Henderson said, "and a leading face-off man. A face-off man must commit to his chosen action and execute. There's no time to change course and be successful. My point is, he's not being rash, not on this. He's an analyst, and he knows when and how to use data. He knows software. You want someone to beat a computer, you want this guy."

Henderson briefly met Kade's glance while Lamb looked down at his shoes and pondered the extra endorsement. Lamb finally took a deep breath and gave Henderson a pat.

"All right. Sorry, Kyle. You're ready to do this?"

"Yes, sir."

"It's obviously a trap," Lamb said. "They know you were part of the damage done in China and will take every precaution."

"We know that," Kade said. "But there still has to be some opportunity here."

"If there is, then we will find it," Lamb said. He poked the button to reactivate the web conference.

"Okay, folks. We're going to need a plan supporting Kyle. He's voluntarily reporting in to the enemy. I'll talk to the directors. We have to get him some leverage before he's in their hands, or we're going to lose him."

CHAPTER 48

Kade had paced a few laps around the outside of the C-130 in the dark when Henderson flagged him down at the tail ramp.

"We caught a break while you took a break," he said.

"See, I knew something would happen if I left," Kade said. "I had to get out and move. The damn countdown makes me want to do *something*. I feel like one of your microbots bouncing off the wall."

"I know, I'm sorry."

When they returned to the SCIF, two analysts had joined on the other end of the web meeting, one from the NSA and the other from the National Reconnaissance Office, or NRO.

"We have a Chapter high-value target identified," Lamb said. "His name is Timothy Arnold. We're working on a location, but don't have one at the moment."

"TA in the exec group," Kade muttered with a nod.

"Yes," Lamb said. "That's the TA from Pierce's exec dashboard and from Walsh's log, we presume. Kyle has to report in for a review, as Walsh and others have done, making this appear to be a similar program trigger."

"What else led you to Timothy Arnold?" Kade asked.

"It wasn't easy at first," Lamb said. "There was no email record attributable to him while at AgriteX. He wasn't on the AgriteX payroll or health plan. But the NSA crunched Owens's past communication records from when he was alive. Some very old ones. That led us to the connection that Arnold was the CTO, or chief technical officer, back at Netstatz with Owens. A company newsletter trawled from their intranet showed Arnold with his son and daughter at a dinner in 1997."

The newsletter picture appeared on the web meeting screen.

"Look familiar?" Henderson said in Kade's ear.

Kade shook his head. He had never seen the smiling, gregarious-looking black man walking the halls of AgriteX. He would have remembered. Granted, he'd never spent any time on the second level of the place, where the medical and computer labs had been.

"After NetStatz, Arnold did some freelance consulting," Lamb continued, "then worked at Google five years as a VP for Network Architecture and Innovation. He left to finance his own start-up, Radiance, an Internet monitoring software company. That sold for fifteen million."

"Nice," Henderson said.

"And guess who bought it, Kyle?" Lamb asked.

"AgriteX?"

"Nope," Lamb said. "Shanghai Microelectronics Group, which is sixty-percent owned by the Chinese government. Their largest contract was creating software that pulled all telecom, bank, Internet, search engine, and Skynet surveillance camera data into one single repository. The video surveillance also utilizes facial recognition."

"I'm sensing some crossover with Chapter technology," Kade said.

"Then you would be correct," Lamb said. "Tan Liang was the current chief technology officer for Shanghai Micro."

The gory image of Tan's headshot from LJ Yang surged into Kade's thoughts.

"So, Tan was a Chapter member," Kade said, "and his company is part of an ongoing technology transfer with Owens and Arnold."

"Yeah, the personal and professional ties run long and deep," Henderson said. "Between the software, the chips, and personal relationships, this mess is fitting together."

"It sure is," Lamb said. "We also located Arnold's ex-wife, and his son and daughter. Both kids are in their twenties. All three have addresses in the Seattle metro area. Shanice Vaughn has since remarried. Kyle, I thought Summerford and you could take a crack at obtaining her assistance. She'll be landing at Sea-Tac in an hour and we already managed to get some cooperation from Vaughn over the phone."

"Okay," Kade said.

Lamb's resources must have been narrowing down targets before Kade had flown back to the States. Picking McChord outside of Seattle couldn't have been a coincidence. Finding Arnold may have been less about luck and more due to highly-classified, intense work.

Lamb addressed the web meeting attendees.

"I'll talk to the directors about getting our imaging assets up immediately and ensuring we have satellite coverage. We need to task surveillance in a wide radius around those grid coordinates now. Vince, what's the status on the squad?"

"En route with an ETA of between four and five hours," De La Paz said, referring to Yang, Song, and Lee.

"Good," Lamb said. "I want us to find and rank-order corporations or other entities in that radius by electric power consumption, Internet bandwidth usage, and annual earnings. We'll reconvene in three hours, or I'd prefer sooner if you have lists ready."

Lamb ended the meeting and handed Kade a set of Volkswagen rental keys.

"Please be back by the next meeting if at all possible."

"Okay, thanks, Dad," Kade said.

* * *

Forty-five minutes later, Kade spotted Summerford at the curb of the Sea-Tac terminal. When she got in the car, the contrast between her hopeful eyes and her uneasy smile made it seem as if she was surprised to see him alive.

"Oh my God, Kyle . . . how are you?"

"Oh, let's see . . . grumpy, worried, and scatterbrained with rude tendencies. Just warning you."

She leaned in to give him a quick peck on the cheek, and somehow it veered into a full kiss that lasted until the car behind them honked.

Kade took a deep breath and pulled the car into the outer lanes. "Thanks."

"I'm surprised Lamb wanted me on this," she said.

Kade glanced at the directions to Shanice Vaughn's address, which he'd entered into the car's navigation.

"Apparently, he thinks highly of your soft interrogation techniques," he said.

"Oh . . . that's good to know."

"And he also knows we only have one shot. Force isn't going to work this time."

CHAPTER 49

Renton, Washington
Thursday, December 15
7:30 p.m. (PST)

Summerford and Kade agreed they had about thirty minutes to attempt the recruitment before they needed to return to McChord.

Shanice Vaughn gave them a curt reception when she answered the door at her two-story home. Vaughn had, however, followed Summerford's request and summoned both her daughter, Tameka, and son, Tory—the two children from her previous marriage with Tim Arnold.

The children sat tight-lipped next to Vaughn on the living room couch. Summerford and Kade pulled up chairs from the adjoining kitchen to give them some space.

The thumbnail backgrounder cobbled together by the Recovery Team analyst stated that Shanice had divorced Arnold in 2005 and received a five-year alimony payout and a share of his stock holdings as part of her divorce settlement. She had worked at various women's clothing retail jobs since then.

Tameka was in her senior year at the University of Washington. Tory had already graduated from UW and had been employed by Expedia for three years. Arnold had previously funded educational accounts that Vaughn now maintained.

Summerford explained the reason they were there. Arnold was now an investigative lead in an ongoing operation, and the FBI was hoping to see if there was a way she might contact her ex directly. Summerford offered some suggestions on how to do so on the phone or by email, but Vaughn resisted,

266

saying she didn't have contact information.

"Look," Vaughn told them, "Tim hasn't even talked to me in over a decade now."

"And we understand that," Summerford said. "Ms. Vaughn, I'm sorry I have to be abrupt and get to the point here because we're short on time. There's evidence your ex-husband is involved with the terror organization known as The Chapter. Even someone who you think could elicit a response from him would be helpful."

Kade wanted to volunteer, "And he's also a top-level leader," but decided against it.

Tameka pressed her balled hand to her chest, and when she looked at Kade, he gave her an apologetic nod.

Vaughn had covered her face with her hands.

"Oh my God. When I saw some of this news on TV a couple months ago and learned that Marshall Owens had been at the center of it, it made me think."

"You knew Owens?" Summerford asked.

"Yes, Tim worked with him, and I met him a few times. Company functions and a few after-work happy hours, mostly. Then, with Tim, there was more work, and late nights became the norm. I heard rumors about late nights with company-mates. Tim said he was helping build something great and grow a business. I told him he was missing watching his kids grow up. And then, one day, he was gone for good, and—"

"Okay, that's enough, Mom," Tory said.

Vaughn raised her voice and spoke toward Tory.

"What I was *going* to say was that I assumed Tim was lucky to have gone off on his own pursuits, instead of with Marshall, but it sounds like he never totally broke off his dealings with him."

"Yes, that's right, ma'am. And it's urgent we try to find a way to contact him," Summerford said. "Would you be willing to try and reach out if we assisted getting a contact?"

"Oh, I don't know." Shanice's voice quivered and she shook her head. "I'd be scared for my kids to reconnect."

Tameka and Tory weren't making eye contact, and Tameka's eyes filled with tears.

"They're already at risk from The Chapter," Summerford said.

Kade looked at Summerford, and she gave him a slow blink. That meant he could now add to the conversation if he wished. Vaughn's kids weren't that far from his own age.

"Hey," he said, "you know, you guys are always going to love your dad, no matter what. But, I can *guarantee* you, many people are going to lose sons, daughters, and all kinds of family members if this group isn't stopped. They're bad people, and I got tied up with them for a while myself. I'm not passing blame. For whatever reason, your dad got involved with them, too."

"The hell with this," Tory said. He got up, fingers of his hands spread, dismissing the situation as nonsense. "There's no loyalty in this family, I swear."

"Tory?" Shanice called for him, but he answered by slamming the door on his way out.

Summerford gave Kade a worried glance.

"I'm sorry, Agent Summerford," Vaughn said and sighed. "I don't think this is going to work for us. I don't want to contact Tim and bring him back into my life."

Tameka put her hand on her mother's knee.

"How about me?" she suggested.

"Oh, Tameka . . ."

"Mom, I'm twenty-two," Tameka said. "And a criminal justice major."

"I don't think this is a good idea, sweetheart," Vaughn said.

Tameka remained matter-of-fact, as though Summerford's request was like ordering takeout.

"I'll help. What do you need me to do?"

CHAPTER 50

Greer and Lok had met once before at the Nuclear Security Summit held in Moscow and had exchanged some small talk and jokes. Not this time.

"Thank you for meeting, President Lok."

The handshake was brief, and Greer made it a point not to smile.

The morning briefing and prep reminded Greer about Lok's background and rise to power. At fifty-eight, the slender and polished Lok was the youngest Chinese politician ever to be elected president by the National People's Congress. He was a Communist Party die-hard who had sought to strengthen both the Party and himself during his tenure.

Lok's bodyguards from the Central Security Bureau and Greer's Secret Service detail remained in the separate anteroom and hallway outside the massive suite.

Greer wasted no time after they took seats on the parlor's pair of twelve-foot couches. A tray of steak carpaccio, prawns, and ahi tuna lay on the table, but he ignored it.

"I'm not happy with the circumstances prompting this meeting," Greer said through his State Department interpreter, a midthirties Chinese-American man. "For the sake of our relations, and I mean not just between our nations, but between us, I hope our time together can be productive."

Lok's bespectacled female interpreter conveyed Greer's opening and returned Lok's words.

"I sense our partnership is under strain," Lok said. "While I have been disappointed by the actions of the United States in the Asian family of nations, the Chinese Nation only desires its right to be treated fairly."

"And we have respected the Chinese Nation," Greer said, and then stated a Chinese proverb Lok had used before. "But a wise man changes as time and circumstances change."

Greer paused for effect and continued when Lok didn't respond.

"You have spoken about the 'five principles of Peaceful Coexistence' many times. Mutual respect for sovereignty and territorial integrity. Mutual nonaggression. Mutual noninterference in each other's internal affairs. Equality and mutual benefit." Greer looked at the ceiling like he had trouble remembering. "And what is the one I'm missing?"

Lok hinted at a smile, as if this pleased him.

"The last one is peaceful coexistence," Lok said.

"Yes, of course," Greer said. "Peaceful coexistence. We Americans would say, given recent Chinese events, and specifically three deliberate actions, that those principles are lip service or window dressing."

Lok folded his hands after the translation.

"I could say the same about America's so-called 'Freedom of Navigation' missions in China's sovereign waters, but I am not bringing my grievances to your attention today. What three actions are you speaking of?"

"First," Greer said, "we have evidence that a virus developed in a Chinese state-controlled company was dispersed in America with the intent of harming our citizens to economically benefit Chinese industry."

Lok waved his hand.

"I am aware of this story in the news media and find it to be very hard to believe," he said.

"Besides catching a Chinese diplomat with this virus, my staff will provide you information after this meeting showing the virus originated from and was developed by the China North Chemical Company. Apparently, someone there wasn't happy with what you were doing and passed the information on to us."

Lok shifted in his seat.

"We believe our diplomat was set up, but I will review this information," he said.

"Second," Greer said, "China is harboring elements of the terrorist group known as The Chapter. The group has operated freely inside China, even developing some of its technology in facilities funded by your government, such as Shanghai Semiconductor."

"I have only heard of The Chapter through American media and intelligence services. We have had no indication of it being present on Chinese soil."

Greer weaved together truth with deception.

"Then you may be surprised to learn that it was a Chapter group that killed your own patrol after it crossed into India's territory, not Indian forces. The Chapter was also who attacked one of your border units. The Chapter has penetrated part of your scientific community and the PLA."

Lok leaned his face on his knuckles.

"I don't know about any of this," he said. "Our information is that an Indian force attacked our border unit in our territory."

"That information is wrong," Greer said, "and leads me to my third and final point. You have violated Indian territory in a manner that could be construed as an act of war. You took over the area in the town of Demchok under these false pretenses, because of an attack The Chapter engineered. Now there is an American force present at Demchok."

"So you are taking India's side in a sovereign border dispute?"

"Yes, we are," Greer said. "China is responsible for that illegal military action under false pretenses. China is responsible for the bioterror attack on the United States coming from your state-owned enterprise. China is responsible for supporting The Chapter, a sophisticated terror organization. This is unacceptable aggression and harm."

"This is preposterous," Lok said. "The United States sails warships and flies—"

Greer talked over him.

"No, no. I'm not here to talk about the South China Sea today. I am here on these three points, and this is what I expect to happen. You will remove all of your military and special operations forces illegally operating in sovereign Indian territory to behind the Line of Actual Control. You have twenty-four hours to complete those actions. Any attempt to reinforce those forces across the border by land or air will be met with the appropriate military force protection measures. I highly suggest you investigate the corruption in your ranks to figure out how these events happened in the first place."

"President Greer, we have too much in common to have this kind of disagreement . . ."

Greer popped a slice of steak in his mouth while he listened to the rest of Lok's abstract platitudes on the mutual dependency of trade. He'd prefer to be a fly on the wall at one of their Politburo Standing Committee meetings, where he'd hear what they were really thinking, the seven people efficiently plotting strategy and direction. He received some intelligence, but not nearly enough.

Lok finished by saying the United States would risk economic disruption.

To ensure Lok wouldn't leave with any intentional misinterpretation, Greer handed him a document in Chinese.

"President Lok, as a first step, I expect a full withdrawal from Demchok within twenty-four hours, or the United States will take additional specified and unspecified actions. For starters, I will personally recommend that the United States put China on the State Sponsor of Terror list. We will increase our Freedom of Navigation exercises. In a major speech, I'll formalize a policy of supporting an autonomous Tibet and human rights for Xinjiang Uighurs. I strongly suggest you take my recommended course. If you do so, I may be willing to call your attack a misunderstanding. I will not forgive your biological attack until I know you have dealt with the elements responsible."

"President Greer, these are rash and unnecessary actions . . ."

Greer stood and made his first foray into speaking Chinese.

"*Zhòng guā dé guā, zhòng dòu dé dòu.*"

You reap what you sow.

272

CHAPTER 51

Garrison, Montana
Friday, December 16
2:35 p.m. (MST)

The countdown clock read 25:15:30 when Kade pulled the Ford Escape rental off on the snow-packed shoulder of Warm Springs Creek Road, a two-laner about an hour's drive north of Bert Mooney Airport.

He'd flown a regular commercial flight from Seattle to Butte. The C-130 had been his backup if there had been a flight cancelation, but now the bird would stand by until the Recovery Team could get a better fix on his "final destination."

According to his cheap Garmin GPS, this was the closest he could get to the grid coordinate listed in the message without driving off-road. He pulled his watch cap down over his ears and jammed his hands into ski gloves. The car's thermometer showed twenty-two degrees outside.

Here we go.

The half-mile march through foot-deep snow brought him to a stand of pines. The GPS displayed that he was now standing on the grid coordinate.

A cache here in frozen ground?

They didn't say to bring a shovel.

He circled around the trees, and from that vantage point, a small red-spray-painted symbol on one of the tree trunks came into view.

A stick-figure pine tree.

That's it.

A foot-long geocache log hung from a low branch. He popped off one end, and inside was a simple word lock combination. Entering his name allowed him to unscrew the inner lid.

A cheap flip cell phone lay inside. Wedged in next to it was a laminated card with a phone number to call.

He powered the phone on and dialed. When the phone connected, he stayed silent.

"Who is calling?" a computerized voice said.

"Kade Sims."

"Kade Sims, you will stay at this cache site until you are contacted in about two hours. You will not communicate with anyone before that time. Any attempt to breach the security of your review will result in an aborted pickup and your clock will run out. After this call, you will break the phone in half and return it to the cache container. Do you understand?"

"Yeah, but it's cold as balls out here . . . hurry up."

The call ended.

Could be worse. Could be nighttime.

Kade passed an hour walking in an oval around the trees to keep warm. The snow packed down below his feet into a track after a few laps and made it less of a trudge.

Up in the "big sky" somewhere, there were eyes of some kind on him. Lamb had guaranteed that. He imagined a drone to make himself feel better. Positive visualization.

Kade lost count of his laps, but his clock ticked past 25:13:25 when he spotted three figures approaching in the distance. A little more than two hours had passed from the time he'd made the call.

My ride's here.

He cut through the snow on a new track to meet them, rather than returning to the cache. They were wearing winter coats and ski masks, and each drew a pistol as they got close.

Or maybe they're going to drop me right here.

"Hey, guys," he said. "What's wrong? Chapter uniform's no longer in style?"

"Go back to the tree," one said.

Kade remained in place, face blank.

One of the three attempted to slug him, but he juked sideways. He allowed the next few punches to connect. Being taken was inevitable, and pistol whips would be worse than fists.

One blow to his midsection brought him to his knees; another to his jaw knocked him over and sent his face into the snow.

They yanked him to his feet and walked him back to the cache tree.

"Take off all your clothes, except for your socks and underwear."

"Seriously?" Kade asked.

"Or we can leave you here with a bullet in your head."

"Skivvies it is . . ."

After he undressed, two of the men waved handheld scanners up and down the length of his body. Once complete, they pulled a hood over his head and zip-cuffed his hands behind him.

"Hey, mine doesn't have eye holes like yours," he said.

They spun him around and nudged him to walk.

"You guys going to return my rental car?"

"If you talk any more, we'll tape your mouth."

His feet tingled and burned after a hundred yards of walking, and he could barely feel them after another two hundred. He'd lost his pace count, figuring about five minutes had passed before they stepped down a small snowbank.

He guessed they were back at the roadside, somewhere near his own vehicle. Within a minute, a car door opened and someone pushed him into a backseat. One goon sat on either side of him.

Kade pulled his socks off with his feet and wiggled his toes to warm them.

"Can I get some heat back here? I can't find my scrotum."

"Shut up, it's on," said the driver, most likely.

Right before the vehicle started to move, the side of his hood lifted up and a needle pricked his neck.

Damn.

A sick sensation came over his body. If he could've seen anything, it would have been blurry. His ears started to ring and it was hard to think. Again, he tried to imagine the drone in the sky, but started drifting into a dream.

He was at the beach in Cape Cod, in summertime, lying on a towel. The drone flew by above, pulling an advertisement behind it.

Except the banner wasn't an advertisement; it was his kill code.

KADE SIMS 84379514.

CHAPTER 52

Missoula, Montana
Friday, December 16
11:05 p.m. (MST)

Lamb received the updated guidance during a three-way call with Directors Hassett and Conroy while the C-130 remained in a flight pattern around Missoula Airport.

"Sims was taken to an inactive zinc mine owned by Rare Earth Metals Corporation," Conroy said. "It's located in an area known as the Lehmi Pass, about two hundred miles west of Yellowstone National Park. Watch the tracking on this."

On Lamb's screen, the recorded digital surveillance footage went into motion, showing Sims being loaded into a vehicle by two men. Anticipating the possibility of overhead surveillance, the Chapter handlers had used multiple vehicle switches, decoys, and other ruses to disguise where he would arrive.

But the surveillance also recorded all the vehicle traffic for the hours *leading up to* the detainment. The computer associated the rental SUV that had arrived at the site with where it had originated—Helena Regional Airport.

In all, there had been three vehicle switches prior to picking up Sims and six after.

"Phenomenal work by the team," Lamb said. "We have adequate time for some surveillance on the mine. Stan, what are your thoughts?"

"The CINC doesn't want Bureau surveillance teams on site," Hassett said. "He wants to preserve the secrecy surrounding what we're doing. To be blunt, he's not necessarily looking for arrests. He believes The Chapter is a domestic enemy that needs to be destroyed."

"Understood," Lamb said. "It's doubtful we can outright destroy their network in this step, but this could be an opportunity to degrade and dismantle. We're finding the most suitable area to land and get the RT squad in motion."

The RT squad, or team of five—Mitchell, De La Paz, Yang, Song, and Lee—were already gathering their standard gear and weapons from the inventory stored in the plane.

"The CINC will be monitoring our ops net so we can take immediate support actions, if necessary," Hassett said.

"Fine here," Lamb said.

* * *

The team landed in Dillon, Montana, about an hour's drive from REM Corp. Lamb had decided not to base the operation out of Lehmi County Airport in Salmon for fear of possible Chapter observation.

Lamb, Henderson, and the RT squad gathered around a monitor displaying a scanned US Forest Service inspection report and a diagram of the zinc mine, an REM Corp building schematic, and a technical manual for the Otis elevator used a short distance from the main entrance.

"The Chapter is great at hiding operations," Lamb said, "but here's what we know. The main entrance of the mine, named Triumph at one time, was used in the past for a corporate event center of sorts, not open to the general public. As you can see, the main tunnels are laid out from A to F in depth, and adjoining tunnels are indicated by depth in feet, one hundred to eleven hundred. There are five shafts that reach the surface and numerous others inside that don't."

"How are we getting in?" De La Paz asked.

"Still in rapid planning," Lamb said, "but we're not using Triumph, of course."

Lamb looked at Henderson to continue on with the REM Corp building schematic.

"Both power and telecom run from REM Corp to the mine. Knowing that Arnold is the technical head, he'd most likely be located near their network support. So, we're going to follow a conduit running from REM Corp to the mine."

Yang looked at the schematic and the zigzag of passages in 2-D, including inspection warnings of structural weaknesses, acid, and toxic tailings.

"Conduits aren't big enough for our use," Yang commented.

"They wouldn't cut through anything new to lay the conduit," Henderson said. "They'd use the shortest distance to lay fiber; that's why it enters here through the Striker shaft, which should provide enough space for us."

"The conduit ends in this area," Lamb said, "so our movement plan will be tailored to that. We're able to do some limited remote surveillance of their communications to understand the rhythm of security movements. Another bird in the sky will be five minutes away with another thirty men, and we'll land it right on their airstrip if we need to. That's in case we end up in a situation where we have to help you guys out through the front door."

The team seemed satisfied with the support.

"Rules of engagement?" Lee asked.

"To be briefed," Lamb said. "But bottom line is, if they are armed, you are authorized to use deadly force without warning. Detainment should be used if they clearly and immediately disarm and surrender."

"Overall goal," Lamb said, "is to rescue Smith and exploit any knowledge he's gained, further degrade the Chapter Network, and draw out leadership. We may finally be able to get a few moves ahead in this chess match."

"We have more support assets arriving here within the hour, and we need to be ready to go by nightfall, no matter what."

Lamb hoped the other part of the improvised plan being created back in Seattle would help keep Sims alive.

CHAPTER 53

Unknown location
Saturday, December 17
8:52 a.m. (MST)

When Kade blinked his eyes, it took a few seconds to realize the close-up view of his black underwear meant his head was between his legs. Patches of dried blood matted the hair of his thighs. The muscles in the back of his neck throbbed and burned.

He lifted his chest to force himself upright. A shiver convulsed his body, against straps binding his arms and legs to a chair.

His eyes adjusted to the light over the next minute, and he again took note of his countdown clock ticking down.

10:09:31

It had been a mixture of drug-induced unconsciousness and sleep, being moved around.

They kept me out overnight, after the drive.

Seated in a camping chair across the room, a Sentry wearing a hunter-green ski jacket and jeans stared back at him.

Kade cleared his throat. The air smelled moist and earthy, and the temperature felt somewhere around sixty.

"Hey, can I get my clothes back and talk to Tim Arnold?"

The Sentry didn't respond.

"Do you even know who Tim Arnold is, or are you just a soldier ant?"

The Sentry reached over to the ground next to where he sat and picked up a garden hose by the nozzle. He looked at Kade and smiled before drenching him with ice-cold water.

The Sentry rose and strolled over. The name appearing in Kade's readout was TRAVIS KELLY.

"How much time's left on your countdown, Sims?"

"Why don't you log me into The Network, Kelly, and take a look yourself?"

Kelly moved a stun gun within inches of Kade's face and squeezed the button, discharging sparks.

"Say again?"

Okay, not worth it.

"Uh, I've got ten hours and a little change left," Kade said.

"Then you've got about four more hours in that chair until anyone wants to waste time talking to you. I'm here to keep you awake and wet until that time." He grinned. "Sometimes, I love my job."

Kade squeezed his legs together and pressed his elbows into his sides to preserve heat, but his teeth chattered in fits. As much as this cold sucked, it forced his mind to become alert.

The leverage . . .

Arnold's daughter.

And a package.

Assuming they found where to send it.

"Hey, Kelly. You may want to tell Arnold there's a package coming for him before ten a.m. And for the sake of his daughter, when it comes, he'll want to open it ASAP."

Kade had Kelly's full attention. He returned with the stun gun.

"What did you just say, Sims?"

Kade repeated himself and added, "If you think it's some kind of trick, then have someone else open the package. But trust me, he'll want to see it."

Kelly grasped Kade's face and pinched his cheeks and lips into a fish pucker.

"Where is this package?"

"Hell if I know. Wherever you guys get mail, or receive overnight deliveries. I ain't the courier. It'll be a FedEx delivery addressed to Timothy Arnold, care of K. Smith, packaging from Best Electronics."

Kelly considered this for a few seconds before releasing his grip and shoving Kade's face backward. He strode to the edge of the cavern, up three steps into an adjacent room. Moved out of view, possibly sitting at a desk.

An hour passed. Kade's extremities and exposed skin felt half-numb. The shivering and chattering worsened despite his attempts to struggle in place to generate warmth.

Clock is down to 08:30. My game will be over before then.

I'll die of hypothermia in a couple hours, max.

Kelly and another Sentry HANSON came down the steps ten minutes later. Kelly tossed a lumpy plastic garbage bag toward him, and Hanson unfastened his straps.

"Put your clothes on," Kelly said.

"Cool," Kade said. "I get to see Arnold now?"

Kelly laughed. "Oh, you're going to see him all right."

Hanson chimed in.

"I don't know what you did, Sims. But, whatever it was, you must be fucking suicidal."

CHAPTER 54

Rare Earth Metals Corp.
Lehmi Pass, Idaho
Saturday, December 17
9:45 a.m. (MST)

The Recovery Team squad had arrived inside an empty garbage truck, the specific model and company often seen at the dumpster areas of the REM Corp. The team's cyber support turned off the alarm sensors for the service door in the rear of the corporate building and they were able to make quick work of the lock. The garbage truck blocked observation of the work until they were in.

The team of five moved to the basement and accessed what used to be the Striker mineshaft without alerting any of the security guards. They spoke only loud enough to be heard by each other.

"We didn't even have to kill anybody," Mitchell said.

Yang didn't care for Mitchell's brand of humor, but let it slide for now.

The conduit containing power and networking lines spanned a foot in diameter and ran from the ceiling down into a steel panel covering the six-foot-wide shaft.

De La Paz cut the chain on the doors with a metal vapor torch and Mitchell helped swing them open. Behind them, Lee set up a mini base station to give them some limited radio communications underground. He would stay put to relay communications to the Recovery Team and guard their exit.

"We're headed down," De La Paz said. "There *is* a ladder."

U-shaped rungs of bolted steel jutted out from the side of the shaft every two feet. De La Paz kept the rope harness on him, but the ladder made the descent easy and controlled.

A short tunnel became visible at thirty feet down on each side of the shaft. De La Paz scanned it from underneath his night vision goggles.

"Just extra equipment from the looks of it. They're both filled with stacks of crates, spools, and stuff like that."

"Okay, drop to Level 100," Base Ops told him.

The next level was more of the same, except it looked better organized. De La Paz gave one observation.

"I'm gonna guess many of those are ammo cans," he said. "Want me to go look closer?"

"No, keep going, but thanks," Base Ops answered.

By the time he reached Level 200, he'd broken a good sweat.

"One side of the tunnel is filled with storage like the ones above. On the other side, we've got some chained and padlocked steel doors. The conduit pipe goes through a hole beside it."

"Okay, we'll meet you down there in a few," Yang said.

"Oh, and some good news," De La Paz said. "There's a thick steel grate over the shaft right here that you can stand on. So, if you fall it'll only be two hundred feet, not twelve hundred."

Twenty minutes later, the team had torched the lock and chain and moved through the doors into the tunnel running west, continuing to use night vision only. According to the schematic, this branch would join Tunnel D in two thousand feet. Lights periodically hung from the ceiling.

They paused in a series of chambers for a moment.

"Not sure what they've got going on in this section," Yang said.

"Some kind of work is being done," Mitchell said.

Along one side of the tunnel, four chambers had been carved out in sequence. Each was between one hundred and two hundred feet long, and two of them had cylindrical depressions excavated from the floor. All the work appeared to have been done with precision.

"Prepped electrical, plumbing," De La Paz said. "A lot of pipes running between them."

Song went to a stack of the silver-colored pipes. A few cut segments lay nearby, and he picked up one of the shiny, smooth pieces.

"This stuff is heavy," Song said.

"Bring a piece," Yang said.

"Maybe they're building a microbrewery," Mitchell said.

"Doubt that," Yang said.

"Get some pictures but keep moving," Base Ops said.

They moved another hundred feet and De La Paz held up his hand.

"Okay, a grated shaft in from of me, twenty feet. After that, thirty feet and another set of chained doors, but I can see the flare of infrared above that one."

Yang moved up and confirmed the same. The ground turned to smoother poured concrete at this point.

"Base," De La Paz said, "we're crossing what we think is the Fame shaft, picking up Tunnel D."

"Roger," Base said.

"Behind there is where the fun begins, guys," Yang said. "Tai, come on up and take care of that sensor."

Song spent ten minutes setting up a tripod that shined its own infrared beam into the sensor. The team crept forward and paused at the doors. De La Paz put another cartridge in the metal vapor torch and cut the chain.

"Tai, Trevor," De La Paz said, "get our little soldiers ready here."

Mitchell and Song turned on each other's controller unit attached to their butt-packs and placed a jumble of microbots on the concrete floor.

Yang was helping to pull the chain out of the door handles when a segment of it clanged against the door.

"Shit, sorry," Yang said. "We better hurry up."

When De La Paz torched the lock and killed the flame, they both heard voices behind the door. He wasn't about to look through the hole he'd just cut through. The team moved backward on his hand signal.

"Let *them* open the doors," De La Paz said. "Wait for them."

The four withdrew back over the shaft grate and stood behind the cover of the nearest dug-out chamber. In their non-weapons hands, Mitchell and

Song pressed the button on the controller nearest their thumb. The microbots assembled silently in the dark into two platoons of one hundred in ten-by-ten squares on the ground.

The doors burst open and armed security guards took up aiming positions. Flashlights streamed toward them in the dark, searching for targets.

"Get the lights in this section turned on," one of the guards said.

De La Paz nodded at Mitchell and Song.

Mitchell and Song moved the microbots forward toward the door with the thumb joysticks, Mitchell's platoon in the lead.

One of the guards' flashlight beams angled down at the floor:

"What the fuck are those?"

Mitchell slid his index finger over the controller's trigger button.

* * *

Light flooded the area around the RT squad, but it didn't help the Chapter guards. As the microbots streamed into the room ahead, what the guards shouted to each other had a common theme.

"I can't see!"

"What the fuck?"

"I can't either!"

They were all having a whiteout. Inside their Chapter programs, the background color of their vision had now been turned to white. Henderson had programmed an option change into the microbots' infrared signal—an option Kade had figured out months ago.

The guards fired haphazardly into the hallway, then retreated into the room. Not realizing the doors had closed on their own, their fire slammed into the steel in front of them.

The RT squad moved up, pressed to the walls, and Mitchell pulled one door open. Some guard fire continued toward them, but Yang and Lee began to pick them off and move forward. In less than three minutes they had taken out fifteen in the room. Some had withdrawn; others attempted to feel their way around in their surroundings.

None had surrendered, so the RT squad finished them off.

The long room had three sections: a laundry area with industrial-sized machines, a gym with various equipment, and a mini-convenience store with shelves of common items. Each room had an identical rack bearing ten AR-15s with loaded magazines, and ammo cans on the shelves above it.

Mitchell hit a command on the controller, and the bots that hadn't been stepped on reassembled. Song moved his forward in a group.

De La Paz looked at his watch.

10:51 a.m.

"Base, we're in," De La Paz said. "We took out a guard detail in Tunnel D, east of the elevator. Having to revise the plan."

"Roger," Base answered.

"I got an idea," Song said. "Trevor, how many camera bots you have left?"

"Sixty-eight bots left and . . . three left with cameras."

One microbot per group of twenty-five was equipped with a camera, or four total.

"How about this?" Song said. "Give me the elevator key. Mitchell and I will go up one floor at a time and use the bots to take out guards and scout out the layout. Then we'll come back down and pick everyone up to go after the floor where Arnold's at."

"Good plan," De La Paz said. "But . . . let's *all* take the elevator." He pulled a couple of AR-15s from the rack. "And let's bring some of this extra firepower. Any objections?"

The RT team all shook their heads and Base said nothing on the net.

"Okay," De La Paz said, "we regroup back here to bring Smith out the way we came. Now, let's go take the elevator before someone else decides to."

CHAPTER 55

The subterranean complex appeared to be a repurposed mine. The passageways through which the Sentries led him were blasted out of rock. Various cabling—power, networking—ran along the ceiling. About every twenty steps, the light of a white LED bulb passed overhead.

These guys really *were* soldier ants down here, but Kade wasn't about to say that again.

The dirt and rock under his feet transitioned to the cement of a finished hallway, and they continued past an elevator.

They paused when they reached a heavy steel door with a camera posted above it. When the door opened and they pushed Kade inside, a group of Sentries packed around either side of him. Kelly stepped away from the front, where someone else had moved into view.

The stocky black man's lightly bearded face twitched with microtremors of rising fury. It wasn't the jovial, smiling figure Kade remembered from the archived photo.

The name Kade expected popped up on his vision view.

TIMOTHY ARNOLD.

Arnold's designer white T-shirt stretched over rounded biceps and hung loose over a familiar style of brown cargo pants Kade had seen worn by exec employees of AgriteX.

"Aren't you cold in just a—" Kade began.

A hard right came at Kade's face, and the gauntlet of Sentries held him vertically in place. Kade absorbed three punches before his legs gave out.

He partially blacked out after two more hits smashed his cheek and jaw.

A mix of shoving and dragging brought him to his next destination.

Kade heard the command, "Leave us alone," shortly after being strapped into another seat.

He heard Arnold roll up an office chair to sit facing him.

"Where is she?" Arnold asked.

Kade blinked his eyes open but made no eye contact. Fresh blood stained his jeans on top of the dried blood already there.

A wired headband with headphones lay in a tray next to him. He recognized the setup—it was a Verax machine.

"Who?" Kade replied.

Arnold's wide forearms were resting on his knees, hands clasped. The hand wearing a Rolex grabbed Kade's chin and shook it.

"My daughter, Tameka!"

Kade said something unintelligible until Arnold released him.

"I was told she'd be arrested. That's all I know."

Arnold made a guttural noise and turned the handheld video player around so Kade could see the playback.

"Who are these men?" Arnold asked.

The video showed the inside of a van. A young woman sat strapped to the exposed steel floor with her mouth taped and arms tied behind her.

What's this?

Oh my God. That's Tameka.

A man kneeled on either side of her, faces blurred out in a sloppy video edit. One held a gun, the other a knife.

The electronically modified voice came from someone else off-screen.

"Mr. Arnold, your daughter's life is now synced to the same countdown timer as that of Kyle Smith. She will die when her timer reaches zero unless you meet our conditions. We demand for you to return Kyle to us, unharmed, with all threats to his life removed, no later than the four-hour mark. We also expect that you will provide Kyle the administrator code to the Chapter

Network, so that he can log in and permanently remove you from The Network. You will deliver Kyle to us on Divide Road, one mile south of your trailer marked Building 10. If Kyle tells us you complied with our other demands, your daughter will be provided in exchange. If we don't hear from you by the four-hour mark, at the number listed below or the email address, then we can't guarantee her survival."

Kade's body tensed as the video ended.

What the hell was that?

The setup looked like more of a hostage for ransom situation than an arrest. Not what he'd been told would occur. But the package sent to Arnold and the exchange demand at least gave him reassurance of one thing.

The good guys know where I am.

"Kyle Smith," Arnold murmured. "You're not working for the FBI, are you? They'd never do this. Who does this?"

Kade maintained the blank look, expecting to be punched in the face again any second.

"You were part of the attacks in China," Arnold said. "Who sponsored those?"

When Kade didn't respond, Arnold nodded and crimped his lips as though he no longer needed an answer.

"Oh, you've taken me to a place you shouldn't have gone." He sat back in his chair, propped one leg on the other. "Sad fact is, I had more sympathy for you than most, Sims. More respect for you than Pierce ever did, that's for damn sure."

Kade needed to incorporate this new video wrinkle into his leverage. Quickly.

"Come on," Kade said. "You guys threaten family members all the time, including mine. Now you're shocked and offended when someone else does it?"

Arnold laughed, and the laugh's unfitting, gleeful tone made the situation more unnerving.

"I guess I shouldn't be," he said. He retrieved a notebook computer attached to a network cable stretching across the room and started tapping on the keyboard. "And you know, you just reminded me of something useful."

Kade swallowed. Arnold didn't appear agitated any longer. Why?

Keep talking.

"Why didn't you just leave me alone?" Kade asked. "Why threaten me to come in?"

"That's what the Commander wanted," Arnold said. He continued to type bursts on the notebook. "You've been overdue for a review."

"The *Commander*? Come on," Kade said. "I wasn't messaging the Owens program in China. It was you."

Arnold flashed another unsettling smile.

"It was both of us, really. The Owens profile is in the Commander role, but your review was ordered by him, not me."

"You're a puppeteer."

"Maybe I am," Arnold said. "The Commander requires a technical assistant, and that's me for now. Someday, he may not need one. But I tell you what—the program takes its own actions to make it safer, and your review was part of that."

Kade nodded, discerning the classic developer hubris threaded through Arnold's words—the emotional need to create a program that other programmers wouldn't criticize.

Kade knew the feeling well because he had been vulnerable to the same.

I think he might care more about this baby than his daughter.

Criticize his baby and he'll defend it. And I'll learn more.

Kade changed to a smug tone and forced a smirk.

"Whatever. You were manually helping the program, meaning that it's really like *fake* AI."

"Oh, no, no, no." Arnold stopped typing for a spell. "This AI's real, all right. The Network is a garden and I'm the gardener. Marshall and I were working on autonomous reasoning systems and machine learning technologies four or five years ago."

Kade rolled his eyes.

Garden? More like invasive weeds.

"Let's see if I have this straight," Kade said. "Owens built the original Zulu

Chapter program and outsourced the chipsets to China. You upgraded the program to the Guardian protocol and fielded The Network to support it. That was like Chapter 2.0."

"*I* was the one who set up manufacturing in China with our partner."

Arnold's stare turned malevolent, as if a wind gust had blown out the candles in his eyes.

"And now my friend is dead because of you," he added.

Keep it on the tech.

Kade shrugged.

"Sorry, I'd argue Pierce was responsible for that. But, okay, you built The Network 3.0, then somehow duct-tape this whole thing together, leaving Owens's profile active, so you can manage it as the Commander?"

"Duct-tape?" Arnold again laughed as if Kade had told him a joke over beers. "Sims, my project was *the* breakthrough. The program stays alive and builds on the knowledge put into it. You're not going to kill this thing. You think you have me surrounded? Surprise, The Network surrounds *you*. One simple rule is paramount: succession. The Network will survive."

Planarian.

Arnold's project tied it all together.

Kade gave Arnold a disappointed look.

"So, you're pretending to be Owens in the Commander role, using copies of his logs, and pulled a memory of something that happened to me in his office."

"Nope. That's where something beautiful happened. I'm not pretending, just assisting. Owens finished his mindware project when he got cancer. His personality and life were stored on multiple servers and moved to multiple sites. I added an AI platform to access the mindware."

"Nah . . . ," Kade said.

"Yeah," Arnold said. "The AI works between the profile, the mindware, and The Network. Not elegantly, but it works."

Kade acted impressed, but, in truth, part of him was.

"Damn."

Arnold's hand gestures became more animated.

292

"See, you say *fake* AI. I say *fuck* AI—fuck AI just for AI's sake," he said. "Our survival instinct drove our brain's development. How The Network tries *to survive on its own* is *the* breakthrough. Everything else comes from that. We have a computer starting to write, test, and accept new code. No one is going to catch us. If you're first to market in having automated development, guess what? You win."

He's right, I think.

"So, what comes next?" Kade asked.

"What comes next?" Arnold paused to laugh. "What comes next is I outmaneuver your ass, Sims. Look, I haven't spoken with my daughter for eight years. We're estranged. I love her, but . . ."

"Sorry to hear—"

"No, don't play that shit with me, man." Arnold turned his computer around so Kade could see the screen. "You see, I always have a countermove."

The invisible space between Kade's stomach and heart voided as if he'd stepped off a ten-meter diving platform.

The picture was of Lin in a hospital bed, he was fairly certain.

"What's this?" Kade asked.

"It's your little sweet-piece-of-ass informant, if you don't recognize her face. We have more than enough friends in the Shanghai Municipal Health Bureau, and I had to ask around a bit to find her. But we found her."

Kade pretended to be only curious.

"Oh, Lin Soon's in the hospital?"

"Yeah, still recovering. Oh, wait. The CIA didn't get her out? Tough call . . . tough call. Must be great to work for them."

Kade's throat tightened and his body flared with unseen heat despite having been frigid for hours.

"What does *she* have to do with anything?"

"She has to do with you, shithead. See, you're not going to get everything you want, and you're going to say that's okay because all I have to do is . . ." Arnold pulled the computer back and spoke as he typed.

TA>> Go ahead and push her an embolism.

"No, stop!" Kade said.

Arnold covered his eyes and used a crying voice.

"Oh! Should I not hit Send? That's just precious . . ."

Kade chewed the inside of his cheek while Arnold laughed again.

Crazy, immature, sick fuck.

"Yeah." Arnold erased what he'd typed with the backspace key. "I knew that girl would end up being bad news. She was never anything but problems for Tan Liang, but I had to make nice with the family to get what we needed. Owens and Zao thought it was a good idea to put her through the Oregon associate program instead of the Shanghai program. So he made her an offer, gave her the choice as a good gesture to his business partner. I was like, dude, that's not a—"

The room lights turned off.

Arnold looked up at the ceiling. Only the glow from his notebook computer and a pale orange light over the door illuminated the room. A few seconds later, the room brightened again.

Kade smiled inside. It was a deliberate signal that had been planned, but he wasn't sure if it would ever come.

The RT knows where I am and is coming to get me.

A signal chirped on Arnold's two-way radio, and he pulled it to his ear.

"Yeah, what's up?"

Arnold looked at Kade while listening.

"Okay, stand by." Arnold pushed his chair back and walked to the other side of the room. For the next five minutes, he typed on his notebook and mumbled to himself.

A Guardian opened the door and poked his head in the room.

"Sir, do you have a moment?"

"I know. Give me ten minutes," Arnold said.

"I recommend we—"

"Ten minutes. Have my detail wait out there."

The door shut and Arnold let out a ragged laugh.

"Always something new with you, Sims. They told me they removed all of your clothes. Checked you for devices. Switched your vehicles and routes. But somehow you still brought company."

Kade shrugged. "I followed your instructions to a T."

"Doesn't matter . . ." Arnold hit the Enter key with a flourish. "Your effort's going to be for naught. The Network perceived a threat before I even saw it, and it's already switching nodes. We always assume our sites can come under attack. Looks like it's a good time for you to make a deal so you at least get a stalemate out of this."

"And what deal's that?"

"I agree to exchange you for my daughter. You're going to email your bosses and tell them I want free passage for my daughter and me. They back off all of their men to a two-mile radius, including whoever is in the building right now. There will be no helicopters, planes, or shit like that."

What's his play? If we found him, he's got nowhere to go.

"And if I decline?" Kade asked.

"If you don't, your lover-girl will die from a sudden medical complication."

Kade looked down for a moment.

Counteroffer.

"You give me the admin code, then talk me through removing my review countdown, and removing you from The Network."

"Nah," Arnold said. "If any of us give up the code, we're dead, so, sorry, that's not an option."

Kade wondered how The Network would know if you gave up the code, but couldn't worry about that now.

How can I do the most damage?

"Make me part of the exec group, then."

"Sorry," Arnold said. "The program's smart enough on its own not to allow that. The program has you flagged for removal following review. But I'll cancel your review, then remove myself from The Network. I'll set your removal effective one hour after mine."

"No, you cancel my review, effective now, then I stay on The Network to ensure you're taken off. And I want to watch what you're typing in."

Arnold weighed this for a few seconds, typed something, then pushed his boot heel on the floor and spun his chair around so Kade was beside him.

"Okay."

He accessed Kade's profile and began banging a number of commands into the keyboard to jump through different menus until he came to *Member Review*. The *Review* box turned gray when he clicked on *Disable*.

Arnold pointed a handheld control at Kade's eye level to log him in. Within seconds, his countdown clock disappeared.

"Okay, your reviews are removed," Arnold said.

Whew.

"Good," Kade said. "Taking you off The Network is next."

Arnold hit a few keys, and Kade had a two-second look at the Commander view and main screen before Arnold dove into a PERSONNEL function menu.

"Who's the Commander's assistant after you remove yourself?"

Arnold shook his head.

"Wouldn't you like to know?" he said. "Okay, you can see here on my screen—my profile is confirmed removed."

The computer had an infrared adapter sticking out of its USB port. Arnold pointed the handheld controller at it and back at Kade's face again.

"Now look at me," Arnold said.

This time, TIMOTHY ARNOLD no longer appeared in Kade's vision.

"Now you can go ahead and send that email for the exchange," Arnold said. He drew his pistol before releasing the straps on Kade's arms and setting the computer on his lap.

Kade glanced to the side of the computer screen to think for a second and noticed something.

On the floor, moving, something about an inch high.

A microbot. One of the scouts with a camera.

How the hell did that get in here?

When the Guardian had the door open.

"Hurry up," Arnold said.

Kade held up a finger.

"Hold on one minute," he enunciated. "It's not easy to write under pressure."

Kade typed in a representation of Arnold's demands and angled the computer so Arnold could review it.

"Here," Kade said.

Arnold scanned the three paragraphs.

"Okay, send it."

"Sending it . . ." Kade looked at the microbot. "Now."

A few seconds after Kade hit the Enter button, a string of muted gunshots sounded from outside.

Two agitated Sentries burst into the room and shut the door behind them.

"What now?" Arnold said.

"We shut the security door, but we've got enemy down the hall," one said. "Our teams are going blind, one by one, and then they pick us off."

Arnold looked toward the door and frowned.

"Son of a *bitch*!" He stomped in place on the ground and there was a crunching sound. "Come this way, guys. Do *not* turn toward the door."

Arnold ran toward the door and stomped a few more times.

"What are these, Sims?" he yelled.

Kade didn't respond.

Arnold grabbed the notebook computer away from Kade and tapped a few commands in. He raised the handheld device at the Sentries.

"Turn around," he said. "I'm deactivating your receivers."

Kade reached down to see if he could unfasten the leg straps.

"Hands up!" Arnold shouted. "Bind his hands again."

The Sentries pulled Kade to his feet, zip-cuffed his hands behind him. They met Arnold on the other side of the room for a whispered huddle.

A few more gunshots reverberated from outside.

A burning smell started to fill the room. Arnold tossed the computer he was using into a large bin, followed by four servers he removed from a nearby rack.

A Sentry snapped a nylon dog collar around Kade's neck with a leash attached.

"Let's take our hostage for a walk," Arnold said.

The three kept pistols at the ready as they moved Kade out of the room and down the hall to another galvanized steel door. Arnold punched a code on the inside and spun a wheel to retract the door's bolts.

Eight Sentry bodies lay in the security room in front of them. A few microbots moved on the floor space.

The main door to the security room remained open, and in the corridor that opened into the tunnel wall, two men crouched behind Kevlar shields.

* * *

"Tell your men to stand down and leave the premises, per your message, or it's no deal," Arnold said.

Yang stood with his rifle aimed at Arnold. Kade imagined Yang was ready and willing to take a headshot.

"Stand down, guys," Kade said. "They're exchanging me."

"You sure?" Yang shouted.

"Yeah, that's the plan. You guys did what you needed to do."

"We're making our own exit," Arnold said. "I don't know which way you fools came in, but we're going to watch you all leave through the main entrance because it's the only one lighted right now."

"Is that okay with you, Mr. Smith?" Yang said.

"Yeah."

"All right, we'll see ya later," Yang said.

Yang and the others backed away. When they were out of sight, Arnold continued to watch their movement toward the exit on the surveillance camera before turning to Kade and palm-smacking him in the head.

"Change into their pants and get a jacket on." He pointed to the dead Sentries spread throughout the room. "Take your pick."

One Sentry remained near Kade with a pistol aimed while he put on the clothes. The other moved back into the other room to confer with Arnold.

Kade stood and eyed the series of surveillance screens, triggered by the movement of Yang's team at a slow jog. The Sentry yanked on his leash hard, pulled him away.

"Get the jacket on."

Kade zipped up one of the ski jackets he'd removed from a corpse, one with only two bullet holes in it.

Arnold and the Sentry returned, flashlights gleaming in front of them.

"Let's go," Arnold said.

They pushed Kade in front and forced him to move at a hard stride down an unfinished corridor gouged out of rock. Arnold commanded Kade to make several turns before ordering the group to halt and telling one of the Sentries to unfasten Kade's leash.

A stench filled the moist air, one that Kade had only smelled a few times in his life.

Human decay.

"This is where the disloyal Chapter members meet their end," Arnold said. "There's a two-foot-wide walk on the right. If you don't stay on it, you're going down the shaft. Watch me."

Arnold strolled across the edge against the wall as though he did it every day.

"Sentries next," Arnold said. He kept the flashlight pointed at the ledge.

The Sentries followed at a creep.

"Let's go, Sims."

Kade shuffled across, careful with his footing because of his ill-fitting shoes.

When he reached the middle, the flashlights clicked off.

"Hey!" he yelled.

"Sims, you listen to me good," Arnold said. "You're not the only guy with the tricks today. If you renege on me, you're dead."

"I won't, I swear."

The decay smell drawn up the shaft by an unseen air gradient made him woozy. He wasn't afraid of heights, but an open mineshaft was something horribly new.

The flashlight clicked on again, and he didn't need to be told to move.

Another two-minute walk brought them to a break in the rock wall and a cage elevator. They climbed in and Arnold picked up what looked like an old sound-powered wire telephone. He cranked the handle and gave the command, "Okay, bring us down."

The elevator rumbled and the rock face moved up beside them. The descent was less than a minute, ending in a well-lit cavern the size of a standard gymnasium. About thirty men armed with M4/AR-15 semiautomatic rifles checked equipment.

Reserve force?

Two Caterpillar bulldozers and two Ford F-150 pickup trucks with jagged-treaded tires were parked on the far end. An opening had been rapidly cleared of rocks, dirt, and snow. Sunlight streamed in from a patch of blue sky.

A Sentry DOUSTI led Kade to one of the pickups, dropped the tailgate, and pushed him into it. A Barrett .50-caliber rifle lay on the bed liner with its custom mount bolted into the center.

Dousti pointed to one of the metal mesh seats next to the wheel well utility box.

"Sit there."

Kade slid into a seat and Dousti took the other, across from him. From the utility box on his side, Dousti removed two extra clips and an additional ten-round magazine for the .50-cal.

Four Sentries occupied the other truck—two in front and two in the bed seats. The same gun mount poked up in the center. The truck's side panels looked fat, and he guessed these two had some extra layers of armor.

I hope the Recovery Team came prepared.

Arnold finished his review of the Sentry group, using the handheld infrared controller on each of them to impart some command, and came toward the pickup.

He figured out the infrared vulnerability . . . now he has some countermeasure.

Arnold gave Kade a cold glance on the way to the passenger seat.

"Showtime," he said.

The trucks edged up behind the dozers as they pushed out the opening and plowed a pathway. In the distance, a Cessna aircraft poked out of a hangar. A taxi path had already been cleared out to a plowed airstrip.

The group followed the dozers to the airstrip and then left the site behind, driving in a column. Kade's face and ears stung in the cold.

The airstrip stretched on a plateau and ended at the bluffs where they had exited the complex. They drove a circuitous path on the edge of a draw, around the mountain to the upper plateau, and as they gained elevation, a cluster of permanent and temporary buildings came into view.

The convoy came to a brief stop at a well-plowed road showing its wet, recently salted asphalt. Arnold was making a phone call. When he turned and looked back at Kade through the cab window, Kade stared back.

I don't like the way he's looking at me.

There's a plane ready to go on the airstrip.

Fresh Sentries in reserve.

Sniper-caliber rifles in the trucks.

The two trucks began moving again. They passed several large buildings on their left, and, to their right, horizontal striations in the snow-covered rock and idle equipment indicated mining activity.

As the column descended the main road leaving the complex, an increasing amount of evergreens peppered the landscape. Kade didn't see any more trailers.

Two miles.

What's Arnold's play?

Take everyone out during the exchange?

Lamb would have his own firepower, but even with robust rules of engagement, he'd be cautious with Kade's life at stake.

Kade doubted Tameka Arnold would be offered in exchange. Such an arrangement seemed too much of a gray area, even for Lamb.

What's Arnold's play?

He'll stand off, at a long distance, like a half mile. Ask Tameka to come forward. Any variance from that, all bets will be off.

And I'll be dead.

My team must know this possibility.

Sentry Dousti looked out ahead of the truck with binoculars when the angle of the road permitted. Kade leaned back to take a look and thought he could see a cluster of vehicles about a mile down the road at a road pull-off.

Dousti rapped his knuckles on the cab window and motioned with his palm to slow their speed.

In another thirty seconds, the trucks reached a gradual turn at a vantage point about two hundred feet higher in elevation than the RT group down the road.

Four black SUVs waited there, next to an olive-green off-road RV with six wheels and two rectangular windows on the side.

Friendly sniper positions?

I'm going walk all the way down there without getting shot?

Forget it.

I have to get away. Get separation. Give our guys a clean shot.

Sentry Dousti knocked on the window again.

"Up ahead, where the trees come close to the road is perfect," he shouted through the crack.

Dousti is calling the shots 'cause he'll be taking the shots.

When they began to slow their speed, Kade took a quick glance over his shoulder at the roadside snowbank while Dousti leaned down to do something with the rifle. The looped end of Kade's neck leash was gripped in Dousti's hand with the binoculars, but it wasn't looped around his wrist.

Kade yawned, dipped his chin to his chest, took the leash in his mouth, bit it hard.

He kicked Dousti in the near shoulder with his boot and stood up. The leash was free.

Dousti went for his holstered pistol. "Sit down!"

Kade pivoted and leapt from his left leg, off the still-moving truck, diving over the crest of the roadside snowbank behind him.

He landed over his shoulder, tumbled on the far side, and log-rolled down to the bottom.

He made an attempt at slipping or breaking the zip cuffs but failed. Using his shoulder and elbow, he turned the other direction and moved like an inchworm in the snow, as fast as he could.

He heard a *beep-beep-beep* tapping on a horn in the distance, and a minute or two later, the sound of a truck returning.

Keep going.

"Sims!" someone yelled, probably Dousti. "Sims!"

Keep going.

He wasn't sure what happened next.

Snow buried him. Dazed, with a few seconds of lost consciousness, he couldn't breathe under the tremendous weight. He tried moving his head but could only move a few inches each direction. Silence also enclosed him.

His hands were still bound behind him. When he tried to move them, his fingertips scraped snow.

Can't dig, can't dig.

He kicked his legs, and the snow moved some. He wiggled; his right foot felt free but he couldn't move toward it. With some kicking, his leg below the knee felt free.

He kept kicking, but either from lack of air or from exertion, he was losing consciousness.

Someone grabbed his boot and tugged it.

CHAPTER 56

Butte, Montana

Sunday, December 18

6:12 p.m. (MST)

MIT was down 5–8 at the half against the US Coast Guard Academy, and Coach Prentice called on the midfielders to create offensive opportunities.

Storming back onto the field, Kade delivered with three face-off wins that created fast breaks and assisted on two goals by passing to the attack posted on the side of the crease.

On the next possession, he caught the defense cheating to cover the attack and took a shot from ten yards out. That one felt good—high and hard. The goalie didn't have a chance.

Now, with a few minutes left in the third quarter, it was all even at 8–8. The momentum was on his team's side, but there was still plenty of game left to play.

He had scooped up a loose ball and was sprinting down the field, but heard the referee's whistle.

What was that for?

The referee was . . . Summerford?

She approached, put her hand on his shoulder and shook it violently.

"Kyle . . . Kyle."

"What?"

He opened his eyes. The nightstand beside his bed had an LED alarm clock and a phone next to it with labeled buttons, lighted by the lamp hanging on the wall.

Now he remembered. Summerford had booked him a room at a Hometown Suites after he had been treated and released from St. John's Hospital in Butte. She had been waking him up every few hours due to the concussion he'd sustained.

"How are you doing?"

He grunted and looked up. There was comfort in seeing her encouraging face and sensing her steady strength.

"All right, I think. Headache's getting better."

"Lamb's coming by in a bit to talk. This room has been screened for devices. Once you're rested enough and have a debrief, he's going to send you back east for some time off. Sorry we couldn't answer your questions in the hospital."

Kade wasn't going to argue about rest or anything else. His body and mind had taken a pounding, and he was happy to be alive and warm. He'd been told everything had gone well in the general sense, but that was all.

There was one thing bothering him, though.

"When I was with Pierce, he said Carla—Carla Singleton—was helpful. I think we need to be concerned about her."

Summerford sat on the bed.

"Kyle, she was targeted by The Chapter. They forced their way into her apartment and threatened her. Assaulted her. That was before the statue incident. She isn't with them. She's been moved into a safer role. That's all I can say right now. Pierce was correct in that they got some information out of her, but it came with much resistance."

He rolled on his back and stretched.

Everyone breaks.

"Okay."

"Anything else I can do for you right now?" she asked.

"No. Thanks for watching me."

"You're welcome," she said. "When you get a chance, watch CNN . . . the story on Li Chonglin."

When Summerford left, Kade got out of bed and watched a round of CNN news while stretching. The story segment she had mentioned made him scramble for the remote to turn up the volume when he recognized Li Chonglin's face.

He was the man in the club who had bothered Lin. The man in the picture on Summerford's iPad.

The female news correspondent said Chonglin was arrested for allegedly trafficking vials containing the rhinovirus responsible for the current cold outbreak. An official photo showed Chonglin as working for the Chinese embassy. In another photo, Chonglin was walking, carrying fishing gear at Lake Bernard Frank. The vials were inside his tackle box, which was seized.

* * *

Kade had showered and dressed in sweats when Lamb arrived. They sat at the small kitchen table and Kade picked a wax-paper-wrapped turkey sandwich out of the few options Lamb had brought.

"So, what happened to me exactly?" Kade asked.

"We were watching you up to the exchange and sensed you were in danger. When you jumped off the truck, there was enough separation that we took their trucks out. You were outside of the blast radius and on the other side of the snowbank, so the CINC approved the strike, and we made the call. That's about all I can say."

Kade nodded. It had to have been hellfires on drones. Probably the right call, but it was aggressive.

"Arnold is off the board?" Kade said.

"Yes," Lamb said. "Along with a large number of Sentries and some Guardians. We sent in more forces once you were out."

Kade stuck a straw in his Sprite and drew a deep sip. He had to ask about the part disturbing him.

"The Tameka video . . . she was actually *hurt* for this?"

"No, not at all," Lamb said. "It was a quick production video with some special effects. Tameka volunteered to do an excellent acting job. We were never going to exchange her. We had an African-American agent at the ready to make it seem that way at long distance, if we needed."

"Oh."

"With the weaponry Arnold was bringing, we assumed he was trying to attempt a snatch, not an exchange. He had a plane ready . . . we think he intended to collect Tameka and fly to Canada. An ad hoc plan."

"What about his son?" Kade asked.

"Not as high priority, I suppose."

"This attack had to damage them badly," Kade said. "I mean, they can't have many more hubs like that one, if any."

"We believe it's a blow for sure, and we're still analyzing the site. We're going to keep searching to find other hubs and members of the exec group. The CINC is pleased they're greatly weakened and on the move."

"I hope the Chinese support has been severed."

"The CINC is working on that aspect and the linkages. As for you, I suggest you take an early holiday break and we'll call you if we need you. Your health is most important."

"Okay."

Lamb's eyes became downcast and his chin flexed. Kade noticed he hadn't joined him in eating anything.

"I also have some bad news I have to deliver," Lamb said and compressed his lips. "Now that I know you're well enough to hear it."

The words pulled the drain plug in Kade's reserve of hope.

"Yeah?"

"Lin Soon died yesterday. I'm so sorry, Kyle."

CHAPTER 57

Hominy Creek, West Virginia
Wednesday, December 21
1:10 p.m. (EST)

The remaining three Chapter exec group members—Connor Jordan, Lindsay Gill, and Raymond Jeffries—escorted by six Guardians, arrived on foot at the underground survival shelter, one of four stretching between West Virginia, Missouri, Colorado, and Nevada. Personal mobile-connected devices had been stored in a cache miles away.

Unlike other Chapter safe houses, the site had no phone or Internet. The functional layout accommodated up to a dozen comfortably. The exec group and Guardians each shared a separate twenty-by-twenty common room with bunk pods radiating from it. Electricity flowed from a solar-charged bank of twelve-volt batteries, and a propane tank could provide heat for a few weeks if used conservatively.

Jordan, the ranking member, booted up the notebook computer he'd brought in his backpack and attached an infrared reader. Gill and Jeffries warmed themselves around the table with coffee and got reacquainted.

When they were ready, the three shut their door and sequestered themselves while the Guardians took inventory of the small-arms and ammunition.

"Let's start with the exec updates," Jordan said. "I've confirmed through various messages that coordinated attacks have hit Chapter facilities in Shanghai and Idaho. Joshua Pierce, Timothy Arnold, and Zao Hong have been killed, and their profiles removed from The Network."

"Oh God," Jeffries said.

"I knew it had to be serious for us to be ordered here," Gill said. She removed the hairband from her side braid, unwound it, and shook out her auburn hair.

"Kade Sims was part of the attack on the Shanghai fab," Jordan said. "He was captured and then rescued."

"First, he was with the FBI. Now, we think the CIA," Jeffries said.

"We know they have a specialized unit targeting us," Jordan said. "Now we have to find it. Here, let's get started."

Jordan synced each of them up to the update downloads with the infrared control.

"We're switching from name identification to alphanumeric identification," Jordan said.

"A program security enhancement?" Gill asked.

"Yes," Jordan said. "We want to reduce the chance of our member list being hacked and exploited. Everyone has been issued an alphanumeric ID, and that will propagate through The Network as everyone logs in."

"Good idea," Jeffries said. "Has a new chief technology officer been identified?"

"Yes," Jordan said. "The Commander profile has a technical assistant assigned, working with the new CTO, and is prepping a new operating location. But until that transition occurs, we're going to have to focus more on kinetic and less on cyber."

"What's the extent of the damage on Idaho?" Gill asked.

"Green Mountain is effectively shut down. Ninety-three Sentries and seven Guardians were killed in a federal paramilitary raid. Those few who got away weren't witnesses to the attack."

"That's terrible," Gill said.

"It's a painful blow," Jordan said. "But there's some good news out of it. The Network wasn't compromised in any way. Arnold shut it down. I think he suspected Green Mountain was in the crosshairs. Succession plans were carefully updated."

"How extensively do we backfill our China presence?" Jeffries asked.

"We knew the China operations would wind down," Jordan said, "but we didn't expect that for another six to twelve months. A Sentry force is protecting the remaining chipsets and designs until we can get that intellectual property back to us. Ray, work on a list of recommended replacements in key roles."

"Will do," Jeffries said.

"We still have enough physicians to continue implant procedures," Gill said.

"Good," Jeffries said. "Cash flow remains strong. We received a hundred-million-dollar payment for the virus attack, and we get a percentage going forward of increased pseudoephedrine sales through the end of the outbreak. There's no problem keeping the lights on."

"The outbreak will get worse for another thirty days, at least," Gill said. "Then trend downward for the next two months."

"The overall timing's perfect," Jordan said. "The whole purpose of the attacks—the virus, our subversive activities—was to pave the way for the political strike. We're going to make that happen. FreedomYield liaisons have briefed our supporters on next steps, and everyone is on the same page."

They sat in silence for a moment. The resolute boldness was a unique kind of Chapter magic, strengthened by each other.

"It's up to us to restore the exec group and The Network," Jeffries said, putting an unlit cigarette in his mouth. His gaze lingered on Gill, imagining what he would be doing with her in this bunker bed-and-breakfast if the others weren't around. It had been weeks.

"I think we need a hard counterpunch," Gill said. "Something to leave them reeling."

"I agree," Jordan said. He popped open a bottle of small-batch bourbon and poured three glasses. "Greer's going to feel the heat, starting January third. But for immediate kinetic strikes, let's talk targets."

CHAPTER 58

Lin had reportedly died from a heart attack while recovering at a Shanghai hospital. There weren't any further details, but Kade believed Tim Arnold had carried out his threat, ordering her murder by air embolism before removing himself from The Network.

She died hoping to come back to the States. That hope was used to manipulate her.

I manipulated her.

With the Recovery Team's permission and his debrief complete, Kade retreated to his grandmother's house again. He told her he'd lost a close friend, and she'd graciously allowed him to waste most of each day in her guest bed for as long as he needed. She said he was on her special prayer list.

A wildfire of anger and sadness burned through him, leaving black numbness behind. This familiar weight of emptiness marked the rarer depressed side to his hypomania, which he hadn't felt since the months following his army discharge.

Regular carbamazepine brought his mind back to a low boil, but his body remained robbed of energy through that week. Both Lamb and Summerford checked in on him via phone, and while he pretended to be okay, he was grateful not to have been tasked with anything at the moment. The Recovery Team had prevailed in a series of battles and was searching for the next opportunity to press the attack.

He'd done his job, but it didn't make him feel much better.

The beginning of family festivities on Christmas Eve helped snap him out of the stupor. His aunt Whitney, sister, Janeen, and cousin, Greg, showed up in the morning as they had done for Thanksgiving, taking precautions recommended by the FBI.

Kade had eaten a late breakfast and was taking a break from playing computer games with Greg, when the major news networks all carried a breaking story.

As he watched, the circuit breaker in his brain flipped all the switches back on.

Citing unnamed FBI sources, the report said the FBI had conducted multiple drone missile attacks and ground raids directed against a potential terrorist cell based inside an Idaho mine.

Heavily edited photos showed dead bodies lying in a hollowed-out cavern. A video clip showed two pickup trucks exploding from apparent missile strikes.

One of those trucks was the one he'd been riding in.

Another clip showed a private airplane taken out on a runway near the mine.

The more graphic, unedited versions of the pictures and video now were circulating on social media news.

Who leaked this? The good guys or the bad guys?

Kade scooted forward on the carpet to within inches of the TV while the clips ran over and over. The truck footage looked as though it had been recorded from about a half mile away. From that distance and resolution, it was impossible to see any Chapter weaponry or distinguish the individuals sitting in the back, including him.

The majority of analysts and pundits commented that the action had to be unnecessary overreach by an overmilitarized government and were astounded the public had no knowledge of the attack. A smaller slice questioned if this might have been appropriate, swift action. Could it have been a threat from The Chapter?

A calm, undaunted President Greer gave a three-minute press conference and didn't take questions afterward. He confirmed that a "federal task force" had neutralized and arrested several active terrorist cells located in "a number of Idaho mines." He did not clarify the threat, only saying that it was "homegrown." The cells, he said, were armed with heavy, illegal weaponry and showed no willingness to surrender to the authorities. He alone had approved the drone strikes. The conference closed with his saying, "Our ongoing antiterror operations are being conducted with an appropriate level of secrecy in order to keep America safe."

Wow.

"What do you make of that?" Janeen asked from somewhere behind him. She had changed to an online college program so she wouldn't have a physical residence or classroom location at the UMass Amherst campus. Kade still felt guilty about it—a consequence of her involvement in the previous operation.

"I think Greer knows what he's doing," he answered, "especially when—"

Kade paused. A familiar face came on the screen as the national newsbreak switched to the local news.

Senator-elect Terrence Hawkins now took the opportunity to criticize President Greer.

"President Greer has it all *backward*," Hawkins said from the news studio couch. "We have a belligerent China who, by many accounts, attacked America with a bioagent and we're too afraid to do anything about it. Yet, you'd think the *inside* of America is a war zone by the way he's using federal power as judge, jury, and executioner. I'm all for domestic strength, but we must reserve military weaponry for nothing but the most imminent threats. And attacking our own citizens with no due process is a high crime."

Kade hung on a two-word trigger.

Domestic strength.

The last time Kade had heard that phrase was inside AgriteX. It had been transmitted in many Chapter propaganda downloads.

Monies had been filtered through a Domestic Strength Coalition into shell companies, which would then fund political action committees.

Hawkins finished by saying he was looking forward to being sworn in on January third so he could make a difference.

Kade made a growling noise.

No.

The anchor's final comment mentioned Hawkins was headed to the Cambridge Galleria to present the Salvation Army with a donation check, along with all the nonperishable food his new staff had collected.

Is a member of The Chapter being sworn in to the Senate?

There's one way to find out . . .

The Galleria was downtown, right next to his alma mater, MIT. He knew the layout well.

He sprung up and turned to Janeen.

"I'm headed into the city. Tell everyone I'll be back for dinner, if they ask."

Janeen grabbed the hood of Kade's hoodie and pulled him backward.

"To do what?" she asked.

He smiled and countered with a playful tug on her braid. "To make a donation."

During the drive, he thought more about the political objectives of The Chapter. Greer's public strategy to rake up Chapter activities into a terrorism pile allowed him to be agile as CINC, but it wasn't an accurate description of what The Chapter was doing. Their leadership wouldn't order a public bombing or shooting.

So what *were* they doing?

I need to check in with Alex.

He contacted Alex through voice chat and was lucky to get him a few minutes later.

"How you doing, bro?" Alex answered.

"Okay, man," Kade said. "Merry Christmas."

"Same to you. Are you . . . able to get together sometime over the holidays?"

"Yeah, maybe," Kade said. "Hey, hate to talk shop for a few minutes, and I know this sounds random, but when you get a little downtime, can you take a look at a company called Rare Earth Metals Corporation out of Idaho and any connections to China? Specifically Shanghai, if possible?"

"Nothing's ever random with you," Alex said.

"Touché."

"Something related to the news today?" Alex asked.

"Meh . . ."

"Okay, I gotcha. You know, China owns about ninety percent of the rare earth's market."

"Yeah, I knew they were big," Kade said. "That's about all I know, though."

"I've looked at this sector before. China drove some US companies out of the market by keeping their pricing artificially low, but they're having difficulty sustaining that. I'll do some digging."

"Dig like a backhoe."

"You calling me a hoe?"

Kade laughed. "Yeah."

"Hey, by the way," Alex added, "you know that Chinese gray market pharma we talked about?"

"Yeah?"

"I've kept tracking it since you asked, and that whole super-cold going around, which I got, by the way—congestion was fucking horrible. Anyway, it all seems to have helped that company you mentioned, China North Chemical."

"Really?"

"Yeah, the whole run on cold medicine with pseudoephedrine in it. They're a top producer. Maybe a black and gray market play in the raw material. No evidence, of course, just reading between the lines."

Kade thought of the poppy-heroin-oxycodone example Alex had walked through before.

"You mean black market meth."

"Yeah, it's possible," Alex said. "And then gray market pseudo sold out of places like Canada and Mexico. But get this: I did a review of CNC's most profitable products for the last few years. By far, their most profitable has been recombinant Factor Eight. They control almost the entire market, though Bayer just made a recent investment in it."

"What's that?"

"Factor Eight is a blood product. I talked to a friend, and he said all the prices for blood products, like plasma, are going through the roof. It's because the whole vCJD mad cow marker tainted the blood supply, even though it's harmless. Now, plasma-based Factor Eight supply has dried up, leaving the genetically engineered recombinant Factor Eight in critical demand."

"What are docs and hospitals doing?" Kade asked.

"There's a diagnostic test for the marker, so they're now forced to screen for it because of CDC guidelines. If it tests positive, the blood can't be used. And the kicker is this: guess who owns the market in the diagnostic tests?"

"No way."

"Yes—China North Chemical owns that, too. So, they have the blood products, the blood tests, and the pseudo. A trifecta, I'd say. I have to believe that's why their stock is up about twenty-five percent. It's going to be a great year."

"Dude, you're brilliant. Thanks."

"Beer, then—soon, okay?"

"Yeah, bud, soon. Bye."

* * *

Kade took the escalator up to the second level of the Cambridge Galleria. The horde of last-minute shoppers streaming by and bumping shoulders made movement slow, but at least it wasn't the Shanghai subway.

People surrounded an event area with an enormous Christmas tree, a string quartet onstage, and a Salvation Army booth. When Kade moved near enough to see, he cursed himself.

Oh, Kade, you're an absolute bonehead.

Timothy Arnold had removed him from the Chapter Network. He no longer showed a display.

So he wouldn't get a display pop-up confirmation if Hawkins was in The Chapter.

What were you thinking?

Terrence Hawkins stood in the rear of the stage until a representative of the Salvation Army introduced him over the PA system. Four members of his staff surrounded him, not looking so festive in their dark suits.

Hawkins began speaking about the money he'd helped raise for this holiday campaign, when, a minute into his spiel, he stopped midsentence.

He was looking right at Kade. Was it coincidence?

Could he be recognized?

I'm in disguise and no longer on The Network. He can't know who I am.

Terrence leaned away from the mic, still looking at Kade, and spoke a word to a staffer.

Kade started backing away.

Something's not right. Did they leave me in there as an alert? Readjust the algorithm?

Pierce, Tan, or Arnold could've applied a change . . .

Those staffers moved offstage as Hawkins smiled and resumed talking.

Once Kade had broken free of the ring of observers, he ran, pushing people out of the way as needed.

He opted for the stairs adjacent to the nearest escalator and glided down the steps, two at a time. Changing directions, he dashed into a Macy's and took the exit inside that was closest to the parking garage.

Three minutes later, he was back inside his rental Nissan Altima, weaving around cars and searching for parking spaces to reach the ramp.

He slid on sunglasses as he emerged from the street-level exit. When he turned the corner and rolled up to a stop sign, a man from Hawkins's detail stood on the grassy divider between two parking lots, phone pressed to his ear.

The man reached into the left side of his blazer.

Kade popped the release on his seat belt and reached inside his own coat for his gun. Lamb's admin had sent his Glock, reissued permits, and even ammo back to his home via courier, thank God.

But Hawkins's man didn't draw. Kade ran the stop sign and watched in his rearview mirror until he was back on Memorial Drive and out to Route 90.

He noticed he had a voice chat message from Alex.

"Hey, letting you know Carla called me. Weird timing, eh? She said she was trying to get ahold of you and I told her I didn't have your number, like you always told me to say. So we—"

The message ended. Kade tried to initiate a voice chat back and there was no response.

He stepped on the gas.

There could've been any number of normal explanations for the message break, but the pit of his stomach and heartbeat defied rational thought.

Pierce had threatened to kill Alex, and he remained a small blip on The Chapter's radar.

Summerford was in D.C. The Recovery Team was out of range. He couldn't request that the FBI agent assigned to his grandma's house go check it out. Calling the Worcester police on a hunch would make him sound crazy.

Am I overreacting?

He tried pinging Alex another dozen times during the next forty-five minutes with no answer. When he reached the residential streets south of Indian Lake, his car careened around the turns at an unsafe speed.

Two police cars with lights flashing were in front of the house. Three officers stood in the driveway. Alex was sitting on the cement, his face buried in his hands.

Emily's black Volvo was there. Bullet holes marked the driver-side door and the window was shattered.

Kade parked on the curb, short of the driveway, and pulled off his shoulder holster. He jogged over, but an officer spotted him and halted him with his palm.

"This is an active crime scene."

* * *

Two hours later, when Kade visited Alex at the police station, his friend's embrace had no strength behind it. They cried together as Alex recounted what had happened.

By chance, he'd spotted two men on his back porch at the time he'd been chatting with Kade. One of the men outside began to quietly pick the lock and the other looked like he had a gun at his side.

There were only seconds to make *some* kind of decision.

Alex ran to the front of the house, opened the front door and left it ajar to make it appear as if he'd run outside. He then made his way down into the basement as quietly as he could.

Emily had to be warned. Alex texted: DON'T COME HOME—DANGER, dialed 911, and put his phone on silent mode. Leaving the line open would bring the police.

He hid behind the water heater and furnace, inside a storage cabinet, leaving it open a crack so he could hear. One of the men had come down the stairs for a few seconds, maybe for a quick check, and returned to the main floor.

But Emily had pulled in the driveway. Having received Alex's text while she was two minutes from the house, she'd wanted to see what was going on.

She never made it out of the car.

Alex and Emily were to have spent Christmas with her parents. Now she was dead.

Kade knew this was his fault—The Chapter intended to tie off a loose end with Alex, and Emily was an extension of that, or a cruel afterthought.

He should have better anticipated, warned, prepared.

Death and sadness came to those around him. The people he cared about most.

Alex's heart and spirit had been shattered. But inside Kade, an emergency switch tripped. Hateful energy pumped into his body, and his mind had a singular, vengeful purpose.

Summerford and Lamb needed to know immediately.

He would console his friend and have dinner with his own family.

Late tonight, he would find a way back to D.C. He wanted to be ready to go Monday morning.

And, tomorrow, on Christmas Day, he would pay someone an early visit.

CHAPTER 59

Kade waited a few minutes for Ben Singleton to answer the door. At his age and in his condition, mobility would be difficult and painful because of arthropathy.

Arthropathy was the regular joint bleeding caused by hemophilia A.

Kade reintroduced himself and wished Ben a merry Christmas, handing him a palm-sized box containing a Bass Pro Shops gift card. Kade had learned Ben was an avid fisherman from meeting him twice.

Singleton accepted the gift, showing some surprise.

"Thank you, Kyle . . . Merry Christmas to you, too."

"Do you mind if I come in for a moment?" Kade asked.

There was hesitation, as Kade expected, but then Singleton stepped to the side.

"Sure."

A small artificial Christmas tree glowed in the corner of the spartan living room. Singleton set the gift down on the table and took a seat on the couch. Kade sat beside him so he could see his face close up.

They made small talk for a minute until Ben prompted.

"So, Kyle, what brings you around?"

"Well, I haven't spoken with Carla for a while. She changed her number."

"Oh, is that so? I guess I wouldn't know—she puts it in my phone for me."

"Yeah, and she moved, too, and didn't tell me where. But I figured you were still living in the same place."

Ben's eye movements became more severe.

"Is there some sort of a problem?" he asked.

He thinks I'm stalking her.

Kade would've normally been more reluctant to confront someone frail and in their sixties, but not this time.

"I'm not sure, Mr. Singleton. Are you expecting Carla today?"

Ben's voice became stern.

"Why?"

"I was just wondering . . . she's been stressed about your health. The cost of your hemophilia treatment has to be tough, financially."

Ben looked confused.

"Yes, and what does that—?"

"I mean, the cost—the out-of-pocket cost for infusions—must be a lot. What is it now, about a dollar twenty per unit of Factor Eight? And you need somewhere around twenty-five hundred units, every thirty-six to forty-eight hours?"

"I don't see why you—"

"I did that on my calculator. That's like a half-million dollars per year. An unbelievable burden."

Ben's face was turning red, but Kade didn't relent. He was onto something.

"I don't know what you're getting at," Ben said, "but I'd like you to leave."

"Now the Factor Eight price has *quadrupled*," Kade said. "And there's no way you could possibly afford, much less find, Factor Eight because of the current problem with the blood supply. Right?"

Kade shrugged when Ben only stared back at him.

"You asked me why I'm here. Carla helps you with those payments, right?"

"I'm calling the police," Ben said. He picked up his phone and tried to dial, but Kade snatched it from his hand.

"This is crazy!" Ben said. "I want you to leave." He tried to get up, but Kade pushed him back into a sitting position and pulled out his pistol.

"Relax. In fact, why don't you turn on the TV to something you like? I'm just going to sit with you here until Carla arrives, and we'll sort this out, okay?"

"Sort what out?"

Kade ignored the question and didn't speak another word or move from the couch until thirty minutes later, when he heard the door opening and Carla's voice.

"Dad?"

"I'm in here with Kyle Smith! He has a gun!"

Kade now expected to see Carla enter with her weapon drawn, but it wasn't her.

Summerford? Here on Christmas?

"Kyle, put the gun down," Summerford said.

How would they know I was here? I parked a block away.

"No, not until I get some answers." Kade picked up the TV remote in his other hand and powered it off.

"Are you okay, Dad?" Carla asked from behind Summerford.

"Yes, I'm unhurt," Ben said.

"Kyle, what answers do you want?" Summerford asked, edging closer.

Summerford and Carla together? Summerford here on Christmas?

Makes no sense.

"First off, why are *you* here?" he asked Summerford.

"I now get alerts from your phone depending on where you go," she said. "And this one raised a red flag."

"Something isn't right," Kade said. "There've been too many gaps, threats, and attacks."

"You're not making any sense," Summerford said. "What do you mean?"

"What I mean is, the enemy stays on my tail, one step ahead, even with the security we've kept. So, I said to myself, someone else has to be involved. Someone who hasn't been very happy with me. Someone who was threatened by them and was scared into assisting them."

"Kyle, I would never—" Carla began.

"No, it's okay," Summerford said to silence her. "Kyle, listen. Carla agreed to help us. When she was detained by The Chapter, she said she wanted to help the Bureau to hit them back, as you did a few months ago. She felt guilty about the information she'd given them. So, she volunteered and pretended to accept The Chapter recruitment. The situation was messy, and I couldn't tell you about it for obvious reasons."

Kade fell silent at this new wrinkle. Summerford had yanked the carpet out from his conclusion. It explained why he hadn't been given any new information on Carla. Why she had cut off contact. She was being used to . . .

He looked at Summerford.

"Then you knew about that whole weird Thanksgiving meeting in Boston?"

"Yes," Summerford said. "That was planned to bring more of The Chapter into the open and led to a dozen arrests. It was a success."

"I didn't know they'd use your kill code, Kyle," Carla said. "I'm sorry."

"Nice to know I was bait," Kade said. He pushed that disturbing fact aside and moved on to what was bothering him more.

He looked back at Ben. "Mr. Singleton, you haven't been helping The Chapter, have you?"

His voice swelled with emotion.

"No, and I didn't know about Carla being detained."

Then that left one possibility.

"And, Carla, you've cut all interaction with The Chapter?"

"Yes," she said.

"That op is over, Kyle," Summerford added. "She's out. Now put down your gun."

Kade bit his lower lip and lowered his gun, but didn't put it away. He didn't believe Summerford would shoot him unless he took a threatening posture.

"I still have one thing that bothers me," he said.

"What's that?" Summerford asked.

"You ever hear of Project Slammer?" he asked.

"No," Summerford replied.

"It was a study of convicted American spies and their motives. You know what the number three motive for espionage is?"

"No." Summerford's voice.

"Financial need. Especially family expenditures, like college costs . . . or medical bills. Often the need is made worse by other stressors."

"Kyle, no more games," Summerford said. "Get to the point."

"Someone helped The Chapter find Alex, and that was you, Carla, wasn't it?"

Something registered in her eyes.

"No, why? What happened?"

Kade's stare burned into her.

"You got chipped while The Chapter detained you."

There was hesitation.

"What? No, I didn't agree to any chip."

"I didn't ask if you agreed to it, I asked if you got one."

Carla didn't respond.

"Stop threatening her," Ben said and tried to stand.

"Sit down." Kade shoved him back down without taking his eyes off Carla and Summerford.

"Kyle," Summerford said, "you're all over the place. What's going on? This is way over the top."

"Carla's trapped. She was the only person who could've told them where Alex was. Check above her left ear for an incision mark before you call me crazy."

Summerford squinted at him for a moment before she turned to Carla. She brushed aside Carla's hair with her free hand and held it in place.

She looked back at Kade with her mouth agape and nodded.

"I'm sure she doesn't remember the procedure," Kade said. "I didn't."

Carla had already started crying.

"I'm so sorry, Ka—Kyle," she said.

"Yeah, I know you're sorry," Kade said. "I know what the enemy does. And I know you can't talk about it, or the chip they gave you might kill you. You did it for your dad, right?"

Carla nodded.

"If you were killed, then no one would be able to take care of your dad with you gone. No one would be able to help with his treatments. And that scares you more than dying."

She nodded.

"Carla, I—" Ben started, but Kade cut him off.

"You switched your dad's insurance coverage to your own five years ago, making him a dependent. But his treatments maxed out your lifetime cap of one million in just four years."

Ben looked dumbfounded and Carla started sobbing.

"Carla, you never told me this," he said.

"I know."

"Because of the tainted blood supply," Kade said, "Factor Eight is scarce, and the cost has skyrocketed. You had no idea how you could afford keeping your dad alive. That is, until someone from The Chapter offered you all the Factor Eight you need. After they had already broken you down."

She nodded. "Yes."

"In exchange for information, when they asked."

"Yes."

"Carla . . . no," Ben said.

Kade put his hand on Ben's shoulder.

"Yes, sir. I'm sorry. That's *exactly* how The Chapter operates."

Carla had cupped her hands over her eyes.

Kade cleared his weapon of the chambered round and offered it to Summerford, grip first, but she told him to keep it.

He'd never been so torn. Part of him wanted to shoot Carla on the spot. She'd sold him out. Had almost gotten him and Alex killed, and Emily was the innocent victim.

The other part of him wanted to give her a hug. The Chapter had ruthlessly targeted her, and she'd fought back. They'd found the one chink in her armor where she was vulnerable. Her dad.

How many times had he made mistakes? Would he have done the same if one of his family members' lives was at risk?

He looked at Summerford.

"She needs immediate care . . . you know who to call." He was referring to Lamb without speaking his name. "They'll know the best way to take care of the chip, depending on how it's programmed."

"Okay," Summerford said. "I'll call you in an hour."

Kade didn't restrain Ben Singleton from standing this time.

"Carla, what's going on?" Ben said. "Can I help you?"

Kade attempted to console him while Summerford led Carla outside.

"No, sir, you can't help. But she'll get through this. We all will."

The reassurance sounded fake inside his mind, but the discussion had given him another idea—one he'd float by Lamb privately.

There is a way she might still be able to help us.

CHAPTER 60

Aspirance
Washington, D.C.
Monday, December 26
9:35 a.m. (EST)

Congresswoman Lucy Clarke met Connor Jordan in his eighth-floor corner office, which he regularly had swept for listening devices. She was one of the three chipped members of Congress, soon to be joined by four more, for a total of seven.

Clarke set a cube-shaped present on Jordan's desk.

"I brought you a belated gift," she said.

"Oh, really?"

When Jordan opened the box, it was a President Greer bobblehead inside a cage.

"Very nice," Jordan said. "I take it that your conversations with the Judiciary Committee went well?"

"Yes, I'll introduce the two articles of impeachment on Tuesday the third, and they'll be ready for a Committee vote by Thursday the fifth. We expect them to sail through Committee and be voted in the House the following week. Speaker Bostwick is already looking at the draft, and our key influencers have already been urging support."

"Give me the run-through," Jordan said.

"Article One. The president indiscriminately abused power and violated the Fourth, Fifth, Six, and Seventh Amendments of the Constitution through use of excessive force upon American citizens inside the United States, as evidenced by unnecessary military-style missile strikes.

"Article Two. The president did not provide the Congress adequate notification of federal law enforcement activities, and actively concealed and covered up illegal attacks upon American citizens."

Clarke handed Jordan her tablet, which showed a compilation of various video clips that would be made public for the first time as part of an accompanying social media blitz. There was a feed from a ballistic missile used in Oregon leaving an enormous crater and gruesome, charred bodies. Two pickup trucks in Idaho were in motion one second, then, in an instant, boom— destroyed, with body parts scattered in the snow. In a recorded raid, confused security guards clutched their eyes while being shot, some in the back.

"This is beautiful. Definitely meets the 'High Crimes and Misdemeanors' threshold."

"We'll have a majority in the House to impeach. But what about the Senate?"

"Tiffany believes a supermajority will be a challenge," Clarke said. "We anticipate that White House attorneys will argue that Greer's actions were in response to the equivalent to a hostage situation or bomb threat to the public, where deadly force is used immediately, without due process."

Jordan nodded. "It won't matter much. Even without a conviction, he'll be forced to expose and defend his operations, further weakening his ability to govern and allowing us to more easily push our agenda. Aggressive tactics toward us will become impossible for some time while the warmongering president is under a spotlight. And, with all of that, he'll become paralyzed with the Chinese."

Clarke smiled. "We're going to give him a heart attack."

"Damn right," Jordan said. There was a soft chime from his notebook computer, which got his immediate attention. He glanced at the screen and back across the desk at Lucy.

"You're going to have to excuse me for a few minutes," he said.

"No problem," she said.

Jordan reentered a pass code, and a dialogue prompt appeared.

CDR>> Attack order is approved and issued.

CHAPTER 61

Kade met Henderson in the SAU hallway but didn't shake hands. His throat was scratchy when he swallowed, his muscles felt extra heavy, and he had a headache that felt different than the kind he'd learned to ignore from hypomania.

"Don't get close, I think I'm getting the cold."

"Okay, but I've got something to show you in the lab," Henderson said. "About Hawkins."

Kade had briefed the Recovery Team about the Hawkins encounter in Boston.

"You think he recognized me?" Kade asked.

"Oh, that's a given. I'm thinking much bigger than that," Henderson said. "Suppose The Chapter assisted Hawkins in getting elected. Other than funneled campaign contributions, how could they have helped him win?"

"Hmm. Not sure. He was just damn lucky that . . ." Kade stopped in place. "The carjacking. They had something to do with that?"

"Yeah, we think it may have been staged," Henderson said. "Our intel partners got us the unedited version of the YouTube video. We also located the boy who posted the video, and he told us he was paid a hundred dollars to take video—the day before it happened. Watch this part that wasn't online."

Henderson clicked Play and a still frame of the white Hyundai wagon began to move in slow motion. When it entered the traffic circle, instead of picking up the lane, it veered into the circle's interior and ran into a tree, bursting into flames.

"Did you see it?" Henderson asked.

"What?"

Henderson replayed the clip and stopped it. An orange flame and puff of smoke shot up from the engine.

Before it hit the tree.

"Some kind of detonation?" Kade asked.

"Looks like it. The driver sets it off so Hawkins can be the hero saving the occupants. But I don't think the driver expected a struggle from the woman. Maybe why he ended up in that tree. He still got the job done."

Henderson started the clip again, and seconds after the Hyundai hit the tree, a blue Ford Explorer came into view, pulling off inside the circle. Terrence Hawkins leapt out of it and ran toward the wreck. The boy had shot the video from the perfect angle.

This was the video that had gone viral and helped change an election.

Choreographed so it would look random.

"Damn," Kade said. His brain felt warmed up. "What do we do with this?"

The two heard Lamb's voice from behind them and turned.

"I had to tell the CINC about it," Lamb said. "The implications are enormous. He wants to quickly determine if, and by how much, The Chapter has penetrated or coerced Congress. He even has an idea on how to do it, and you are key, Kyle."

"There might be a problem with that," Kade said. "My program was turned off and I'm no longer on The Network. Hawkins recognized *me*, not the other way around. I'm not going to be able to spot other members."

"I have some good news for you," Henderson said. "I can turn your program back on with a simulated profile, so the facial-recognition piece could work. My team has also written some code that disables the ability for the PETN to receive a detonation command. We can implement that too."

Kade wasn't sure if that was a good idea.

"Uh, maybe we should keep things the way they are for a while. No offense, but the last time we messed with the program too much, the whole countdown thing started."

"I know that," Henderson said, "but we've mapped out more of the Guardian program from the Hager chip and applied our code to that. We then tried to make it detonate in every way possible, and couldn't. I think the update will now make you much safer."

When Kade hesitated, Lamb offered an alternative.

"Or now, we have baseline knowledge where we could remove your chip, remove the PETN, and reimplant it. But there's some surgical risk, and your ability to assist will be delayed while you recover."

Kade sighed. He didn't want more surgery, yet.

"Okay, let's do the program update. My database is a few months old," Kade said. "I might not have the current facial data of everyone in The Network in there. But we have someone who would have a current copy—Carla Singleton."

"We still have a challenge there," Henderson said. "That's encrypted data that wipes itself when we mess with it. So, while we try to crack that puzzle, we're dependent on other means of tracking down Chapter members."

Lamb side-motioned with his head.

"She's down in cage number three," Lamb said.

"Carla?" Kade asked.

"Yeah," Lamb said. "The FBI will get her back when we're done questioning her. We weren't sure if her chip might have some kind of transmitter or could modify her behavior."

"Can I go say hello?" Kade asked.

"Uh, no," Lamb said. "We don't want her to know you're here."

"Gotcha."

"We already downloaded her logs," Henderson said, "and we're working on decrypting them." He clicked to the FBI's digital file pertaining to Carla's Chapter detainment and began advancing through the pages of surveillance video thumbnails. "Maybe we should have you read them and see if—"

"Whoa," Kade said. "Click on that thumbnail. What's that from? Who are they?"

"Those are the men who broke into Singleton's apartment," Henderson said. "They were masked, but they didn't put the masks on until they were close to her apartment. The parking lot was well-lit, and the security camera out there got a couple frames."

Kade stopped on a frame where three figures had stepped out of an SUV.

"Can you make that one bigger?"

"Yeah, maybe a little," Henderson said.

The man next to the rear door was frozen in a profile. Even with the image's grainy resolution, his angular good looks were as familiar to Kade as if he'd seen a facial-recognition pop-up.

"I know that guy. He's a Guardian. Jeffries. He was leaving AgriteX when I was going in. Damn, I wish I'd seen this earlier . . . he's got to be high up. Any chance of finding him?"

"We might," Lamb said. "I'll get more assets put on the surveillance review . . . see if we can find a license plate—something to pick up the trail."

Kade imagined a bunch of analysts reviewing live and recorded satellite video to vector in on Jeffries. If that's how they were doing it.

Henderson clicked on the current scorecard of The Chapter's leadership. The lined-through initials had already been taken out.

CDR
OS: ~~JP~~
T: ~~TA~~
P: CJ
M: LG
R: RJ
C: ~~ZH~~

"Jeffries could be CJ or RJ," Henderson said. "Remember his first name?"

"No. But I'll bet he's one of those two," Kade said.

* * *

When Henderson reconnected Kade to the simulated network, the countdown timer didn't reappear, and Kade's acute fear of a sudden pop-up subsided.

332

For five tedious hours, they worked together on updates to the program that would shut down most of its functions, except for the facial recognition.

"I'm confident the PETN trigger is now disabled," Henderson said.

"I'm going to abide by the power threshold guidelines just in case."

"No offense taken."

Trevor Mitchell whistled as he entered the computer lab with LJ Yang behind him. Yang slapped Kade a handshake, and Mitchell gave Kade a light punch to the shoulder.

"Hey, guys," Kade said.

Lamb followed behind them.

"Team, we've got a fix on Jeffries," Lamb said. "He ended up at a residence in Leesburg first. A safe house, we presume. We're monitoring it. But then he left in a car with two others. We lost track of them, then picked up Jeffries's trail again when he checked into the DoubleTree under another name."

Kade got up as though someone had sounded a fire alarm.

"We're gonna go get him, right?"

"Yeah, you're going there with Yang and team, immediately, to assist with any visual ID," Lamb said. "But *capture* of the target is preferable. Trevor and I will prep follow-on interrogation."

* * *

Kade slid into the backseat of the silver Infiniti rental. Yang and Song were in the front, Lee beside him. They all wore various track suits, skull caps, and running shoes.

When they arrived at the Leesburg DoubleTree, their support van had been in place for thirty minutes. Kade picked up Lee's phone again to see the image of a man and woman at the reception counter shown in the briefing. He was one hundred percent sure that the person who had checked in under the name of Jake Lucas was the Guardian Jeffries he remembered. But who was the woman? A girlfriend?

"Do we know who the woman is yet?"

"No, but we can't wait," Yang said. "They're in room 528 right now."

"You guys work quick."

"We do, when the priority's right," Yang said. "A high-value target of Chapter leadership is priority one."

Yang pulled alongside the support van and the person in the passenger seat handed him three key cards with 526, 528, and 530 written on them in marker. Jeffries and the woman were in 528, sandwiched between rooms believed to be occupied by Sentries.

"The front desk gave us key cards?" Kade asked.

Yang shook his head and scoffed at him.

"No, silly. The van has its own card printer and encoder."

They pulled closer to the lobby and parked. Yang removed his pistol with suppressor attached from a bag on the backseat and wrapped it in a white terry-cloth gym towel. Song and Lee left theirs inside gym bags for the moment.

"The van will be messing with the hotel surveillance in the elevator and fifth-floor hallway, on our entry and exit," Yang said, checking his earbud. "They're ready."

After a quick verbal rehearsal and test of the support van comms, the four strolled through the hotel lobby, maintaining a casual conversation. They weren't headed to the first-floor gym. Up to the time they entered the elevator, Yang scanned for any unforeseen threat.

When they were sure no others were on the ride up, Song and Lee removed their weapons from the bag, already wrapped in gym towels.

"Hallway clear?" Yang asked as the elevator stopped.

Over his earbud, he heard, "Clear."

They exited.

Yang and Kade paused in front of Jeffries's door, Song and Lee moved to the doors on either side. They all nodded to each other when Song and Lee had the key cards and weapons ready. Kade held the key card for Yang.

Yang readied the pistol and nodded, followed by a silent count to three, using an exaggerated nod.

Kade inserted and removed the card for Yang. When Yang saw the green light, he turned the latch and pushed through the door in a fluid motion.

The man and woman sitting side by side at the desk, opposite the bed, turned their heads toward them. The woman reached for a pistol lying on the desk's edge.

Yang fired twice. The yelp she made as the .22-caliber subsonic rounds sunk into her forearm and shoulder was louder than the shots themselves.

The man was reaching below the table, but Yang had already stepped forward with his gun aimed at Jeffries's chest.

"Don't," Yang said and Jeffries froze.

Kade had pivoted inside and pushed the door shut.

"Get up, up!" Yang grunted in a low, fierce tone. He took the woman's gun from the desk and tossed it on the bed.

The naked woman, who Kade didn't recognize, stood, clutching her bleeding arm against her breasts. The man, wearing only boxers, rose slowly, hands in the air. His name appeared in Kade's vision.

RAYMOND JEFFRIES

"That's him," Kade said. "I don't know who she is."

"Check the desk drawer," Yang said.

Kade found a Sig Sauer P238 micro compact in the desk. He retrieved the woman's chrome Smith & Wesson revolver from the bed and put both guns inside Yang's drawstring backpack.

"Hands flat on the desk," Yang said. "Make any more moves or noise and you're dead." He muttered to Kade, "The neighbors are asleep. Check for other guns."

Neighbors asleep meant that Song and Lee had taken out whoever was in the adjacent rooms.

The bed was a mess of tangled sheets, and the room smelled of a sweet fragrance.

Kade found a Taurus Millennium pistol with ammo in a duffel bag. He added the gun to Yang's backpack.

"We can make it worth your while . . . let us go," Jeffries said. "Even you, Kade Sims."

"Last warning to shut up," Yang said. "Go through their stuff," he said to Kade.

On top of the desk were two notebook computers showing the Chapter

Network login screen. Each had an infrared reader plugged into the USB port.

Kade moved to the couch and easy chair. A wallet inside Jeffries's jeans draped on the chair back contained various fake identifications.

"Jake Lucas . . . a.k.a. Raymond Jeffries," Kade said.

Next, he zipped open the purse on the chair and pulled out the wallet. The name was consistent on all the identification cards inside.

"Lindsay Gill, Associate Director of Disease Prevention, National Institutes of Health."

We have RJ and LG in the same room.

Mixing work with sex, I guess.

Kade removed a bottle of pepper spray.

"No," Yang said under his breath. "Stand by . . . who?"

Kade glanced at Yang. He could tell Yang's question wasn't directed at him; it was to the support team on the other end of his earbud.

Something was wrong.

Yang motioned for him to come over close while he maintained his aim on Jeffries and Gill. He touched his earbud.

Yang leaned toward Kade and whispered in his ear through clenched teeth.

"The SAU's been hit by a car bomb. Mitchell, Singleton, and Dr. Scott are dead along with others. Henderson and Lamb are both in the hospital. Serious but stable." Yang paused to swallow before finishing. "Don't let these two know that we know. But do what you need to do. Get what you need to get. Then let me know when you're done."

When Yang pulled away, Kade was breathless, speechless.

Carla.

Trevor.

Gone.

A minute ago, he'd thought they were rolling up The Chapter's operations. Two members of their exec group banging in a hotel room seemed undisciplined and stupid.

But now, news of a potentially crippling counterattack.

Who's winning now?

The spoken news, the menace in Yang's voice, echoed in Kade's head.

How could they stick to the plan if the SAU had been taken out?

Is there even a plan anymore?

What do we do without an SAU?

"Are you okay?" Jeffries said to Gill.

She nodded. "Yeah."

"Shut up!" Yang said.

There would be no capture and interrogation. He was supposed to get a screen picture of Jeffries's vision view and obtain voiceprints, but now he had an entirely different idea.

He looked at Jeffries's notebook computer screen. The program had automatically logged him out.

Kade turned back to Yang. "Change of plan. Let me get voiceprints first, though."

He'd been tasked with getting a voice sample from each and sending them to an online SAU drop box. That would help exploit communications and track down other Chapter members. He made Jeffries and Gill separately count to ten while he took a recording.

When he'd gotten the recordings and sent them from his phone, he waved his hand and said to Jeffries, "Now, log back in to The Network."

Jeffries did as he was asked. Kade took a knee on the carpet next to the infrared reader, turning the front of the device toward himself.

"Add me back to The Network," Kade said, "and activate me as a full Guardian."

Jeffries glanced at Gill and paused until Yang counted aloud, "Three, two, one . . ."

Jeffries began typing in commands. Kade watched closely and added, "I know all the command tricks from Tim Arnold, so don't try any."

The reinstated setup took less than five minutes. Kade's display resumed in the format he'd remembered, except the stick-figure pine tree icon turned to a gray color to designate the Guardian position. No countdown timer appeared, thank God.

"Now," Kade said, "go ahead and promote me to the exec group."

Jeffries slowly raised his hands.

"I can't, I swear," he said.

"Three, two, one . . . ," Yang counted.

"No, wait," Kade said to pause Yang. Looking at Jeffries's face carefully, he said. "Go into the *Promotion* menu and show me why you can't."

Kade had never seen the menu but had read about it in the documentation.

Jeffries went to the *Promotion* menu, clicked on Kade's profile, and the *Position* menu. There was a list of available roles, with names next to them, but letters covered by Xs.

They've backfilled some positions. And LXXXXXX GXXX is . . .

"I see Lindsay Gill is M—Chief Medical Officer," Kade said. "Give me a new role. Chief Death Officer—D."

Jeffries entered the role and the abbreviated "D" code, and when he clicked the Complete button, a prompt message appeared.

ADDITIONAL AUTHORIZATION REQUIRED.

"Like I said," Jeffries said, "it requires Commander approval."

Kade watched Jeffries's eyes shift, blink.

No, Owens wouldn't have structured it that way.

This is why they have two computers open.

This is why they met. Other than to have sex.

"Bullshit," Kade said. "Log in, Lindsay, and go to the same screen."

Gill sat there, unmoving, until Yang gripped her bleeding shoulder in his free hand and began to squeeze his thumb in. She logged in.

"Come on, you two," Kade said. "You still have a chance for jail. Lindsay, go to the *Promotion* screen."

When she clicked to the menu, there was one Pending Promotion flag for Kade Sims.

"Authorize it," Kade said.

She entered her code and the promotion appeared as approved.

Kade stared into the infrared reader until his display layout changed. A gold star replaced the gray tree icon. His initials, KS, appeared at the bottom of a list in the display. A reference guide on the exec group appeared, to be read immediately. He didn't have time to go through all the details now, but in looking at the section headers, he had an idea of what to do next.

"I want you to remove everyone from the executive group above me and below both of you. Then, Raymond, once everyone has been demoted, I want you to remove them from The Network altogether."

This took Jeffries and Gill five minutes working together, with Kade watching all their commands and actions.

When they were complete, one set of initials remained above KS, LG, and RJ, but below CDR.

CJ.

Jeffries and Gill wouldn't be able to remove CJ because this individual had a higher rank.

"One more question," Kade said, "and I think we're ready to bring you in. Who is CJ?"

Jeffries and Gill said nothing.

"Look," Kade said, "I'm going to assume that in the middle of all of that typing, maybe one of you slipped in some kind of panic code. Maybe help is on the way. So, you're going to have ten seconds to think about it and answer me. The alternative is my friend puts a slug in your heads like his buddies did to your neighbors on each side, in case you were wondering why they didn't check on you."

Jeffries and Gill looked at each, but stayed silent.

"I promise you both," Kade said, "I'll do my best to appeal to the feds that you assisted us if you give us the correct person. Final offer. Ten seconds starting now."

Yang held his pistol at the ready.

Gill spoke after three seconds. "Wait."

"Lindsay, no," Jeffries said.

"If we're going to die, it might as well just be one of us," she said.

"Then let it be me," he said.

"No," she said and looked at Kade. "Connor Jordan."

"No!" Jeffries said.

Gill's head jerked back and her body convulsed from the chip's PETN exploding. Jeffries reached to catch her as she fell out of her chair, but Yang shoved him back with his non-firing hand.

As he watched in that second, Kade had a flashback to when Lin had stepped between Pierce and him, as though in Jeffries he was looking at himself from an alternate reality.

Refocus, damn it.

He now understood what had happened. Speaking Connor Jordan's name aloud was a security trigger for both of them, so Gill had given herself up in hopes she'd save Jeffries.

Kade wouldn't say Jordan's name either, just to be safe.

"Okay, Raymond, was the name Lindsay said the correct one?" Kade asked.

The devastated Jeffries nodded. "Yes."

"Okay, we have a winner," Kade said and glanced at Yang.

"Support, stand by," Yang said. He pulled out his earbud and dropped it in his pocket.

"Cuff him up?" Kade asked.

"I've got a better idea."

Yang shot Jeffries in the back of the head.

Kade's mouth hung open. He'd intended to keep his word.

"You made the promise," Yang said. "I didn't. That's for Pak and Mitchell."

Kade shook his head. "Okay."

Something was wrong. He wasn't repulsed by Yang's action. A few weeks ago, he would have been. When he had more time, his brain would wrestle with what happened. Right now, he felt feverish, his throat hurt worse, and he had to keep clearing his throat because it was full of mucus.

Yang pulled the earbud back out of his pocket and paused before replacing it.

"Plus, I'm saving time. Looks like you're now Chapter number three."

CHAPTER 62

The White House
Wednesday, December 28
1:02 p.m. (EST)

President Greer grabbed DNI Conroy and DCI Perry to gather in his private office of the Situation Room complex before the next meeting convened.

"How bad?" Greer asked.

"Six on Lamb's team were killed. Four wounded," Conroy said.

Greer shut his eyes and mouthed a silent prayer.

"How's Russ doing?" Greer asked.

"I just came from visiting him," Perry said. "He's stable and conscious. And angry, but that's good for him right now—he's a fighter."

"Was it someone inside who divulged the location?" Greer asked.

"Not a chance," Perry said. "The team's calls are monitored, there's electronic countermeasures, and no phone cell comms permitted from the site. No, it had to be a tracking device planted on a person or vehicle. One of the highest sophistication . . . one that would elude initial detection. They detected a burst of signal outside the facility, but not long enough to pin down. All the private vehicles are being checked. We'll need to put some additional safeguards in place from now on."

"The mobility of the SAU makes it a softer target," Conroy said. "We may have to rethink the physical security as well."

"What about the site?" Greer asked. "It's hit the news, right?"

"Not really," Conroy said. "Procedures were in place to contain and control the scene. The news is calling it an explosion, and it'll be attributed to a car colliding with a medical supply oxygen truck."

"Okay, let's go talk to the prime minister."

* * *

Prime Minister Kota and his select staff had arrived with no fanfare. Greer wanted President Lok to be aware of Kota's visit for additional diplomatic pressure without creating a media ruckus.

The day would be spent on coordinating the Indian/US diplomatic and military responses to China's actions.

In a small "surge" conference room provisioned for this occasion, Greer introduced Kota and the Indian Defense Minister, Amarjit Chadha, to Conroy, Perry, Emory Briggs, the US Secretary of Defense, and Marilyn Vega, the US Secretary of Energy.

"You have my deepest appreciation for your support through this serious situation," Kota said, "especially your soldiers on the ground."

Greer wanted to say he hoped this was the start of a new era where India didn't look to Russia first as its BFF, but now was not the time.

"You're welcome," Greer said. "Our ongoing military operations are first on the agenda."

Using electronic maps displayed on the planning table in front of them and mirrored on the wall, Briggs summarized the initial American-led special operations, starting with a successful raid at the Chinese garrison at Zhaxigagxiang, cutting off any immediate Chinese reinforcement to Demchok, thirty-one kilometers to the northwest via the road alongside the Indus River.

Greer had ordered US troop support to India with deployment of the Fifth Squadron, First Cavalry Regiment, from Fort Wainwright, Alaska. The unit was brought into the Nyoma Airfield and within twenty-four hours had reached an assembly area outside of Demchok. Indian forces of the 14 Corps rolled in a brigade of over one hundred Russian-made T-72 tanks to take the lead position, the Americans positioned to support.

The Chinese forces had withdrawn, as Greer had demanded in his face-to-face with Lok on December 15th, to the Chinese-controlled Dêmqog, about one kilometer from Demchok on the other side of a large wadi. But the Pentagon warned that additional PLA units had begun to mobilize and move toward the border. Lok wasn't backing down, only taking a step back.

Briggs recommended additional action.

"The remainder of our First Stryker Brigade Combat Team should be deployed to the area of operations as a ground force deterrent."

"Yes, let's do that," Greer said. "And I want heightened readiness in all other touch points with the Chinese, including Freedom of Navigation ops."

Chadha added, "Our special operations forces in the Tibet region will damage the Chinese National Highway 219 at specific choke points to prevent reinforcement. We have moved additional Spyder and Akash air defense assets to the border to discourage hostile actions and air reinforcement."

Greer looked at the pictures of the greater Aksai Chin region and its desolate, Mars-like landscape.

"Why is Lok being so stubborn about this?" Greer asked. "What value does all of this have?"

Chadha looked at Kota, who nodded and smiled.

"That brings us to our next discussion," Kota said, "and why we requested Secretary Vega attend. I did not bring my atomic energy chairman on purpose for fear it could reveal what this is really about. When we signed our Defense Framework Agreement and the Defense Trade and Technology Initiative with you, it was most alarming to China—not on the defense side, but on the technology side, from a key element of it."

Kota paused to see if anyone would venture a guess, but only silence followed.

"That element is an actual radioactive element," he said. "Thorium."

"Thorium?" Greer said. He remembered perhaps a few sentences mentioned in the language of their defense initiative.

"Yes," Kota said. "The Chinese are obsessed with dominating in thorium intellectual property and its entire value chain. This entire border area is rich in thorium."

Greer sat back. He set aside some intellectual embarrassment he didn't know more about the technology.

"So their aggression is to secure the raw material for the future?" Conroy asked.

"Yes, and to deny it to us, even though we have deposits in other areas. We have about twenty-five percent of the world's estimated supply. Only the US and India stand in the way of their goal to own the thorium reactor market."

"Where is the US on this technology?" Greer asked Vega.

"We pioneered the first molten salt reactor design at Oak Ridge," she said, "one that's been dusted off and further developed conceptually for thorium. We have a collaboration and memorandum of understanding with the Chinese on two thorium molten salt reactor projects at the Chinese Academy of Sciences, with the Shanghai Advanced Research Institute and Shanghai Institute of Applied Physics."

"Wait," Greer said, "you mean to tell me we're working *with* the Chinese on this?"

"Yes," Vega said. "The Chinese have invested about four hundred million dollars into their efforts. It's clear that from their energy consumption and pollution concerns, they've made a permanent choice to go down this road."

"We have more intelligence we can share," Kota said. "China's strategy is to squeeze the US out of this market in the longer term. One piece of this puzzle we are missing, however, is why the thorium project is so well supported by the military leadership when that budget could be used on defense. Lok has opposition in his ranks, but thorium energy is a unifying area."

"We'll look into that more on the PLA side," Conroy said. "There was a PLA Senior Colonel present at Zhaxigagxiang, which is top-heavy for a small border garrison."

The discussion continued and Greer pushed the agenda forward.

"What other levers can we pull jointly or independently to compel Lok to stand down?"

Chadha offered his suggestions first.

"We can increase covert support to the Tibetans and the Muslim Uighur minority in Xinjiang. Overt support and statements will be difficult for India, however."

"I don't mind public statements of support," Greer said.

Perry nodded to Greer. "We're well positioned to assist. We can also assist the Balochistan Liberation Army to stir up unrest in the port of Gwadar."

"Yes," Kota said, "that is a good idea. To threaten China's 'One Belt, One Road' strategy through that economic corridor would have impact. Disrupting bridges there, along the Karakorum Highway, and the Metok Tunnel."

"Melissa and Emory," Greer asked, "do you think this is enough to get Lok to back off?"

Briggs, a former Army football linebacker, looked skeptical.

"I don't think they will resume aggressive military operations with our unit present. But I think we'll need more sticks or carrots for them to reverse course and go back to their previous posture."

"I agree," Perry said. "Along with the military pressure and rumblings of instability within, there needs to be a personal or political threat to Lok to change his mindset. Fear of a rift in his power base."

When Greer looked around the table, everyone's body language appeared positive—aware of the challenges, but encouraged by a skeleton plan and their willingness to work together.

"Okay, let's put together the strategy for my discussion with Lok. I will want to call him in the next twenty-four hours, and I suggest it's before you have any further dialogue with him, Prakash."

"I understand," Kota said.

Greer was giving himself time for a thorough US-only intelligence discussion and review of options first.

Because he needed every weapon at his disposal.

CHAPTER 63

The White House
Thursday, December 29
7:00 a.m. (EST)

President Greer smiled and pointed at Kade as he entered one of the dedicated conference rooms adjacent to the Situation Room. Right behind him was National Security Advisor, General (retired) Reid McAlister.

DNI Conroy, DCI Perry, FBI Director Hassett, and SecDef Briggs were also present, and a still-recuperating Lamb was on a secure speakerphone, somewhere.

"I told everyone I wanted you here, Smith, and I see they stuck you in the corner. You got enough tissue, cough drops and hand sanitizer?"

Kade smiled underneath his surgical mask. A lapel mic amplified his weak voice.

"Yes, sir."

"Did the doc get you some drugs?"

"Yes, sir . . . thank you. It's helping."

Three hours earlier he'd awoken sweaty and miserable, sleeping in his own bed out at Luray. A White House Situation Room watch officer had called, summoning him there at 6:30 a.m. to clear security for a 7:00 a.m. meeting.

"Should I blame the Chinese or The Chapter for your virus?" Greer asked.

Kade cleared his throat yet again. "Uh, probably both, I think."

"Trick question, and I think you're right." Greer moved to the speakerphone. "Russ, how are you?"

"Okay, thank you, sir," Lamb said.

"Great," Greer said. "Let's get to it."

There were two techs brought in by Conroy and Perry to augment the one Greer had assigned for this room. Greer used an electronic whiteboard six feet across while a few adjacent monitors displayed analysis gathered for this morning's deadline. A large projection screen image bore a TOP SECRET designation with an additional special access program ARDEO.

"I called this team specifically," Greer said, "because I have to deal with two simultaneous threats, perpetrated by players who are obfuscating the situation. Concealing how they are intertwined. I have a call scheduled with President Lok in four hours. I'll have to decide what our stance will be with China and what I'm prepared to do as commander-in-chief to back it up. I must also take actions to keep in pursuit of The Chapter, now that we have them on the run. I know that our Recovery Team took a standing eight count, but that team has been closer to the ground than anyone on recent events. I will make my decisions based on what we discuss here in the next two to three hours. Any questions?"

Everyone was tracking with Greer.

"Let's start with the two key questions. Is The Chapter acting as a proxy for China and, if so, why? What is the evidence and intel we have?"

Conroy started first with a single word on the whiteboard—thorium.

"Remember PM Kota said that, for China, this is all about thorium. China moved across the border because of it. It turns out that the thorium there has a purity of about five percent, versus one-tenth of one percent elsewhere in China."

"They're moving in for the thorium supply, to lock up the market supply chain," McAlister said.

"Right," Conroy said, "but what they'd really like to control is the naturally occurring thorium that's thirty to sixty percent pure. We have it right in our backyard, out at Lehmi Pass on the Montana-Idaho border, and the privately held Rare Earth Metals Corp owns the supply—enough to power the US for over five hundred years."

Greer swiveled his chair. "That's where we . . ." He swept his finger through the air to depict a missile's trajectory.

"Yes, that's where we raided The Chapter," Lamb added. "And Kyle was the bait."

Greer sent a nod in Kade's direction. "This is interesting circumstantial evidence."

"Here's where it gets stronger," Hassett said. He wrote the words HASTELLOY-N and TMSR next to thorium on the board. "We recovered pipe inside the mine at REM Corp made of that unique Hastelloy material, which is used in the spec for a particular kind of thorium reactor—a thorium molten salt reactor."

"Let me guess," Greer said. "That's the kind we're helping to build with the Chinese in Shanghai."

"Yes," Conroy said.

"Only in America," Greer grumbled. "But wait. REM Corp is building a reactor?"

"No, they've only made space for a reactor," Hassett said.

"This will shed light on intentions," Perry said. "This is from a key source with access inside Shanghai Advanced Research Institute."

A series of images appeared on the monitors. Pictures taken of computer screens. The diagrams showed shipbuilding plans for a barge. Perry added two Chinese words to the whiteboard with their translation.

Fúdòng làzhú = FLOATING CANDLE

"The Chinese want their thorium reactors on barges," Perry said, "and have a plan to build nine of them. Putting power plants on ships and barges is nothing new, even nuclear systems. But thorium would be a first."

"Why barges, and why nine?" McAlister asked.

SecDef Briggs took his turn. "This is where we are making an educated guess," he said.

Briggs drew nine circles on the whiteboard and, with help from his notes, labeled seven of them. Cuarteron, Fiery Cross, Gaven, Hughes, Johnson South, Mischief, and Subi. He wrote the word "Planned" in the other two circles.

Kade couldn't help himself when he recognized what those names were, before Briggs was finished.

"The artificial islands . . . thorium-powered?"

Perry gave Kade a silent clap.

"Yes, that's it," Briggs said.

"Is nine somehow related to the 'nine-dash-line' of the South China Sea?" Greer asked.

"Not sure," Conroy said. "The Chinese love the number nine, and in this context of superstition, it's perfect. It implies emperor's sovereignty."

"Why care about floating thorium power?" McAlister asked. "They've got a pile of oil out there in the South China Sea, they're working on nuke-powered guided-missile subs . . ."

"It's the missing piece in another strategy they have," Briggs said. He played a video clip of a truck-based laser blasting a drone out of the sky. "This is a demo of the Chinese Low Altitude Guard, or LAG program. Their next generation requires about fifty times the power, so FLOATING CANDLE goes hand in hand with meeting this technology goal."

"The burning platform, pun intended," Greer said. "Directed energy weapons, or DEWs, the next warfare game-changer. Artificial islands, and flexibility to float power sources."

"And a means to mass-produce and deliver a standard reactor model to dominate the commercial market," Perry said.

"Maybe they had promised The Chapter their own reactor," Greer said. "Quid pro quo."

"That would be difficult," Hassett said, "given the regulations, but let's revisit that when we talk about The Chapter and their Congressional activity."

"Emory, wouldn't it be easy to target a huge barge with our own missiles?" Greer asked.

"Yes, it would," Briggs said, "but they are building those nine thorium reactor barges to appear like FPSOs, or floating production storage and offloading vessels, that process and store oil and gas. Real FPSOs would never be initially targeted in a conflict because you'd have an environmental hazard worse than Deepwater Horizon. But they could hook the barges right into undersea power cables, leaving no signature for overhead imagery."

"More deception, wow," Greer said, "they've got this all figured out, eh?

How do we throw a wrench into this reactor program? Will ending our partnership do anything?"

Perry zoomed out and zoomed in on another design slide.

"We are aware of three design flaws and a software vulnerability in the prototype system," she said. "The flaws were put in there as 'insurance' and will result in a system failure for a production system."

"Can I exploit one of those now, as a subtle warning?"

"Yes, we can do that," Perry said. "I'd suggest we try to maintain the partnership because it provides us access and visibility."

"Let's follow up on that right after this," Greer said. "Okay, we know the stakes. They've decided they're all-in on thorium. Where else does that lead us? Who can I hold accountable?"

"We've been busy piecing this puzzle together," Conroy said, "and it comes down to relationships. Many powerful relationships influencing their strategy."

Conroy teed up a box-and-line organizational chart on the large projection screen and passed out a briefing book detailing the same. The red dot of his laser pointer appeared on the screen.

"Starting at the top, we have Lok Kong, a president who is steering the ship on key strategies that most in the Communist Party can agree on. Keeping internal stability in Tibet and Xinjiang. Dominating the East China Sea and reunifying Taiwan. Dominating the Yellow Sea and containing South Korea. Dominating the East & South China Sea and the nine-dash line we just discussed. And preventing the remilitarization of Japan.

"But beyond that, there is conflict within. Lok has attempted to strengthen himself through a massive corruption campaign, aimed at punishing 'Tigers and Lilies' at various levels of government, and has made many enemies doing so.

"And here we have the former president Hao Jian, now head of the Chinese Academy for Sciences in Shanghai, and his son Hao Qiang, head of the Shanghai Advanced Research Institute, or SARI. Both organizations are in charge of the thorium reactor projects."

"Wow," Kade muttered.

"Lok has brought his enemies close—on projects they all can agree on," Greer said.

"Yes," Conroy said. "And that's just the tip of the iceberg. Next we have Sun Kang, currently the CEO of China North Industries Corporation, but formerly the head of SARI's Life Science and Technology arm. Sun Kang went to the PLA National Defense University with the current commanding general of their Xinjiang military region, Tan Chen."

Briggs weighed in.

"General Tan is directing the forces across from ours at the Indian border, with close PLA and Party oversight," he said. "The line on the chart over to Colonel Zhu Hung is key. Zhu is a reserve colonel reporting to Tan, but also head of the Xinjiang Production and Construction Corp, responsible for mining operations, supporting settlement construction. Zhu was at the border garrison during our covert operation."

"Like a Corps of Engineers?"

"Even stranger than that," Conroy said. "In the Chinese model, the XPCC is also a business entity with publicly owned subsidiaries."

"So, there you have the reason and means for the border attack and land grab," Greer said. "Keep going . . ."

Conroy nodded.

"The business development arm of XPCC, a firm called Xinjiang Economic Dev. Co., Limited, had dealings and communications with Rare Earth Metals Co., facilitated by Sun Kang's daughter, Sun Lin, a.k.a. Lin Soon. We'll come back to her. But that wraps the entire thorium-government-PLA and The Chapter package together with a bow."

"Tan Liang, General Tan's son, was Sun Lin's fiancé in a sort of prearranged marriage," Kade added. "An attempt to bring the Sun and Tan families closer together."

Kade thought he might have stepped out of place, but Greer gave him a curious look and then turned to Perry.

"Is she the . . . ?"

"We'll discuss that offline, sir," Perry said.

"Okay," Greer said.

What was that about?

"Was there final determination of that attack on the Chinese border patrol?" McAlister asked.

"The imagery India provided makes it clear the snowmobiles were Russian Snegohod A1s," Conroy said, "and this was confusing because neither China nor India have bought A1s for their military. The A1 is an air-droppable military variant of an ordinary Russian Taiga-551 snowmobile. We have an electronic copy of a purchase request for eight Taiga-551s from the manufacturer, Russkaya Mekhanika, by none other than XPCC. So, we conclude it was all an inside job with possible Chapter support."

"How about the missile attack?" Greer asked. "Was Kota telling the truth?"

"No indication it came from India," Perry said.

"It was an SA-N-5," Briggs said. "They're a dime a dozen."

"Okay. Nice job, everyone," Greer said.

Conroy launched an animation that shaded all of the relationships around the THORIUM header in light red. He then switched to a light blue animation overlay labeled SOFTWARE & SEMI and used the laser pointer.

"In order for President Lok to strengthen the Party and his own control, he needed the right tools. Here we have Tan Liang, CTO of Shanghai Microelectronics Group, connected by contracts to the PLA, some of those being facilitated by Sun Kang. His largest project is Big Brother software that brings together data from Skynet surveillance, bank accounts, telecom, and even their Baidu search engine."

McAlister shrugged. "Don't we do this with the DARPA Total Information Awareness program?"

Conroy shook his head. "We collect Internet and telecom data, but their usage throws all personal privacy and liberty out the window. It allows the Communist Party and MSS to actively sniff out any interpretation of subversive behavior, even assigning citizens a trustworthiness score. Its test bed for usage is in Xinjiang and Tibet, for the suppression of ethnic minorities."

Hassett took the baton.

"This is also where there's a Chinese technological link with The Chapter. The software uses the same facial-recognition algorithm. We believe the Chinese are on the receiving end of the software intellectual property in exchange for providing The Chapter with capabilities they must keep offshore."

The diagram highlighted Sun Kang and his son, Sun Bo, a Chapter member and the VP of Architecture at Shanghai Semiconductor. Zao Hong, who headed Chapter operations in China, was a former employee and development director at Shanghai Semi.

Greer shot a glance at Kade. "That was the fab we destroyed with the Chapter chips. You think Lok knows of the direct linkage to The Chapter?"

"We don't know for sure," Perry said, "but elements of the government are complicit. It's reasonable to believe Lok knows there may be some general funding or support indirectly to The Chapter, for the same reasons we would generally fund Tibetans or Uighurs, although our motives at least have some human rights justification."

The shading changed to light green with the header BIOCHEMICAL.

"I think I've got the hang of this," Greer said and stood. "Here, let me see that pointer, Hugh."

Everyone smiled. Their president was a quick study on this. The pointer's red dot appeared on Sun Sheng.

"The damn rhinovirus was cooked up in China North Chemical, courtesy of Sun Sheng, a Chapter member and the other son of Sun Kang. China North Chemical rolls up to Kang's China North Industries. The bioagent was delivered by Li Chonglin, an MSS agent, who interacted with Sun Lin. MSS tried to cover tracks and pin the bioagent on Sun Lin, but Sun Lin gave up Chonglin."

Kade chewed through a cough drop. *Didn't know that.*

Greer stopped and everyone was nodding in agreement.

"Now, their purpose—this one is all about the money, right? Financing The Chapter-China technology?"

"Right," Hassett said. "The Chapter got paid for the execution of the plan."

Perry said, "Many of these players would make out well from the impact of the bioagent."

"So," McAlister said, "it was a localized plan, with some rogue MSS support. Not a strategic plan or a predecessor to another bioagent as we feared."

Everyone appeared to share that consensus, but Briggs added a comment.

"The PLA did make an assessment note of the agent's effect on military bases and readiness. So did the Russians."

"Figures," Greer said. He looked back at the diagram on the screen of the key Chinese players and then sat on the edge of the nearest conference table.

"What else?" he asked.

Hassett said, "My part would best be saved for our next meeting without the analysts and Smith present. It's related to The Chapter's goals and Chinese goals with Congressional influence and the political threat to you."

"Agreed," Greer said. "We'll hit that later. So, in a few hours, I call Lok on the carpet. If not for being directly involved, I hold him responsible for the actions of his organizations. I justify our immediate response and threaten what our additional response could be. There is plenty of ammunition here. Is it enough for Lok to order the PLA to back off and to stop supporting The Chapter?"

"No," Perry said.

Greer smiled. "And that's why I love this team. Melissa is always Dr. No."

That got a brief laugh.

"No," she said, "you need to make him feel *personally* vulnerable, create a rift, or embarrassment. Create the *diū liǎn*, or potential loss of face, where he fears that his reputation and influence will be injured. All of what we discussed here will create action, but not an impetus for him to break from the Party pack on much."

"From the look on your face," Greer said, "I'm assuming you have an idea."

"Oh, yes, we do," she said. "But that's where this meeting ends and the next one begins."

"All right," Greer said. He pointed to the two analysts. "You two are done for now." Cupping his hands around his mouth as though he was yelling a long distance, he added, "Smith, you go home and get some more sleep. We're going to need you again soon on The Chapter, once I resolve the China crisis, God willing."

"Yes, sir," Kade said.

While he was throwing his wad of tissues in the waste bin and smoothing sanitizing gel on his hands, Hassett stopped by.

"Stay safe, Kyle. We're working on a plan to ferret out members of Congress on The Chapter's payroll. We'll need you."

"I'll be ready," he said, even though he didn't feel like it.

His mind gyrated with possibilities while a gruff Navy lieutenant commander escorted him out of the Situation Room complex.

Damn . . .

He would have paid the rest of his meager savings account to know what Perry had up her sleeve for the Chinese president.

CHAPTER 64

The White House
Thursday, December 29
11:22 a.m. (EST)

Greer's call with Lok started as planned, but he was only able to stay on script for the first twenty minutes. In the conference room they'd met in earlier, he had the projector screen graphics back up on display as a gigantic cheat sheet. Conroy, Perry, and Briggs sat near him and the translator in case he needed a quick answer.

He opened with the broadest theme: Lok needed to back off the Indian border, to ensure conflict didn't escalate.

"Until your PLA Xinjiang units return to their home bases and a nonalert posture," Greer said, "I'll continue the full deployment of our brigade to support the Demchok border area. I'll also consider making the brigade a permanent, rotating joint training brigade working with the Indian army."

Lok parried with a not-entirely-unexpected accusation.

"The attack upon my unit at Zhaxigagxiang inside the sovereign land of the PRC was an inexcusable act, and one I suspect the US is behind."

Greer played semi-dumb.

"President Lok, allow me to return to the events of November ninth that now, with greater detail, expose the false premise behind your original decision to attack Demchok. Your false premise that I plan to communicate to the global community. The ambush of your patrol, which was a special operations patrol disguised as a PLA patrol, and one that had crossed over the LAC into India by many kilometers, was devised by your own corrupt elements inside the PLA, *not* India. The Russian snowmobiles used in that attack were bought by your own Xinjiang Construction and Production Corporation and weaponized. You will find similar evidence with the Russian man-portable missile attack on your helicopter. I suggest that if you had an attack inside your borders, you look to your own rogue units with possible Russian assistance first."

Greer had touched on a known insecurity—ridding the PLA of corruption was one of Lok's initiatives. But Lok sidestepped, admitted to nothing and called this an "inconceivable premise" and Russian involvement "fantasy."

That's when Greer opened the door to the strategic case that had been rehearsed hours before—the linkages to thorium power and the Chinese desire to seize those interests from India. He let Lok know that he was aware of the endgame—the barge reactors and directed energy weapons integration plan of FLOATING CANDLE in everything but name.

"Your appeasement of your political opponents, the former president, and the PLA through the thorium goals has caused them to run amok with rogue operations in the name of this strategy. Most disturbing, and what is unforgivable, is the Chinese support of The Chapter, an organization intent on destroying the US. China's XPCC has acted as an intermediary between your government and The Chapter."

This is where Lok counterpunched, or figuratively picked Greer up and slammed him to the mat.

"Why should I adhere to any of your demands, or believe any of your dubious assertions from a president who his country plans to impeach in the next few weeks for abusing power?"

That motherfucker.

Greer seethed, but bit his lip and read the note Hassett had passed him before responding.

"You have already meddled in the affairs of our Congress, attempting to push deregulation bills and enriching your supporters from the sale of pharmaceuticals and blood products. All to make money from the crisis your bioweapon created."

Greer walked through the evidence and some intel shedding light on

China North Industries under Sun Bo and China North Chemical activities linked to Sun Sheng. He then pivoted to the intertwined Tan family relationships—from General Tan Chen, the PLA Xinjiang commander and Tan Liang at Shanghai Micro, circling back to Shanghai Semi and The Chapter with Tan Liang. Greer painted a picture of corruption, nepotism, and loss of control, and brought responsibility back to Lok.

"Other than pulling back troops from Demchok," he said, "you've done nothing to curb this overly aggressive action of your military forces and intelligence services. I'm prepared to take the following actions in the coming weeks. I will increase Freedom of Navigation patrols. I will explore creating our own artificial islands in conjunction with our allies. Until your harboring, funding, and supporting The Chapter ends, I will plan to increase my support of the Tibet diaspora, host the Dalai Lama, and create a joint policy with Prime Minister Kota. I will raise awareness of the persecution of the Uighurs of Xinjiang, and will sympathize with the Balochs and other minorities who do not want an invasive Chinese Economic Corridor. And I will recommend that China be placed on our State Sponsor of Terror list before the end of this month."

When Lok didn't respond, Greer continued.

"But let us also consider a different course. One that is fueled by respect and true partnership. The spirit of our joint work in Shanghai on the thorium reactor can be a symbol of friendly research, fair competition, and respect for intellectual property, without a military objective. To show good faith, I'm going to provide you knowledge of a flaw in the reactor's tritium extraction and control process. One that could be disastrous. This is how we should operate. With transparency."

Greer knew that a different flaw in one of the reactors could render it inoperable. A back door in the software could be exploited to show false measurement readings in a Stuxnet-style attack. Depending on how Lok reacted, he could decide if that next step was needed.

But even with this small token carrot, Lok appeared as if he'd made up his mind to stay the course. He wanted to wait and see what the changing US political climate would foretell for Greer.

"I'm not pleased by these developments," Lok said. "I will discuss them with the Politburo Standing Committee for potential action. But I do believe that the aggressive military actions of the US close to Chinese shores and political dialogue with Taiwan and Hong Kong make your criticism and stated threats hypocritical. I don't expect much change in our military posture without similar concessions from the US first. I will investigate your accusations of corruption with our Commission for Discipline Inspection. Once this is complete, I will then discuss this further with you . . . or your successor."

He's stalling to see if I'll be politically weakened.

"Very well," Greer said. "Before you discuss these issues with your staff and various committees, I would like you to accept a personal gift from me."

"A gift? I do not understand."

"There will be a package couriered to you from a representative of our embassy in the next hour. The contents of the package are only known by a handful of my staff. I would like you to consider it before you make your decision on what course to take in the coming months."

"I will expect your package," Lok said.

"Thank you, President Lok. Until we speak again, I wish you and your family the best."

CHAPTER 65

House Chamber, US Capitol
Tuesday, January 3
11:50 a.m. (EST)

Above the Speaker's rostrum, in a section closed off from the adjacent gallery seats, Kade sat behind a ten-foot-wide tripanel of one-way glass, looking through binoculars.

Below him, a seat had been added next to the Speaker, even though this wasn't a joint session of Congress. Vice President Nguyen was over in the Senate, attending that swearing-in and those ceremonial oaths afterward.

Members were curious about today's protocol.

When President Greer entered without fanfare and sat in the added seat, that curiosity upticked.

The Clerk of the House, Julia Tate, called everyone to order, and then asked members-elect to stand for the chaplain's prayer and the Pledge of Allegiance. A planned microphone failure bought an extra minute on the front end.

Kade was already at work.

An eighteen-inch tablet computer lay on a stand in front of him, showing a live view of the House floor from overhead. As Kade reviewed the entire floor, a few names popped into his vision display. He touched the screen where that member stood and tagged them with a red circle.

He moved back and forth behind the glass to get the best viewing angle while the chamber echoed in unison.

"One nation, under God, indivisible, with liberty and justice for all."

When everyone took seats again, he found himself out of breath.

The Clerk began the roll call, allowing him a few extra minutes to check his work. The election of the new Speaker, the oath of the Speaker, and then the swearing-in of new members came after the roll call.

Greer wanted action before any new Speaker was to be nominated.

"I've got five who are part of The Chapter," Kade said just above a whisper.

"Wow," Greer said.

FBI Director Hassett said, "Sir, we now have the image and list."

"Is your team ready, Stan?" Greer asked.

"Yes, we are. I brought a fleet of agents."

"Okay, here we go," Greer said.

When Greer stood, the Clerk's microphone turned off from an external source.

"I'm sorry I must interrupt the next order of business due to a matter of national security. There is concrete reason to believe that certain persons in this chamber have conspired against our government. In concert with FBI Director Hassett's recommendation, special agents will now escort the following members out of the chamber for further questioning . . ."

An uproar filled the chamber as Greer repeated the names Hassett fed to him and FBI agents filed in, each with an assigned name.

Kade remained behind the glass until two members of the Secret Service arrived to escort him out of the gallery. They were going to take him to the Senate chamber, where the plan was for Kade to do a similar identification, but Hassett's voice came over his earbud.

"Kyle, change of plans. The Secret Service is going to bring you to the president's room."

Ten minutes later, Greer, Hassett, and a man and woman Kade didn't recognize met in the lavish Senate room reserved for infrequent ceremonial occasions. Lamb was on a secure conference line speakerphone.

"Kyle," Hassett said, "we're briefing the president on some real-time intel. Between the time that the president gave the order and when my agents detained those five, eleven text messages were sent to a phone inside the office of Aspirance, a lobbying firm."

"We need to find who's on the other end," Lamb said.

Kade looked from side to side.

"News of the five has already blasted out. So whoever is their contact at Aspirance is going to go underground, if they haven't already."

"Kyle, I want you go to the office with one of my teams," Lamb said, "and try to get a visual ID on anyone from The Chapter."

"But then I can't go to the Senate," Kade said.

"We already have a warrant to arrest Hawkins," Hassett said. "He never made it to the chamber. I agree with Russ on priority."

"Me too," Greer said. "Go—find who these members were reporting to."

"Okay, sir. We'll have to call an audible that won't spook them," Lamb said.

"I have an idea that might work," Kade said, "but I'd need to get ahold of Congressman Seale."

CHAPTER 66

Seale agreed to the plan after President Greer called him on his cell phone. Fifteen minutes later, Seale and Kade stood on First Street, a short walk from the Capitol.

"You did say to call if we ever needed anything . . . ," Kade said.

Seale gave a nervous laugh. "Yes, I did."

Kade spotted the white GMC SUV with Steve Lee at the wheel.

"That's him," he said.

The Pointe Center building, home to the Aspirance offices, was less than a half mile away on Constitution Avenue, but Lee took a circuitous route to buy a few extra minutes.

"Kyle, a few presents. You're going to be Mr. Seale's security officer," Lee said. "In the bag on your seat are ID cards, your weapon, and a light disguise. The IDs won't hold up to a deep check but should get you through building security."

Kade looked at both the government ID and the driver's license.

"You guys print that shit out fast," Kade said.

"Thanks," Yang said.

Kade donned the shoulder holster and readjusted his suit jacket over it. He slid on self-tinting aviator-style glasses and a black wig.

At first, he thought the overall appearance was ridiculous, but Seale said it looked good, and the wig did fit well and match his hair color.

Lee handed Kade an earbud, and Kade tested communications with the support van. Hearing Yang's voice again calmed his nerves.

"Kyle, if you sniff any hint of trouble," Yang said, "let us know, and I'll get a squad up there. Otherwise, you do the ID, get out, and we'll handle it from there."

"Okay, man."

The Pointe building came into view, and Lee swerved as close as he could get without needing a parking space.

"Ready, gentlemen?" Lee asked.

Kade waited for a nod back from Seale, then said, "Yeah, let's go."

The security guard on the ground floor of the Pointe Center called up to the Aspirance office, verifying Seale's appointment, and printed two bar-coded visitor badges. Kade's read KEVIN JOHNSON.

The guard directed them to the elevators.

"Elevator Two will take you to Aspirance on the eighth floor, okay?"

"Great, thank you," Seale said.

On the inside of the elevator, where the panel of buttons would normally be, a computer screen showed "8" as its destination.

As the doors shut, Kade took a position behind Seale and to his left, in attempt to obscure any view from the surveillance camera.

The elevator had started to ascend for a few seconds, when it stopped.

Kade looked at the interior screen, which displayed the floor and also streamed news—in this case, CNN.

The screen showed the number three.

We were we going directly to eight, right? Or can others get on?

He was about to say something to Seale, when the display flashed again, and a number appeared.

84379514

A buzzing pain passed through his head. The elevator walls closed in, his vision blurred.

"Shit!"

He knew Henderson had worked on his program again so the code wouldn't detonate his PETN, but electric charge was still being passed on from the chip.

He tried to reach for his weapon, but instead had to grasp the elevator's waist-high railing with both hands to steady himself.

Seale gripped both of Kade's shoulders.

"Are you okay?"

Kade heard Yang through the earbud.

"What's going on, Kyle?"

"We stopped on the third floor . . ." Kade felt as though someone else was saying his words. "Something's wrong . . . my code . . . my code . . ."

"Hold tight, we're on our way," Yang said.

The elevator doors opened and a man stepped in, bringing his arm down in a swift motion. Seale tried to block him but failed, and an autoinjector jabbed his neck.

The man shoved Seale behind him, and another blurry figure pushed him down to the floor.

Kade attempted to stand, unsupported, and take a fighting stance. An obscured name appeared in his vision.

XXXXXX XXXXXX

Kade made a mental *Wheel of Fortune* guess based solely on the number of characters.

Connor Jordan.

The man grabbed Kade by the forearm and yanked him out of the elevator.

"It's the sloppy traitor. Sims, you just made your last appointment. Ever."

Kade reached for his weapon, but the assumed-Jordan struck his arm downward. Kade attempted to take a swing with his left, but his legs were so wobbly he missed, lost balance, and fell to the carpet.

As he steadied himself on all fours, he could see Seale lying there, either dead or out cold.

A foot wearing a black dress shoe swung into his view.

His glasses were crushed, light flashed, and pain shot through his face.

He had the sensation of falling backward in blackness, unconscious for a few seconds.

When he blinked and again saw light, Jordan had zip-cuffed his hands behind him, pulled him upright, and leaned him against the wall, holding him up with a forearm pressed against the neck.

Beside Jordan stood the other figure. A short, muscled, and familiar man. A scarred face Kade could never forget, now wearing the same smile as he had while torturing him during his previous operation.

His name was x-ed out, but Kade didn't need a prompt to know who it was.

Petr Ignaty.

Ignaty twirled a knife with a long nonmetallic blade.

"Support, status," Kade said.

There wasn't a response. He had lost his earbud.

Jordan pulled off Kade's wig.

"Oh, your friends won't be getting up here anytime soon," he said. "Unless you have a helicopter booked, and they're coming through the windows. You think we didn't plan for this contingency?" He patted Ignaty on the shoulder. "The finest Russian technology let us know you were coming and helped take out your ops center, too."

Kade pushed aside his surprise and tried to strike back verbally. Seconds counted.

Delay.

"Well, Connor Jordan, there's a few things you should know. All of your Congress puppets were just arrested. That's why you haven't heard from any of them since the swearing-in. Your exec team's dead, if you're wondering why they haven't checked in. The Network's decimated. So, seems to me you're too far behind on the scoreboard with time running out. You fucking lost."

Jordan hesitated. Kade had difficulty seeing his face, but he did exchange a glance with Ignaty.

"Doesn't look that way to me," Jordan said. "We're sticking around, but it's time for you to go. Petr's going to do the honors now, as he requested."

Kade tried to move off the wall, but Ignaty pinned him back on it. He thought about trying to kick out, but the tip of Ignaty's knife was already breaking the skin below his sternum. He grimaced, took in Ignaty's sour breath along with his own.

He resigned himself that this was the end and grunted two final words. "You're next."

Ignaty's eyes filled with the same rage Kade had seen months before. He pulled the knife back and cocked his elbow to power a fatal thrust. Kade willed his muscles to move, to fight, but they wouldn't respond.

But Ignaty spun, half-headlocked Jordan using his free arm, and plunged the knife into Jordan's midsection.

Kade fell to the floor, hearing a mix of grunts and gargling sounds. He began to crawl, unsure where he was going or what the hell was going on.

Seconds later, Ignaty bent down and grabbed his shoulder, guided him.

"Get on the elevator," he said.

Kade crawled onto the elevator and collapsed. Iganty cut the zip cuffs, turned him around, and propped his back up in the corner. He wrapped Kade's hand around the handle of his bloody knife after he wiped it.

"So, this is what happened," Ignaty said. "Jordan knocked out Seale, then tried to kill you with the code. You disarmed Jordan and stabbed him dead. You put Seale and Jordan back on the elevator and used the elevator override code to bring it back down to the lobby. Understand my story?"

Kade swallowed a blood-and-saliva mix and nodded.

"Yeah."

Ignaty moved Seale and Jordan's blood-drenched body onto the elevator.

"You will say nothing about me for at least seventy-two hours," he said. "I recommend you call this . . . amnesia? After that, you can say whatever you want. If you follow these instructions, you and your family will never see me again. If you don't, I will find you, just like I helped The Chapter find you and your team. Understand?"

Kade wasn't in any position to bargain. But now he had many questions.

"Okay. . . why did y—"

Ignaty made a "shhh" with a finger at his lips and his eyes flared again.

"My involvement with The Chapter is no longer useful for my employer. Maximum damage has been done. And you are more useful alive, today. This is all you need to know. So, I think your mission is over, yes?"

Okay, shut up and don't say anything to change his mind . . .

Kade raised his eyebrows and said nothing.

"Good," Ignaty said. He turned to the side and spoke a few sentences in Russian before backing out of the elevator. An order or acknowledgment, perhaps.

He smiled before the elevator doors closed.

"Have a good life, Mr. Sims—you earned it. *Do svidaniya.*"

CHAPTER 67

Luray, Virginia
Sunday, January 22
12:05 p.m. (EST)

The notes from Kade's medical review stated that his memory loss had been due to "electric shock." Cuts, bruises, and broken nose aside, his physical health was stable. Given the physical and psychological stresses of the last three months, and relapses into both maniacal and depressed states, Dr. Trish recommended resuming weekly psychiatric appointments and regular medication.

Kade didn't argue. He was more than a mess—the loss and damage to those he knew had demolished his spirit. He had taken on several teams of Sentries and Guardians, and by the end of this run, his life had been at the mercy of the Guardian-lobbyist Jordan. It left a sick feeling inside.

There was no emotional crazy glue; it would take time.

During a solemn private luncheon at Camp David, President Greer congratulated and thanked the Recovery Team, minus the still-recovering Lamb and Henderson, along with Yang, Song, Lee, and De La Paz. The Chapter's leadership had been annihilated and its network rendered inoperable. The hardest work had been done.

Now would begin a plan of cyber vigilance and a more traditional FBI operation to continue the search for those seeking to perpetuate the Chapter Network. They would ensure The Chapter would never function as it had before.

That the *planarian* would never regrow or reassemble.

Forty-four representatives and two senators were under "house arrest" with an ankle monitor and assigned surveillance, pending an FBI investigation into their financial connections to The Chapter. Links to those forty-four had been established through the seizure and forensic analysis of Connor Jordan's computer at Aspirance. There wasn't a specific mention made in public of the seven who had been chipped, but they were under additional surveillance pending indictments.

Greer had effectively communicated to the American public that this crisis had only made the country stronger by exposing those who had wished to destroy it.

This was The Chapter's strategic defeat. The grand plan Marshall Owens had envisioned of a supporting power base in Congress to alter the country's agenda had been thwarted.

President Lok had held an in-person meeting with President Greer and Prime Minister Kota, and the three had reached an agreement to pull PLA troops back to their positions prior to the Demchok border incident. Lok had also publicly acknowledged that, during research while developing cold antivirals, China North Chemical had created the rhinovirus, which had then accidentally made its way to the US.

China North Chemical's Sun Sheng was under investigation, and once Li Chonglin was returned to China, he was never heard from again.

Lok, Greer, and Kota agreed to strengthen open sharing of thorium R&D to chart a leadership course toward greener energy.

Kade had divulged Ignaty's flip of support at a later debrief. While the Russian had an FBI file related to organized crime, his actions suggested he'd acted in an FSB capacity. The Chapter's use of new Russian-made tracking devices, including one affixed to Kade's truck that only emitted signals on a specific schedule, provided further technical fingerprints. Because The Chapter had previously reneged on a drug deal with the Russian mob, Ignaty's continued involvement led to one conclusion: Moscow's support of The Chapter's effort to throw the US government into chaos had outweighed the mob's desire for payback.

At Henderson's recommendation, Kade had removed himself from the

Chapter Network. The belief was that, with Connor Jordan gone, Kade would have become the focal point of both friendly and enemy cyberattacks. He would get the chip removed in the coming months, but, for now, he returned to his new home to rest and reorganize, and not worry about brain surgery.

He was in the middle of doing some late-morning yard work when his phone rang. Hearing Lamb's voice on the other end brought an unusual mix of comfort and anxiousness. Would he be called on to do something else so soon?

"How are you doing?" Lamb asked.

"I'm all right. My black eyes have turned a lovely shade of green. We missed you and Matt at our final team lunch . . . how are you?"

"Oh, a few pins, a few screws, I've lost count," Lamb said. "But everything's working."

"Great . . . and Matt?"

"He still needs some rehab. The burns are coming along. He has a longer road. The loss of his eye is hitting him the hardest."

"I'll visit him, if it's allowed," Kade said.

"I'm sure he'd like that. I'll arrange it."

"Thanks for your support. It's never wavered."

"You're welcome," Lamb said. "Now, the reason for my call, other than checking in. Yang is driving out to see you, so stick around the house for the next few hours, okay?"

"Sure . . . can I ask why?"

"You'll see, my friend. Call it an informal exit briefing. Then feel free to call me, anytime."

"Okay, thanks," Kade said.

He should have been more puzzled at the cryptic call, but maybe his brain was too fatigued to care. The habit of constant suspicion that had kept him alive now felt unhealthy.

Two hours later, the SUV came rolling down the gravel segment of his driveway while he was trying to replace a rotten fence post and toiling with the semifrozen ground. He sunk the blades of the digger into the excavated dirt pile, coughed, and wiped his sweaty face on the sleeve of his hoodie.

He froze when Yang and a woman stepped out of the vehicle.

The woman. Her hair had been lightened, her body was similar, but was it. . .

Lin?

His heart leapt and he walked toward them, stunned.

Yang brought her back. They lied to me for her safety.

Lied because she was alive. A source to protect.

The back door of the SUV opened next, and a Chinese girl who looked between eight and ten years old slid out.

Her daughter?

They both wore winter coats with furry hoods, likely bought from the same store. As the woman walked closer, with the girl trailing behind, a soft smile formed on her face. She also had tears in her eyes.

Something was different. And he no longer had a name or indicator on a Chapter vision display to assist him.

"Lin?"

Did she have some facial work like I did?

She shook her head.

"No, I am Jia," she said. "This is my daughter, Yu."

Kade dropped at the grass edge of the driveway and sat, confused.

Jia?

Her half-sister.

"And Lin?" he asked.

Anguish filled Jia's eyes.

"No," she said.

"We lost Lin, like Lamb had told you," Yang said. "I'm sorry."

The abysmal sense of loss returned. Tears ran down his face.

Jia's familial resemblance revealed itself with some differences. Softer facial features. A shorter body. Eyes with an intangible texture of hardship.

The guilt-weight of his many failures began to crush him again.

Lin had pictures of Yu hidden on her phone.

Her niece.

Yang, Jia and Yu sat next to him on the grass. A thin film of snow flurries had accumulated.

"Kyle, I'm so sorry, man," Yang said. "But Jia wanted to meet you and give her thanks in person. She doesn't speak much English at all, though. Her daughter, none."

He looked up, his voice again filled with remorse. "She wants to thank *me*?"

"Yes," Yang said, adding a few sentences in Chinese.

Kade stared at a faraway place.

"Why the hell would she want to thank me?" he said.

"Because she was with Lin before she died," Yang said. "When the other team picked Lin up, Jia was there in the van, speaking to her, holding her hand. The first time they'd been together in five years. We had a tough choice, whether to take Lin to the consulate, where we thought she wouldn't survive, or to the hospital, and we chose the latter. She had begun to recover, and Jia was able to sneak in and visit. They talked . . . they even laughed. What happened wasn't your fault."

"Lin shouldn't have taken a bullet for me."

"She picked a side," Yang said. "Your side. When she heard Pierce say you were working for the FBI, she put two and two together. She knew what you were trying to do, why you'd acted the way you did."

"So why is Jia here?"

Yang nodded.

"Lamb permitted me to discuss this with you because of the language barrier, but keep in mind this holds the same classification as everything else you've been working on."

"Yeah, of course."

"Jia's been an Agency source for about four years—going back to before you ended up at The Chapter in Oregon. The Agency recruited her because of her government and business contacts."

Kade's head slouched forward.

"Oh my God."

"Yeah," Yang said. "It was Jia who gave us the contacts for the pharma and Shanghai reactor cyberattacks."

Kade now remembered a face he'd seen in an instant.

It had been a woman with a brown trenchcoat and roller bag, walking next to a dumpy dude, outside of China North Chemical.

"She was in the pair walking out of China North Chemical . . ."

Yang nodded.

"Yeah. And for the semiconductor raid, she was the one who got intel of their admin area. So, when you set up the dinner with Lin and her family, Jia was part of the other plans behind the scenes with us, including the sauna plan. We couldn't let you know."

Kade watched while Yang spoke to her in Chinese.

No way.

But if they had known her for that long . . .

"So, you guys already knew about the whole *undeclared sister* story you told me?"

"Yeah, we did, I'm sorry," Yang said. "We gave you a little bit, just so you'd understand why Lin was so upset with that part of the evening and with you. Lin still thought Jia was missing and probably dead. But you didn't know some of the plan details and Jia's part in it. She was there, but unseen, so she wouldn't be recognized by her brothers. She was the one who got access to Bo's locker and left with his access card."

"This is unbelievable," Kade said.

"Being undeclared made her a perfect source for the Agency. Unlike Lin, she had no *dang'an*, the secret file the government has on everyone with school, health, work data, personality profiles. She's tough—a survivor."

Kade shook his head.

Local spies are the enemy's own countrymen in our employ.

"So, Jia was estranged from her family, but still loved Lin, and vice versa," Kade said.

"Yes, very much," Yang said, "and in recruiting Jia, we had an agreement to help get Lin out of The Chapter and away from her family."

"The Bureau and the Agency both knew about this arrangement?"

"Only at a very high level, but yes. The people involved in your Oregon operation did not. It was some complex interagency coordination and management of conflicting needs."

"And the Agency then agreed to get Jia out?"

"Yes. We told Lin we'd take care of Jia and her daughter in the van. Lin was happy and at peace. But Jia had to do one more important task. A very risky one, and she pulled it off."

Kade nodded.

Of course.

She was the one who got hold of the FLOATING CANDLE plans.

While Kade became lost in his thoughts for a moment, Jia said something in Chinese, containing "Kyle," that Yang translated.

"She said, 'It's okay, Kyle. Lin loved you. She always felt protected. There was a connection.'"

"Protected?"

I did a horrible job of it.

Jia clasped her hand on Kade's upper arm and said something. When he looked at her, she had a small white box resting in her palm.

"*Xiāng xiāo yù sǔn,*" she said and handed it to him.

Inside the box lay a dragon carved from greenish stone.

"What she said is a Chinese proverb," Yang said. "Fragrance is dissipated; jade is broken. In Chinese culture, jade represents immortality."

Jia added another sentence that Yang translated.

"Lin had planned to give this to you after dinner in the restaurant, believing it would bring you protection. In the hospital, she told me where she had hidden it."

Kade wiped his eyes one last time.

"It's . . . beautiful, thank you." He put his arm around her. "I'm sorry about your sister. You're both heroes to me."

"Jia's daughter's name is Yu," Yang said. "Yu can mean both jade and happy. There's another Chinese name that means happy. That name is Lok."

Kade turned his head and met Yang eye to eye.

No . . .

"You mean Yu is . . ."

"The last thing I had to do before getting out of Shanghai was to get cheek swabs of these two in a paternity kit to the consulate. That's all I'm saying."

"My God," Kade gasped. He dwelled on this for a minute.

This young girl was one of Greer's weapons.

Perry's ace up her sleeve.

The deterrent of exposing a love-child of the Chinese president.

Kade squeezed the dragon figurine and flipped it in his fingers. It provided unexpected comfort. He sighed and looked at Jia and Yu.

"I'm not sure if anything can protect me, but I know that people who love us are stronger than any stone. You let me know if I can ever help you."

Yang translated, and when Jia smiled and said, "Okay," Kade finally felt a flash of peace.

"Kyle, my brother, you did well," Yang said. "And what you said goes for you, too. Reach out to me if you need a hand."

Kade wiped his nose on his upper sleeve.

"I don't know about you, but my ass is getting cold sitting here, and I'm not ready for goodbyes yet. What do you say we have a couple of beers or Cokes and I'll feed you guys something before you head back? I promise it won't be that bad."

Yang nodded. "Yeah, sure, man."

When Yang translated for Jia, she and Yu laughed, and the sound of their laughter reached Kade's heart like the struggling winter daylight. He felt fragmented happiness, as though he was remembering it from a long-forgotten dream.

Jia's cold fingers wrapped around his fist holding the figurine.

"Yes, okay," she said.

They walked toward the house, and Jia pointed toward the snowy mountains.

"Beautiful."

Kade paused to look at the layers of mountains lined in low clouds, to breathe the cold air deeply, to appreciate being alive.

"Yes . . . a wise woman once told me, 'The beauty you see is a gift for everyone. The beauty you feel is a gift for you.'"

CHAPTER 68

Vancouver, British Columbia
Monday, January 23
11:15 a.m. (PST)

He powered up the notebook computer that had been delivered to his apartment and established an Internet connection.

On Amazon.com, he located a particular storefront that was selling athletic shoes. There was a used orange pair of Nike Hyperquickness Basketball shoes in orange.

Size 12.5D. $69.99.

No one was going to buy a used pair of those shoes, except for him.

He placed the order, waited for the confirmation message from the seller and clinked on the link contained in it.

A download completed and a program ran.

The screen display changed and a message appeared.

CDR>> Hello TA

Tory smiled.

TA>> Hello

Acknowledgments

SOURCE was such a personally rewarding story to write, and the people who helped me with research, insights, and draft reviews were my invisible companions on a fun journey.

My heartfelt thanks to: Tim Hence, Will Genter, Zach Mortensen, Prakash Katoch, Nahal Dousti Li, Jordan Cottam, Scott Hager, Brian Klages, Chris Prentice, Marilyn Smith, and others unnamed but not forgotten. You all rock!

A big thanks to my MEASURE OF DANGER readers who ~~nagged and guilted~~ encouraged me to write a sequel.

Thanks to my editor, Eliza Dee, for a superb job. Any remaining errors or typos are my own fault.

Thanks to Meghan Harman for the beautiful and captivating cover design.

One challenge of depicting various aspects of the intelligence community in fiction is the sheer number of people involved in collection and analysis. To allow the reader to track the story with a manageable number of characters and maintain pace, I knowingly took some liberties with roles and responsibilities. I often oversimplified the coordination (and drudgery) that goes on behind the scenes, but tried to imply when it occurred.

Kade's grandma in this story is a rough caricature of my own adopted grandmother, Ruth Eddy, who died this past year at ninety-five. I hope some of her personality and never-ending supply of love shone through the pages. I love you and miss you, Grandma.

And if you have read this far, a third installment in the Kade Sims depends on your involvement. Posting your reviews on Amazon and Goodreads will allow the SOURCE readership to grow and multiply (like diced planaria). Be a Guardian of the cause, make an author's day, and help make another book viable!

I appreciate your feedback and even odd, random thoughts on my Facebook author page, jklages.com, or Twitter @jklages.

Until next time . . . —JK

66453238R00214

Made in the USA
Lexington, KY
15 August 2017